D1030376

To Joe —

the best dad in

Jackson

Merry Christmas

2008

FRESH
FROZEN

[signature]

Ponder House Press
Jackson MS

Copyright © 2008 Darden North, MD

Layout and Design by The Gibbes Company

ISBN-10: 0-9771126-3-2

ISBN-13: 978-0-9771126-3-0

First Edition

Printed in Canada

Previous novels by Darden North, MD

HOUSE CALL

POINTS OF ORIGIN

To Rogue and Tuxedo:

We miss you.

Acknowledgments

No doubt I have inadvertently omitted someone in this essay of gratitude, but I have been helped along the way by so many and from so far away that this tribute could be a book in itself. While this novel belongs entirely in the fiction genre as advertised, I have strived for accuracy as much as possible; however, surely I have made some mistakes. Of course, there is nothing wrong with plausible fiction, I would think, even though it does not necessarily need to come true.

Victoria M. Sopelak, Ph.D. and William H. Cleland, MD, of the University of Mississippi Medical Center Department of Reproductive Endocrinology and Infertility and James W. Akin, MD, of the Bluegrass Fertility Center in Lexington, KY, were instrumental in my creation of the Van Deman Center in *Fresh Frozen*. To be clear, the imaginary deeds of my fictional place in no way cast disparity on the actual work done at those and other fine healthcare institutions.

Fresh Frozen spirited me deeper into the world of forensics, and I owe much to Captain Farris Thompson of the Rankin County (Mississippi) Narcotics Unit in that regard. Once again, Ricky Dawson of DK Digital Designs, computer guru Bill Staples, and personal stylist Darrell Wilson were invaluable in my research as was pathologist George Sturgis, MD.

My editorial team of Evelyn North, Mona Evans, Karen Cole, MD, and Sally North were overly patient with me. (The literary world would benefit greatly if tireless Mona Evans worked in that venue full-time.) Denton Gibbes, Craig West, Wade Rico, and the rest of the talented team at The Gibbes Company in Ridgeland, MS, are once again unmatched in cover and book design as well as with marketing and maintaining my website *www.dardennorth.com*. I am also indebted to my publicist Nanette Noffsinger and literary agent Sheri Williams for taking me on and to Kathy Spurlock, executive editor of *The* (Monroe, LA) *News-Star* for her insight regarding this novel.

The following individuals have been influential in promotion at specific events including literary panels and festivals as well as at book signings and in publications: Syble and Shell White, Cheryl Oleis, Wanda Jewell, Elizabeth Hadwin, Tammy Lynn, Lane Carrick, Darlene Herring, Paula Jackson, Geneva Donaldson, Vince Valruvnek, Angela Kestenbaum, Becky Wooley, Claire Aiken, Jo McDivitt, and, of course, Mary Shapley as well as fellow authors Billy Watkins, Joyce Dixon, Margaret Fenton, Steve Stubbs, Alice Nicholas, Joe Lee, Gayden Metcalfe, Martin Hegwood, Helen DeFrance, and Marta Stephens. I am also grateful to the growing list of bookstores and libraries who have welcomed me to signings and readings, as well as to their shelves, and to the publications who have featured reviews or articles about my novels. Also, special thanks go to the real Coco Ihle.

Also, I would also like to thank Margo Grace and Mike Giesbrecht of Friesens Corporation among others for consistently producing a fine product and everyone at BookMasters and AtlasBooks for their work with distribution and promotion of my novels.

I am one fortunate guy to have two fulfilling careers: practicing medicine and writing, and at the risk of sounding corny it does my heart good to be appreciated in both. My ultimate thanks go to my family and to the other physicians and staff at the Jackson Healthcare for Women, P.A. In fact, I'm told that my nickname around Woman's and St. Dominic hospitals is *Dr. McNeedy* (a name probably just as befitting at home), although some nice lady at a book signing somewhere called me *Dr. McDreamy*. I think I like that second nickname better.

SOMETHING WANTED INSIDE.

Carrie prayed that the something was God,
but she was certain it must be the Devil.

Contents

FRESH FROZEN

•••

DARDEN NORTH, MD

Chapter
1
•••
THE BRUNETTE

"Hey, you out there. Toughen up! Throw up on your own time."

Dr. Knox Chamblee had already spotted the struggling woman through the plate glass window and fought the urge to join her. Probably somewhere around his age, the sick woman looked as attractive as anyone could in that predicament, as she worked to drown her disgrace in a row of tall, overgrown shrubs. Despite the dense wall of ligustrum leaves, she was miserably unsuccessful.

The shrubbery bordered the property of Coco Ihle's Fitness and Body Camp, an in-demand exercise and physical conditioning facility in Jackson, Mississippi, that approached the level of a posh torture chamber. The indoor exercise space was filled with computerized treadmills, elliptical bicycles, and stair steppers as well as free weights, simulated rock-climbing obstacle courses, and various other athletic training equipment. The machinery required an engineering degree to use properly, or at the least, detailed instructions. Adjoining the aerobic and physical training facility were indoor tennis, basketball, and handball courts. The establishment was commandeered by Miss Coco Ihle, a taut, black-haired, five-foot-four personal fitness trainer certified by the National Institute of Sports Medicine and Therapy.

And Ihle loved what she did and lived to do what she loved.

"Come on, you rookie. Wipe up and get on back in here. *The meek will inherit the Earth* is a bunch of crap!" Ihle yelled again through the opened door that abutted the floor-length window as the row of ligustrum remained unshaken by the outburst. The sick woman had prayed that no one would see her as she slipped away from the exercise session, towel in tow, covering her face and mouth. However, Coco Ihle never missed a thing. She was determined that her students get the full value of their 125 dollars per week.

The thick-leaved shrub gave up; it was no match for the drill sergeant, failing miserably in its attempt to hide the retching woman. Even though its long branches strained to cover her shockingly pale face as she stood bent on the sidewalk, the plant could not shield the woman from Ihle's barrage and the resulting humiliation. Growing with abandon for years against the chain link fence that marked the property, the ligustrum had witnessed, and witnessed often, such extirpation at the hands of other fitness trainers. Some had been lighter than Coco Ihle, few tougher.

As Knox forced his attention to the mileage and speed of his treadmill, he assumed that by now his fellow student was beyond embarrassment and thankful for the relief. The pretty woman out there in the bushes hid the shame well, although Knox realized that any sign of humiliation would have left her face as quickly as did the contents from her stomach.

In truth, the slim, brown-haired woman in the color-coordinated exercise outfit was not at all surprised by her broiling stomach. One time before, the same injections had turned her inside out, just as the chemicals were doing now, although during the former treatment cycle she had not exercised as vigorously.

The severe training sessions had begun two weeks ago, and the nauseous brunette, like Knox, had been there from day one. He first noticed her at registration, at a time when she was much

more composed and attractive than now. She was thin, but
not skinny, tall, but not taller than he, with an age somewhere
between 30 and 35 and a figure that stood out even under a
tailored workout jacket and pants coverup. She wore no wedding
ring, not even a simple gold band, but that meant nothing.

Like most everyone else, the woman had paid for the six
weeks of physical pounding at registration with a credit card.
Standing directly behind her in the sign-up line, pen and personal
information form in hand, Chamblee fought the urge to introduce
himself as he strained in vain to see her name on the registration
form and credit card receipt. To have struck up a conversation
with the striking woman would have broken with the norm since
no one else seemed sociable at that moment. Collective chatter
between the participants of the course was a waste of valuable
energy, no one was there to hook up. Everyone was there to
concentrate on his or her own body, no one else's.

When Coco Ihle's clients did talk, it was with tongue-in-cheek
groan, referring to their voluntary, paid-for experience at *Boot
Camp*. Since its inception two years prior, the popularity of Boot
Camp had exploded as many of the forty or so participants per
class had finally worked their way to the top of a waiting list.
In the central Mississippi area, Ihle had rapidly established
a dedicated following of professional types: doctors, lawyers,
nurses, bankers, local entertainers, as well as manicured
housewives and house husbands, happy to trade financial well-
being for physical and verbal abuse. The abuse was all for the sake
of being physically fit, or at least for trying to be.

And from the perspective of the person wielding the verbiage,
each one of Coco's clients wanted to be with her, needed to be
with her – why else would they have paid the $750 six-week fee,
not to mention bought two pieces of the required issue eighteen-
dollar cotton tees labeled *Coco Ihle Fitness*? Certain that a Coco
Ihle body could be recognized anywhere with or without her

obligatory tee, the diminutive but determined master wanted every pupil of the class to receive maximum benefit from her program. There was no other choice.

"Come on, you guys. Pay attention to whatchur s'posed to be doin'. Move your asses!" Ihle blurted to Knox and his classmates once they had switched to the elliptical bicycles nearby.

Like Knox, the others in their section of the class were still concerned over the vomiting brunette in the ligustrum. The Hippocratic Oath as well as the spirit of being a good Samaritan summoned him to stop his bike and attend to the sick woman, although he knew there were several other doctors around him who had sworn to the same oath and should possess a similar conscience. He decided he would let someone else make the first move. Besides, the woman was trying to be as discreet as possible as she continued to shield her bright yellow *Coco Ihle* tee shirt from the mess. Should one person, even a doctor, leave his post to come to her aid, she would be even more embarrassed. Knox was sure of it.

Beginning with Boot Camp registration and during the ensuing two weeks, the woman had kept strictly to herself, arriving immediately before startup and leaving with Ihle's final whistle. Her pattern had not altered on this day either. Knox had seen her speak to no one earlier that morning when she was arbitrarily assigned to his same exercise section.

Chamblee knew that he could no longer ignore her. Somebody needed to offer a cup of water or a cold cloth for her forehead and neck, at least show some sympathy. Just as he was about to halt the elliptical trainer and slide outside to help her, she seemed to regain composure as the retching waned. As Knox observed her straighten up and move slowly to re-enter the building, Coach Ihle settled the issue: he would not move; he would stay right where he was and keep his legs spinning.

"Hey, you rookie," Ihle repeated, loudly enough to be heard over any machine. "Glad you decided to get out of that poor shrub. I thought you might kill that old thing. Like I said, throw up on your own time – and in your own bushes!" Chamblee sped ahead on the elliptical, expecting the brunette to sprint back out the door after Ihle's outburst, escaping not merely for the day, but for the remainder of the session, never to return.

Today's incident was not the first time this particular classmate had received the main brunt of Ihle's attention. A couple of days previously, the class had been split into five groups, then assigned to an obstacle course laid out on a freshly refinished, indoor basketball court. Each participant, rookie and veteran alike, was then required to push a basketball nose-first around a series of Ihle yellow, cone-shaped, thick plastic markers – the type commonly used to block off parking areas but usually constructed in orange instead. Other than the color, the dramatic difference between these cones and those used elsewhere was the Coco Isle Sports emblem stamped on the sides in large black letters.

"Remain on all fours, back parallel to the court floor, nose on the basketball, do not stop. I repeat. Do not stop!" bellowed Ihle, the instructions demanding everyone's attention as the exercise began on the obstacle course. The fate of the draw had placed the attractive brunette first in line, her confusion over the directions painfully obvious when she initiated the routine with an immediate stumble. Nevertheless, she continued down the course, only to stumble again.

Witnessing the third, and blessedly final, infraction of one of Ihle's favorite workout routines, another reminder of the proper technique erupted. "Woman, I said, remain on all fours, back parallel to the court floor, nose on the basketball, do not stop. I repeat. Do not stop! " And then with a brutal laugh, Ihle berated her, "You are the blondest brunette I've ever seen!"

With that, the brunette, who remained strikingly attractive even with beet-red face and damp hair, turned limp on the court for a few seconds before coming to her feet with hands on hips. Standing but a short distance from the instructor, she turned to Ihle and delivered a lethal stare that could have lasted only seconds but seemed much longer. Next, she threw down her arms in frustration before turning to march toward the restrooms.

Ihle immediately waved up the next participant to the starting point, then yelled at the sweaty brunette as she moved away, "Hey, Blondie, wouldn't you like to hit me?"

Chamblee was sure that the entire class was just as surprised as he that the blonde/brunette returned for the next day's 5:00 a.m., hour-long session. However, there she was in a new exercise outfit, no less, and she had returned each day thereafter leading to her marathon in the shrubbery outside.

"My grandmother can lift more weight than you. Come on! Put out!" The command exploded in his right ear as a river of sweat made its way from his scalp down the side of his head. As instructed, Knox had moved to the weight lifting section and was unaware that his female master was looming over him.

"Uuuunnnhhhh!" he grunted as he forced a smile at the five-foot-four dynamo.

"No sexual noises!" she responded. Ihle was outfitted in trademark yellow exercise gear. Her brilliant white Adidas tennis shoes with matching yellow shoe laces supported a pair of rippling calves. The calves led to firm buttocks that, though flat, still supported breasts that rose above her clingy exercise top. The firm, symmetrical breasts were too large in proportion to her torso to be considered real, but still not so oversized that they lost appeal.

Earlier that day when Ihle was near but not looking in his direction, Knox had made a careful study of her physique: not an ounce of cellulite visible anywhere on the exposed areas of her body, no puckering, and no lumps. As he struggled to push eighty pounds above his head, Knox wondered if there ever had been any cellulite on those exposed areas of Ihle's body or, for that matter, on the few non-exposed spots. He doubted it.

"That's enough, Rookie." Unknown to Knox, Ihle had slipped back to his area, startling him so that he almost lost his grip on the weights. "Give me a wiggle, Rookie, and move your ass back over to the treadmill."

After remounting the weights on the stand, Chamblee hesitated momentarily to catch his breath and swipe his forehead with a towel. Ihle moved closer and popped him gently on the rear with the palm of her right hand. "I said, give me a wiggle." With that, he grabbed his towel and made for the treadmill station, unknowingly leaving Ihle to admire his moves, her pleasure masked by a characteristic stony expression.

Satisfied, the coach turned her attention across the room, "OK, you vets, get off your sweet asses," she demanded of the others as she moved away, her directive designed to shame the repeating students who should know better than to waste a moment. However, the broadcast was an admonition to the whole group, with each individual hearing and feeling the sting of the warning but too spineless to look away from his or her assigned position to acknowledge it, must less argue.

"Show these rookies a thing or two!" Ihle yelled even louder as she moved closer to accost another group that had once before taken a round of her classes. Although her interest was now directed to those doing squats while holding 10 and 15 pound weights, she paused to yell back at Chamblee, who had obeyed her earlier directive. "And, Rookie," she shouted, her shrill, strong voice easily audible above the exercise equipment and the users' groaning, "Didn't I teach you the first day to hold your back straight while you're on the mill? Don't let me catch you slacking, and turn your damn machine up a mile or two. I wanna see those buns glisten!" Dr. Knox Chamblee followed the updated orders and punched the arrow on the gauge, then for good measure upped the elevation control a notch as well.

As the coach moved away, redirecting her attention elsewhere as if making a zigzag pattern of medical rounds, Knox managed to muster the energy for a sigh of relief. Reciprocating the admiration, he reevaluated her figure, this time entirely from the rear. Ihle was unquestionably short by fashion model standards, very strong but still indisputably feminine, a shapely cut that should fill a bathing suit or cocktail dress just as nicely as the tight workout clothes she wore now – the perfect proportion of feminine muscles and curves.

"OK, you guys and girls doing the squats over here," Ihle screamed without stopping, weaving further to approach another section. "Whatcha think you're s'posed to be doin', half squats? Damn, if you don't wiggle it on down to the floor, then we're, I mean **you're**, gonna bear crawl up the back stairs with those hand weights like we did a couple of days ago."

Hearing that, Knox pushed it up another half mile. "Come on! Let me see some nice squats, you sissies. Put your hearts into it!" Ihle let out a haughty laugh, laughing alone at her metaphor of human anatomy.

Knox grabbed the water bottle waiting for him in the cradle of the treadmill control panel. While reimagining his female coach nude, screaming at a bunch of sweaty bodies that were electively paying for growing physical and mental abuse, he caught a glimpse of the drained brunette. As a fresh drop of sweat trickled through the corner of his right eye, he blinked it away and noticed that the still pale-faced woman had slipped back into the gym to resume her place a few treadmills over.

The young doctor charged ahead on his, trying to blend in with the crowd and avoid any of the teacher's attention. As his mileage tenths registered in green fluorescence, Chamblee reassessed his own reason for registering for and hanging with boot camp and remained grateful that his present physical condition had held up thus far. The effort was but one step in his plan to revamp or literally reshape his thirty-five year-old life: lose some weight, tighten the abs, energize, forget the old girlfriend – not an original plan, a simple out with the old, in with the new.

Sometimes such catharsis is the direct result of that change in spouse or girlfriend. But in the case of Dr. Knox Chamblee, the girl was not the primary focus of the change, but losing her had come only secondarily.

From a social standpoint, the change had been a relatively simple process. Chamblee benefited from a single man's ability to pick up and go, with or without the girlfriend. His incompletely furnished house, which included no live-in, made it easier to move. All it took to reorganize his life was leaving a growing general obstetrics and gynecology practice in his former home in much smaller Montclair, Mississippi, for a couple-of-hours' drive south, where a new opportunity for even greater career advancement waited.

As doctors immerse themselves in the bedrock of science, a certain degree of naïveté is bred among physicians, a trusting attitude that finds no place for secrecy and mistrust in the practice of medicine. Dr. Knox Chamblee's own overwhelming trust in taking things at face value landed him at the Van Deman Center of Reproductive Technology, located not directly in Jackson, the state capital, but a few miles north in Canton.

After 24 years of formal education and three years of previous medical practice in Montclair, he had changed course, maintaining status as a physician and a gynecologist, but dropping the labor and delivery part. He wanted to be there from the beginning of conception, not just a handler of the precious by-product. At the Van Deman Center he would not be a voyeur or even an explorer of sexual behavior, for Chamblee wanted a greater challenge.

Much like the torturous obstacle courses that Coco Ihle laid before her groupies, Knox had chosen the additional dare of tackling the obstacles to human fertility. He knew it would be a tradeoff – the predictable day-and-night exhaustion brought on by the unpredictable hours of delivering babies exchanged for the less physically taxing, but often more mentally draining, task of solving infertility issues for patients.

The decision that led him to this career change had come easily and felt good, felt simple, not naïve at the time: he would borrow some more money, take unpaid leave from his now abandoned medical practice, and pursue specialized training in human infertility. To disrupt a career as a sought-after doctor headed for continued success had been a gamble and had been met with astonished argument from the other physicians in his original practice. But like Knox, the physicians in that practice anticipated his acceptance for additional training into a reputable reproductive endocrinology fellowship program. His résumé from medical school and obstetrics and gynecology residency, not to mention his medical practice experience, was there to back him up.

Nevertheless, once the sabbatical for his infertility training fellowship was completed, the former partners in Montclair were hit hard by his decision not to return as planned to their practice. As the two-year fellowship drew to a close, the physician headhunters had planted the idea of his relocating to the Northeast, the Midwest, the west coast, or to one of several sites in Florida. One recruiter even mentioned an opening for an infertility specialist in London.

Considering the prospect of a medical practice far beyond
the confines of his upbringing made returning to a smallish
community or to any other place in Mississippi no longer enticing
or even remotely appealing. However, the appeal did resurface
when Dr. Henry Van Deman and his cache of medical and surgical
advances found Dr. Knox Chamblee.

The new practice opportunity was new for Chamblee but
also new in the sense that Van Deman was utilizing proven
advances in infertility management in his practice even as he
commercialized them. With the initial offer to join the Van
Deman Center, Chamblee could see and feel the concept but
was unsure if he liked it: the idea of medical merchandising in
which the provision of medical services can seem like no more
than a commodity.

The old partnership never had a chance at getting him back
home. Even before completing the postgraduate training, Henry
Van Deman, MD, had already plucked Chamblee from the other
candidates enrolled in infertility fellowships, naming Knox
Chamblee, MD, as his first physician associate and potential
partner in the Henry Van Deman Center of Reproductive
Technology.

"Ditrification, that's the future, Knox ...... ditrification," Van
Deman emphasized when interviewing Chamblee for the position.
"*Frozen embryos.* Well, we all know that concept was everything
in the eighties," Van Deman continued with a chuckle, a charming
affectation that rose well above colored business know-how or
the simple art of persuasion. A medical pioneer in interventional
human reproduction as well as an astute businessman, Van
Deman had seen the impending explosion of assisted human
reproduction that had progressed well beyond simple *in vitro*
fertilization or IVF, the process commonly referred to in the
introductory years as test-tube babies.

As Van Deman was well aware, exotic methods to reproduce had become a staple for television and magazine exposés. There were twins born with silver spoons but to separate birth mothers; sixty-plus-year-old, no-longer menopausal women giving birth to one or two or more babies at a time; and same sex couples receiving egg, sperm, or embryo donations involving various assortments of surrogates, depending upon which of the same sexes was involved.

Knox was already familiar with ditrification. "Right, sort of like freeze-dried embryos," he responded during one of their initial talks.

Van Deman chuckled. "Yes, Doctor, you might rephrase the technique in those terms. And I have done just that for lay people who are slow to understand the process. Actually, ditrification is quite simple: viable human embryos are processed through a rapid freeze technique employing a hyperosmolic fluid."

"The embryo survival rate is said to be better than present ..."

"Oh, yes, Knox," Van Deman interrupted in his excitement. "Embryo survival rates are 90 percent with ditrification, much better than the more commonly used freeze-and-thaw technology. Once the embryo is dehydrated, it is secured in a sealed plastic tube, and then plunged into liquid nitrogen. All our technician has to do is top off the liquid nitrogen tank as evaporation occurs, and we've got a nice supply of embryos."

"*A nice supply*. That's a novel way to put it," Knox remembered his reply at the time, given with a smile that bordered on smirk.

"That's correct. A nice supply. With this superior embryo survival rate, we can advertise our superiority over other clinics in assisting infertile couples. As long as there is a uterus at their disposal, a couple can have a baby. It's that simple. Our patient base will span between New Orleans and St. Louis, and very likely beyond. I'm certain of it."

As Knox continued on the treadmill and took another slug
of water from his plastic bottle, he recalled mulling over Van
Deman's offer versus returning to his old practice in Montclair.
The last ten months with the guy had indeed been interesting, no,
more than interesting, fascinating. Notwithstanding, Knox could
easily remember the challenging mental debate over accepting
the position with Van Deman versus resuming the security of his
former practice. As he topped four miles, he felt a hint of the sour,
nervous stomach that erupted over the concern of potential failure
during that self-debate, a gastric debacle that was nowhere near
that of the writhing brunette.

"What about the egg donor program?" Knox had asked during
another interview and discussion with Van Deman. "Isn't that
still hot?"

Van Deman laughed softly. "It's not at all hot; it's frozen,"
he said, laughing louder, proud of his play on words. "The
International Fertility Standards Bureau still considers freezing
viable human eggs to be experimental, but I prefer the term
investigational. In fact, the IFSB will continue to label the
freezing of human ova experimental until 100,000 births have
occurred birth defect-free — what a shame, typical bureaucratic
red tape. Hell, my research group in New York produced
hundreds of babies using frozen human eggs, not one case
with an adverse birth effect, except maybe an extra digit on the
extremities here and there.

"The market for frozen eggs exists, Knox, just waiting for us. All
these single, professional women who want to put off childbearing
until they meet Mr. Right will jump at the chance to freeze their
own eggs at a younger time of life, or they still could prefer to
obtain a donor and freeze some embryos for later use," Van
Deman continued with a satisfied smile. "But as far as the
frozen egg program goes, when that rich, handsome guy and

his sperm show up and the woman is too old to conceive or has otherwise lost the ability to do so, her eggs will be ready for a thaw and fertilization."

Knox contributed, "Since the eggs would have been harvested at a younger maternal age, there would be fewer chromosomal concerns, too. Couples would worry less about mental retardation issues like Down's and other congenital deformities associated with older women giving birth, not to mention the higher risks of miscarriage."

Chamblee was becoming more convinced of the technology's potential value to patients as well as to Van Deman and himself. But shortly before making the final decision to accept Van Deman's proposal, he wanted to feel more certain about the true demand for the high-tech reproductive services. "What about the average-income patient?" he asked. "Do you think people in Mississippi will spring for this?"

"Well, first of all, our facility will be able to offer a frozen egg cycle at just over half of what my former colleagues in New York were charging. As I said before, we'll draw clients from everywhere: lots of career women in their mid-thirties, female doctors, lawyers, investment bankers and the like, who suddenly wake up with no natural sperm donor in sight," Van Deman replied with anticipation. "They'll want to put something aside until their early forties when recycled husbands start making their rounds. Of course, alternative lifestyles will come into play. Besides, we can store the frozen eggs and embryos for our clients for three or four hundred bucks a year, adding to our profit margin."

"The AIDS scare could fuel the success of a frozen egg program, as well, I would think," Chamblee added. "HIV killed the fresh sperm donation programs."

"Your thinking is right on track, Knox," Van Deman said with a smile. "Soon the feds will restrict fresh egg donations and require the same six-month waiting period that they do for sperm. If the donor remains HIV-free for six months after the egg harvest, then she's a go, but, of course, the eggs would be nonviable unless they had been frozen. This is a win-win prospect! Rewarding for everybody."

"Seems like it." At the conclusion of the last one-on-one personal interview, a convinced Dr. Chamblee signed the employment contract with Van Deman. He no longer felt averse to the concept of such progressive medical commercialism that had troubled him during his initial contacts with Van Deman. Mainstream medicine had long embraced the informality of community-based advertising, such as seminar presentations to women's groups, free blood pressure and cholesterol screenings at malls, and television interviews about the latest and greatest in this or that medical care.

Knox was converted and ready for the next level. Now more than a year later, he felt even more comfortable with medical marketing and the profitable results. No longer did he shrink at the prospect of medical websites that he had begun to consider no more than expensive yellow page ads, nor did he find distasteful highway billboards portraying smiling doctors whose physical appearances had been so digitally enhanced that they were nearly unrecognizable.

As the morning's session was coming to a close and the dashboard of his treadmill beamed 7.2, 7.3, 7.4 miles toward the goal of 8.0, Chamblee felt even greater satisfaction about his current medical practice situation with Van Deman. Knox was young enough to embrace changing concepts in medical commercialism which he realized would not seem foreign to doctors even younger than he. Through these changes, the medical mainstream would parallel measures of profitability and competition with patient outcomes and satisfaction. Dr. Henry Van Deman espoused the doctrine that the business aspect of medical care should reach clearly beyond superficiality.

Under the Van Deman principle, gone would be traditional lip service slogans used in advertisement of medical services. Such offers as *no appointment necessary* which really mean *you're going to have to wait several hours for the doctor anyway* would become obsolete as patients universally schedule their own appointments online from a personal computer. *Locations all over town* which actually means *before it's all over, you'll probably be sent somewhere else for additional tests or treatments* would be meaningless in a world where multi-specialty medical care all under one roof became standard.

Further, Van Deman believed that the reach of reproductive medicine and resolving human infertility was exploding into a lucrative cash business – one that soon would surpass the need for petty advertising and the limits imposed by medical insurance companies and blue collar pocketbooks. As Knox reached for his yellow Coco Ihle towel to wipe his forehead and neck, he felt pleased that the well-educated, well-trained, savvy Van Deman had seen some promise in him. Reaching beyond mere diplomas and recommendations, the late Cullen Gwinn, MD, had seen that same promise when he hired Knox for his former practice in Montclair. Equally important was the fact that Van Deman was an astute businessman. Since Knox had made the jump to reinvent his medical career by narrowing the scope of his practice, he was resolved that the gamble was softened by Van Deman's abilities.

However, from a financial perspective, it had been unnerving to Knox that his self-directed change of plans and promising new association in medical and surgical practice with Van Deman would focus on a much smaller percentage of the population, only those few who could afford him. The need to remain financially comfortable and become even more so was as important to him as it was to any other professional – or to anyone else for that matter.

Walking away from the treadmill toward the men's shower and locker suite, he smiled at the memory of contract signing day when he sealed a new physician employment agreement with the Henry Van Deman Center of Reproductive Technology. As though clairvoyant, his new boss had squelched any of Knox's ambivalence over personal work satisfaction and the gamble about continued success.

Over drinks to celebrate the commitment, Van Deman had been reassuring. "Your practice with me will be limitless, Knox, especially if you consider the cyber patients."

"Cyber patients?" Knox remembered asking. "That sounds like something out of a Schwarzenegger movie."

"By *cyber patients* I refer to those patients we attract by long distance, either via our reputation, our own website, or links to other websites. You know that when we first started our discussions, I mentioned that I chose this location for commercial reasons but that I expected my – our – reach to extend well beyond Mississippi and the Deep South. Hell, we might even produce some infomercials," he laughed with a great degree of perception as he sipped dry his third pomegranate martini. "They'll fly in or drive in from everywhere to see us. Patients always want the latest, greatest thing, and from the Henry Van Deman Center, they'll get it."

Knox remembered suddenly feeling his eyebrows rise, his face become pale, and his underarms moisten as did the palms of his hands. Maybe this whole thing was going to be a little much, he feared. But Van Deman was convincing.

"In fact, I anticipate other physicians will want to train with us. I have plans to put in an endoscopy lab that utilizes fresh cadaveric tissue for technical skills development, real hands-on surgical training on real human tissue, almost as good as that on live patients, except if the MD makes a mistake ... well, you know, no harm done and no malpractice suit!" he laughed as he switched to a vodka tonic. "We'll develop the highest level of virtual reality physician training and, naturally, become the best in fifth generation robotic surgery."

Knox stopped for a minute to study his reflection in the full length mirror of the men's room, deciding that his ex-girlfriend would have enjoyed the improvements. The career change had cost him that steady relationship, and he had opted out of others since.

I did make the right decision, didn't I? Leaving Montclair for more training and then leaving Montclair for good? he wondered. Losing the ex had only been a small part of the equation. Although he had enjoyed delivering babies and providing routine medical and surgical care for women, there had been no way to return to his previous practice once he had embarked on this new adventure and was introduced to what Henry Van Deman had to offer professionally.

From the start, Van Deman had promised a career of concepts that moved past traditional infertility treatments, even past cryopreservation and frozen embryo transfer. The guaranteed opportunity to return to his old practice in Montclair, to the practice of general obstetrics and gynecology, was simply no longer a challenge.

As he stepped into the shower and reached for one of a choice of several plastic containers of scented body wash, Chamblee still believed that he had made a carefully considered, rational career move in leaving a soon-to-be-lucrative physician practice in sweet little Montclair, Mississippi. He had done this simply because his interests had shifted. The change of direction was not a total 360, just a narrowing of objectives.

Chapter
2

◆◆◆

THE SURVEILLANCE

Just get all of it was the order. *I don't care how you do it – just get all of it* was printed in black ink on white paper. The planning was left to the imagination, and Tinker Murtagh was known for his imagination. No one had to tell him how to steal. As it had been in this case, his hire typically started with nondescript instructions, often sounding desperate, delivered to him by aloof individuals who were just as nondescript. From the appearance and actions of the messenger, Tinker Murtagh judged the kid to be truly unaware of the subject of his errand as well as happily ignorant as to the identity of the sender; he was merely a runner, and a dense one at that.

Unlike the courier, Murtagh found nothing trite about the directive or the place he had been watching as a result. If he had assumed so, then he would have passed on the project since the promised fee fell well short of his usual take. Although the payoff would be slim in comparison, the job's description garnered his attention since it was not a typical heist. "This little stint will add nicely to my repertoire," he decided while refolding the brief note and enjoying the use of a fancy word. What was truly delicious was the promise of money, any money, as the message burned a hole in his pants pocket.

The past twenty-one days of Tinker's vigilant espionage in preparation for the heist had been intriguing for him, intriguing in the sense that he did not understand the motive of his anonymous client. Money must not be the reason, he had decided, only emotion, maybe vengeance. Why else would someone want him to steal a set of human embryos, frozen ones at that?

Murtagh considered himself no different from any other professional; he was in business to make a living, although it never hurt to earn a few kicks along the way. The video of the past three weeks collected at the Henry Van Deman Center for Reproductive Services had become such entertainment, making the meager compensation much more tolerable. Before accepting this job, Tinker had been clueless that the medical procedures he had witnessed were even possible, much less actually performed, but was not surprised to find rich people eager to take part.

The bulk of the espionage had been nothing more than electronic voyeurism, a brand of boredom made bearable only by mentally fingering and counting the reward until he could smell it, taste it. The rather slight cash retainer was quickly spent on updating his computer software, enabling Tinker to accomplish the surveillance with the stroke of a few laptop keys. "A piece of cake," he muttered. "Damn, I'm good!"

Now that the spying was complete and he was ready to move, Murtagh realized that the project could have been shortened to fewer than two days, although the orders had been specific: *Watch for three weeks, no less. You need to be sure that everything works out OK.* After breaching the building's security system, monitoring the night watchman was a study in predictability. By the second night, the security guard's ritual had been nailed, and Tinker could have foregone the rest had it not been for fear of a 48 hour paycheck.

"You just can't let the clients know that these jobs are sometimes too easy. It really doesn't hurt to stretch it out and let them think they're getting their money's worth," he often said aloud to himself.

Murtagh was surprised to find a lone guard assigned to perform the Center's nighttime security duties, particularly skimpy coverage for a commercial facility of the size. The security officer's night off turned out to be Sunday, and even then the guy who filled in for him followed the same pattern on lockup rounds. After checking the main entrance to verify that it was properly secured, a systematic golf cart ride around the renovated, older building with stops at one exterior door after the other accomplished the task. Next, the guard noted on a steno pad the license plate numbers of vehicles left standing overnight in the parking lot, which typically were few, if any.

The security patrol for the interior of the facility was much the same. Like the outside, Tinker could practically set his watch by the night patrol's punctuality and monotonous routine as the low-light surveillance cameras transmitted live video feed to him. Since the security guards spent little time studying the bank of video monitors in the closet-sized room designed for such, Murtagh judged that the digital computer server for the surveillance system was merely preserving the action for later review.

Murtagh's own computer software detected no other remote log-in to the live or stored feed of the security cameras. As an around-the-clock spy in cyberspace, he was the only one there, except for the infrequent spot-check by the on-site guard. While closely analyzing the span of each camera and saving, cataloguing, and timing the video for later reference, Tinker was able to memorize the floor plan of the building complex, learning every square inch of each nook and cranny, including every laboratory and patient examination room. Try as he might, Murtagh was unable to access the private office belonging to one of the physicians, the older one. Initially he decided that the camera placed there was no longer operational, but after analyzing the design further he realized that no surveillance camera had ever been installed in Dr. Van Deman's own office.

Tinker assumed that the value of the tiny, high definition cameras – at least 64 by his count – lay in some sort of strategic design that went far beyond snagging an individual who had stolen away for a smoke. And despite the posts throughout the interior and exterior of the complex, including the employee break area on the rear patio which blared as tastefully as possible *THE VAN DEMAN CENTER AND PROPERTES ARE SMOKE-FREE FACILITIES*, Tinker continued to spot live Marlboro Lights and their residue. He could not hold back. He smoked right along with them.

Murtagh reasoned that the saturated surveillance in and around the building might extend beyond prevention of theft or bad habits but could be considered routine in any such elaborate and supposedly secure site. It seemed nothing more than a standard precaution. Maybe the system was a requirement for casualty or liability insurance coverage, or instead, a mechanism for compiling information for some sort of science documentary. He supposed it possible that someone or some security group planned later to use similar remote access to the site via the Internet.

Surely, he decided, no one would install such an elaborate internal video spy network in a facility and not put it into play, particularly one that rivaled, albeit on a lower scale, RealEyes, Homeland Security's real time surveillance system. Judging from what he had already learned regarding the detail of the Center's physical plant, Tinker assumed that there had to be another party interested in acquiring round-the-clock surveillance of the medical facility.

Maybe these two doctors just got sold a bill of goods. Looks to me that this system is overkill, Tinker thought a few nights after taking the job and observing the night patrol. *If I owned the place and was paying for all this electronic security, I sure as hell would log in with my computer, at least now and then, to keep tabs on that ol' fart.You just can't depend on nobody.*

Within the Van Deman Center was a security office, meant to serve as headquarters for the ol' fart and his slightly younger counterpart who worked the alternate shift. The area measured no less than five by seven feet, no bigger than a walk-in closet by some standards. It was tucked in an out-of-the way corner alcove of the building and boasted a bank of six lonely, fourteen-inch flat screen monitors. The security office was lonely in the sense that its observation deck was never manned continuously; in fact, it was seldom staffed at all. Flirting with any one of the female employees or finding an excuse to visit the break room or men's room was an easy distraction from the cramped, dark quarters that provided only a single metal folding chair for seating.

The visual reach of the security guards' surveillance had been programmed to include only those sections of the infertility treatment complex where security would typically be an issue: each entrance and exit, the employee lounge, the business office, and the patient waiting areas. The security cameras streamed a predictable live feed of various scenarios. There, along with patients walking in and out of the building, the two physicians moved from one room to the other, looking important and either dictating into hand-held digital recorders or typing on thin laptops.

Also visible were employees processing credit cards or receiving checks along with the occasional cash payment from patients who did not appear to fret at all, while other employees stole away to the outside rear patio to talk on cell phones and smoke or to the interior break-room to drink coffee and soft drinks and to gossip. Of course, there was no audio to the spying, but the guard knew there was gossip. As far as the security guard on duty was concerned, the six monitors rotated through a predictably dull routine – just business as usual.

However, from the privileged observation point of Tinker Murtagh in his motel room, a view that extended far beyond that of the hired security guards, business at the Henry Van Deman Center never seemed usual. As Murtagh began to map out the burglary, his daytime surveillance had become much more intriguing than tracking the rote maneuvers of a pot-bellied night security guard. Curiosity over the intricacies of what the two doctors were doing with and to their patients became a near obsession as he remained glued to his laptop screen, recording everything within and circling the building, then neatly filing it away in his hard drive with a backup to the jump drive he wore suspended from his neck.

The detail of the electronic security coverage for the Van Deman Center of Reproductive Services never ceased to impress Tinker Murtagh. Barely a square inch of the property, if that much, was left uncovered by the panorama, except, of course, Van Deman's private office, although that of Dr. Chamblee was ripe for the picking. Murtagh even had full access to the facility's digital video recorder, allowing him to monitor any of the camera's stored footage in addition to the live action. To hack into the video surveillance system, it had first been necessary to steal the Center's IP (Internet Protocol) address so that his computer could communicate with those purchased and installed by Henry Van Deman. After acquiring the Center's computer address, picking up the user name and password had been somewhat simpler, but not as simple as earlier in his career.

Technological advancements had become as much a hindrance as a help to modern burglary, even when the sly perpetrators considered themselves more than tech savvy. A few years back, Tinker's prepping for similar jobs literally involved driving through the business or residential neighborhood of interest, searching for Wi-Fi wireless computer networks. While the use of this wireless Internet "sniffing" was only a hobby for some and had reached beyond the art of DXing (radio scanning by amateur enthusiasts), what was termed wardriving had become a profitable occupation for Murtagh and others. Tinker mastered the concept from an Internet site where not only were operational instructions provided, but also all the necessary software components were available for order from a short list of ready and willing vendors.

Armed with a laptop bulging with downloaded software, external wireless card complete with pigtail appliance attaching it to a small antenna, and handy GPS device to map all wireless access points, warrior Murtagh could then detect and record every single stroke made on a targeted computer keyboard. Parked curbside, secure within his "company" van with *WE PAINT MISSISSIPPI* emblazoned across the sides and a directional antenna slyly mounted rooftop, Tinker would then become a virtual user of the networked computer system inside the targeted business or home. Once he had the location and status of the wireless network marked, it was simple for him to pull up the IP address from the targeted computer. The victim's user name and password easily came next. With all of this supposedly secure information at his disposal, Tinker could then hack into his target's computers from anywhere in the world as long as he had access to the Internet.

Tinker had built a bank of clients through referrals that included corporate executives and managers, advantaged but jealous housewives with entrée to substantial checking or savings

accounts, and lagging-in-the-polls politicians or their backers.
A quick and often-used application for this curbside wireless
espionage had involved piercing corporate communication
systems so that executives away from the office could peek from
the outside looking for an embezzler or underling otherwise up to
no good.

Much like watching a reality television show, the goal of
snagging an employee's indiscretion or wasted moment or two
was often accomplished by Tinker Murtagh. In those early years,
he often was called a computer genius. Of course, since Tinker
saw no conflict of interest in turning the tables, some of those
same executive clients fell prey to the reverse process initiated by
their peers or spouses.

For Tinker Murtagh business remained good. Nevertheless,
widespread use of security-enabled wireless software in private
homes and businesses had made the ease of wardriving by Tinker
and others ancient history. Without a change in *operandus* of his
wireless computer surveillance service, Tinker's ability to unearth
secrets electronically would have been no more productive than
emptying the contents of a vic's mailbox. A self-taught survivor,
Tinker Murtagh prided himself on the extent of his computer
knowledge and in maintaining cutting-edge, brilliant, and
unbeatable abilities – a self-perception likely widespread among
hackers. He liked being thought of as a computer genius.

Because of the introduction and widespread use of security-
enabled wireless Internet systems, there was indeed a challenge
to staying in business. Tinker could not argue that he enjoyed
hacking into computers, but to do so unhindered he needed to
maintain the ability to gain access into the pool of static Internet
protocol addresses. Through the back door of another Internet
site specializing in wireless computer networking, Murtagh first
obtained and then implemented certain Internet auditing software
that remedied his dilemma, putting him back in business.

Afforded an individual or corporate static IP address, he would continue to have access to an online surveillance system from anywhere in the world, just as if he were an authorized security guard, corporate executive, business principal, curious home owner ... or whoever. Retaining the ability was necessary to satisfy this client who was so interested in the Van Deman Center. In completing every previous job, he had gotten by with only virtual on-site presence. However, this assignment was different. Once he had seen what he needed to see inside the medical facility, he would physically have to break inside to get it.

Opening the monitor's screen, Tinker commanded the console to display a nine-screen matrix devoted to the Henry Van Deman Center of Reproductive Technology, optioning down to a show of only four. Four cameras, top-of-the-line, with a nighttime resolution approaching that of crystal clear daylight and assisted by a multitude of unobtrusively-placed, but effective, exterior lights were serving Murtagh and the security guard well – that is, they would have served the security guard well if he had taken more than a cursory glance at them. However, the building's exterior lights were not needed at the moment; it was a few minutes after ten o'clock in the morning.

Camera number three's display was to the lower left of the matrix and offered an overview of the facility's expansive front parking lot. Tinker reasoned that the camera was mounted on one of the security light poles rising from a landscaped planting bed but then realized from the surroundings that it was perched in a tall, live oak no doubt indigenous to the property. From whatever its height, the observer could appreciate the detail and lavishness of the property's landscape.

In a random but uniformly timed sequence that still provided equal coverage to each area, the surveillance software automatically altered the directional view of the exterior cameras.

Through his online ability to override each programmed position, Murtagh redirected number three's tiny robotic arm to scan the lot thoroughly along with its periphery, briefly zooming in and out to improve the detail but at the same time resisting idle play. Although he still believed there was little to no live observation of the site other than his own study, too much magnification of the camera's typical view, no matter how slight, could alert security. Again, from what Tinker had observed from the lackadaisical security guards, he was not overly concerned, actually not concerned at all.

The landscaping surrounding the parking area boasted nearly mature trees, transplanted at a height that blended smoothly with the existing landscape. A group of fairly young hardwoods standing in close proximity to the building itself had miraculously survived the modernization and expansion of the original physical plant, an abandoned Masonic Lodge. This third camera captured the effects of a soft breeze that bathed the area, creating a relaxing, gentle sway in the tree canopy. The ferns and azaleas planted beneath the healthy trees moved in unison.

But nature's ambience was lost on Tinker Murtagh.

"There ain't a piece of trash nowhere," he said aloud, continuing his inspection of the exterior by highlighting the panel for camera five and then redirecting to another, number eight. "Nothin' goin' on back here either," he determined after scanning the rear exit, which included a camouflaged garbage receptacle area. "Hell, not even a cigarette butt thrown on the ground, not a single one."

Returning to his study of the building's front exterior, Tinker no longer marveled at the building's red brick façade, no doubt meant for those who appreciated renovated Greek revival architecture. Ornate china-white columns supported an expansive porch lined with color coordinated china-white rocking chairs meant for an inviting air but unused, or at least not during the time of Tinker's three-week watch. Breaking the middle of the porch were oversized English ferns flanking the main entrance. Although the plants did not appear artificial, he had never noticed an attendant watering or grooming them. Never was a frond out of place.

To the right and left of the steps leading to the grand porch were meticulously manicured flower beds, each living thing in its place as though nature had created it there with pleasure, never to be disturbed. The fact that the fussily managed seasonal plantings were free of encroaching weeds or foreign grasses as well as bird or other animal droppings was completely lost on the Internet voyeur. Tinker also failed to appreciate the aesthetics of each strand of pine straw or black-stained woodchip and the deep green ground cover which masked the bare areas of soil.

Despite the camera's high-definition capability and resulting brilliant display of organic harmony, the splendor of the landscape's architectural design was clearly not an issue for Mr. Murtagh. Instead, Tinker focused on the return of the light yellow Mercedes S550 that suddenly rematerialized in the top right corner of his monitor. The matrix for camera number two continued to hold that place of honor. Having spotted the vehicle on other occasions, he had somehow missed the driver each time but made note to check the video archives. Today he surmised that the Mercedes must have slipped onto the property through the main highway entrance while his attention was directed toward the rear garbage receptacles and the check for cigarette butts.

Highlighting camera three's panel, Tinker brought the view to full screen. He watched with interest as the Mercedes approached the dark red, slave-made brick front steps which beckoned to the expansive front porch. In near military style, the doorman descended from the porch, marking each row of steps of the sweeping staircase with precision, tipping his hat to the driver in anticipation. Much to Tinker's surprise, the vehicle did not stop there for valet parking but instead pulled into the left side of the parking lot, where its driver chose a vacancy not far from the smiling doorman.

Given only a brief glimpse, Tinker realized the driver was female. The feminine aura projected by the vehicle was an irresistible influence in making that decision, not to mention the doorman's chivalrous attitude as the car flew by him. Tinker longed for a facial close-up, impossible until she stepped from the car. "Hell, who does she think I am, the paparazzi or somethin'?" he chuckled sarcastically as the face remained obscured from the live camera and Tinker's eye.

Despite switching to the camera lens hidden under the eaves of the front façade and redirecting it toward the mid-section of the parking lot in an effort to hit the subject full frontal, Tinker could not define her facial features. Even the magnification and zoom option proved useless as she kept her looks obscured by dropping her head. With the middle finger of his right hand, Tinker thumped the encasement of the laptop in angry frustration. He wanted a closer look; he needed a closer look.

Was this the one? Tinker wondered, trying to control his growing anger as he outlined her figure on the screen, his index finger directing the cursor first to the shape of her chest then descending to the buttocks as the woman turned her back again to the camera. She reached back into the car and produced her purse from its place on the front passenger seat. As the woman shut the driver's door and finally completed her exit from the car, long blonde hair swung in sync with the door's movement as she stepped quickly away. As though trying to escape Tinker's facial study, she kept her head lowered while walking briskly but purposefully toward the entrance to the Center.

"Blue? Were her eyes blue?" He further adjusted the camera angle seeking the answer and then continued his electronic trace of her body, turning next to the form of the blonde's right leg, reaching her spiked heels before doing the same with the left. By the time he was to her left shoe, the woman had reached the bottom of the steps where the doorman, and oftentimes valet, remained at smiling attention, as though in anticipation.

"Mornin', Ma'am." Tinker missed the doorman's greeting but noticed the blonde toss her head a few degrees or so in the man's direction as she gracefully moved past him to ascend the steps to the entrance. Cheryl Choice was not about to introduce herself to the attendant, and his attempt to learn her name or that of any of the other clients or visiting families would have been met with immediate termination. The Van Deman Center was a private place.

To assure her privacy whenever she visited the Center, Cheryl Choice disguised herself with a long blonde human hair wig that looked as natural as that of any frosted blonde. Cheryl was a natural brunette, as Knox Chamblee had noticed when he saw her daily at boot camp. When she was not throwing up as the result of Coco Ihle's punishing routines, her rich, nearly olive complexion and classic facial features radiated without the need of much makeup. She flaunted this look around Jackson and had done so throughout the country when she once traveled extensively with her husband Gregg. In contrast, her beauty was never on display at Coco Ihle's Fitness and Body Camp but instead was generally drained to a pale display of sweat and the matted locks of her natural hair.

Up to that point, Knox had still not formerly met Choice on the exercise floor nor had he come face-to-face with her at work. Unknowingly he had assisted with her treatments and egg harvesting procedures at the Center as he would have done for any of the other patients primarily assigned to Dr. Van Deman. That was his job and his new career. Had he indeed seen her in person or noted her patient file photograph, there would have been no chance of recognizing her as the unfortunate woman who had regurgitated in the bushes and had been the brunt of Coco Ihle's insults.

Just as she did when attending workouts, Cheryl Choice left her structured, designer street apparel and emerald and diamond jewelry at home when keeping her physician appointments, adding to her blonde alter ego a wardrobe of loosely structured, costly outfits that approached the provocative. The jewelry became heavy costume items that were always color-coordinated. The thick makeup applied to her face, arms, and chest lightened her exposed skin, making her almost unrecognizable without detailed study. In this altered look for her donations at the Center, even a close friend or associate would have walked right past her.

As Cheryl Choice began to climb the steps ahead of the doorman, remaining focused and purposeful, she managed a silent smile in acknowledgement of the attendant. Tinker watched the guy literally trot up the steps to head her off at the handle of the front door and wait to open it for her.

Studying her near-seductive climb to the building's front entrance, Tinker was jealous of the doorman's unobstructed view. He was angry that the guy had the advantage of touchable, face-to-face scrutiny while his entertainment unfolded behind a cold camera, keyboard, and cursor.

"How old is this chick anyway – twenties, thirties, or maybe even a well-preserved early forties?" he guessed aloud. The high-def, multi-pixel resolution of Tinker's electronic study could not overcome the angle of this particular camera and the shyness of the subject who would not cooperate by lifting her face. Maybe she did not want to cooperate.

If she let the doorman see her, thought Tinker, *why wouldn't she let Tinker Murtagh see her?* "Stuck-up bitch," he muttered. "She doesn't want me to get a good look. Well, we'll see." The solution was a full 200% camera zoom as he pushed his effort.

As expected, her body moved closer to Tinker as it glided across the brick porch toward the front door. The answer to the age question, or maybe the assumption, was a quick tease for Murtagh. Passing through the building's entrance, she seemed to glance upward into the camera and even grin at her new observer.

"Thirtyish! Yeah, hot chick's in her thirties, early thirties – no, maybe late twenties. But she looks damn good wherever she is. Walks good, too!" Tinker shouted in his motel room.

Cheryl Choice had indeed moved through that entrance on multiple occasions and in similar style, picking her associations there carefully and with marked discretion. The aloofness she exuded each time was a feminine quality that attracted the doorman in contrast to what Murtagh now saw as raging sexual energy begging to be released.

"Mornin', Ma' am," the doorman repeated unanswered as he held the door open for Choice and from his angle watched her upper thighs elevate and lower the crowning buttocks as she walked through the door. Just as much as Tinker, he wanted to grope but would never get the opportunity.

As Choice entered the enclosed foyer and vanished from the doorman into the patient sign-in area, Tinker switched to a different camera and shook his head in vexation. Understanding the facts did not make him happy; this woman was out of his league. Besides, Tinker had business to take care of, no more time to play around with computer-age fantasy. To supplement the interior and exterior blueprints of the building which he had stolen online, he needed to wrap up the fine points of his surveillance. The job was coming to a close. His fee was fixed, no bonus for early completion, although a satisfied customer generally meant repeat business.

This particular heist was certainly unique for him as it would have been for any of his peers. Tinker Murtagh prided himself in a smooth operation: systematic, well-orchestrated, and clean. This job was a definite challenge, an enigma all its own.

After all, never before had he been hired to rob an infertility clinic.

Chapter

3

◆◆◆

THE SCENARIO

The 2:00 a.m. trip to the hospital emergency room in Jackson
was an emotional shock both to Wesley Sarbeck and his wife
Carrie, and would become a hemorrhagic one for her. The
entrance to this particular ER had become nothing more than a
revolving door where the triage nurse knew the Sarbecks by name.

When the emergency room doctor reviewed the results of
the first round of blood tests and announced that Carrie was
pregnant, Wesley immediately assumed that his wife already knew
it and suspected the reasons for her secrecy. He rationalized that
his wife of 15 years was consumed by dread, hoping to prevent
another round of regret for herself as well as for him.

The last 12 years of trying to have a baby had been a mentally
crushing and financial upheaval for Mr. and Mrs. Wesley Sarbeck.
To compare their emotions and personal experiences to a roller
coaster ride would be to make light of the situation. Wesley
assumed from the Bible that God meant for propagation of the
species to be a perfectly natural thing, but for some reason He had
chosen to omit Carrie and Wesley Sarbeck from that plan.

"I guess I'm just made of piss-poor protoplasm!" Carrie

Sarbeck had screamed one morning when another conventional infertility treatment had failed and the home pregnancy test kit read *negative*. Out of frustration she turned to her only living relative, a childless, widowed maternal aunt who also lived in Jackson. Carrie hoped for the consolation that commiseration can sometimes bring, although the aunt's barren state in relation to that of her niece was more out of coincidence than anything else.

From that teary conversation, her aunt revealed that her own husband had abandoned her after ten years of marriage, not because of infidelity as she had once told Carrie, but because of her own infertility issues, and choked in prayer with Carrie that her husband would not do the same. With some element of fact, Carrie's aunt began to assume genetic blame for the endometriosis that had blocked Carrie's childbearing efforts.

"When my husband divorced me, the court was generous. Much of what I gained has remained in a liquid investment account. I have been saving the money for a special need, and I believe that I have found that," she announced between sobs, much to Carrie's surprise.

Neither Wesley nor Carrie was totally reserved in accepting the financial gift, regardless of whether or not there existed a true link between Carrie's inability to have a baby and her dwindling family's health problems. "Go ahead and let your aunt get some relief from her guilt. Why not?" he responded when Carrie first shared the news of her aunt's financial offer. The couple happily and gratefully accepted the money and recycled it in a revolving door of reproductive specialists.

However, the pregnancy that had landed them in the emergency room with Carrie in mortal danger had somehow occurred unscheduled, a product of the couple's spontaneous sex life and Carrie's libido, which much to Wesley's relief, had survived the aura of artificiality surrounding their difficult and unsuccessful road to parenthood. Even through the resulting diagnosis and treatment of her clinical depression, Carrie had miraculously retained her interest in sex.

"You're lucky she got to the hospital when she did," said the doctor Wesley had not seen enter the cramped waiting area. Located down a short hall from the hospital operating suite and recovery room, Wesley intentionally sat removed from the family members of other patients. During Carrie's surgery, he had forced himself to look at a well-thumbed hunting magazine left from several seasons ago, but actually he could think of nothing but his wife and her survival.

In a tone laced with the forced politeness of professionalism, the doctor continued, "Had your wife sought medical care earlier in the pregnancy, then the ectopic might have been diagnosed before its rupture." He paused a moment before adding, "Then we might have been able to do more."

Wesley expected the doctor to shake his head at him in disgust, but the denouncement never came. He looked over at the thick plastic badge hanging cockeyed from the collar of the physician's white lab coat and read the name *Van Deman, Henry* printed under a reasonably decent and recent photograph.

Once the emergency room physician had taken Carrie's menstrual and obstetrical history as it related to the development of sudden, severe abdominal pain and dizziness and compared it to the positive pregnancy test, an easy assumption of an ectopic pregnancy was made. This consulting physician had been hastily called in to evaluate and care for Carrie, the physician being, as the ER doctor explained, an infertility specialist who could not only solve the emergency but perhaps also give them hope for a healthy baby in the future. Wesley was given a brief moment with Van Deman immediately before his wife was whisked away to emergency surgery, oxygen mask in place with an IV in each arm and a soft bag of blood transfusing through both.

"Fortunately, we were able to save your wife's uterus," Dr. Van Deman explained once the surgery was completed and Carrie was safely recovering in the intensive care unit. Other than the relief of learning that his wife had survived, the medical heroism was lost on Wesley. "You see, Mr. Sarbeck, the out-of-place, or ectopic, implantation site of your wife's pregnancy was in the cornual area of the uterus." A look of non-comprehension emanated from the husband, who unbeknown to Van Deman had actually assimilated a decent level of layman's medical knowledge through all of Carrie's unsuccessful infertility treatments, nevertheless lacking the fine specifics. "The cornua is the area of the uterus where the fallopian tube joins the uterus," Henry Van Deman continued.

The tall, distinguished-looking doctor could at the moment add little to Wesley's bank of medical concepts since his level of anxiety blocked out anything more than that Carrie was alive. This new doctor had lost the distraught husband on the specifics, and Van Deman knew it.

"As the pregnancy grew in size," he continued with practiced patience, "it quickly distended, or stretched, that area of the uterus, which is naturally quite thin." The husband's stare remained blank but at the same time was clouding. "You see, the stretching of this thin area of the uterus by the abnormal attachment of the pregnancy resulted in excessive bleeding into the tissues, which was not self-contained."

Despite his best efforts, the infertility specialist saw no comprehension in the husband's blank stare. Nevertheless, Dr. Van Deman pushed on. "The anatomy there just does not allow a pregnancy to grow as it should. Therefore, as the pregnancy increased in size, the uterine wall ruptured." Still blank, not even a blink. "Well, so with this rupture, heavy bleeding then spread into the area of the adjacent fallopian tube and ovary."

Van Deman again saw no progress with the husband and

decided to rephrase. "The fallopian tube also became involved in the distention, ahh, *stretching*, of the tissues as the bleeding spread, *pushed on*, uncontained, *unstopped*. This led to the rupture of the uterine cornual area and the loss of your wife's remaining fallopian tube and ovary. Somehow, my partner, Dr. Chamblee, and I were still able to save your wife's uterus."

Drawing on his best bedside manner, Van Deman worked to mask his frustration over the husband's stone-faced response. His explanation of the surgery performed and its indications had been methodical and accurate but unabsorbed. As an alternative, Dr. Van Deman abandoned the detailed medical rhetoric and went for the primitive.

"Everything just blew apart. There was nothing else that Dr. Chamblee and I could do. She lost all of her female organs, except the uterus. I'm sorry."

Beads of sweat had begun to erupt on the pale, high forehead of Wesley Sarbeck. "Doctor, is my wife dead, or something?" he wanted to ask, but could not for fear of the answer. Defeated, he merely stared at Van Deman in silence.

Through his bewilderment he saw in the surgeon's demeanor a muddle of professionalism, fatigue, concern, and indifference. It was the deep concern in the doctor's facial expression that alarmed him, for there was one aspect of this doctor's family waiting room discourse that was missing: Sarbeck feared that the surgeon was bracing him for the ultimate in devastation.

Unlike others before him, this doctor had not entered the room after Carrie's surgeries with a cheery *Your wife made it, Wesley, my friend. She's doing just fine, just fine.* Through all the initial rhetoric about hysterectomy and fallopian tube and ovary, Wesley wanted to beg for reassurance that his young, beautiful wife had not been left brain dead or even just plain dead. And if either had been the case, the devastation would have been his fault, his reward for getting her pregnant without some doctor's magic formula.

The silence between doctor and distraught family member was broken when a gasp erupted from around the corner in the family waiting room. A robust woman in her mid-fifties, dressed in a flowered tunic with a miniature silver cross hanging from a taut left ankle bracelet, had positioned herself behind a partition a few chairs over from the aisle, fanning herself with a well-worn copy of *People* magazine. The frequent visitor treasured the communal nature of the family waiting room, which on this night was particularly entertaining. Her eavesdropping on the one-sided Van Deman/Sarbeck dialogue reached, if not surpassed, the theatrics of one of her favorite medical television dramas, not to mention the magazine article she had been reading. Her only wish at the moment was for a volume control that would prevent her from having to lean sideways to hear the doctor's lines.

Ignoring the interruption, Dr. Van Deman lowered his voice a few decibels out of sensitivity for Mr. Sarbeck's privacy and elaborated further. "As I said before, fortunately we were able to save the uterus." Another fitful gasp from around the corner brought a frowning pause from Van Deman as Mr. Sarbeck remained motionless, expressionless.

His annoyance suppressed, Van Deman continued, "As I was saying, Mr. ... Sarbeck, luckily, we were able to halt the hemorrhage before a hysterectomy became necessary. Removing the remaining fallopian tube and ovary and halting the bleeding facilitated our suturing the rupture in the uterus. Thus, we saved your wife's uterus and her life."

"A hysterectomy?" Wesley asked almost rhetorically, jerked back from his fear that Carrie had not made it through surgery at all. Earlier that evening as his wife was carted away on a gurney to what he assumed was simply another procedure, he had never considered the finality of that possibility.

"Oh, dear God, no! She's too young!" a feminine voice erupted from behind the partition. The outburst was followed by another deeper gasp, sounding like a plea for the Heimlich maneuver.

Unlike the around-the-corner eavesdropper, Wesley's own concentration on the doctor's words was much more scrambled. As he continued to drown in confusion over his wife's medical condition, the memory of their years of marriage replayed in reverse before jerking his mind through a blurry futuristic fast-forward. In what seemed to be a poorly focused video, he could not recognize Carrie's face at all, much less imagine faces of any unborn children.

This foggy visual of his never-to-be family was interrupted by a repeat from around the corner, "Oh, dear God, no. She's too young!" in a guttural, defeated, but at the same time prayerful tone. Her own follow-up question for the doctor of *"What about IVF?"* trailed off as she looked up reverently toward the discolored ceiling tiles, her magazine flattened between her closed palms.

Ignoring the interruption, Van Deman continued, "Yes, at the beginning of your wife's surgery, as we saw the extent of her internal bleeding, we thought that a hysterectomy was unavoidable." Wesley shook his head reflexively, bringing his face back toward that of the doctor, trying to fight imagination for reality.

Upon still receiving no verbal response from the man before him, Van Deman felt the need to repeat himself. "During the procedure to correct the ruptured ectopic pregnancy, we were concerned that removal of the uterus would be necessary to stop the bleeding and save your wife's life. Happily, things turned out differently."

"Differently? Happily?" Wesley jerked back to attention as though jabbed in the ribs with a fireplace poker. His response was one of edged anger mixed with frustration.

"Oh, God, yes. There are still options for the two of you," the emotional surrogate sitting around the corner reacted, this time in whisper, though still audible to Van Deman and Sarbeck. The continued interruption was nothing more that her effort to propagate a boiling melodrama.

"You see, Mr. ..." Van Deman paused momentarily, glancing down to reference the slip of paper handed him by the operating room nurse, a printout of both the patient's name and medical record number. "You see, Mr. Sarbeck," he pushed on undeterred, "with today's medical advances, preserving the uterus, even though both fallopian tubes and ovaries have now been lost, represents an important feat." One of the most renowned reproductive endocrinologists in the United States then paused again, waiting for some sense of comprehension, the person before him maintaining a half-blank stare.

Unabashed, the infertility surgeon plunged forward, adding a tone of the more dramatic, as though he were heating things up for the eavesdropper around the corner and preparing for the upcoming television ratings sweeps. "Tonight, we saved your wife's life, ripping her away from death due to an acute pelvic hemorrhage. And now, given our cutting-edge medical and surgical reproductive options, she, that is, both of you, can still have a family if you like."

"But how? She doesn't have any tube or ovary left. She lost the other side a couple of years ago, and, Doctor, you just said that you had to remove her last one. Didn't you?" Wesley asked, already knowing the answer.

"Yes, yes, unhh, hunhh. I heard him say that. Yes, yes. I did. Oh, God!" The *People* magazine was now clutched tightly to the woman's chest, the antics of the British royal family, David Beckham, and the Spears family long forgotten.

Pretending sudden concern that the doctor and the poor

husband near her in the waiting room might sense her presence,
the rapt audience of one mouthed her next response without
losing the intense drama. "Oh, there are still options to have
a baby. There must be!" she intoned, her facial expression a
contorted plea, learned from any of several day- or nighttime soap
opera actresses.

Despite the silence from around the corner, Van Deman was
sure of the constant intrusion as he stood stiffly from his seat
across from Wesley and stepped around the corner. "Miss, may I
help you with something?" As if she were oblivious to the Sarbeck
plight, the gesture was greeted with a spread-open edition of a
much fresher *Us*, the change of magazine covering the woman's
round, reddening face and surprised open mouth.

Not having expected a reply from the intruder, Van Deman
stepped back around to his patient's husband without missing a
beat in his medical/surgical discourse. "You see, Mr. Sarbeck,"
he said, once again referencing the tiny sheet of patient ID
information cupped in his right hand, "given today's technological
advances in reproductive medicine, uterine preservation is
important even after loss of both fallopian tubes and ovaries."

"OK, Doctor. I guess I understand." Wesley was breathing a
little easier, the sweaty forehead drying a bit. "The fact that my
wife is alive is really what's important to me right now."

"Oh, Lord, thankya, Jesus," was next mouthed by the woman
around the corner as she dropped the *Us* magazine to clench
her fists nervously against her pursed lips. As she wanted so
desperately to scream aloud in relief for the poor man around the
corner, her head shuddered in reprieve as the magazine settled
askew on the floor.

Van Deman paused momentarily at the brisk rustle of paper,
fully expecting a snooping comment to follow. Surprised
at hearing none, the surgeon lowered the volume a bit and

commented, "Right, Mr. Sarbeck, that is definitely what's important – your wife's life, of course." Up to that moment, Wesley had forced composure he considered befitting a city policeman: steely professionalism, almost military at times, mixed with a vow of cordial public service. Now looking away from the doctor, he dropped his eyes to the white Styrofoam cup half-filled with coffee and held tightly in his right hand. Wesley was flabbergasted to find the liquid quivering. Embarrassed, he quickly brought his left hand to the opposite side of the cup to stabilize it. He wondered if the doctor had noticed.

The doctor had not. On the other hand, what Dr. Van Deman could not miss were the man's moist eyes. "Mr. Sarbeck, I know this has been terribly difficult for you, as well as for your wife." The doctor reached toward Wesley's knee and patted it reassuringly. The sincere gesture made Wesley feel uncomfortable for a moment. Carrie's emotionally stricken husband stared deeply into the black liquid in the Styrofoam cup that grew even colder as it continued to shake subtly.

"May I call you Wesley?" the doctor inquired gently. By now the name was clear to Van Deman. He no longer needed his cheat sheet for reference.

"Sure, Doctor. Wesley is fine."

"So, you see, Wesley, the two of you as a couple still have options, modern options. Fortunately, in reproductive medicine we have made great strides in defeating human infertility. My associate, Dr. Knox Chamblee, and I, along with our highly trained staff, would like to have an opportunity to discuss these medical advances with the two of you."

"Good God, man. What are you talking about?" Wesley Sarbeck blurted, his stoic policeman's demeanor vanished. "My wife just had surgery for God's sake, Doctor. She was on the brink of death. All I care about right now is her!" Sarbeck reacted, shaking his head in a mixture of disgust and surprise at what he perceived as insensitivity on the surgeon's behalf.

Glaring at this man outfitted in a neatly pressed, blue-colored scrub suit, a man he had just met, a guy who had just ripped open his wife and wanted credit for saving her life, he suddenly wondered if perhaps he was misjudging Dr. Van Deman. Surely the busy doctor took pride in his work. Through his professional medical insight, Van Deman was simply giving recommendations on the next level of patient care, Wesley decided.

Officer Wesley Sarbeck understood the meaning of professionalism – hard work and ethical standards. To date, the officer's law enforcement career had included a smattering of car wreck investigations, even a brief gun battle at the termination of a high speed car chase with a fleeing bank robber, and another at a motel on Highway 80 in south Jackson. At a rest stop off the interstate, he had apprehended and then shot, although not mortally wounded, a man holding his estranged wife hostage at knife-point. Those events had been the dramatic highlights of a career that typically was much more mundane. Academy training films had definitely been more explicit, much more horrific, than anything he had ever witnessed on active duty as a Jackson, Mississippi, city policeman.

But nothing he had ever seen go down or even studied in training had been as heart-wrenching or disturbing as what he had experienced that evening. The terror of watching his pale, nearly unresponsive wife being lifted from the emergency room examination table by a bunch of scrub-suits and then strapped to a gurney for a race to the operating room still sickened him. The doctors and nurses had not even given him a chance to kiss Carrie goodbye before whisking her down a corridor to an operating room. He had felt deserted, left standing in the disheveled ER cubicle. In his left hand was a printed sheet of paper pinned to a clipboard, meant to serve as legal consent for his wife's emergency treatment and surgery while a cheap plastic signing pen waited in his right.

Once Carrie vanished down the gray hall to surgery, the only other detail Wesley remembered was the sudden materialization of an ER unit secretary. "Please go ahead and sign the consent, sir," she pleaded coolly, gesturing to the pen he had been handed. "My shift'll be over in fifteen minutes so I gotta get all this paper work straight. Cordelia comes on after me, and she'll be pissed if all this ain't done by the time she clocks in."

Henry Van Deman had ignored the temper flare before him. He expected some husbands and partners to react in certain ways to certain treatment outcomes. After all, that was ordinary human nature – a gut-level mixture of anger, grief, and hopelessness scrambled with worry over medical costs. Even so, in the best interests of the Sarbecks and the recruitment efforts of his practice he remained unabashed.

"My reproductive center would like to help you and Mrs. Sarbeck," Van Deman said. "Since your wife was lucky enough to retain her uterus, Dr, Chamblee and I can do all kinds of things for the two of you. Your wife can still carry and give birth to a baby since the exciting technology is endless: frozen or even fresh embryo transfer using donor eggs, fresh or frozen, fertilized with your sperm or, if you prefer, a sperm donor," Van Deman detailed to a husband whose expression had returned to blank, although a faint gasp from around the corner signaled the eavesdropper's diversion from an *Entertainment Weekly* article.

Who is this guy, anyway? Wesley began to wonder. Despite a burgeoning receptiveness to the doctor's presentation, Wesley's comfort zone was assured by the certainty of his wife's safety, not in the long-held desire to produce offspring with her. Finally learning that Carrie had survived the emergency surgery due to her, to their, ectopic pregnancy had been an overwhelming relief, although through his growing calm, Wesley Sarbeck still felt the horror of her possible death from a pregnancy he had caused her.

Quickly setting the cold coffee on the plastic wood grain table near his chair, Wesley lowered his face into open, clammy hands to cover his tears. The possibility of yet another bag of blood flowing into his wife's slight arm made his head pound, accompanied by a wave of nausea. Suddenly, Wesley could think of nothing but Carrie's life-saving blood transfusions administered earlier in the emergency room. The sight had been agonizing: thick red blood cells filling two lines of intravenous tubing crammed into his wife, red blood cells donated by someone they would never know, maybe someone with a terrible, undetected disease. This blood would serve only temporary residence in his wife's veins, running quickly to her heart before being pumped through her arteries to a hole in her pelvis, a hole that would not have erupted had he not gotten her pregnant.

Wesley Sarbeck grew sicker with the thought and feared he would soon vomit before Van Deman. He doubted if he could make it to the nearest men's room. He fought the vision of Dr. Van Deman and the other surgeon – was the name *Chamblee*? – dodging streams of pressurized blood spurting from his wife as they cut open her belly. He swallowed deeply, forcing the bitterness down his throat, trying not to lose it, and fighting the urge to punch-out the know-it-all MD sitting in front of him. Even with that, Wesley looked around for a garbage can, just in case.

"Look, Doctor, I appreciate your saving my wife's life," Wesley managed to respond, trying to regain composure as he swallowed hard and breathed slowly. No, he was not really going to throw up, he decided, then thought differently as a shot of acid spurted up from his stomach, forcing a cough when a trickle dropped down his trachea. "But, Doctor," Wesley managed to say to Van

Deman, "I think you're going a little too far with all this other infertility treatment crap, all this magical stuff that you say your practice can do for us, especially when none of Carrie's other doctors has ever mentioned any of that stuff to us – frozen this or fresh that."

Van Deman sat there motionless, expressionless, waiting out the husband's frustration. "Hey, look, Doctor ... see, the way I feel," he swallowed deeply, fighting his bitterness against life as well as the churning in his stomach, "for God's sake, my wife, she almost died. That possibility was all I heard from the ER nurses and doctors when we first made it into the emergency room before you got here. I really think you're kinda out-of-line right now talking about anything else. All I needed to hear from you I've already heard – that my wife is OK and that she's going to stay that way."

Wesley had said enough. He would fight the display of further aggravation, relying instead on the professionalism of his training in dealing with the public, the minor lawbreakers, and the whiney insistent ones. He wondered if this Dr. Van Deman's story about having to remove Carrie's last ovary and fallopian tube as a life-saving measure had been just that, a story, a story to avert a malpractice case.

The doctor had gotten his point across in absolving himself and the other physician of any careless surgical or medical care regarding his wife. At the same time Van Deman had touted the overall successes of Carrie's surgery and the possibility that she could still have a baby under his watch. Needing to do something with his hands, Wesley reached for the cup of cold coffee and picked it up with his right. He needed to be honest with himself about what he really wanted out of life and what he really believed. Wesley did not blame the doctor for what had happened tonight, nor did he blame his wife. This time Carrie must have been in denial about being pregnant. That's why his poor wife had not told him: she was trying to avoid more disappointment – for herself as well as for her husband.

Wesley was ready to be left alone to wait for some nurse to come for him. She would announce to him as had been done so many times before, "Sir, you may see your wife now. Please come with me."

In dismissal of Van Deman, he pushed, "I just said, Doctor, we've just been through a lot tonight. I don't need any other information 'cept that my wife is all right."

Henry Van Deman took a deep but quiet breath, one that hid his exhausted patience. Having been subject to similar past responses received from the sexual partners of patients, he assumed that the specialty of his services was wasted on the ignorant, blue-collar brick wall sitting before him. The advanced training and progressive medical practice experience which followed had landed Henry Van Deman, MD, in a position of technical authority; it was the emotional or psychological authority over Sarbeck that was presently lacking.

Regardless of his superior education, Van Deman's better judgment saw the futility of one-upmanship with Mr. Wesley Sarbeck. On the other hand, the reproductive medicine specialist wanted to retort, "Well, if you and your wife had sought earlier medical intervention by even a few hours, then her situation likely would not have been as critical." But common sense ruled that consideration as purely antagonistic and bordering on cruel. Whether the fault of delay in her pregnancy care resided with the patient, the husband, or both of them, Van Deman was unsure; it certainly did not matter now.

Nevertheless, he felt that his surgical skills and mental expertise should never go to waste. "Mr. Sarbeck, I know this has been a rough night for you and your wife." Van Deman rewired his tone and composure to one of great compassion and understanding.

"Anyone in your situation would be as upset as you are fatigued. However, it would be negligent of me not to explain the current options open to patients who are meeting difficulty in having a baby. The things that I alluded to earlier are, of course, purely optional." The Van Deman medical marketing program was in full force.

"Yes, Doctor, I understand," Wesley acquiesced out of exhaustion. He was anxious to distance himself from the doctor. "I know. You're just trying to do your job," he added in a stretch of surrender, followed by a stretch of the truth, "and, anyway, I'm not trying to be a wise-ass."

Van Deman answered with a smile of professional acknowledgment. "Thanks for saving my wife, Doctor – Wesley referred to the physician name badge after a second of hesitation – Van Deman." Annoyed, Van Deman wanted to correct the guy's pronunciation from *Van Day'mun* to the proper *Van' Duemon*, but decided against it. "Even though she – we – wanted to have a child, to have a real family, I guess we should just give up. It just isn't meant to be, just isn't in the cards." Wesley's voice was steady, though clearly dejected.

He could see the sympathy in the doctor's face and manner; his own expression was desolate. Wesley cringed at the thought of his wife Carrie as she lay recovering from surgery in some impersonal, sanitized room surrounded by austere, dingy white walls, her body connected to monitors streaked with thin, colored lights. Fighting to regain consciousness in a cacophony of beeping equipment noises mixed with the hushed voices of scurrying scrub suits, his poor, beautiful wife was probably, no certainly, in some degree of pain, maybe even a lot of pain, but alive nonetheless.

"I – we – just can't keep goin' through this," Wesley managed to continue. "I – we – can't do this anymore." The availability of other infertility treatments, other options, as the doctor had said, should be emotionally uplifting for him and for Carrie, once she learned about them. As a result, their future as parents should seem brighter. Wesley knew that he should give his thanks to God for his wife's survival and not to Dr. Van Deman. A thick cloud of trepidation darkened Sarbeck's visage as he silently prayed for surrender to God's will, fighting his recent assumption that God had abandoned the Wesley Sarbeck family.

Consternation as well as grief abruptly vanished from Wesley's eyes, and Van Deman saw it. With this came resolution as Wesley rebounded from hopelessness. As though he had originated the concept, he blurted, "I guess we'll just have to adopt. Sure, we'll just adopt a baby. That's what we'll do! Give a child a good home, a loving home."

Van Deman had witnessed the scenario many times: the identical screenplay, same scene but with different characters playing identical roles. A renewed marketing window materialized before the human infertility specialist, a slight variation to a plot that would lead to a persuasive climax. "Well, certainly, Wesley," he responded kindly. "Certainly you can adopt. But adoptive babies are hard to come by unless you look overseas, that is. China, Russia, Africa, Romania – there are several sources outside of the United States, but there's a lot of red tape associated with a foreign adoption. And wrapped up in all that red tape is a lot of expense. Of course, with all the political upheaval in the world right now, bombs popping up in all kinds of places, you never know what can happen." The *political upheaval* remark was a new one. Van Deman liked the way it sounded. He would use that again.

The husband seemed to be listening closely, drinking it all in as the specialist continued. "Of course, even here in the U.S., Caucasian babies are hard to come by, what with legalized abortion and all. Of course, you could choose to reach outside your race. You might even consider a biracial or even multiracial child." From his silence, Van Deman wondered if Sarbeck was even listening at that point. Maybe the target was wondering how oriental or black features would blend into a family portrait or among the other kids in his neighborhood.

Van Deman glanced at his Rolex. He was beginning to weary of this conversation. It was just after 5:00 a.m., and he had to be back in the OR for a scheduled surgery case at seven. Fortunately, he had the afternoon off and would sleep – one definite advantage of having signed Knox Chamblee into the practice. Knox would cover for him by seeing the afternoon patients and supervising the critical work in the infertility lab. Van Deman decided that this encounter was a lost cause and that perhaps he had come across as too persuasive. He decided to let it go, but not before one last effort at recruiting.

"But please, Wesley (use of the husband's first name was again thought better for bedside manner and once again lifted from the patient information sheet), there are very real options that I think you should consider, options that will enable you, as a couple, to give birth to your very own child. A baby that could look like you."

The offer penetrated Sarbeck's silence. Wesley surprised even himself as he took the recasted bait. He pulled his face upward from tired, sweaty palms, his eyes now as bloodshot as they were wet. "OK, Doctor, go ahead. I don't really understand what you're talking about. How can we have our 'very own child' when my wife barely has any of her female organs?"

"Well, we have the ..."

"Tell me some more, Doctor, about what you mentioned before: donors and all that," Wesley interrupted. "I think Carrie will want to know about them. She'll have a ton of questions, and the first person she'll ask is me."

"Yes, you two darlings have got to explore your options. Let the doctor help you, please!" The shrill reverberation from around the corner was by a now a contorted, distressed mix of facial muscles, covered by unwanted hair and sagging, plump skin. The woman had not missed a syllable of the discourse and anxiously awaited the next installment.

"Certainly, I'll be happy to tell you some more, Wes. Fortunately, you and your wife can benefit from meticulous medical research that has produced remarkable advances in biological parenthood. My reproductive endocrinology practice can offer these successful advances right here in Mississippi." Van Deman reached into his top front pocket and produced a business card. "Once your wife heals from her surgery, I or my associate, Dr. Knox Chamblee, will be happy to see both of you in consultation. We'll go over everything again at that time, put all your options on the table."

The name Sarbeck was now ingrained in Van Deman's memory. He would instruct his secretary to anticipate a call from the soon-to-be-grateful Sarbecks. "Just call for an appointment. My office will take care of it. Like I said, my associate, Dr. Chamblee, or I will be delighted to see you. Dr. Knox Chamblee and I now work as a team."

From around the corner the engrossed eavesdropper sensed that the doctor was rising to leave and would pass in her direction. She tossed her last magazine aside and, as fast as noisy flip-flops would allow, scurried to the restroom. Henry Van Deman, MD, initiated a parting handshake, the professionalism not lost on Wesley Sarbeck, who at the moment felt unsure of his feelings – tremendous relief or the confusion of mental overload. The doctor's smile did seem all-knowing, reaching beyond a well-practiced bedside manner to project a demeanor that stirred emotional comfort in Wesley.

Carrie Sarbeck would live, this doctor had said so. The handshake was not one of goodbye.

As he anticipated the relief of holding his wife's delicate frame and pressing tightly against her, Wesley realized that the doctor's words were part of a never-ending story. There was still more that could be done in the Sarbecks' drive to have their own baby: more hope, more tests, more doctor visits, more surgery, more frustration, and more money. Propagation of his branch of the Sarbeck line remained possible, not merely in the adoptive sense, but by truly mixing his and Carrie's bodies together – their own flesh and blood. There was still hope. This guy, Van Deman, would be able to help them become, as he had said, *biological parents*.

Wesley's mind played victim to the doctor's explanation of their options, the fine print. As he had listened to the physician's discourse on how a baby with his wife was still possible, he had heard what he needed to understand, suppressing his knowledge that Carrie Sarbeck's line would be excluded from the propagated Sarbeck gene pool, a fact that present day science could not change.

Herself an only child, Carrie's parents had died several years earlier in an automobile accident, leaving behind only Carrie and her mother's childless sister. Once Carrie Sarbeck came out of her post-anesthetic trance, she would learn that as a result of the night's surgery, her genetic line had died. As far as reproduction of the human species, her body could serve only as an incubator. Yet, Dr. Van Deman and his associates could help her. To have a baby, another woman's chromosomes would have to be mixed with those of her husband, leaving Carrie Sarbeck as a bystander, a receptacle, a feeder, a nobody.

Chapter

4

◆◆◆

THE TRANSGRESSION

On the surface the Van Deman Center was no different from any other place of business. There were the few employees who arrived earlier than necessary and those who managed the time clock as though it were a slot machine. Shortly after she was hired, the practice administrator noticed Mia Evans' ritualistic early arrival and promptly enlisted the new employee as keeper of the key to the rear door, a duty that garnered no extra salary but was appreciated nonetheless by a much less eager administrator.

Although her official responsibility was to facilitate morning access to the building for the other employees and any supply deliveries, the distinction of being first on-site soon evolved into a self-appointed employee break-room/kitchen cleanup duty, assuming that the after-hours effort of the professional janitorial service had been perfunctory at best.

In truth, anyone else would have considered the compact kitchen provided for the employees to be clean enough once the evening janitorial crew had completed its blitz. Despite what those professionals considered their best effort, she still envisioned the area as disordered, as nasty. Mia Evans could not rest until the room was returned to her immaculate standards in preparation of her peers' arrival to work.

Evans lived up to her own expectations. Each morning in near obsessive fashion, she brewed the coffee, replenished the community refrigerator with soft drinks from the storage closet, and sanitized the break table with cleaning tissues borrowed from the patient examination rooms – thin sheets of paper saturated with hazardous liquid chemicals that annihilated bacteria or viruses on contact. The sterilizing wipes were drawn from the top of a cylindrical plastic container resting near each exam room sink that resembled similar products used to wipe babies after diaper changes.

Mia's reliability with her assumed early hour cleaning duties and first-to-arrive status continued to be appreciated by the practice administrator. Despite the gratitude, Evans' responsibilities grew without regard to a parallel rise in her pay.

Once a week a nondescript white van arrived at the rear entrance to the Van Deman Center, a vehicle similar in color to that of Tinker Murtagh but roughly three times the size and scripted with legitimately painted lettering. Instead of *WE PAINT MISSISSIPPI* scrawled across the side, this van was neatly designated *SPECIALTY CHEMICALS, INCORPORATED – Dallas, Birmingham, Atlanta*. Finding the Jackson area an easy stopover on Interstate 20, the thoroughfare connecting its corporate locations, Specialty Chemicals, Incorporated delivered a fresh supply of liquid nitrogen to the Center every Wednesday morning. Ready and waiting at the back entrance to sign in receipt of the delivery and admit the delivery technician was the punctual Mia Evans.

"Here to top things off again? Huh, Frank?" Mia asked Frank Rizzo, the Specialty Chemicals technician assigned to the Van Deman account.

"Yeah, Mia, but I'm running a little behind with this drop-off."

"Behind? You're always here at 7:45, give or take a minute or two, have been ever since I started working here."

"My problem is they've added another delivery stop for me on the way over to Dallas. Some new medical clinic in Monroe has started to use our products, and the extra time there will put me late getting back to the main plant," Frank explained with some hesitation as he handed Mia his laptop for her signature. Even though she had signed in receipt for the chemicals on multiple occasions, she still fumbled with the stylet, trying to apply just the correct amount of pressure for her signature to display on the screen. As Frank watched her awkwardly scribble *Mia Evans*, he wondered if he should push his plan with her.

"My wife already complains enough about this job I've got, what with all the traveling back and forth between Dallas and Atlanta and back. Of course, I'm gone two or three nights a week, and she has to help with the kids' homework all by herself. You know, says it's a real pain, but really, she's kinda good at stuff like that since she's a teacher's assistant. Anyway, the extra hour with the new customer in Monroe – that's the real bitch for me. Puts me an hour late getting home on the nights I make it home – another hour for me to be away from my family. The wife says she's sick of being a single parent. Might as well be divorced, the wife said crying the other night on the phone while I was stuck in a motel just outside of Birmingham."

"Gosh, I'm sorry, but ..." Mia responded handing the laptop back to the delivery man.

"Look, you look like a responsible gal," Frank carried on as he looked down the short hall of the rear entrance, at nothing in particular. "The company'll have my ass if my delivery production falls, and my wife'll have my ass if I don't make it home more. She's about to cut me off, anyway, if you know what I mean. A guy's got to have a little ..."

"Wait a minute!" Mia threw her hands up, palms forward.

"No, really, I'm just trying to get a little help here," Rizzo countered.

"I'm sorry, but you're reading me the wrong way. I'm just here doing my job; I'm meeting you here every Wednesday morning to get the delivery from the chemical company, just like I'm s'posed to."

Frank looked puzzled, not with the eyes of someone sexually rebuffed as Mia expected. "Damn, girl, you're reading me the wrong way," he pleaded as Mia turned to walk away, planning immediately to report the incident as sexual harassment to her administrator. She then remembered that her superior had a dental appointment for a root canal and planned to take the day off. "Wait, this could be good for both of us," he called out to her.

"I told you I'm not ..."

Rizzo interrupted Mia. "What I'm talking about is paying you, on the side, of course, if you'll ..."

Mia then interrupted him in turn, stopping to turn halfway back toward Rizzo. "You know, Frank, my boy, you're a real oversexed asshole. Gosh, did you have me fooled. I thought you were a nice guy. Comin' here every week and all, bein' real friendly to me. Now I know why." She turned back toward the employee kitchen, remembering that she had forgotten to wipe out the microwave with the bacterio- and viricidal "baby" wipes. First, she would need to scrub out the splattered food stains as a result of yesterday's late afternoon leftover lasagna snack, then sanitize the entire interior surface with the special wipes.

"No, Girl. Like I said, you've got me wrong!" Frank called out to her, and then lowered his voice, not wanting to attract attention. He was fairly certain that few, if any, of the other employees were in the building at such an early hour, but could not be certain. He needed this girl's help, help that could cost him his job while at the same time save his marriage. He would up the ante of his proposal, make the help worth her while.

Mia decided to ignore him, her thoughts now immersed in double-checking the staff kitchen for dust particles and other disorder that would escape the superficial sight of every other employee. In returning to her obsessive concern about cleanliness, she slowed long enough for Frank to continue his plea. His tone was hushed, compellingly secretive. "This is what I'll pay you to do. I can show you how to top off the tanks with the liquid nitrogen. It's really easy to do, a simple process. You just have to do it kinda slow. That's why I'm in such a mess over the time."

"What? I can't do that!" Mia exclaimed, first amazed at the guy's audacity, then alarmed that her screaming response had been heard all over the building. Then she remembered that, of course, she and Rizzo were the only two people there.

"Yes, you can. It's really easy to do," he countered. "I'll drop off the containers, even pull the cart around to the embryo storage chamber. Then you'll do the rest. The pay'll be worth it to you. I guarantee it."

"That's not what I'm talking about. There's security involved. No one has access to that chamber except the doctors and the laboratory director and her assistant. I'm really not sure that Dr. Van Deman has even given the new doctor the authority to go in there yet. He probably has, but I'm not sure."

"You're correct about the security; I knew you were a smart girl. But all that's standard," Frank explained patiently. "For sure, there's a voice recognition system and a backup fingerprint program in case the voice entry fails. All I have to do is give you a recording of me saying my name *Frank Andrew Rizzo Junior* and that's all there is to it. I've got one of those little digital recorders right here." Frank Andrew Rizzo Jr., produced a small, handheld voice recorder from his right front pants pocket. "Picked this thing up at Wal-Mart yesterday," he announced proudly, as though demonstrating a unique discovery. "This'll do the trick," he said with reassurance, feeling that Mia was warming up to his proposal.

He next motioned for her to follow down an adjacent corridor that narrowed just as it wound toward the embryo storage vault. The vault was indeed housed, as Mia had touted, in a restricted zone of the building complex, that is, restricted to physicians, certain laboratory personnel, and delivery persons with security clearance. From her new employee orientation of over a year ago, Evans recalled the administrator's stern admonition regarding the sensitivity of the area and its off-limits status to low-status employees like her.

The mysterious shroud hanging over the operations of this section of the Center was propagated by those warnings and became a central item in each new employee's job orientation, falling in line immediately behind learning the location of the restroom and that of her personal locker. Feeling a mistaken sense of immunity to the simplified "hands-off, stay-away" rule associated with the embryo culture lab, Mia nervously accepted his invitation and followed in the forbidden shadow of Frank Rizzo. His security status was granted as a bonded employee of Specialty Chemicals, giving him green-light authorization to proceed through this section of the building. Of course, that green light did not extend to Mia Evans.

Mia's pulse quickened over the certainty of dismissal if she were discovered penetrating the guarded area; the *if* being the issue, *if* she were caught. *The lowly likes of Mia Evans*, she thought. *I'm such an unimportant employee, nothing but kitchen help, a step-and-fetch-it for the administrator of this place. She herself is nothing more than a glorified medical office manager, too lazy to get up out of bed every morning and unlock the building herself.*

As Mia lurked closely behind Rizzo, she wondered if Dr. Van Deman was aware of how truly lazy his administrator was. Surely, when he hired her to manage the practice he had not realized that his chief officer would let him down in such critical matters as receiving important supply deliveries, like the stuff Rizzo was pushing down the hall on a dolly. Van Deman's a smart man, she thought, deciding that he must be intelligent to do the kind of work he did.

Walking forward, moving closer to Frank Rizzo, staying within his protective shadow, Mia envisioned the administrator standing before her, shaking a finger in disapproval if she were caught, and then pointing that bony finger toward the permanent exit door. Her supervisor was normally a pleasant woman and, though lazy in Mia's opinion, was still a stickler for rules, as far as everyone else was concerned. That was one of the reasons Mia had taken the position at the Center: she initially liked the woman and her systematic approach to things. But Mia Evans' inquisitive nature had overcome her at the moment, altering her perception of right and wrong.

No doubt her getting caught snooping around in the restricted area would garner a swift kick out that permanent exit door and all without a penny of severance pay. "Flagrant disregard for the Center's policies results in immediate dismissal," the woman's words were clear and crisp at Mia's hiring, as the administrator entered Mia's social security number in a blur across a computer keyboard.

Remaining on Rizzo's heels, Mia thought again about her first day on this job which predictably began with employee orientation. Sitting at attention across from the woman who every two weeks would electronically deposit a desperately needed paycheck into her checking account, Evans had heard, "Many of our patients have been all over the South to other infertility clinics, even all over the country, until they wisely selected the Van Deman Center. These patients have been riding an emotional roller coaster trying to have a family: highs and lows, ups and downs, twists and turns. A lot of them have divorced over their ordeals, borrowed more money that they could ever pay back, had multiple surgeries and other procedures by other less-qualified doctors – all because of trying to produce a baby. Fortunately, most of the patients we get here have plenty of resources to pay us cash in advance for all of the things we can do for them."

The administrator had continued to deliver indoctrinating new-employee phrases as she punished the keys of her Dell, the information derived from Mia's completed *New Employee Information* form sliding permanently into the free space of the hard drive devoted to Mia Evans. "You know, ahh, yes," she scrolled back to the *Employee Name* section, "yes, Miss Evans," placing emphasis on the referenced name *Evans*. "Miss Evans," the administrator continued, making a stronger mental note of Mia's name this time, "the Center for Disease Control and Prevention over in Atlanta keeps detailed national statistics related to the success rates of fertility centers. The Center updates our data with them at least every two years. And our first rankings were extremely high."

While she pretended to be impressed at the time by the statements regarding the ethical feats of her new employer, Mia's immediate need to receive a steady paycheck seemed guaranteed by the promise of a steady stream of patients through the practice's front foyer. Recalling the espoused laurels of the Van Deman Center and the admonishment of *We adhere to strict quality control over our supplies, equipment, and procedures* quickened her pulse as it seemed to skip several beats behind Frank Rizzo and his dolly.

Suddenly Mia caught the reflection of her flushed face. She and Rizzo were approaching the shiny, chrome-surfaced door leading to the forbidden embryo culture lab and its sophisticated support equipment. As austere and imposing as the seal to a financial bank vault, the entrance was branded *Unauthorized Access Strictly Prohibited.* The idea of being caught violating any of the rules of the practice normally would have garnered at least a skipped heartbeat or two. In contrast, Mia surprised herself with an abrupt emotional rush from this flagrant violation of boundaries. She saw excitement in committing an act that could mean certain dismissal and possibly worse.

The climate control system clicked on with a jerking noise that diffused air automatically from the ceiling vents overhead. Normally such a sound would have gone completely unnoticed, or at least ignored; however, the break in the surrounding silence jolted Evans. The swish of fresh, flowing air encircled her as the reverberation echoed back and forth across the corridor as well as ahead of and behind her. Rizzo seemed oblivious to the disturbance as Mia was jerked back to the reality of the risk she was taking and how her actions could change her life forever. She forcibly repressed her second thoughts.

Already her early morning assignment to unlock the rear of the building had distinguished her somewhat from the other non-medical staff, a distinction unattached to a salary increase. The office administrator had implied a little extra Christmas bonus for her trouble, and somewhere below "a little" is what she received.

Forgetting that it was her personal choice to arrive early to work that had landed the self-appointed kitchen duty and resulting extra chores, Mia mulled over her disappointing Christmas salary bonus as she continued to follow Rizzo down the deserted corridor unabated. *Stingy bitch!* she thought of the combination administrator/personnel director as she pushed closer to Frank.

Any remaining guilt was rapidly fleeting, her violation of company directives seeming more and more justified.

Encroaching on the actual entrance to the off-limits area, Mia began to feel a harmony with Rizzo: his ideas were becoming more and more plausible, more and more sensible. As a nitrous oxide delivery specialist, he would save time and his marriage while Mia Evans would pocket some extra cash. The extra money would come close to making up for her twelve-fifty per hour before taxes, plus benefits.

Stingy bitch! she thought again, this time smiling at the thought of betraying the administrator's trust, a betrayal that was more than justified; it was deserved. Mia Evans' sentiment was now completely devoid of guilt, replaced with the fear of getting caught. Stingy or not, Mia was certain that the administrator would fire her on the spot if caught entering this area. While the thought of possibly being arrested for trespassing in the embryo lab was horrifying, Mia could imagine nothing worse than losing her job. Mia needed a job.

Her chest fluttered at the thought of being fired, as second-guessing her decision to join Rizzo resurfaced. The short run of skipped heartbeats, or anxiety-induced PVCs, and the dizziness which followed made the walls of the corridor seem to bend and sway. It was a struggle just to step forward behind Rizzo. Mia fought against gasping for air, fought against passing out, fought against falling to the floor to be discovered by an angry Center administrator. Rizzo, no doubt, would feign ignorance. With the fingertips of her right hand, Mia grabbed for the pulse in her left wrist, reassured that she was still alive and conscious. Thankfully, her cardiac rhythm had steadied as the PVCs resolved. Her breathing became less labored as she refocused on Rizzo's torso ahead.

"You OK?" he asked, pausing briefly in response to the deep, uneasy breaths behind him. Turning his head back toward her, he noticed that her complexion had lightened a couple of notches and she had fallen behind a bit. "You look like you've seen a ghost."

"Oh, uh, I'm OK – just stayed up too late last night watching Jimmy Kimmel."

"You're not having second thoughts about this are you?" Rizzo asked, seeing through her lie.

"No, well, I ..."

"Look, there's no one in this building but us right now. You said so yourself, and it's been that way at this hour ever since I've been makin' these deliveries." Rizzo's reassurance that the two were the Center's sole occupants somewhat soothed her fear of discovery as she envisioned the clueless security guard encircling the building's exterior in a golf cart. Mia's grasp for justification in breaking the employee code of ethics twisted her reasoning beyond the stingy administrator to the stingy doctors.

All Dr. Van Deman and Dr. Chamblee care about is making lots of money and keeping it all for themselves, she thought. *They should be sharing more of it with me and the rest of the employees – particularly with me since I've taken on extra duties.* The office secretary's growing resentment over lack of compensation for the extra work she had assumed was buried in that very fact: she had voluntarily assumed the extra duties. Her desire to get to work early had been a personal choice and the unlocking-the-back-door thing a prerequisite to that. Mia had often wondered why the Center's administrator had not enlisted the nighttime security guard to unlock the rear entrance for the early morning employees and deliveries, but decided that not only was she more reliable, she was cheaper, too.

"Are you sure that nothing's wrong?" Rizzo asked again, noticing that Evans was still standing in the middle of the hall, no longer following on his heels. Mia could not muster an answer, fighting a mounting tremor in her tense muscles that she hoped to defeat. If she had tried to answer him, her embarrassing fear would have been obvious.

Turning back around to face the awaiting closed door, Rizzo shrugged his shoulders and swiped his magnetic pass card almost absent-mindedly through the security control port embedded in the wall just to the right of the entrance to the lab. "You won't need this card. No, not really," he mentioned, not anticipating a response.

Mia immediately regained her composure, gathering nerve to move closer and absorb his instruction. "Now, what did you say I'm s'posed to do to get though this door?" she asked, steadying her voice as much as possible.

"It'll be a piece of cake. Since you won't have my pass card, you can just punch in the six digit security code right here on this metal key pad," he explained the alternative, pointing to a compact bank of shiny, grey numbers and symbols arranged in standard fashion and positioned adjacent to the card receptacle. "Of course, you'll only have to fool with this if the voice recognition system is on the blink, like it's been for the past few weeks," Rizzo added, pointing to a microphone inconspicuously recessed above the other devices. "Before I leave, don't let me forget to give you the digital recording of my ID info. Hey, it won't earn me a Grammy, but it'll gain access for you on my dime."

Because of the resentment she had mustered against the Center's doctors and practice administrator, her facial muscles aborted her attempt at a smile, her lips flattened against cold front teeth. She could not even render a nervous grin. Somehow she forced acknowledgement with a nod, albeit a weak one. Each step toward the embryo storage vault had heightened the rush she felt over the risk she was taking. But her excitement over the secrecy and sophistication that had drawn her to this wing of the building continued to be overshadowed by a fear of being fired or arrested.

She knew she should stop, beg off from the scheme, and tell this Rizzo guy that she was just pulling his leg, that she had changed her mind. Her actions were bordering on lack of professionalism, she knew, and then decided that there was no *bordering* about it. Mia knew that she had instantly violated professional decorum by ignoring the restrictions established for this section of the Center. Then she reconsidered her salary in the face of her rich employers. "Professional?" she nearly questioned aloud. "Hell, these people that sign my check consider me nothing more than a clerk, an errand girl, a nice voice on the other end of the phone, a smiling face at the front desk, a smiling face with pretty white teeth." Mia was defiant under her breath, her voice barely audible enough for Rizzo to perceive, assuming he was really paying any attention anyway.

Her insubordination justified, Mia's muscles relaxed with guiltless ease. Her pulse remained steady, and she smiled pleasantly. Mia Evans was determined that she choose curiosity over professionalism and doubted if any of her sisters in the clerical staff would act differently. Feeling the relief of peace, Miss Mia Evans was hereby vetoing the bitch's dictums; after all, the supervisor really didn't think that professionalism applied to a stupid paper pusher, did she? In her twisted push to justify the morning's actions, Mia had overlooked the true value and appreciation of her type of daily work at the Henry Van Deman Center of Reproductive Technology. Without the routine that she considered so mundane and the wages she viewed as so grossly inadequate, the patient schedules of both doctors would never run smoothly and the Center's higher-end technology would never take place.

As Rizzo proceeded through the final security maneuvers to get them into the embryo lab, Mia hoped that at least her workdays would no longer be bathed in boredom. As she entered this sacred place, she was soon to discover what patients were receiving at the hands of Drs. Van Deman and Chamblee. She would soon be privy to what really went on behind closed doors. Mia had no intention of violating specific patient confidentiality – she was professional in that regard – but was warming up to the possibility of becoming more involved in what the Center was doing to help the unfortunate, infertile people, all the while making a little extra money on the side at Rizzo's expense.

Unlike the other members of the clerical staff, Mia would no longer be left to endless hours of pecking on a computer keyboard. Oblivious, her peers would remain on the cold, banal outside. They would tragically be stranded to converse among themselves, exposing the commonplace drama of ordinary lives – boyfriends, children, ex-husbands, ex-boyfriends, girlfriends of ex-husbands, girlfriends of ex-boyfriends, poor finances. They would also dwell on the mundane such as where to purchase the most attractive scrub suits or what was new at Target – all a circle of stagnation broken only by the infusion of an occasional new hire or two and the attached fresh gossip.

Mia felt true remorse for her clerical sisters, but was certainly not sorry enough to trade places with them. In making patient appointments or posting patient treatment charges, they would remain miserably frozen at their computer screens, unaware of the sophisticated technologies playing out behind the closed doors of the Center, one of which was beginning to open under the direction of this nitrous oxide delivery man.

Evans breathed even easier. Having a grasp of the inner sanctum would add meaning to her work, even though her regular salary would remain a pittance. Once more, she would still be able to keep this job since no one was watching her enter forbidden ground.

But to the contrary, someone was watching Mia Evans creep along the corridor to the embryo culture lab and was delighting in every minute of it. During a furtive glance or two as she worked through her diminishing guilt and fear, Mia had stared directly into the looming eyes of Tinker Murtagh via the lens of the security cameras tucked into the ceiling air conditioning vents. Believing correctly that the exposed security cameras were in place as safety measures at the entrances and exits to the building as well as to protect the parking areas, Mia and the other employees remained unaware of the intricate in-house spy network that Dr. Van Deman had installed. Furthermore, the Center's administrator and Dr. Knox Chamblee, in addition to the security guards, remained ignorant of the widespread placement of additional live cameras.

As Tinker Murtagh electronically scanned the sectors in range, he was curious about the young woman, the first person to enter the building each morning. He was not at all interested in the security guard still spotted outside the building, who at that moment was violating the property's no-smoking rule. The snooping eyes of Tinker Murtagh had already judged her fairly attractive and physically fit. *Probably works out*, he thought again. *I wonder if she puts out*. Tinker's appreciation of the opposite sex transcended racial barriers.

Since the digital video feed was black-and-white, Tinker could only reason that the girl's complexion was a rich caramel color, definitely not ebony. Her coarse-looking hair had been well relaxed so that it fell down to her shoulders, making Tinker long to touch it. He liked thick hair and wondered how much time or money it took to get the girl's hair to behave that way.

Her anxiety was obvious. Studying her under magnification,

Tinker judged the girl to be in her very early twenties and much more appealing than was his first impression. Definitely cute, he decided, and not too shy, definitely not shy, but probably hot – yes, hot, but not shy, no, not at all shy. The caramel-colored, cute, hot, uninhibited female was for some unclear reason following the delivery guy, whom Murtagh had noticed in the building the week before when he reviewed the recorded video of that morning. Tinker felt growing excitement that he was experiencing this particular morning's action live.

"What're this guy and girl doin' together, all alone in this medical building, just the two of 'em?" Tinker asked aloud. *Is the chick looking for a little tryst with this guy she's trailing? A little video porn action comin' up, maybe? Probably on the soft side?* he wondered in anticipation of a break in the monotony of Internet video surveillance, a morning wakeup spectacle for Tinker Murtagh. The two in the corridor were moving toward the central infertility lab, an area visited only by the same two doctors and a couple of regular laboratory technicians who generally did not appear there until somewhat later in the mornings. On some days Tinker had spotted others in the perimeter of the area and assumed them to be patients.

Tinker's pulse quickened in anticipation as he leaned into his computer screen. A clear deviation from the morning routine was unfolding before him, something over-the-top, perhaps. Never before had he spotted this particular girl in this usually quiet part of the building, nor had he noticed her as nervous. Not even a heterosexual male could deny the good looks of the physically buff guy that the nervous-looking girl was following, as Murtagh continued to look on with envy concerning what he was sure the couple was going to do. He might even want to magnify the action up close on the screen.

"Frank Andrew Rizzo" emanated from the tiny speaker that

was no more than several dark slits marring the smooth finish of the wall. Seeming to engulf the entire corridor, the sound was heard only by Rizzo and a startled Mia as she jumped back several inches from the wall. She shuddered again as the latch to the thick metal barrier popped loose on cue.

While Tinker remained glued to his computer monitor and switched screens in anticipation of the next step, Rizzo moved purposefully into the room as Mia fought her last-minute reluctance to follow. "Stop here and put these on," he said, reaching into a plastic bin that served as storage for disposable shoe covers, a collection of commonly-used surgical supplies that resembled a pile of light-blue-colored wads of corrugated paper. Rizzo tossed her a pair which, unraveled, revealed an extra shoe cover.

Puzzled, she separated the elastic-lined material and raised the third cover with her right hand as she held the remaining, pair in her left. "They're to keep the floor clean since the people 'round here don't let the regular housekeeping crew in to clean up after their sloppy asses," he chuckled, understanding her question from the confused look. "These people are real worried about security and crap like that. But, screw that – here you are – here we are. So much for all that expensive security."

Tinker continued to watch in earnest as Mia gently returned the third shoe cover to the bin as though it would break and clumsily stretched the remaining material over her low-rise pumps. "Hey, are you OK?" Rizzo asked as Mia realized her suddenly colorless fingers were trembling. She imagined Dr. Van Deman or Chamblee or any of the nurses putting on their own shoe covers with much greater dexterity, a procedure they no doubt performed many times a day. *Dr. Van Deman, Dr. Chamblee*, Mia thought again as a wave of guilt overcame her.

Reconsidering her earlier criticism of her employers, she

recalled Dr. Chamblee's kind greeting for her a couple of times when passing hurriedly in the hall, though he had never called her by name. She had seen Dr. Van Deman a few times as well, and though he had not acknowledged her existence as had the younger doctor, she reasoned he was simply too busy to do so. On behalf of the doctors, the administrator did pass along a birthday bonus and automatic payroll raises, seemingly not based on merit but apparently linked to showing up for work.

Unexpectedly Mia felt hollow, a fleeting feeling usurped by one of fear. Her curiosity over the intricacies of the infertility lab and the proposal to make a little on-the-side money as this fellow Rizzo's assistant no longer seemed important. She felt foolish; she felt stupid. As she watched Rizzo move across the brilliant white, vinyl-covered floor of an area that was off-limits to the inconsequential likes of Mia Evans, her pulse quickened further as she fumbled for her cell phone to check the time. Remembering that others would be entering the building in a little more than 15 minutes, maybe less, her hands trembled so that she nearly dropped the phone.

She clumsily slid the thin cellular device back into her jacket pocket as Rizzo rolled a slim mat ahead of his dolly. Mia understood this action as one that served the same purpose as the human shoe covers. Shortly ahead of Rizzo was a trio of shiny, aluminum-colored, shoulder-high canisters topped by a series of ringed metal tubes contorted into Dr. Frankensteinian-lab style semicircles – an incongruous grouping when compared to the sleek, molded appearance of the rest of the infertility laboratory. Crowning the tubes every foot or so stood a fifties-era-style mechanical gauge that Mia assumed played some role in Rizzo's purpose for servicing the facility and topping off the level of the embryo freezing medium. Remembering that a close study of Rizzo's work was the reason she had entered this lab and violated company policy in the first place, Mia fought her returning anxiety and focused on the subtle complexities of the sanitized surroundings. Despite Rizzo's demonstration and instruction that the first thing she was to do was to connect the cable to this flange, describing it as the ol' tried-and-true male to female mechanism, Mia's curiosity was drawn elsewhere, ignoring his sexual metaphor. Unknowingly, Rizzo shared the opinion of Tinker Murtagh regarding the girl's subtle allure that could be really hot in the right setting. As he analyzed the correct amount of nitrous oxide needed for the first canister, he hoped that maybe that venue would come later. That would be a really nice way to consummate a business deal, he decided.

Continuing to ignore her instructor as he spouted instructions to his audience of two – one having no sound capability and the other mesmerized by the furnishings of the oblong section of the room where she stood nervously – Mia kept her feet firmly planted in position as though to move them would have yielded discovery. She swiveled her neck to survey her surroundings thoroughly, twisting her waist uncomfortably as she kept her covered feet in place. Mia was mentally inhaling all that she saw.

Just across from where she stood a short distance from the canisters were the words *Embryo Culture and Laminar Flow Lab: No Unauthorized Admittance*. The imprinted sign was affixed to another solid-appearing door that, though Mia had not touched it, exuded the weight of the highest level of security. The periphery of the door was lined with a rubberized seal that extended beyond the limits of the door itself, overlapping any space between the closed door and its frame. This airtight fitting was designed to eliminate any foreign particle contamination within the embryo culture laboratory. Had Mia been able to invade the Embryo Culture Lab as well and open the small pass-through chamber leading from that facility into the adjacent egg-retrieval room, she would have initiated a one-way, positive-pressure air blast rivaling a mini-tornado.

Mia reveled in the sleek and orderly appearance of the infertility lab, an obsessive-compulsive's dream – a sharp contrast to the remainder of the building's cushy, inviting interior. The only medically-related furnishings that appeared remotely familiar to Evans were the flat screen computer monitors that stood in sleep mode at uniformly placed intervals along the counter surfaces. In juxtaposition to Mia's clerical section of the Center, which invisible to the patient eye had remained cluttered despite the practice's extensive electronic medical record system, there were no mounds of paper or stacks of files weighting this area's working space.

Much to the relief of her strained neck and waist muscles, Mia summoned the nerve to take a few steps away from Rizzo, who by now was preoccupied with hurriedly finishing the service call and infusing the embryo freezer with nitrous oxide. She moved slowly along the main section of the lab toward the juncture of the L-shaped space.

Meanwhile, disappointed about no secret tryst between the couple, Tinker Murtagh had turned to the pages of his morning newspaper. The girl's sudden movement caught his attention just as he was enjoying Marshall Ramsey's cartoon on the editorial page of *The Clarion-Ledger*. She seemed to be looking around as though making a real study of the joint, he decided. In fact, and much to Tinker's surprise, she again stared directly into the security camera he had accessed, seeming to pause for a moment. *Did she wink at me?* he wondered, before laughing at himself for a few seconds. He then turned the next page and took a loud slurp of coffee from the thin Styrofoam cup. He was certainly correct that there was no way she could have spotted the security camera in that high tech, well-organized space.

The truth was that Mia Evans was even more fascinated by the sanitized aroma of the lab than the austerity of the furnishings or the procedures possible behind its closed doors. The scent was an odor of cleanliness, not typical of any cleanser or disinfectant that Mia had ever used or seen. Remembering what Rizzo had said about the lab being off-limits to the routine housekeeping crew, she assumed that the infertility lab technicians did their own cleaning and sterilizing with some specially derived formula, maybe one not available to an ordinary medical office, much less the general public. "That crummy kitchen would be immaculate, not a germ alive anywhere. Nobody in this joint would ever get sick if I could use this Formula XYZ or whatever they call it," she decided aloud.

"Hey, did you say something?" Rizzo blurted without turning his head in her direction. Time was growing short, and he needed to get going – finish this job and move on to the next stop. "Are you watching what I'm doin' ?" he asked over his shoulder, again not turning to check to see if the girl was even paying any attention to what he was doing with the cables, valves, and meters that controlled the flowing nitrous oxide and maintained the frozen human embryos. "Maybe bringing this chick in on this wasn't such a great idea," he muttered under his breath. "This frozen stuff won't have a chance if I turn this over to her. Bad idea, Rizzo," he ascertained.

Mia heard Rizzo call out but was too fascinated by her surroundings to bother. As she continued to walk through the central area of the lab, she neared a corner that led to the foot of the dogleg space. The plain white walls were lined with more counters hosting more thin computers, some of which had come alive with blinking cursors and lists of words, some sounding familiar, a few more vague. The catch phrases included *media of the day, ICSI, IVF, follicular aspirates, oocyte observations,*

*number of eggs denuded, sperm processing, embryo
development, transfer date, cleavage (yes/no), embryo
status (abnormal or damaged).*

"Where is the cleaning closet in here?" she whispered, still
curious about finding the specialized supply closet and the source
of the area's smell. Slinking alongside the counters, Mia came
across several old-fashioned clipboards branded with names of
pharmaceutical companies. Pinned to the clipboards that were
scattered among the thin video monitors and their flashing
medical terms were common-looking paper charts.

While penciling answers to the newspaper crossword puzzle,
Tinker glanced at his own monitor finding nothing of interest at
the moment. Meanwhile, Mia looked around awkwardly although
she was positive that no one was watching. Rizzo was still around
the corner at the other end of the lab; she was completely alone.
No one would ever know she was prying as she picked up one of
the clipboards.

Typical of any other medical facility, the sheets mounted to the
plastic clipboard were designated with a series of numbers printed
in the upper right-hand corners. Lying flat on the counter a few
inches away was a separate gray folder, constructed of heavy-
weight material but still much thinner than the standard-sized
patient charts which Mia sometimes still shuffled back and forth
within the building. The numbers on the outside of the chart
matched those imprinted on the sheet topping the short stack on
the clipboard.

Patient anonymity potentially blown by the carelessness of a
hurried laboratory technician, who had left the chart turned face-
up, Mia picked up the material as she hurriedly looked in Rizzo's
direction. Not only could she not see her accomplice, but she had
also crept to a distance where hearing him could be impossible as
well. Realizing that she should rejoin Frank Rizzo, since he had

probably finished working and was preparing to exit the infertility lab, she was just too curious to leave.

"How did she hear about us?"

Mia's startled reaction to the unfamiliar, feminine voice was to toss the patient chart back to the gleaning Formica counter, but she stopped herself before doing so. That would have made too much noise. Panic is often a sobering insult, dashing one's delusions of grandeur, thoughts of diversity, or just plain stupid curiosity. Instead, Mia softly returned the patient record to the counter, trying to position it exactly as she found it, a difficult task in that her hands were trembling uncontrollably, the writing on the chart nothing but a blur. She stared at her hands in self-disgust as she then quickly replaced the clipboard as well atop the short stack of others. *Why had she placed herself in such a predicament?* she wondered, wanting to kick herself. She needed this job and was just about to lose it.

Mia looked toward the sound, moving closer and closer to her, as it was joined by another voice, the second voice male. "Van Deman plans to handle everything himself, considers her a super-private patient. He doesn't even want you to know who she is, and I'm sort of surprised he even told me," Dr. Knox Chamblee shared with the chief laboratory technician. "Anyway, the patient's stipulation for coming to us was strict confidentiality, even among our own staff. You won't have to lift a finger. How about that?" he added to the tech responsible for the day-to-day operation of the infertility lab as well as the embryo and egg storage facilities.

As she listened, the chief technician shrugged her shoulders in indifference.

Part of Mia's surprise was realizing that the infertility lab must be larger than she first thought. She could tell from the direction and gradual increasing volume of the voices that the individuals were coming toward her from another hall, apparently a short one

extending past the next corner near where she stood frozen
in fear.

The voices from the deeper part of the lab were coming closer.
One of them was definitely Dr. Chamblee; Mia was sure of it.
He was always so nice to her when she passed him in the hall or
talked to him on the phone, or at least he used to be before he
was sure to find her in the wrong place and fire her. Youthful,
handsome Dr. Chamblee even sent polite intra-office emails with
little smileys attached to his signature. He probably did that with
all of his emails, but Mia considered it a special gesture on hers,
nonetheless. She was sorry she had tossed those negative thoughts
toward him earlier in the morning.

Since Chamblee had never called her by name, Mia wondered if
he could even put her name with a face – probably not, since he
had never addressed her personally when passing in a corridor –
one of the corridors where Mia belonged. "Hey, how's it going?"
he would ask in greeting. Another salutation that was not meant
for an answer other than a smile and nod was *Things going OK
up there in the front office?*

Whether or not Dr. Chamblee knew her by name was moot
at that point. He was getting ready to get the shock of his life,
unexpectedly catching the likes of Mia Evans in an off-limits
area, and then would fire her on the spot, no name needed. As
Mia glanced hopelessly around her, grappling for an escape,
she hoped that Chamblee would at least recognize her as an
employee and not as a burglar or someone who had wandered in
off the street. Maybe that would keep him from calling the cops.
Getting fired was no longer the issue; staying out of jail seemed
extremely important.

Mia needed to run, but instead she hurriedly tiptoed back
toward the entrance to the fertility lab. Even though the voices
were growing closer, their volume remained soft, professional,

and not nearly loud enough to mask running or panting. Clumsily, and in only a second or two, Evans reached the spot where she had first watched Rizzo begin to service the embryo freezing unit.

He was gone. Rizzo was gone.

"Oh, shit! Where is he?" Mia screamed through clenched teeth so that only she could hear, glaring back toward the direction of the encroaching voices. The people coming toward her continued to chat away, unaware of their audience.

"She's flying in tomorrow from California, Henry told me – made her flight arrangements from L.A. into Jackson himself," he explained to the chief infertility tech. "Oh, I guess I shouldn't have said *L.A.* That might tip you off to her secret identity," he joked.

The tech shrugged her shoulders again in indifference. Each day was simply another payday for her.

"Surely that woman is not flying commercial," Chamblee stopped for a moment to mull over what Van Deman had divulged in confidence. "Someone like her must own a jet, at least a small one, not to mention a personal pilot," Dr. Chamblee mused aloud as he sprang forward to catch up with the technician. "Well, whoever this prima donna is," she contributed, "the chick probably figured that the Jackson airport was so small that no one would ever recognize her, so small that no one would ever expect a famous person to be flying into our airport." Chamblee did not argue.

"Hah!" the tech continued. "I wonder if Miss Special Pants realizes that we have movie theaters down here in Mississippi, even DVD and MP-3 players?" she asked sarcastically.

"Yeah, not to mention cable and satellite TV and indoor plumbing!" Knox played along.

As Mia heard the two laughing, she nearly spun around in place looking for a place to hide. She was afraid to try the main door for fear of setting off some type of alarm. Besides, she could see the same type of security apparatus to the right of the door that Rizzo had accessed to gain their entrance.

Relieved, she spotted another alcove jutting in another direction off the main section of the infertility lab and darted for it, returning to tiptoes and hoping for an exit. She soon reached a nondescript door next to a compact, waist-high counter that housed another computer monitor and work area. Just as Mia grabbed for the doorknob, she noticed a microscope and a few other pieces of laboratory-type paraphernalia lined along the counter next to a wire rack housing test tubes. In her terror what Mia did not notice was an unobtrusively placed, imprinted sign mounted to the right of the door and abutting a wall cabinet. The sign read *Masterbatorium*.

"Thank God," she gasped as the door easily opened. Quietly she closed herself inside the dark room which she sensed was about the size of a janitor's closet and stood perfectly still, pressing her right ear against the door. There was no sound. The door was thick, but Mia assumed it still possible to hear if Dr. Chamblee and his companion approached her sanctuary. She remained motionless except for shallow, quick breaths, her concentration so intense that her ear ached from the firm pressure against the door. She switched sides for relief, and the left ear revealed nothing else. There was no sound from the doctor or the female. They had not followed her.

Those few moments standing motionless in the dark with two burning ears afforded Mia the opportunity to reconsider the enormity of her predicament. No one knew exactly where she was, she was sure. Even that worthless service technician, yeah, Rizzo was his name, Frank Rizzo, was not exactly sure where she was. Apparently, after enticing her to join him on this cockeyed scheme, he had left her stranded in an off-limits area and couldn't have cared less where she went or what happened to her.

Trying to remain motionless and undetectable in the dark
room, Evans nevertheless shook uncontrollably, tightly, like a
housecat just before pouncing on an unsuspecting prey. Her skin
felt clammy as she held her arms folded tightly against her chest.
Beads of sweat erupted on her forehead and began to trickle into
her eyes. Claustrophobia, much less achluophobia, had never
before been fears of hers, but swiftly she was afflicted with both.
The oppressive walls of the dark prison were quickly closing in
as her every breath sucked the last few ounces of oxygen from
the room.

Mia felt that unless she was released from the darkness soon
she would begin to scream uncontrollably, like a madwoman. She
had to be sure of where she was, of what could be behind her, or
worse, *who* could be behind her.

Assuming correctly that a light switch was positioned
somewhere along the wall adjacent to the door, she groped in
vain until her trembling hands reached the frame. She found
the control switch with the fore- and middle fingers of her right
hand, then hesitated briefly before turning on the light. She
reconsidered the fact that being discovered would mean losing
her job, or perhaps getting arrested, though she really did not
believe that the doctors or the administrator, that ogre, would
turn her over to the police. They would want to shun such
negative publicity.

Mia Evans needed some time to think, and she desperately
needed to get out of the darkness. Then she realized that the area
outside the door was well-lit, likely preventing a beam of light
from appearing under the door into the lab area.

"Come on; you're a smart chick. Get hold of yourself," she
whispered, as she chose to go ahead and flick the switch.

Mia closed her eyes in dread as she followed through with
resolve, impulsively holding the doorknob from turning with her

left hand as she popped the light switch up with her right. The room was filled with light, but not only from the fluorescent unit recessed above her. Just as Evans released the switch, the door knob turned, overpowering her feminine grasp. An unathletic-looking, light-skinned, balding man who looked to be in his late thirties was standing in the now-opened doorway, holding a small plastic sample cup with screw-on cap. Mia wanted to scream, and tried, but nothing came from her throat.

"Wow!" the man exclaimed. "I was expecting a few dirty magazines, maybe a poster of Heidi Klum or Katherine Heigl – maybe even a selection of adult videos if I needed them. But wow, not a personal assistant!" Fortunately for Mr. Wesley Sarbeck, a quick nap after his 4:00 p.m. to 2:00 a.m. police patrol would help him satisfy his half of the fertility equation.

Mia threw herself from the room designed for male sperm-donor collection, nearly knocking down the gentleman who stood smiling in surprise, still holding his empty specimen cup. She rushed toward the direction from which Dr. Chamblee and the female had appeared, hoping to find a door to the outside of the building and no one in her way. To her relief, Chamblee was nowhere in sight, and the tech who had admitted Wesley Sarbeck for his specimen collection was engaged in another far corner. The same woman, who had been talking with Knox Chamblee shortly before, was now performing the morning ritual of powering-up lab equipment while humming a Broadway show tune, unaware of the blur that was Mia Evans running by her in tiptoe fashion.

Just as the nice-looking girl bolted out the exit to the rear parking lot, Tinker Murtagh looked up from his freshly completed crossword puzzle. "This place is a surprise a minute – never know what's gonna happen next," he remarked as he finished his coffee with a final, loud slurp.

Chapter

5

◆◆◆

THE CATALOGUE

Cheryl Choice left the Center quickly after her appointment. Some visits there required a few minutes, some a few hours. Today's had been one of the in-betweens. Despite the mild discomfort and queasiness, the procedure had become easier each time. As usual, her post-donation instructions included an admonition to avoid driving for 24 hours, a restriction she continued to ignore since her yellow Mercedes could practically drive itself home.

Cheryl was different from most of the others who participated in the program in that she was a bit older. She was tall for a woman, beautiful by most anyone's tastes, and smart, almost regal in appearance, the kind of person who looks and acts wealthy even if not.

But Cheryl Choice was rich. And once more, she liked the new process of human egg harvesting touted on the Van Deman Center website. She liked the words *cutting edge technology* that the recruiter used when she answered the ad online. Seeming genuine and objective, the recruiter had helped Cheryl make comparisons between this new facility closer to home and her unpleasant previous experience in another state. Cheryl was thrilled to place herself in someone else's hands, to have another chance at donating her eggs and feeling fulfilled.

The doctors at the infertility clinic in Georgia would assume no responsibility for the problems she experienced there, instead blaming Cheryl's body for overreacting to the medicine routinely given in ovarian stimulation. As a result of the ovulation-inducing injections, her ovaries overproduced, unexpectedly yielding multiples of eggs and causing painful abdominal swelling. In addition to her swollen stomach, she was miserably puffy all over. She had lost her looks; she felt wretched.

Cheryl had lied to her husband Gregg that she would be shopping in Atlanta only for the weekend, so the several-day hospitalization in Atlanta jeopardized her alibi. Fortunately, an otherwise preoccupied Gregg Choice bought the need for her to extend her shopping excursion for a few extra days. "My watering holes are dry this time, Gregg darling. I need to check some new spots out," she had told him in a brief cell conversation. He was too busy with work to press for details or to care about them. As usual, his wife would simply send him the bills.

However, there would be no bills from the stores of Lenox Square or Phipps Plaza, or from the Georgia hospital. Instead, Cheryl was treated free-of-charge for abnormal levels of electrolytes in her blood, a condition which resulted from overstimulation of her ovaries. "Your ovaries were simply too sensitive to the follicle-stimulating hormones we gave you," the chief reproductive specialist and head of the egg donor program had explained to a groaning Cheryl Choice as the technician inserted more IVs into her arms. "Excessive fluid has accumulated around your organs as a result of ovarian hyperstimulation syndrome. This situation should completely resolve in a short time," the doctor assured her as her abdomen felt like a water balloon. "You know, we told you this could happen. It's listed under *Potential Complications* on your consent form."

Cheryl never lent much importance to medical terms. She counted on medical people to deal with those issues and placed her full confidence in same. Nonetheless, when assumed to be dozing in her room, Cheryl's concern was raised when one of her attending nurses murmured too loudly while reviewing her posted laboratory results. "My God! They're way off the charts. Her serum electrolyte levels are sky-high. She could die," the nurse uttered to one of the assistant nurses who had dropped by to deliver fresh towels.

"Don't worry," the assistant consoled. "That just never happens here."

As a result of the medical complication, Cheryl Choice no longer felt comfortable secretly donating her eggs through that facility, even though she fully recovered as her physicians had predicted. But she would not give up; she refused. A quick Google led her to a new facility closer to home, the Henry Van Deman Center, where she could continue to give of herself. Since there would be no children with her husband Gregg, as he was content to toss her beauty and talents aside, she was kept from leaving a part of herself behind. She simply could not and would not let that happen to the world.

During the last year of disguised visits to the Van Deman Center, she was known merely as Cheryl as she worked to blend into the walls, although her getup suggested otherwise. Van Deman's nurse called her Miss Cheryl. No one ever referred to her by last name in that she had been assured of the highest level of confidentiality. Dr. Van Deman himself had personally guaranteed that no one outside the human egg donor program would ever know that she was an active participant and that her true identity would be kept secret even within the facility itself. He stressed further that he and his associate, Dr. Chamblee, did not always know the personal background of the other doctor's patients, much less be able to put names with faces. That brought comfort to Cheryl when she noticed Chamblee at Boot Camp and felt that he had not recognized her there. Anyway, as an egg donor in her Van Deman blonde wig, heavy makeup, and clothing, the true brunette looked nothing like a Coco Ihle fitness student.

Today's visit to the Center had been a little different. Seeing the doctor at every visit had not been required in most instances, because the laboratory technicians and assistants seemed to do all the work. Cheryl believed that they were the busy ones, the smart ones. The doctors may have come up with the idea for all the technology, but the technicians possessed the real brains.

In contrast, she had seen Dr. Van Deman today, albeit briefly. He had done the sonogram of her abdomen and pelvis and inserted the needles right after the assistant administered the Versed, that dreamy little concoction that in itself made the whole process worthwhile. Despite the rules of procedure, the assistant called Cheryl by name – actually by her nickname – CC.

Nevertheless, Cheryl's body had responded well to the day's medicines and procedures except for an unexpected bout of nausea reminiscent of that miserable day at Boot Camp. Lurching for the emesis basin would have blown the persona she had garnered at the Center – cool, beautiful, together, a cooperative guise that was immediately appreciated whether or not her full name was associated with it. The sick feeling had passed before CC could say anything to the assistant, who at the moment was daydreaming indifferently.

Cheryl answered her own question, guessing that the hypnotic relaxation induced by the Versed had been the cause of the nausea, although she had never before associated that side effect with the drug. She had been warned that the thin needle penetrating her peritoneum to gather the multiple eggs could result in nausea, so she judged that to be the true culprit. If she had felt the sharp, harvesting needle enter her, she could not remember it. "Good ol' Versed," she thought.

Maybe it was last night's heavy meal at the new restaurant near the King Edward Hotel that had not agreed with her. Gregg had insisted they go to the eatery's grand opening inasmuch as he had invested heavily in the consortium that had opened the place and jump-started a revitalization of the downtown Jackson area. Because of the next day's clandestine procedure and despite an expensive night out that placed her husband in an amorous mood, she had to beg off having sex with him, using the heavy Italian food as an excuse.

Once again, Gregg Choice had not been happy.

Believing that ringing a doorbell seemed impersonal, she knocked instead. After all, she was expected. This was an appointment, an important one as were all appointments, and punctuality was a Lucille Wax trademark. Consequently, she was there at 2:00 p.m. sharp. She impatiently tapped the toe of her right shoe on the front step of the modest home, not planning to wait long at the door. Promptness was both a personal and professional trait in her business, a profession that revolved around reliability as well as the value of time.

At the sound of the doorbell, Wesley Sarbeck jerked toward the front of the house, then arrested himself to a slow walk from the small staircase landing. He hesitated midway through the compact, neat formal living room and again called upstairs to his wife. There remained no answer, just as there had been silence when he called to her from the bottom of the stairs. Suppressing his annoyance, he continued to the front door to answer the repeating bell. His gait was not fast, nor was it slow, but nonetheless it was drenched in emotional discomfort.

Fighting the beads of sweat forming on his pale, sweeping forehead, he nervously peered though the peephole. Through this distorted, tunneling view, the woman struck him as older than suggested by her phone voice. For an instant, Wesley Sarbeck wondered what kind of first impression his own phone voice had made on her and if it would jibe with that of today's face-to-face meeting.

Without his black, well-fitted policeman's uniform, Sarbeck looked and felt weak and indecisive, a marked contrast to the persona he radiated up and down Jackson-area roads, streets, and highways and during the session with the psychologist that was a prerequisite for this woman's visit. It was not accidental that he had worn his law enforcement garb to the psychologist's consultation during which he dominated the Sarbecks' side of the conversation.

Reaching for the doorknob to greet her, he wished for his policeman's hat and the protection it lent to his finely wrinkled, pink facial complexion. That same hat also camouflaged a scalp crowned with remnants of a disappearing hairline, both of which would soon confront the woman.

As usual, Miss Wax had suggested they meet in the clients' home, believing that a more personal location for an initial visit and an opportunity for her own socioeconomic-sociopsychological assessment. Wesley Sarbeck had assumed that he and his wife would meet the woman in an office somewhere in Jackson. To his surprise, there was no office.

"Generally, I work out of my home," Lucille Wax explained when Wesley called to make the appointment after he and his wife had survived the psychologist's screening. "I do make on-site visits when someone either enlists us to utilize our services or wishes to become an addition to our catalogue – basically an opportunity to get a general feel for health and well-being from all concerned, seen from my perspective, of course," she added before the appointment time was finalized and the phone conversation ended.

"And Mrs. Sarbeck? Is she here?" Wax asked as Wesley opened the door, introduced himself, and invited her inside. After hearing the woman's voice a second time, he appreciated both her eloquent and businesslike tone, but at the same time his thoughts drifted to the countless hours of police work required to take care of this whole thing – even with the financial help of Carrie's guilty aunt. A fresh batch of beaded sweat suddenly erupted on Wesley's forehead, coalescing into a thin, salty stream that ran down into his eyes.

"Yes, Carrie will be right down," he answered, his eyes burning as he awkwardly wiped them with his sleeve. "This whole thing was my idea. I mean that it was my idea to proceed with this next step. But it's really what we both want."

The expression on Lucille Wax's face remained stoic as she stood at the door, although Wesley could not miss the restrained tilt to her head. He recognized that questioning gesture, similar to that of their pet dog when he seemed to recognize a word or two of English.

"Ever since her last surgery she's been really ... uh, she's been really ..." Sarbeck hesitated and then called again to his wife, cupping his hands together in Tarzanian fashion. "Carrie, the lady is here for our appointment. You know, Miss Wax, the one the Center told us to call!"

"Well, may I come in?" Lucille Wax shielded her left eardrum as she walked deliberately through the doorway, not waiting for an answer and repressing her annoyance at the slow start to the proceedings, particularly when other appointments could have been scheduled. She trusted Van Deman's commissioned psychologist and financial affairs department to sort things out long before she got involved with clients such as this couple. However, a client's decision to seek her services when having the resources to do so was psychologically adequate for Lucille Wax to begin the process, and never had Dr. Deman's referrals been inappropriate.

Taking in the living area as she continued forward, she focused on an oddly-shaped, but strangely inviting, sofa positioned below a large plate-glass window that worked to form the backbone of a sitting area. Miss Wax noticed the exaggerated architectural elements present in the moldings and door frames of the 1930s home, many of which were dulled by layer after layer of interior house paint. The home was typical of many of those in the Fondren area of mid-Jackson, a neighborhood and business district self-described as progressively avant-garde and sandwiched between Interstate 55 to the east and the railroad tracks to the west.

Consisting of varying-sized homes generally built in the earlier part of the twentieth century, the area simply referred to as *Fondren* embraced for the most part art deco and other architectural elements now considered eclectic by contemporary standards. The Sarbecks' street was one of those on the western edge of the district that had yet to enjoy the spirit of renovation and cosmetic upkeep that was sweeping the rest of the area, nor had it attracted the attention of new construction that was replacing the razed homes considered hopeless.

As she positioned herself in the sofa's midsection of the couple's living room, Miss Wax pulled the coffee table to her with her right hand while clearing the top of it with her left to make way for an attaché case. She flipped open the tan leather-covered briefcase in the same motion in which she rested it on the table. Despite its similar thin and feminine frame, the case still matched the persona of its important owner. That importance amplified itself as Wesley watched her extract professionally printed and designed documents. To ensure even more space for her materials, she pushed a painted glass figurine carelessly aside.

"Oh, yes, please do have a seat, yes, right there," Wesley said, motioning to the spot already taken by the woman. "And that vase belonged to my wife's late mother. I'll just put it over here, out of the way," he added as he picked up the glass object and gingerly situated it on the sofa's end table.

Lucille took another look at the glass object and responded with one eyebrow raised. "My God, a vase? I would never have guessed," she said under her breath, almost deliberately loud enough for Mr. Sarbeck to hear. There was an increasing sense that the client screening process had at last failed her. Even so, Lucille Wax pushed on.

"Mr. Sarbeck, as I'm sure you understand, our protocol guides us all through a process that is decidedly personal but at the same time totally private, totally anonymous." All of the procedures and policies had been thoroughly explained on her explicit website and then detailed live when Wesley scheduled the appointment over the phone. Wesley saw no need for Lucille Wax to explain anything else. "Our adherence to privacy in the selection process is sure to facilitate the client's making an appropriate choice," she added, nonetheless.

Even though he had completed the online medical, financial, and social questionnaire for Wax Consultants, LLP, and this woman had thoroughly reviewed it with him when he made the appointment with her, he recalled the fine-print disclaimer found at the bottom of its fourth page: *At any time we reserve*

the right to terminate client arrangements with or without
cause, providing full refund minus expenses. Wesley Sarbeck
was a city policeman, a law enforcement officer who considered
himself truthful and forthright, at least most of the time, and
certainly law-abiding. Therefore, his conscience was clear
on the issue. He had not hesitated to disclose any medical or
family history concerns on the Client Medical History section
of the questionnaire, including his wife Carrie's depression and
treatment for such.

The intrusive questions had been answered a few weeks
previously when Wesley sat at the keyboard of their desktop
computer, hunting-and-pecking his way through. The exercise
did nothing but add to the emotional upheaval of their infertility
ordeal, which he hoped had found its resolution. He assumed
that Lucille Wax, president of Wax Consultants, LLP, would
understand the scenario, having no doubt run across it countless
times before.

Besides, his wife had undergone one psychotherapy session
after the other, sprinkled between her many pelvic surgeries, and
continued to see a psychiatrist regularly while still taking the
antidepressant Vasoprene. Wesley hoped that once pregnant with
the aid of the Van Deman Center she would be able to continue
the medication safely.

The relentless tapping on the bathroom window easily
overpowered the knocking at the front door even though the
sound had drifted upstairs. Even if Lucille Wax had rung the
doorbell instead of using the door knocker, Carrie Sarbeck would
still have pretended not to hear it. She knew the appointment had
been scheduled for the afternoon but ignored any other sound,
opting instead to listen to the bird's rhythm.

For several days the blue jay had thrown itself beak-first against
the master bathroom window which was set within a round

wooden encasement at eye level above the toilet. The window
was actually a grouping of narrow panes of glass wedged between
thin wooden tines that fanned from the midpoint like spokes of
a wagon wheel. When she and Wesley first purchased the house
several years ago, the real estate agent simply described it as a
round window containing glass original to the house.

During its first intrusion, Carrie assumed the bird's pounding
against the bathroom window to be random: mere confusion and
disorientation of a crazed animal trying to enter an imaginary
birdhouse. When visiting her aunt's house as a child, she had
seen a flock of sparrows swarm a Savannah holly, heavy with red
berries, eating so wildly that a few strays lost their bearings and
flew head-on into her aunt's thick den window, dropping dead
with broken necks. However, there were no red berries to swarm
this time – just Carrie Sarbeck herself.

She first tried tapping her forefinger in reciprocation against
the bathroom window, initially hoping to shoo the blue jay
away; but the animal was relentless, almost obsessive, in its
attempt to break through. Carrie believed that she understood
the animal's fixation. Its inexhaustible, overwhelming desire
to reach inside for human touch mirrored her own passion, a
passion to reach beyond what she could not have. The animal's
drive to touch her must be meant to hurt her, she decided. Why
else would the blue jay want to be inside her house with her in
this miserable existence?

All day she had waited in the master bathroom, certain that the
bird would return to chip at the glass with even greater fervor.
When it did come back shortly before Lucille Wax arrived at the
front door, Carrie pretended to be startled, and then admitted the
truth. She had known the blue jay would come back. Someone was
trying to reach her to warp her future, to twist the shape of what
was to come, a future that seemed shrouded in total uncertainty

and dread. Unsatisfied that it had tormented her enough, the creature wanted inside, just as Carrie Sarbeck wanted out.

As her husband called for her from downstairs, she tiptoed to look through the panes at the house next store, the happy house next door, the one bulging with an exhausted but fertile married couple and four healthy kids, ranging in ages from six months to six years. Only slightly larger than their home but similar in age, the house adjoining their property continually radiated life while hers reeked of death.

However, the blue jay's relentless pecking had nearly smeared the bathroom window glass beyond visibility, so much so that Carrie Sarbeck could no longer clearly see the neighbors' house, the happy house. That must have been part of the bird's purpose for being here: to keep her from seeing the house, to keep her from wanting a family and a happy home, to keep her from wanting what she could never have.

The weather had been atrocious for the last several days. The ten to twelve inches of hard rain over a few hours the day before had flooded several Jackson streets. But today was different; there was no rain outside, only inside, soaking Carrie's miserable life, her childless life. Finding a couple of inches of clear glass toward the bottom that the obsessed bird had missed, she strained to peer intently through the window, finding some relief in seeing the yard below. Despite the fall season of early October, green leaves and grass still abounded around their property. Thank God for green, she thought.

Then Carrie begin to think about chromosomes and genetics and how those factors – not God Almighty – controlled how life developed and how much green existed in the world. God could not have been this cruel to her; she was sure of it. Maybe it was just bad karma, she surmised, forcing a smile of surrender. Whatever or whoever dished out such cruelty and controlled such things, God or karma or birds, was something or someone she hated.

So many different doctors including her new one, Dr. Chamblee at the Van Deman Center, had explained varied and complex options to her for having a baby, much of which was difficult to grasp fully. During the last few months, she had pored over the printed medical literature and detailed DVDs that he and his senior partner had supplied until her eyes crossed. She had downloaded from the Internet additional information pertaining to infertility treatment, and in countless chat rooms she had commiserated with other infertile women from all over the world. Much to her discontent, Wesley had pulled the plug on her tormented weekly Internet blog site dedicated to Carrie Sarbeck's personal journey through recurrent ectopic pregnancies, multiple intricate surgeries, and expensive medical treatments for infertility – all for nothing.

"Carrie, the lady is here," she could hear Wesley call from downstairs as the bird circled back around to continue to pummel the window. Her husband seemed so removed from her agony. Sure, he wanted a baby, but unlike her, he was not constantly reminded of her failure. After Sunday School, at the grocery store, and especially at Bunko, her peers inadvertently tortured her with debates over the attributes and weaknesses of area daycare centers, preschools, and babysitters as well as the latest clothing styles and stores for toddlers. Out of an assumed obligation arising from friendship, her Bunko group had initially skirted the subject, clumsily changing the conversation from diaper brands, children's books, and pediatricians' personalities whenever she returned to the game after a restroom or kitchen break.

But recently she had perceived her shrinking group of friends as becoming immune to her predicament – or maybe they were just tired of it.

"Carrie, are you coming down? This is getting to be awkward."
Her husband was now tapping at the bathroom door as the bird
did the same at the window. Finding the doorknob locked, he
whispered again, holding back from banging on the door. "I'll
go ahead and choose one if you want me to." Wesley was taking
this all in irritating stride, she realized, as though their having
a baby remained a natural thing. Playing the part of practicality
was simple for him in that her half of the equation remained the
embarrassing obstacle.

Leaving her husband's summons unanswered, Carrie Sarbeck
sprang from the closed toilet and threw her fists against the
window, shooing the crazed bird. Was it God's curse or maybe the
devil's curse? Did God freely wield curses on His children or did
Satan do this? Evil must have cursed her as barren, but God had
granted the gift of crying, hadn't He, crying to bring relief from
the anguish of slowly dying? But Carrie Sarbeck had reached an
exhausted pinnacle where shedding tears could no longer grant
her any relief. Her soul could no longer bear the burden of being
barren, the pain of a childless marriage, as well as the heartbreak
of a childless life.

As she forcibly sat back on the closed toilet below the bird's
window, her heartbeats propelled her tiny, feminine frame
forward, her body pounding in rhythm. The dying organ inside
her chest struggled to keep her alive, at least physically. She
longed to peel away her outer skin, exposing the tissue that she
was sure was rotting beneath. She would throw the skin away,
or better yet, bury it, burn it, put it down the garbage disposal,
or simply flush it down this toilet. Carrie had tried to escape
her body and her life before but had lost the nerve. On another
occasion, her husband had come home early and, unbeknownst to
him, interrupted her final effort.

"I'm such a coward. I couldn't do it," she remarked, looking up

to the window panes which remained free of the banished bird.
While propped on the same toilet as she loosely held a kitchen
knife against her left wrist, Carrie had waited for her dark blood
as she weakly pried open a shallow, crooked slit in her wrist. So
superficial was the self-inflicted wound that it barely required a
Band-Aid and no explanation to her husband when they had sex
later that night.

Abandoning all attempts to end his wife's seclusion, Wesley
returned downstairs to the living room where Lucille Wax waited
with her catalogue of available human egg donors. Mystified
over his wife's unpredictable behavior, Wesley studied the initial
picture in the catalogue. He took comfort in the psychiatrist's
reassurance that treatment would eventually help Carrie. But
getting a baby, Wesley decided, might be the only answer. It had
to be.

The youthful woman in the first photograph was smiling at the
photographer, glancing up as though she had been pleasantly
surprised. Holding a book in her lap, she appeared to have been
reading leisurely, supporting the book by her right hand while
petting a Shetland sheepdog standing to her left. Poised at
attention, the animal's head reached just below the level of her
chair. Its loving, but jealous, eyes seemed to beg for the chance
to leap into his master's lap and dislodge the book from her
attention.

"This one has been one of our most popular. She's a medical
student – in the top 10 percent of her class," Lucille Wax
explained. "If she were a little taller, her fee would be a few
thousand more."

"Has anyone used her much?" Wesley asked, thinking the med
student was approximately Carrie's height and build if the picture
was a true representation. The girl had to be smart; she was in
medical school. "She might just be perfect for us," he added.

"Yes, this donor has been selected several times, and each time with great success," Wax answered as she flipped the page over, revealing a list of statistics: height 5'5", weight 115 lbs, eyes hazel, hair auburn, IQ listed at a number Wesley assumed to be high. "I really cannot divulge any other information about this donor other than to tell you that the transfer of eggs in this case has always been successful."

Miss Wax silently referenced the $25, 500 donor fee listed in code at the bottom of the page. She thought back to the information she had been given regarding the Sarbecks' salary and net worth, feeling certain that this couple could not manage the fee required of the medical student. Her annoyance at Mr. Sarbeck's interest in a donor who extended far beyond his financial reach compounded her displeasure over his wife's absence from their meeting. Miss Wax was becoming more and more certain that this visit was a tremendous waste of her time as she quickly flipped the page.

Lucille Wax was correct about the money. Wesley and Carrie had agreed to spend no more than five to ten thousand on an egg donor, and even that was a pecuniary stretch, particularly if the experience was unsuccessful and they had to repeat it.

"Anyway," she continued after clearing her throat politely as though to avoid embarrassing Mr. Sarbeck, "using that donor in your case is likely impossible. I'm not sure that you are prepared ... I mean ... you see ... her fee may be more than you ... well ... might have anticipated," she detailed with a mixture of a forced smile and raised, questioning eyebrows as she diverted her eyes to the side opposite Wesley.

Miss Wax paused a few moments. "Isn't your wife going to join us?" she asked again as she looked admiringly at the photograph of a striking blonde woman which had followed that of the medical student.

"Gosh, Carrie isn't feeling well. I think she has a stomach virus or something, but she should be coming down in a minute," Wesley lied, still unsure why his wife could not pull herself together for such an important decision, at least for a few minutes.

Prior to scheduling this donor selection meeting, he and Carrie had repeatedly discussed this next step in their plans to have a baby. After all, the psychologist at the Center had cleared them both as sane as long as Carrie took her medication, but Wesley was beginning to wonder if perhaps Carrie had merely fooled him. Beginning to feel uneasy about their plans, he would have cancelled today's appointment with Lucille Wax had he known how badly his wife was going to behave.

"Wait. What about that one?" he asked, reaching forward to stop Wax from moving through the ensuing pages in the catalogue. Sarbeck focused on the blonde's photograph, admiring the woman and wondering if her hair was natural.

"Oh, yes, that's number *OE-5652*. She's unquestionably beautiful, but not always a productive donor." In contrast to the casual rendering of the page before, this woman was dressed as though at an elegant party. Flowers in silver vases were amassed behind her as she seemed to beckon the photographer to come closer and join the fun. Two rows of dazzling white teeth radiated in perfect form from inside regal, flawless facial features.

"But, who is she?" Wesley was drawn to the attractive, vibrant woman, somewhat older than the girl with the dog, but still radiating youth.

"Of course the identity is privileged information. That was explained to you at the Center. At least, I was told that you understood these conditions, and you signed papers to prove it."

The woman in the glossy photograph appeared tall, not too thin and certainly not fat. Her expensive-looking clothes clung to her body, revealing perfect proportions, although the size was subtle, tasteful. A double layer diamond necklace encircled her delicate long neck. "Oh, I mean that I just wanted to know some more information about her statistics," he explained clumsily. For Wesley Sarbeck the situation was not unlike shopping for a new automobile. Even though the price may be out of reach, he still wanted the test drive.

"Is she smart and how old is she?" he asked. He was mesmerized by the photograph of the striking blonde with the beautiful teeth and perfect breasts; at least her breasts looked perfect as they pushed above her gown.

Wax fought to hide her growing annoyance. "This one is 31-years-old," she answered as she also pointed briefly to the respectable IQ listing. "She is expensive, but her fee is quite a bit lower than that of the medical student."

"OK, then maybe this one is not way out of our league. Maybe we can afford this one," the almost childish excitement obvious in Wesley's voice.

Wax let out a weak but unrepressed sigh. She regretted the entire afternoon.

Chapter
6
❖❖❖
THE OLD LODGE

The building on the outskirts of Canton had collected pigeons, vagrants, and drug dealers for more months than Darla Bender cared to remember. It was nothing but a boutique hotel for nomads, human and animal alike. The listing had been an embarrassing failure for a real estate broker whose domain blanketed the northern area of the Mississippi, extending well beyond her native Larkspur. After all, Bender's properties roped in areas of Holly Springs, then up to Corinth, eastward to Tupelo and Oxford and then back westward to Cleveland, Indianola, and Montclair. Her portfolio of real estate offerings swelled when she was able to penetrate the more central region of the state and include Canton, Jackson, and the surrounding communities.

In spite of the army of sales agents swarming under her umbrella and meetings with countless potential buyers as Bender cracked the whip, her company had failed miserably in moving this particular property in Canton. The old Masonic Lodge had once been a hub of activity, attracting members from throughout the southeastern United States, but now was only a monument to handmade red brick and outlawed asbestos. Even though one business enterprise or manufacturing firm after another had toured the property and consulted with architects and engineers about potential development, no deal to move the property ever materialized.

Ms. Bender's tarnished image as the area's stellar real estate broker was enhanced somewhat when she maneuvered a stipend – a relatively meager amount of money, but cash nonetheless – from the federal government to house displaced victims of the Hurricane Katrina nightmare temporarily in the abandoned building. The building's actual owners, who were faceless to Bender, also received a sizeable corporate tax break by opening the inhabitable section of the sprawling brick complex to the Mississippi Gulf Coast and New Orleans residents who lost their homes as a result of the storm's annihilation. However, once FEMA trailers became available months later, the Katrina evacuees were gone, returning the building to complete vacancy and the rent stream back to zero.

Still with no potential buyers by that point, Darla Bender reconsidered another financially successful method of liquidating the client's – and her own – dilemma, one that had worked well before. However, she decided against the extreme. In this case the true client was faceless, the real estate seller's agreement having been signed by a corporate legal firm on behalf of an unidentified third party which seemed to accept the slow market and declined to criticize her sales tactics and lack of success.

Regardless, without the advantage of personally gauging the individual client's own level of desperation, she simply could not bring herself to push the button that had settled dead properties so nicely in the past. Getting rid of a stagnant piece of real estate lent itself to extreme measures – those same measures useful for simply tying up loose ends, whether they be financial, professional, or personal.

For such properties as the monstrosity on Mississippi Highway 36, her use of arson had worked well in the past. However, after a big fire in Larkspur a few years prior that brought down an elaborate lawyer's home, she had sworn off arson, particularly if the reason arose more from emotional retribution than financial. Nothing stemming from the dinner party that night had ever been traced to her, and she had not contacted the arsonist since.

Fortunately for Bender, there was never a need to reinvent the combustible solution for the Highway 36 real estate debacle. The old Masonic Lodge would no longer be home to pigeons, vagrants, meth lab technicians, or asbestosis. The victims of the next catastrophic storm, as well, would have to find somewhere else to go. Henry Van Deman, MD, and his money had come to Darla Bender's rescue, getting her off the hook with the faceless owners of the lodge building before she resorted to having it torched.

Why the physician and the cash had found their way to Canton, Mississippi, was of no real concern to her. Bender had bagged a buyer, a good buyer – one whose check would clear. A quick Google revealed that Van Deman had been a principal in a Manhattan infertility practice and from the images, statistics, and patient testimonials, it appeared to have been a profitable one.

What Bender did not see published on the website was Dr. Van Deman's personal quest to advance the technology of human reproduction. In his many years of practicing in New York City and through the ever-expanding necessity of marketing to the moneyed upper crust to survive financially, Van Deman had grown weary of locking horns with those vying for the cash. Van Deman's laurels had become lost on savvy New Yorkers who, despite the fact that they could have afforded whomever or whatever in medical care services, simply focused on shopping around for the best deal. Judging from the Yellow Pages, the Internet, and television and radio commercials, not to mention roadway billboards and banners affixed to the sides of buses, his native New York had more than enough reproductive endocrinologists clamoring for business.

Even though Van Deman's patient referral base in New York and the surrounding environs had remained steady through the years, sprouting enough green to keep him and a host of peers in business, he felt a need to be in control, to be and remain number one. His ego dictated that he brand his medical commodity with the Van Deman name, the irreproachable last word of authority in the management of human infertility and reproduction.

When initiating plans to relocate his practice, Van Deman did what most red-blooded Americans would do: he went immediately to the Internet and conducted a search of the board-certified reproductive endocrinologists practicing throughout the United States, finding, as expected, most infertility specialists sprinkled in the more densely populated areas. "We'll leave out the quacks," Van Deman chuckled to himself over several glasses of *pinot noir* as he privately critiqued the websites of various infertility centers, making notes in separate electronic files on his laptop, grouping together the attributes and negatives of each facility and physician or group of physicians.

His quiet but thorough research brought him to the relief of the southern United States, where he imagined a casual lifestyle along with professional opportunity, boasting clients who were fairly cosmopolitan but not as impassive as those of his native New York. The original site selection for his new practice had been the New Orleans area. Regrettably, the August 2005 timing was a disaster, courtesy of Hurricane Katrina.

While much of the affluent area of New Orleans still stood after the hurricane and the fallibility of the city's levee system, the area's economy was left bruised and shaken, forcing Van Deman to seek another location for his venture. Fortunately for Van

Deman and his investors, their business attorney had included a cancellation clause with the developer and builder of the proposed elegantly-designed, ultra modern infertility treatment facility, so that in event of a natural disaster the principals could back out of the project and look elsewhere.

The legal jargon had been a lucky break for Van Deman, whose infertility center and its elective, non-emergent medical care could have failed in New Orleans without the support of a healthy cash flow. Besides, the marketing focus planned for his advanced medical and surgical services was targeted to those with disposable income, potentially creating ridicule toward Van Deman given the sad economic plight of so many. Also, many of those with disposable income who had composed the target market before Hurricane Katrina were now among the unfortunates displaced from their homes by the flooding of Lake Pontchartrain or stripped of their businesses either by looters or the flood itself.

Once the New Orleans location was out, Van Deman's relocation decision was reshaped by a renewed desire to be an outdoorsman while remaining a productive infertility specialist who practiced on the cutting edge. Since childhood, he had maintained an interest in hunting and fishing that had progressed to pure fascination because he was unable to master fully the pastime for lack of opportunity in trendy Manhattan. The concentration on wildlife and relatively inexpensive and available hunting land kept Van Deman's relocation efforts concentrated in the South, almost as much as did his perception of the area's need for his medical services.

As far as real estate was concerned, Darla Bender's immediate needs had been met. With Van Deman's purchase of the decaying brick property on Highway 36 and his successful renovation of it, her reputation as Mississippi's number one realtor remained untarnished.

Shortly before daybreak, they slowly approached the field in
a modified golf cart painted entirely in hunters' camouflage.
A local entrepreneur had capitalized on the growing appetite
for such personal playthings, recycling them after they were
discarded by country clubs and other golf courses that desired
newer, untarnished models. Even available were electric or gas
carts customized to match the exterior color and texture of a
personal residences. For that reason, Van Deman had already
ordered another in brick red with optional exterior and interior
lights, mirrors, rear seats, and security system. Cruising one's
upscale neighborhood late on a Saturday or Sunday afternoon in
a souped-up, retooled golf cart seemed to be the thing to do – the
neighborhood ambience made all the more relaxing with the aid
of a glass of wine or a light beer as long as the community security
patrol or, worse, the city police did not call the driver's hand.

While Knox Chamblee had not yet established himself within
such a comfortable neighborhood, the likes of which had been
easily reached by Dr. Henry Van Deman, he nevertheless
appreciated the smooth ride in the senior doctor's golf cart
along the paths of his hunting property less than two hours away.
Once the old lodge in Canton had been acquired through Darla
Bender, renovated to the point of nearly total reconstruction,
and outfitted with the most recent technology, Van Deman
followed through with his self-made promise and joined the
White Tail Hunting Preserve. For the sake of financial resolve,
Henry delaying joining the choice hunting organization until his
progressive medical facility was clearly profitable. The resolve
made for only a short delay.

Located in northwest Mississippi, White Tail was overrun with deer and turkey and opportunities to fish for bass or bream. On occasion, a dove hunt with an old-fashioned barbeque was held on its grounds as well, with skeet available to shoot if the dove did not like barbeque. During the past few seasons, the deer and turkey hunting camp had continued its transformation into an even more highly polished place to shoot wild game; the pathways and trails to its permanent deer stands and other gaming areas now so passable that such party-type vehicles as golf carts or other mini-models had in many areas replaced the need for more rugged ATVs.

Courtesy of Van Deman, today was Knox's first invitation to hunt trophy deer at the Preserve. With gun season not yet underway, Chamblee's option was to bow hunt. And while the reality of his getting a deer with a bow was suspect, it would be an adventure. He would give it a try.

Once he was settled in a permanent hunting stand hidden among live oaks and brush at the edge of a short field, Chamblee wondered if he was anywhere near the stream. There are few babbling brooks in Mississippi, especially during October and following a dry summer, so Knox did not expect to hear the sound of naturally flowing water. It was his understanding that the stream, infamous in certain circles, normally served as a tranquil, picturesque feature of the acreage. Remaining shallow during most of the year, the water still rolled gently over the flat, brown rocks lining its bed as it traversed the heavy woods.

However, one winter morning several years ago, the then frozen, shallow brook was a deathbed for his former physician employer who fell there while deer hunting with a rifle. Like Knox, the late Dr. Cullen Gwinn had been a novice deer hunter. Somehow, both emotionally and financially, Knox had survived the loss of Gwinn, once his mentor and chief proponent in a practice that was slow to promote him once Gwinn died.

Nonetheless, Chamblee remained to practice obstetrics and gynecology in the late Dr. Gwinn's namesake clinic until his plans changed. His desire for specialized training in the advances of infertility treatment and the practice offer from Henry Van Deman finally lured him away.

Chapter
7
♦♦♦
THE NIGHT SHIFT

Wesley's supervisor at the Jackson Police Department dinged him with the night shift that month, an assignment which generally brought disfavor from any of the working uniforms whose beats changed daily. Wesley assumed there was some method to the designation of certain shifts and beats to particular police officers, though he had never figured out the pattern, if indeed one existed.

However, regarding the specific assignment to evenings, the department's night shift supervisor received none of the expected discontent from Officer Sarbeck. Wesley needed to be free almost daily so that during typical business hours he could accompany his wife to the offices of Drs. Van Deman and Chamblee for treatments. The production of a healthy Sarbeck embryo seemed to be going smoothly, the compensated donor selected from the Wax file having provided healthy human eggs, dispelling the fear of an unpredictable performance.

At roll call that afternoon, Sarbeck was assigned a beat in northeast Jackson, an area of Mississippi's capital city north of Lakeland Drive brimming with investment bankers, lawyers, doctors, insurance executives, business owners and the like, as well as retirees and other folks who enjoyed their quiet, mostly upscale neighborhoods.

"Omega 5, 10-8. Beginning mileage 65,258." Wesley's initial communication with the radio dispatcher officially started his evening shift with the first assignment being to monitor traffic flow – that is, to issue speeding tickets. His follow-up of *"10-4"* indicated full calibration of his cruiser's traffic radar device.

The productivity of the mid-afternoon's speed trap was much higher than expected. From the number of speeding citations issued on his stretch of Interstate 55 leading through Jackson north toward Canton, the vehicle mass was in a big hurry. As a bonus, Wesley even racked up a few expired inspection stickers and citations for last-year's car tags. The wise positioning of his cruiser near an overpass had been one reason for the larger-than-average number of tickets written as the vehicle's exterior blended with the shadows of the surrounding grey concrete and steel pilings. The overgrown shrubbery of the landscape periphery did not hurt either.

Well-hidden, Wesley stood near the driver's side of the police cruiser, gently leaning against it and popping his radar gun at each passing vehicle as though he were at a carnival booth. The process also reminded him of a stomach-turning ride at a central Florida theme park during which he and Carrie shot at imaginary aliens. Carrie was definitely not pregnant at the time.

Instead of tabulating points for each alien massacred in Florida, he received a different reaction from his real-life prey on the inner-city section of interstate that afternoon. Wesley found it almost comical that each tagged speeding vehicle would dart furtively from one lane to the other to escape him or waste a vehicular nosedive by pumping the brake pads much too late. Masked by standard-issue dark glasses, the satisfied policeman's eyes topped by raised eyebrows missed not a law-bending driver.

Wesley considered every facet of his job purely professional, that designation challenged as evening approached, clocking one wounded I-55 traveler at 78 miles per hour in a 60 mph zone. "Officer, I feel like a scalded cougar," blared a male voice through the lowered window of the compact, light-colored SUV as Officer Sarbeck approached.

"I'll need your driver's license and proof of insurance certificate, please, sir." To the officer's surprise, the rear of the vehicle was stuffed with boxes brandishing the names of the area's most expensive stores and boutiques, places which Wesley had never visited and certainly hoped his wife had not either. Several women's garments hung from a bar that traversed the length of the back seat. From his initial impression, Sarbeck assumed he had stumbled upon a fleeing merchandise thief or a DUI case or both. However, the situation was soon obvious: there was no influence for the driver to be under; it was pure personality. And the stuff nearly overflowing his SUV was legitimate.

"You've got to understand, sir," the nervous driver continued. Wesley would have considered him well-dressed if flamboyance in men's clothes had been his taste. "I'm on the way to the phone store because my cell won't work." He held an opened, foldable thin yellow cell phone in his right hand as though he had just been using it rather than paying attention to the road. "You see, I've got to have my phone with me at all times because they need me," he added as his eyes flickered from side-to-side almost in unison with his shaking head.

Officer Sarbeck cared not at all who *they* were but was intrigued nonetheless by the character he had pulled over. Relatively long but manicured fingernails had dropped the cell on the car seat beside him, and then the individual's face began to quiver as he frantically waved his hands in front of it. After Wesley examined the license and insurance certificate, he returned them, warning,

"Sir, you must slow down. From a morgue, you sure won't be making any phone calls."

"I would never let my little head rest on my pillow at night without returning a client's call. You see, my job is to make people feel and look good – it's all about being the best you can be. You know – change your shoes, change your life. The last time I couldn't make cell calls, God must've fixed my phone. Thank you, Jesus!" With that, the quivering fellow raised both opened palms up to the heavens.

The statement which followed – *"Please, officer. One more ticket and I'll lose my license, and I can't work without my car."* – was unnecessary since the entertained Officer Sarbeck had already decided to let the weirdo off. Wesley also overlooked, as only part of the show, the presentation of a pair of supposedly antiqued men's cufflinks clearly offered as a bribe.

By five-thirty when the SUV whisked away, it was already dark since daylight savings time was not yet in effect. The flashy cell phone addict who wielded the cufflinks had been one of Wesley's final traffic stops. Before leaving his interstate assignment and moving on through his supervisor's other directives, the police officer decided upon a cup of coffee from one of the gas stations along the Northside Drive exit. He would need the caffeine to complete the rest of his night shift.

Despite the fact that the majority of retail businesses and many of the residential neighborhoods located to the east of the interstate had resorted to private security patrols, the JPD captain had promised an increase in inner city officer patrols. The reaction to rising crime rates, which mirrored those of many other cities in the South and elsewhere, had been a political debacle for the city council and mayor, and Officer Wesley Sarbeck's assigned patrol for the night was one of the token efforts to squelch the outcry for better police surveillance in Jackson.

By eight-fifteen that night, that first coffee had long been
followed by a couple of others, then a sandwich, fries, and Diet
Coke from Wendy's. Wesley would be relieved of duty at 2:00
a.m. and was looking forward to it. Tomorrow was to be the
scheduled embryo transfer, and the paternal donor of the genetic
material for the future Sarbeck progeny felt strangely ill at ease.
His part in the process had been simple. After all, his wife was
the one subjected to the multiple poisons pumped into her body
in preparation for a growing embryo. Most of the medicine made
Carrie nauseous, swollen, and increasingly more depressed even
as her uterus became healthy. But it was Wesley's hope that the
likelihood of finally bearing a healthy child would refocus his wife
toward sanity.

He knew full well that this effort tomorrow at the Van Deman
Center would be the final chance for the Sarbecks to have a baby
naturally – natural in the sense that Carrie Sarbeck would give
birth to the child, even though the maternal half of the genes was
contributed by a thirty-one year-old blonde woman, a stranger,
selected from the Wax catalogue. The medical school student with
the stylish haircut and high IQ who liked Shetland sheep dogs
demanded too high a fee, even though her younger eggs might
have been healthier, as well as smarter. Once coaxed out of their
master bathroom, Carrie had begrudgingly approved Wesley's
choice of the blonde.

While Lucille Wax had purported that the distinguished-looking
blonde was less expensive due to her age and less successful track
record with *in vitro* fertilization, Wesley assumed that the blonde
donor was not in it to make money as was the medical student.
And Wesley was correct.

In any case, tomorrow would be the day. His wife's body was
ready. Under Dr. Henry Van Deman's direction, the beautiful
blonde donor had taken injections and pills to ovulate this time

on schedule, producing several eggs that easily accepted Wesley's sperm in a Petri dish and had been growing and dividing cell-by-cell into his and Carrie's baby.

"Officer Sarbeck," the radio dispatcher disrupted Wesley's thoughts of the Van Deman Center where he and Carrie were scheduled for ten o'clock in the morning. The dispatcher continued, "Possible 10-43 at 1216 Jasmine Terrace in the Eastover subdivision." Wesley jotted the address on a pad in his cruiser. "Caller reported to 9-1-1 the possibility of a gunshot next door. But could have been just a firecracker, caller said," the dispatcher detailed before adding specifics which Wesley absorbed as he turned his cruiser in the direction of the expensive neighborhood.

The residences in the Eastover neighborhood of northeast Jackson were generally positioned on large acre-plus lots, all allowing plenty of footage between homes with few zero-lot line style arrangements except on the periphery of the approximately seventy-year-old development. The woman who made the 9-1-1 call was unsure from which the direction the noise had come, perhaps from the driveway next door.

Before the 9-1-1 operator could disconnect the call, the woman had second thoughts: the sound was definitely a shotgun blast and not just a firecracker. She was sure that it was the sound of a shotgun since it resembled one recently heard at a dove hunt in the Mississippi Delta. She had not hunted that day herself but had been nearby under a shade tree with barbeque and cocktail in hand as her husband fired away at a legal limit of birds, making her well aware of the sound of a shotgun blast. She said that she couldn't possibly be mistaken.

Some sort of teenage prank, the popping of an overloaded electrical transformer, a slamming door, fireworks ... Sarbeck ran through alternate sources of the sound the caller had assumed to be a gunshot. Being in the vicinity, he quickly reached the reported Jasmine Terrace address and turned slowly into the driveway. He noticed the house was dark except for a few strategically placed exterior security lights. As Wesley exited the cruiser, club-sized mag light in hand, gun checked for position, he updated his location to the dispatcher.

Sarbeck then methodically approached the nearly wall-length front windows lining the central section of the front of the house which qualified as a mansion in most vocabularies. He streamed his light through the clear glass in methodical inspection, the pattern of the beam appearing from the interior as flickering signals had anyone been at home to see it. Sarbeck detected no movement within the residence, only a few pieces of furniture and a statue or two ruling a grand foyer – nothing appearing askew, everything appearing expensive.

Next, he walked the periphery of the remainder of the building, entering the rear grounds of the house through a wooden side gate that broke a solid brick and stone fence. All lower level windows and doors were locked and undisturbed; the windows to the upper floor seemed secure as well and also pitch-black. Wesley assumed that either everyone was asleep or, more likely, that no one was at home.

Walking back around to the front of the residence, Sarbeck tried the doorbell. As he would have predicted, there was no answer. Realizing that the caller could have misjudged the sound distance and identified the address incorrectly, he decided to check the next residence down the street and maybe the home on the other side of that of the caller. He would likely be reporting this incident as a false alarm, a case of vivid imagination on behalf of a hunting widow.

The officer returned to his police cruiser, exited the first driveway, and approached the house next door – another building that qualified as a mansion if using the same vernacular. In contrast, this brick and stone manor boasted a security gate at the bottom of the drive that was fully open as if Officer Sarbeck were expected. While the exterior security lights were in place and illuminating the grounds, a smattering of interior lights were also lit in contrast to the previous address. Wesley reported his new position while following the curve of the drive. He planned to park at the front entrance to the home which crowned the top of the circling pavement.

The cruiser's headlights draped the façade of the house as Wesley ascended the incline of the brick driveway, long enough to serve as a short street in many small towns. Slowing as he neared the wide stone steps that beckoned visitors to the front door, his headlights illuminated the rear of a car parked over to the right of the drive in a parking bay of sorts and obscured from the street by landscaping. The front passenger door was open, the interior lights burning softly as Sarbeck stopped his vehicle and cautiously approached the car.

Flashing his mag light across the car in inspection, the insignia of its trunk glowed *Mercedes* – the significance of belonging to the S Class lost on Sarbeck. Reflexively, Wesley radioed another update to headquarters as he moved closer to the sedan and added the license plate number to his report. As he rattled off the last digits of the Hinds County plate, his flashlight was drawn upward to the back windshield.

Law enforcement officers are trained in the mundane, the thrilling, the taxing, and the horrific, and as is true of most occupations the mundane and the taxing aspects typically predominate. On the other hand, it is the thrilling and horrific that become most memorable and stiffening for the professional backbone. This moment for Wesley Sarbeck, lieutenant with the Jackson, Mississippi, police department, was one of the horrific.

A material resembling red gelatin mingled with purple grape jelly glistened in the flashlight beam as it illuminated the blown-out glass that once completely wrapped the rear window of the Mercedes. The substance had thickened in stalactite fashion, appearing as dripstone attached to the top of the frame that once enclosed an intact rear windshield. Questioning his first impression, he moved closer to the back of the Mercedes, choosing to round the right corner to inspect further the rear seat of the S Class.

His flashlight illuminated a 30-06 rifle as it lay tangentially to the right side of the body, not far from the right arm. Without touching the remains, Wesley detected that the top rear of the woman's skull was absent, no doubt displayed in aggregate with the brain matter and other blood and pulverized tissue splattered across the glass of the rear windshield.

Despite his police training and experience, Sarbeck felt revulsion. There was no immediate sign of a struggle within the vehicle; the woman's clothes were not torn or disheveled although there was no purse or wallet nearby for an easy ID, suggesting possible robbery. There were no obvious scratches or bruises on her neck or on the exposed extremities. Even her manicure appeared impeccable. Curiously, the victim's facial beauty had survived the blast, the sound of which the neighbor had mistakenly associated with that of a shotgun.

Indeed she had been a striking woman, thick brown hair, physically fit, probably above average height as discerned by the long slender legs that rested outstretched and slightly spread apart in the back seat. Officer Sarbeck wondered if this good-looking woman had been someone's wife and then thought about his own spouse left home alone, vulnerable to attack from the outside world in his absence. *This job is crap*, he thought, the moisture in his eyes surprising him. No one was there to catch

Lieutenant Wesley Sarbeck quickly wipe his eyes on his uniform sleeve; embarrassed, he glanced around to be sure. He then longed to hug Carrie tightly, to reassure her that what mattered was having her as a lifelong mate. They should just forget about trying to have a baby; they had each other.

Seldom did Wesley's emotions show in his police work, but human tragedy touched him as it should – particularly if children or the elderly were involved. All the same, those feelings never interfered with his professionalism, and fortunately his exposure to truly gruesome crime scenes involving any age had been minimal. This call to Jasmine Terrace just after dark on an otherwise quiet weekday evening would rank as one of the most appalling and saddening of those exposures.

Realizing that he had not yet summoned backup, he turned to his radio and called for a police investigator. His brief report to the dispatcher included the discovery of a fatality related to a shooting, and that as a formality an ambulance was needed. It was not the officer's immediate duty to differentiate between a case of murder or suicide – that would be left to the specialists, although in this instance he had his own opinion.

Signing off with the dispatcher, Wesley remained near the Mercedes, incredulous at what he had discovered. He more closely studied the dead woman's delicate facial features as a feeling of cold curiosity tempered his admiration for her classic beauty and sadness for its loss. Wesley appreciated something even more mystifying about her as she lay there motionless, moist skin remaining warm to the touch, her body still appealing if one could ignore the surrounding gore in a residential area where such things just never happened.

The woman's face exuded an alarming familiarity to him. Wesley thought back to that day in his home, to the initial meeting with Miss Lucille Wax. He remembered her detailed color catalogue of human egg donors, posed smiling and available for hire. Her catalogue ... he had studied it intensely as Wax sat impatiently on the couch. Once he had selected the tall blonde woman with nice clothes and breasts and received a cursory approval from his wife to proceed with the fertilization process, Wesley had not deliberated over the selection.

Strangely, the particulars of each catalogued photograph and the attached donor descriptions now seemed as vivid to him as they had that day in the presence of Lucille Wax, the egg broker. Through clear, dry, startled eyes, Wesley suddenly could see her again – as clearly as when he first held the compilation that Wax offered.

There was no question; he was sure of it. She was the second entry in the series, following the pricey medical student and her dog. She was the rich-looking one standing in front of an enormous flower arrangement as though she were greeting him, measly Wesley Sarbeck, at a magnificent, formal party. At the time, Wesley assumed her personally unapproachable; he would never see her in the flesh, much less touch her. From a morbid aspect, his assumption had been only partly correct. The body lying motionless before him, an absolutely gorgeous face drained of all color except for a few wisps of thick brunette hair, not blonde, matted to her forehead by bloody tissue, was indeed OE-5652 – the second entry in Wax's catalogue – the one whose fee fell within the Sarbeck infertility treatment budget.

––––––––––––––––––––––––––––––––

"I may have something with me that would do. But, what about your Carolina Herrera leather-trimmed black jacket and matching sheath dress? Or you could wear your Stella McCartney belted jacket. It would look fabulous with the Michael Kors smoke and black plaid pencil skirt." Minor Leblanc, personal shopper and stylist, was back in business with an even thinner cell phone, courtesy of the cellular service store in the mall that stayed open past six. Had he not encountered such a forgiving traffic cop earlier that evening, he might not have made it to the mall at all – one more traffic violation would have jerked his driver's license. The incident on I-55 had been reminiscent of a similar close call, but that previous debacle had involved a female police officer in another town who, fortunately for Leblanc, eventually lost interest in him and their arrangement.

The expired deal with that dumpy, policewoman in her twenties had in no way been a sexual one, not even close; but after his encounter with the male police officer earlier that night, Minor Leblanc was gaining confidence in his management of law enforcement. After freeing himself from the police officer that evening, Leblanc released his charisma once again, this time at the mall and upon an impressionable female phone rep. In exchange for levying no penalty for his outside-of-contract cell phone replacement, Minor promised her hours of fashion advice and personal local shopping excursions. So excited was the sweet but terribly plain service representative that she gratefully tossed in a cache of extra minutes along with Leblanc's ultra-slim, updated model phone.

Once relieved to have again at his disposal the lifeline to his profitable personal stylist business, Minor Leblanc was growing to hate himself for repeatedly needing to barter out of jams by tossing complimentary beauty and fashion consultations into the mix. Fortunately, the policeman earlier that night had not been interested, even though Minor Leblanc's consulting services were available to men, but the unfortunate salesgirl at the cellular store was another story. There was not much he was going to be able to do for her; after all, he was not God. Maybe she would not call him, he speculated, but was not convinced. Like the others, she would take him up on the offer, and when she did, he would deliver 100 percent Minor Leblanc.

The sound of his new cell phone interrupted his thoughts. "I hate that noise," he reacted aloud to the standard ring tone, adding, "I'll have to get someone to change it for me. Maybe something gospel this time." With an abrupt turn through the gates leading up to the address on Jasmine Terrace, he simultaneously answered the call. Minor Leblanc knew that he was miserably late for the appointment up the hill. His precious, longtime client Cheryl Choice was waiting, and he assumed that it was she who was calling regarding his tardiness.

"Oh, it's you, Miz Tricia," he added after a hurried hello, surprised that the caller was not Choice. "Look, please don't worry. I am going to take care of you. You shouldn't fret one bit. You'll look fabulous, just like always," he consoled. "I'm driving up into another client's driveway as we speak." He paused a minute to allow a short question. "No, I'm in Jackson right now, but I'll drive back up to Montclair later tonight after this client's appointment." *Oh, Jesus, please don't let this woman take me up on that offer!* Leblanc prayed silently, considering the hour.

"Let's see," he hesitated only a moment, not allowing Miz Tricia to respond. "If that doesn't work, then I'll just be at your house early in the morning – yes, in plenty of time to get you all organized and packed before you and the mister leave for the airport. It won't take me but a sec to pull some exquisite things from that wonderful closet of yours, and you'll be the best looking thing on Fifth Avenue."

Minor worked by the hour, earning healthy commissions for his fashion design and consulting work. His clients were essential to him, and he knew it. Nevertheless, there were some for whom he enjoyed working and some for whom he did not. The inopportune caller in question was Patricia Pennington of Montclair, Mississippi, who was deep into the second category. It was the thought of Tricia's generous tips that kept his aggravation over the last minute summons to a minimum, annoyance warranted by her ceremonial refusal of his earlier-in-the-day offer to pack her suitcase for New York.

During that morning's delivery of a costly dress with freshly dyed, color-coordinated shoes perfect for a Manhattan cocktail party, he practically begged at that moment to arrange her travel things for her. Having worked with Tricia Pennington for several years, he correctly predicted a change of mind and the near tantrum over the frustration of packing a suitcase.

"Minor, I know I should have gotten you to pack for me this morning." Pennington said, the regret obvious as Leblanc's lightly-colored SUV topped the drive. The pleading in her voice built to pure desperation. "You've just got to cancel what you're doing, Minor, and help me. Please!"

The woman was persistent. With chilling accuracy, he could envision the heaps of mismatched ensembles, strewn across Pennington's king-sized bed, hoping to find their way into her Gucci luggage – an impossible task without the skills of Minor Leblanc. He glanced down at his Rolex while nearly running off the driveway into a row of Elaeagnus shrubbery; the time was nine-thirty, not an unusual hour for a professional to visit a client, particularly a professional whose schedule was positioned around the convenience of others. The acknowledgement of that convenience warranted the ample fees.

Solving last minute fashion disasters before important social events was Leblanc's specialty, often jostling him between adjoining communities to scurry through the expensive neighborhoods of those towns. He was already late for his appointment with Cheryl Choice, one of his most prolific clients in terms of the racks of apparel, cases of jewelry, and other assortments of finery she had amassed through him during the last several years. "I'm sorry, Miz Tricia. You see, I can't cancel this client. I'm not like that ... never would do such a thing." Minor was aghast at her suggestion. "Anyway, I'm pulling up in the client's driveway now."

Trying to focus on the path illuminated by his headlights, Leblanc's eyes veered rapidly from side-to-side in silent aggravation as he fought back a stutter of disbelief in his voice. *How could this woman I'm talking to suggest such a thing?* he thought again, reaching the back of the mansion's driveway and parking at the left rear loggia entrance. This was Minor's established drop-off point for a woman who preferred his visits to be confidential, her sources for high fashion highly guarded.

Minor's rush up the driveway and his preoccupation with the call from Patricia Pennington of Montclair caused him to whiz by the patrol car and Mercedes, failing to notice either vehicle parked to the extreme right of the circular drive. Officer Sarbeck was early into his discovery at that moment, still a quiet find, with no flashing blue lights and no squawking radio. Although Leblanc's skills of observation fell short in noticing the ensuing police investigation, Wesley Sarbeck could not miss Leblanc's hasty arrival on the other side of the property. No one could have missed the streaking headlights and acceleration of Minor's vehicle racing to meet Leblanc favorite, Cheryl Choice, a meeting that would not take place, at least not in the usual sense.

"OK," he acquiesced, trying to mask a sigh. "I'll be right over as soon as I meet with this client." By now, Leblanc had stopped his SUV, turned off the ignition, and exited after grabbing a few of the client's expected things. "I've gotta go now. This client has had this appointment for over a week, Miz Tricia. Like I said, I'm running a little late to meet her. Bye!" Leblanc slid his new cell into his front right pocket, a reflexive maneuver that would avoid a shattering fall for his new treasured lifeline.

"Hold it there a minute, sir. I need to ask you a few questions." The intense beam of Sarbeck's mag light as it illuminated Minor Leblanc's dark, startled face might as well have been a bullet. There was a sharp scream, not really high-pitched, but a shriek nonetheless that was somewhere between masculine and feminine, but closer to the latter.

Minor Leblanc stood frozen with hands raised, holding two bulging shopping bags by the handles with flexed wrists – his body forming a large capitalized letter Y in the stream of light, the bags serving as slight downturns to the upper, outer tip of the scripted letter.

"You again!" both men exclaimed simultaneously, although Leblanc's terrified voice was no match for the authority found in the policeman's surprise.

Instinctively, Sarbeck pushed forward, his adrenaline pumping in disbelief over what he had discovered during a routine investigation of a reported noise disturbance: a beautiful woman's brain spattered all over the rear of an expensive automobile and the reappearance of this strange guy he had stopped earlier on a moving vehicle violation. He wished his support had arrived by now.

"Is this your residence, sir? Do you live here?" Officer Sarbeck probed, trying to recall the name from the driver's license while not placing the fellow's address at this present location. He had not demanded that the black male speeder now raise his hands, nor did he tell him to lower them. The shopping bags were swaying gently from forward to back, and Wesley remembered spotting similar packages overflowing the seats of the fellow's SUV.

"Oh, Jesus, no. I don't live here. I'm here for an appointment to see a client."

"An appointment with whom?"

"Miz Cheryl Choice. She lives here with her husband." Leblanc turned slightly and gestured with the packages toward the door to the rear of the house that was softly illuminated. "She's expecting me."

"Sir, please stay in your position, facing me. I need to ask you a few questions. In fact, an investigator from my department will be joining me in just a moment, and I'm sure he will want to question you also."

"Look, Mister Officer," Leblanc stuttered. The packages had ceased to shake, the movement replaced by that of Leblanc's parched, twitching mouth. "Mister Policeman, I was not trying to rob the place. Like I said, I have an appointment with the lady of the house. I don't need to go to jail. The only reason I would consider going near a prison would be to put on a fashion seminar for those poor incarcerated souls." Beads of perspiration had formed on Leblanc's forehead to match those appearing in his armpits. His large, white eyes had returned to a rapid quiver.

"Sir, gently place those bags down at your feet and follow me quietly around to the front of the drive," Wesley commanded.

"Officer, am I under arrest?" queried Minor. Sarbeck did not immediately answer, unsure about his next move except that he intended to settle his immediate curiosity about the identity of the body without disturbing it. *Was the woman lying mutilated in the back seat of the Mercedes this Cheryl Choice?* And if she was, then she was OE-5652, the woman in the Wax catalogue, the genetic mother of his soon-to-be baby.

"Let me see some identification." For the second time that day, Sarbeck inspected the driver's license of Minor Leblanc. "All right, Mr. Leblanc, follow me around front."

"Now, I know my rights. All I do 24 hours a day is try to help people. I was not trying to break into this house. Don't try to put me in any squad car."

"Sir, I have not accused you of anything. Please cooperate with me. Simply walk around to the front of the house with me."

Minor complied, albeit reluctantly, following the officer's directive to walk in front of him. Regardless of what might be presumed elsewhere, Minor was not concerned with present-day racial profiling. He was more concerned over the situation in general, really more confused than anything else and did not feel in danger since the officer was not brandishing a weapon.

"Officer, I think I should ring the doorbell and tell Miz Cheryl that I'm here," Leblanc halted, turning around quickly to face the policeman. He immediately regretted the unexpected change of pace, thinking that he might have startled the officer into drawing his gun.

"Don't think that's necessary, Mr. Leblanc. Nobody seems to be in the house. At least there's no one available or willing to answer the door." Minor stood stone-faced, more perspiration rolling down onto his cheeks. "Just keep walking, please, as I have instructed," Sarbeck continued.

The two were rounding the front corner of the mansion as the sound of a siren oozed in stereo from the distance, increasing the flow of Leblanc's sweat as, rather than quickening, his gait slowed even more in apprehension.

"Head over to that car over there." Sarbeck redirected his flashlight beam at the Mercedes, realizing that his tactics of investigation might not represent proper procedure, but he had to know the real identity of the woman in the car. *Was she Cheryl Choice? And if so, she was OE-5652.* Besides, he was not going to let this strange Leblanc fellow touch anything close to the actual scene, so there would be no compromise of evidence. Anyway, Leblanc was certain to be called as a witness and might be implicated somehow in the death.

As the two moved closer to the vehicle, Minor announced in

surprise, "That's Miz Cheryl's car. She never parks her Mercedes there; at least I've never seen it there – always assumed it to be back in the garage when I've been over here."

"How do you know whose car it is?"

"She's driven me in this car to Memphis and Atlanta a couple of times to shop with her. We've flown everywhere else that was too far to drive."

Wesley Sarbeck made no comment.

Just as a couple of squad cars raced up the driveway with an ambulance wedged in between, the walking policeman and his would-be suspect neared the car. The shock of seeing a shattered and soiled rear windshield completely distracted Minor from the approaching entourage and what he would have previously feared to represent cavalry coming for poor Minor Leblanc. Sarbeck quickly led him around the side of the Mercedes and illuminated the face of the body with his mag light.

"Oh, no. Oh, Jesus!" This time there was no phone or precious cargo being held that could be dropped. Instead, Minor's entire body collapsed on the pavement in an awkward puddle.

———————————————————————

The on-the-scene photographer for *The Clarion-Ledger* was able to make deadline for the newspaper the next morning, so a picture of the corpse stretched on a gurney under standard white drape made the front page. Along with a brief article about the shooting, which included a couple of clipped quotes from Minor Leblanc, was a more flattering file photo of a smiling, brunette Cheryl Choice along with her handsome husband Gregg, holding their prized croquet mallets. The spring before, the Choices had posed as the victors of a couples' charity match, held to benefit diabetes research.

Since the crime statistics of that neighborhood seldom included more than the occasional home burglary or car theft, a gruesome murder in Eastover was not only newsworthy for Jackson but also made headlines statewide. The horrific death of the beautiful socialite and wife to an entrepreneur of rising prominence in the exercise and fitness industry even reached *The Commercial Appeal* in Memphis and *The Dallas Morning News*.

Had Officer Wesley Sarbeck seen a later edition of *USA Today* at police headquarters downtown, he might have seen the Choices' photograph there as well, buried deep in the first section along with an abbreviated cutline. However, he did notice the picture on the front page of his own newspaper as he retrieved it from the foot of the driveway the morning after the shooting. That marked the third time he had seen Cheryl Choice either in a photograph or in the flesh. Wesley had seen her both as a brunette and as a blonde. He had seen her happy, and he had seen her dead.

Chapter

8

◆◆◆

THE DISSECTION

"You know, people die in the most inconvenient places," the young man said, shaking his head half out of frustration and half in amazement, nevertheless grateful that he had been allowed in to watch.

"You're correct. But I don't think this vic had a choice," the pathologist and state-appointed medical examiner responded.

"Well, I guess not," Jimmy Perry shrugged. "But if you'd been the one who had to get her out of the backseat of that car, then you might see my side of it – particularly if the police detective is all over you while you're trying to move the body," he explained.

"They just wanted to preserve any evidence."

"Hey, man, the police took all these pictures at the scene, gettin' the body from every angle. I watched 'em. Then when me and Tom started to remove the body from the back seat of the car and place it on the stretcher, they wanted to take some more shots. Man, I thought they'd never be through."

Jimmy was a likeable guy, attractive, probably too attractive. He worked well with the public, but socially kept to himself since his romance with an older woman doctor ended a while back.

Despite the handsome looks and well-built physique that had
kept him busy during the last several years, Jimmy Perry still
maintained a marketable skill as an emergency medical technician
before returning for additional training as a paramedic. He soon
partnered in business with Tom Henderson, an experienced
paramedic who had once been Jimmy's proctor during his initial
ambulance service training.

Jimmy's arrival at the Jasmine Terrace address was not at the
beckoning of a 9-1-1 call; the emergency was long over. A police
dispatch had directed Henderson-Perry Ambulance Service to the
location, first briefing Jimmy about what to expect at the ghastly
shooting scene. As he commandeered the ambulance up the
driveway of the mansion reminiscent of his ex-girlfriend's home,
the sight was made all the more dramatic by four police squad
cars positioned haphazardly with blue lights revolving, shuttering,
and zigzagging in all directions.

Yesterday had been Jimmy's designated day to head his
ambulance company's EMT team, which was more accurately
described as a duo consisting of himself and the assistant he
and Tom had recently hired from the newest pool of community
college graduates. As a basic emergency medical technician,
an EMT-Is, the new hire was to alternate as Jimmy's or Tom's
assistant – help whoever was on call.

The new hire was thin and looked no older than high school age
– brandishing just-below-the-shoulder length hair of a uniquely
dark hue, swept back carelessly off her neck with the aid of an
oversized banana clip. During her training at Holmes Community
College in nearby Ridgeland, she had received high marks and
from the moment she stepped on the job was expected to be a
reliable, skilled medical worker – and was – until the bloody
scene on Jasmine Terrace. The "thin, young chick" as Jimmy
had called her was indeed reliable and skilled when faced with
aiding old ladies or gentlemen who had suffered a bathroom

fall or a stroke. She even did well with out-of-control obstetrical patients who waited a little too late to decide to go to the hospital. However, the true-to-life horror of a beautiful woman's mutilation ended the chick's career that night with Henderson-Perry. The thin girl and her banana clip got a courtesy ride home with one of the policemen.

"When I first drove up, the police detective said that it could have been a suicide, but it didn't look like that to me," Jimmy continued, watching the medical examiner work system by body system.

"Well, you're probably correct," he responded without looking up from his dissection. The medical examiner was a pasty-complexioned man who appeared to be in his early to mid-sixties but was probably somewhere in his fifties.

Jimmy Perry watched with interest as the ME methodically used a vibrating saw to divide the remaining areas of intact skull. After he separated the facial and forehead region to expose what was left of the brain cavity, Perry asked, although he assumed the correct answer, "You don't expect to find any bullet fragments in there, do you, Doc?"

Swearing off older women, even those with insatiable libidos like the last one, Jimmy Perry had dropped out of the dating circuit over the last several months, turning instead to the Internet for entertainment. Convincing himself that he was enriching his medical education, Jimmy surfed through countless medically-related websites, stopping only to take his turn at ambulance runs. Night after night he bounced from one link to the other until he landed on a website built around interactive autopsies. The video of step-by-step, detailed dissections of the human body performed by someone portrayed as a real-life physician was captivating, particularly when the autopsies were embroiled in forensic investigations.

As the celebrity Internet physician instructed using 3-D animation while tossing in the occasional human tissue specimen for realism, Perry ignored the advertisements for life insurance, herbal vitamins, and voguish diet plans that popped up along the sides of the website. Jimmy was fascinated by the doctor's terminology and graphic descriptions, feeling not at all squeamish; any such feelings were long ago exorcised on the job.

Never considering himself morbid but simply curious, Perry often wished that the website included more real-time video of actual autopsies. As he bookmarked the site on his desktop and returned to it daily, Jimmy even considered trying to acquire a life-size, anatomical rendering of the human body to practice on – similar to the one the celebrity forensic pathologist utilized many times on the Web. His hope was to stumble upon some cast-off demonstration model from a medical school or teaching hospital – and perhaps get one free somehow.

Regarding Jimmy's curiosity about locating any bullet fragments, the ME answered, "No, no fragments expected. Like a missile, the bullet from the 30-06 apparently passed completely through the body and pierced the rear windshield of the vehicle. I'm told by the police investigators that the intact slug is likely embedded somewhere in the front lawn of the victim's home or maybe in one of the many trees on the property."

"What about using a metal detector to find the bullet?" Jimmy asked.

"No luck with that so far, I understand." As he answered, the medical examiner reached above his head to activate the microphone and record some of his findings.

"How'd this woman wind up in the back seat of the Mercedes?" Jimmy continued his inquisition.

"According to the police detective's report, there was no sign of struggle. You probably realized that yourself when you picked up this corpse to bring it. So, assuming that the vic was shot in that location, and every indication is that she was, then she went peacefully or more likely was held at gunpoint by another weapon. The front seat had been pushed forward and left in that position, evidently to allow space for the stock and barrel of the gun. I don't know if you know much about weapons, but since a 30-06 rifle was apparently used, a fair amount of room was needed to accommodate that length," explained the ME.

"Incidentally, the fact that the weapon was found at the scene and belonged to the Choice household makes suicide a possibility. Of course, there were no prints on the rifle except those of the victim; and the police, I'm sure, are looking closely at the husband."

"Yeah, I do know about guns," Jimmy was almost offended by the ME's question of his knowledge of weaponry. "I do a good bit of huntin' – by myself now. I hunted a lot with my cousin awhile back before he was killed. A 30-06 is a good deer rifle, my favorite. I own one myself and would've inherited my cousin's as a spare, but it's still locked away someplace in a police evidence locker. At least that's what the cops say every time I check to see if a family member can pick it up," he complained.

"I s'pect that gun's been long gone from police headquarters and is resting nice and easy in some cop's hunting cabinet. That is, when he's not usin' it." Jimmy considered elaborating on the police shootout of a few years prior that had claimed his cousin's life and spared his, but decided against it. He assumed the doctor to be uninterested in the Perry family history, caring only for the dead stretched before him as practice for his scalpel and bone saw.

"Were there any other guns found inside that big house where we picked her up?" Jimmy inquired, returning to the matter at hand.

Without slowing a bit or even looking up from his systematic review, the medical examiner completed his study of the remaining aspect of the woman's cranium before responding. "You're asking the wrong person, young man," the doctor shrugged. "You see, when I'm assigned a forensic autopsy case, I'm kept in the dark about most of the other investigative details that don't pertain to the actual death scene, at least until my initial findings are complete. I really prefer it that way – makes things more objective, or at least to appear that way."

Perry nodded, although the busy pathologist failed to notice.

"In fact, in the great majority of these cases where I have served as medical examiner, I'm called as an expert witness in the following capital murder trial, unless my findings do support suicide. It's sometimes not until trial when I first learn a lot more about each case, that is, the information that I couldn't gather from the autopsy. The testimony from the other expert witnesses is always intriguing, assuming I'm allowed to hear it or read the depositions or trial transcripts."

"Well, look at this, Jimmy."

"What, Doctor, did you find something else?"

"The victim's trachea is bruised, as though a soft, flat object, such as a scarf, was used to strangle her without leaving much damage to the skin of her neck. Strangulation, particularly in the location of the body's discovery, would eliminate suicide as a possibility. The rifle shot was only a coverup, I suspect."

Just business as usual, Jimmy thought, listening to the doctor recant the routine of his profession. He had been looking at the body as the ME spoke. The woman had indeed been beautiful. Even with the back of her head blown off and after the doctor's dissection of the body, no one could disagree.

Chapter
9
•••
THE MOVIE STAR

While cellular phone service had served him well in his line of business, Minor Leblanc finally did it. He caved in.

Establishing an Internet website, cranking out a blog, and joining several email list servers that cater to high-end fashion clients was a step below what a discerning professional should have to do, at least in the opinion of Minor Leblanc. As he registered the domain of *minorleblanc.com* and the Web address of www.minorleblanc.com came online, he felt a blow to the mystique surrounding the name *Minor Leblanc*. That name, previously attached only to his cell, had continued to attract the types of clients he sought in the prosperous areas of Mississippi and south Tennessee, supplemented with a sprinkling of fashion hounds in Atlanta and New Orleans.

But even as the economy tightened and intemperance faced hard times, Leblanc witnessed the emergence of a plethora of personal stylists, wardrobe consultants, personal shoppers, and whatever kind of assistant one desired. As these novices appeared out of nowhere, he began to realize that he had growing competition, uncontrolled by the lack of training standards or professional licensing requirements. All of these upstart purveyors of style and finery were contending for the same select few clients that could still afford such services, his services.

From a business standpoint, Minor was also concerned about the casual references made by his clients to the more nationally known stylists or makeup artists who blew into town for certain events, such as charity fundraisers or various product promotions. Such comments as *"Oh, Minor, do you know Alexander Rue? He was at my friend's beautiful new house in Bridgewater last week for a clothing trunk show and personal style body makeovers – all to benefit charity, of course. I asked Alexander if he knew you, and he said he didn't. He's really got a great flair for design, something really kind of different ..."* generally elicited a characteristic reflexive eye twitch and a slightly stuttered Leblanc comeback of *"No, I don't know Mr. Rue, but I'm sure he's gifted."*

In fact, it was the Rue saga in the upscale, gated residential development in Ridgeland immediately north of Jackson that pushed Leblanc into cyberspace, even more so than seeing one of his best clients mutilated in the back seat of her Mercedes. Lurking through the chat rooms and email list servers, he was able to monitor the changing fashion ideas that regularly appeared via his two new sources of information: email and the Web. Leblanc was then able to put the jump on magazine print that had up to that point been his major resource.

Through the blast of data sent to him via the registration of his newly acquired email address, he could, and with seeming anonymity, also gather tips from other personal stylists and wardrobe consultants willing to share their views. *Define image* is what he read over and over.

In gleaning information from others, Minor kept his own pearls to himself, never sharing a sliver of his opinions, skills, or client success stories with anyone over the Web. However, Leblanc saved emails and tidbits of stylist banter from others that might apply to his present clients' needs or to those he would like to reach as clients.

Just as he was beginning to question the value of spending an hour or so daily, scrolling the listings and reading the jabber on the Internet, Minor discovered the answer. As a result of someone's carelessly stroked laptop key, he intercepted confidential email sent between a couple of personal stylists working in Los Angeles. One stylist had heard a rumor that during the next week Allyn Saxton would be returning to Jackson, Mississippi, and again under shrouded circumstances. Though there were medical reasons involved, the source could not fathom what a wealthy client such as Saxton could receive in "backwoods Mississippi that Allie baby couldn't get in L.A."

This email not intended for mass distribution along with other such notes sent Minor Leblanc into a tailspin. Allyn Saxton would soon be setting foot on his own turf, and she was certain to look terrible, being terminally ill and all, he decided. From the next several lines he learned that she was bringing no makeup or wardrobe person along to help her through what he was sure was some of last-resort treatment. Leblanc was ecstatic that his home state was going to save the young life of Allyn Saxton and rescue her fabulous talent for the rest of the world.

A healthy Allyn Saxton was synonymous with the epitome of style, unassuming beauty, and effortless elegance. However, Minor Leblanc knew differently. He was certain that even before her illness had been discovered, makeover consultants were constantly studying the pluses and minuses of the celebrity's physical attributes. When Allyn Saxton graced the cover of a magazine or appeared at a movie premiere, she was, in Leblanc's opinion, representing a stylist whose diligence had transformed her and kept her the darling of the media. Maybe there had been a plastic surgical procedure or two, here and there, or maybe even three nips and tucks, but on a daily basis, it was a fashion consultant and stylist that glued Miss Saxton together.

If she truly was coming to central Mississippi, the control of which Minor Leblanc was determined to maintain, this was his opportunity to cement his local stature and maybe even – his eyelids fluttered uncontrollably at the thought – follow Allyn Saxton back to L.A. and work there. The only glitch to this slide into the national and international celebrity stylist market would be Saxton's decision to bring her own personal stylist with her to Mississippi, making Leblanc's services unnecessary.

However, Minor recalled the email that discounted that possibility and realized that stars would likely travel incognito, particularly on trips related to personal business, like the life-threatening, terminal illness that was Allyn Saxton's affliction. Now relieved, Leblanc blotted the sweat from his forehead with a Principessa silk handkerchief pulled from his bag.

Minor was correct. Allyn Saxton would be traveling not as Allyn Saxton the star, and she would be alone. However, he was totally wrong about her reason for flying from Los Angeles to his native Jackson. True, Miss Saxton's visit to the Deep South was not in any way related to the entertainment industry or to the advancement of that career. She was pursuing a different calling, something about which the Internet pundits were ignorant.

Minor Leblanc's heartbreak would lie in the fact that he would fail to meet superstar Allyn Saxton while she was on his home turf. He incorrectly assumed that she was scheduled for admission to one of the large area hospitals for the treatment and cure of what he believed was a devastating illness. But he would never fully realize his otherwise flawless plan. The refusal by his perplexed clients in the medical industry to confirm or deny her as a patient was misconstrued by Minor as nothing but stonewalling, when in fact they were not permitted to confirm or deny his question. There were just some things an eye-twitching Minor Leblanc could not control with offers of personal body makeovers.

Tinker had long since finished skimming the headlines in that morning's issue of *The Clarion-Ledger* and conquered its crossword puzzle. As he placed the last digit in the last nine-by-nine square grid on the last page of the booklet he was holding, Murtagh realized that this was the fourth collection of Sudoku puzzles completed since taking the job. Much to his disappointment, there had been plenty of time to accomplish the feat. The anticipated tryst between the early morning delivery man and the cute light-skinned black girl never materialized.

Fortunately this job would be over soon.

By once again breaching the encrypted Internet scheduling program for the Van Deman Center, Tinker confirmed that the appointment still stood for ten o'clock that morning as specified in an earlier email between Saxton and Dr. Van Deman. Now, if only she would show up.

The more he learned about the celebrity through his Internet research, the more concerned he became about her inattention to detail. Tinker's ignorance of the rigid timetable for her treatment protocol was evident and was causing him undue distress. Any deviation from the plan for Allyn Saxton could determine success or failure.

On his laptop Tinker pulled up a JPEG containing several color images compressed together in no particular sequence and without the benefit of Photoshop, not at all typical of those appearing in glossy entertainment magazines. Tinker was no different from anyone who had an Internet connection or television, or who had been to the movies or at least picked through a grocery store or pharmacy magazine rack.

Along with millions of others, he had been bombarded by airbrushed publicity images of Allyn Saxton's sculptured face and lawfully exposed body parts to the point that in that form he would have instantly recognized her anywhere – slender, perfectly proportioned arms, legs, and ankles – each appendage supporting enough jewelry at any one time to fund global-warming research for decades.

In contrast, the procession of images that Tinker had just resurrected of trips to the gym, corner market, and Hollywood physicians would never see the pages of *Bazaar, Vogue, Cosmo,* or *Vanity Fair* without Saxton's unlikely permission. The persona known as *Allyn Saxton* was unrecognizable in the color digital photos slowly moving across his computer screen, each in an effort to familiarize Tinker Murtagh with the target.

The *au naturel* close-up head shots were interspersed among the full body ones that were clothed but not adorned. Even without a graphic designer's artistry to compensate for the absence of expensive, expertly applied cosmetics, Saxton still remained attractive, but recognizable only with scrutiny. Her well-defined facial features – high cheekbones, clear, wide-set, almond-shaped eyes, perfectly sized mouth, and proportioned lips that had never been plumped – worked well with the rest of her body. All the same, the facial blemishes, inescapable crow's feet, and uneven skin tones from too much tanning bed and sun exposure marked her as an everyday-appearing, thirty-something – one with a lot of potential, but definitely not Allyn Saxton.

The most intriguing group of photographs was those completely free of makeup, hair color, or even the efforts of a hairbrush.

Secretly captured with a telephoto zoom lens, Allyn Saxton was frozen for Tinker Murtagh in her native Malibu in one casual moment after the other, as though her efforts at being casual were just as intense as her cinematic performances. There were shots of her leaving an organic ice cream store, rescuing an abandoned kitten at the animal shelter, and pushing her Hispanic housekeeper's baby stroller. For her, the latter nearly approached the level of obsession as changing baby diapers easily usurped housebreaking the kitten.

In many of the photos at Tinker's disposal, not only had the perfectly-applied makeup and coordinated fashion-designer outfits been omitted but some things had been added. Recently spotted slipping into a Los Angeles pharmacy, Saxton sported a purposeful disguise consisting of a paisley-patterned do-rag and a pair of wraparound Versace sunglasses with a Valentino silk shawl draped across her tall but delicate torso. Maintaining her privacy was not an unreasonable goal, and she might have had a chance except that the bizarre vision of an outlandishly colorful, five-foot eleven, statuesque yet graceful feminine figure was just as out of place in Hollywood as it would have been anywhere else.

Even the likes of Tinker Murtagh could peer through the futility of the smokescreen as he studied the photos that showcased her disguises. The certainly costly but mismatched ensembles only screamed *"Look at me. I'm trying to look like someone that no one could ever recognize or want to recognize!"* Allyn Saxton's effort at obscurity was failing at a frustrating time when she faced the most basic of human desires: to reproduce and become a mother herself.

In the detailed pictorial supplied to Tinker, a detective had spent most of a digital memory card memorializing one particular stroll, or rather hike, in the Malibu Creek State Park 25 miles from downtown Los Angeles. Through miles of streamside trail lined with oak and sycamore trees, Saxton traded her housekeeper's overdone baby carriage, an earlier gift from the star, for a baby harness, and borrowed the baby to fill it. Separating herself from the bird watchers, fisherman, and other hikers who failed to recognize her, Allyn and the housekeeper's baby could not lose the photographer as he missed not one sweaty, unflattering pose.

Following the hike and with the housekeeper still hard at work at her home, Saxton continued the lengthy afternoon with her treasured baby-on-loan by exploring a series of shops, all photographs of which were included in the examples of Saxton's appearance. After such a thorough education in the many dimensions of Allyn Saxton, not recognizing her was incomprehensible.

When Tinker Murtagh accepted this assignment, he was not interested in the emotions that led Saxton to want to have a baby nor in the emotions of someone else who wanted a piece of her progeny. He accepted the job for the money and the challenge.

He had seen the pictures of Allyn Saxton with a baby, but the fact that the baby belonged to her Hispanic housekeeper was not important to him. In marked contrast, the fact was important to Allyn Saxton and would devastate her when a fake green card led to the housekeeper's deportation. The temporary work permit, which had preceded the green card, had been a forgery as well.

The housekeeper's status on American soil was unsalvageable despite the best efforts of Saxton's high-priced Los Angeles attorneys. Born in the United States, the housekeeper's baby could have legally stayed, but Saxton's live-in housekeeper was not interested in giving up her parental rights, no matter how much money Allyn offered. It was then that Allyn Saxton knew how truly alone she had become.

During the earlier part of her adult career, she had endured two failed marriages, both childless. More than a few times

during moments of passion, Saxton's first husband had pushed
for their having a baby, but pregnancy and her then-current
television character would never have mixed. For fear of angering
producers, she refused to stop her birth control, and her first
husband eventually dropped the idea.

For a fleeting moment during the court proceedings of her
first divorce, Allyn wondered if the pregnancy-refusal issue on
her part had ignited the implosion of that marriage. The issue
lingered over the next few months until she confronted her
first ex-husband with the question, even as her future husband
stood beside her. Sipping martinis on a crowded patio at a post-
Oscar party at Spago Beverly Hills below tall pepper trees, the
abruptness of her inquiry was met with a puzzled grimace.

"No, Allie, surely you never took me seriously about our having
a baby. Sex with you was just an exercise for me, nothing more,"
he said as he finished off a classic gin martini and chewed the
olive while gazing toward the patio's passion fountain and the
100-year-old olive trees nearby. "Anyway, you would make a
terrible mother," he zinged, turning away to converse with an
old agent who suddenly appeared beside him with a
congratulatory hug.

By then an Oscar and Emmy award winner herself, Allyn Saxton
was not easily humiliated, but this rapidly drew an immediate
reaction. Her flush of anger was hidden by the deep effects of a
tanning bed as she resisted the urge to level her ex-husband. No
need to create material for the tabloids, she decided. It was at that
moment that Saxton made a decision. She moved closer to her
next husband, put her hand gently on his buttocks, and guided
him closer to the fountain.

The second marriage was even shorter than the first. Her screen
career continued to explode while the new husband's fizzled,
assisted by his sinking sales at the box office and magnified by

two well-publicized DUI arrests. There was no pregnancy with this new marital partner whom Allyn had literally handpicked for that purpose, mistakenly choosing his looks over a growing propensity for booze, cigarettes, and drugs – a threesome at odds with a healthy sperm count. Between the intoxicating parties, his wife's mushrooming career in the entertainment industry, and the guy's growing resentment of his own dwindling status, there was dwindling bedroom time as well. Another divorce ensued.

Allyn Saxton felt as healthy now as she did when she was married. She had given up all intoxicants, only occasionally indulging in a low-tar cigarette and only in a moment of weakness or frustration, but never in public. Indeed, like everyone else in Hollywood, she was getting older but fought age at the spa, health food store, and plastic surgeon's office. Her gynecologist in Los Angeles had assured her that with normal female hormone levels and reproductive organs she could still conceive a baby. She just needed the right partner.

Somehow, through all the years of sexual activity before, between, and after her two husbands and exposure to who-knows-what, her body had been left unscathed, at least physically. The only scars were the emotional ones, and her housekeeper's leaving with the baby had only deepened the wounds.

To fuel both her frustration and desire to smoke, pregnancies suddenly seemed to be popping up all over Allyn's circles. Seldom did a day go by without *Entertainment Tonight*, *E!*, *Access Hollywood*, or *Hollywood Rag* reporting blessed events for dating, engaged, or married celebrity couples, both heterosexual and same-sexed. Nowhere in those announcements, rumored or factual, was the name *Allyn Saxton*.

She longed to be a mother, to hold and love a baby and watch it grow. The desire seemed so simple, so basic, so natural, so unlike many of the things she had done to herself and the people with whom she associated. Some of her later television and movie roles had included playing mothers of various ages, even a grandmother on one occasion – a project that earned her an Emmy. Her varied maternal cinematic experiences were certainly a challenge for any actress who had had no personal experience from which to draw.

But Saxton had imagined it well, easily pulling off stunning performances as gleeful, abused, rich, poor, or devastated – whatever the script and fantasy demanded, all the while affording her a frame of reference. Up until the recent past, she knew that she had put her career ahead of motherhood and time was now running out. She was no longer enamored with the ageless persona of Hollywood. Allyn Saxton wanted more.

The constant barrage of the paparazzi that sought to envelop and expose her life and those of her peers was of growing concern to the international film star. While she was sensitive to the notion that in between films fans deserved a little return for their ten dollar movie tickets, Allyn Saxton was growing more private about her personal desires, which now overwhelmingly included motherhood. Through the same publications whose creators and contributors she generally fought to avoid, she had learned that her two exes were now rumored to have begotten progeny. Hearing about the alcoholic's upcoming fatherhood was particularly frustrating.

Now thirty-four, Allyn Saxton was determined to give birth to her own baby, and with some semblance of privacy. This was something she could not do on the west coast or in New York. She needed to go elsewhere.

That elsewhere was the Henry Van Deman Center of Reproductive Technology located just north of Jackson, Mississippi, in Canton. Forgoing the help of her personal assistant, Allyn did her own extensive Internet research of sites offering infertility and reproductive services. She did not consider herself as much infertile as needing the right mechanism to have a baby and the right sperm source. For the star of both small and big screen, it had come to that: finding the right donor or at least submitting to one.

Allyn even thought about just hauling in another boyfriend. With her star power, preserved looks and figure, doing so would be simple – always had been, even in high school before she was famous. Maybe she should just skip a third wedding, grab a decent-looking male, and go after it night after night, or day after day for that matter, until she got pregnant.

For some reason that she could not define, Allyn Saxton had begun to shun the basic human concept of sexual dependency and any sense of romance, pleasure, or sharing that went with it – heterosexual, bisexual, or homosexual, although her own experience was strictly heterosexual. Something about the concept of emotional or physical dependency on another adult outside of professionalism was now unappealing to her, if it had been at all.

For the first time ever, Saxton, a novice to netiquette, entered anonymous chat rooms inhabited by both satisfied and frustrated childless patients, apparently both male and female. These chat rooms were linked to the various websites built around assisted human reproductive and infertility services. Her sometimes careless access of certain related websites and available links yielded a barrage of unwanted cyber contacts as unexpected emails penetrated her computer's spam-blocking software. Allyn had a wide-eyed and generally disgusted reaction when her email address *wantababynow@ohyeah.com* was showered with unwanted messages offering services ranging from overseas adoptions to offers of breast and other body enhancements.

Allyn considered her time in the chat room discussions to be generally well spent and at times almost therapeutic. The contributors remained as nameless as she, although most were much more verbose and laboriously frank about their experiences, both good and bad, with various infertility centers in the United States and abroad. Even though she had appeared in several medically-themed television dramas earlier in her career, Allyn remained ignorant of many of the medical terms and most of the procedures discussed in intricate detail on the Web. Fluctuating hormone levels, awkward specimen collection methods, punctures of various sensitive sites on the body, and opinions regarding embryo and human egg harvesting and donations were discussed frankly.

Allyn's secrecy extended beyond her name to include the circumstances surrounding her childless predicament, so much so that her level of involvement in the chat rooms and blog commentaries was more that of a "listener" or reader. When Saxton did contribute there was no mention of the worthless, ego-driven, substance-abusing male movie star who had failed to serve as a marital sperm donor when she was ready and the first husband who was not really interested in her as a person.

As a consequence of all that chatter and electronic research, Allyn realized that she no longer wanted or needed to depend on someone's acceptance in this most personal of decisions. Yes, it had come to this. "All I need is a donor. Screw men," Allyn chuckled aloud to herself, the inadvertent pun an encouraging boost as she reached to dial the toll-free number. Privately from her bedroom desktop computer, she had chosen this particular infertility facility from the many websites she had researched.

Ultimately, Allyn's choice of the Van Deman Center was the result of her experience with *Facebook* using an assumed identity. A chatter's reference to her own registration on the social networking website enticed Allyn to scan a photograph of her ex-housekeeper, tag it with the fake name *Maria Sanchez*, and submit it as her own. The *Facebook* member immediately honored Allyn's request to be a friend. The deception and its harmless intent did not stop there.

Unbeknownst to Allyn, her new *Facebook* friend, the thin-faced, simply-dressed, dark-haired woman with the asymmetrical pageboy haircut, was really the more feminine partner of a same-sex male couple. The same-sex status had been dropped from the dramatic story in which a sister of the more feminine of the two male partners volunteered as a surrogate mother but was then unable to ovulate. An egg donor selected from a catalogue was then enlisted to jump-start the family for the gay couple Allyn assumed to be heterosexual as the other male partner donated his sperm. The woman with the egg-donor catalogue had been recommended to the secretly homosexual couple by the infertility practice that had agreed to help them.

As promised, the egg broker had arrived at their condo with color photographs of inviting, healthy-looking women, mostly in their early twenties with one or two appearing to be just over thirty, their garb relaxed in some instances, structured and costly in others. The selections were dominated by Caucasians with one or two of African-American or Asian descent. The payment required for the egg donors varied, Allyn's *Facebook* friend explained during one of their many conversations, Allyn's assumption being incorrect that all of the participants were in need of money. While she did not consider the amounts required by the egg donors nor the commission charged by the egg broker to be exorbitant, Allyn did find incongruous the descriptions of the expensive-looking clothes and jewelry that donned a few of the donors.

Her curiosity about the motives and social background of the egg donors was short-lived. Important to her was that these people existed, that there were options. Allyn had found her answer in these options, her options. In great detail, the process of getting pregnant with as much artificiality as needed had been mapped out for her by a person whom she had met only on the Internet, someone whom she judged merely by a misleading photograph laced with emotional dialogue. What she had read and absorbed felt quite straightforward to her, a woman who was not short on resources but in fact had much more at her disposal than most with similar problems. Allyn Saxton had only lacked direction in how to solve her predicament and become a mother. In a defining moment, she had found direction.

Up to that point, Allyn Saxton's career had taken her all over the world, a place that she had come to consider as shallow and superficial. She had been sipping a glass of pinot noir while she read the last comment from her *Facebook* friend. The happy ending to that couple's saga had been overwhelming for her and might still have seemed so if she had known the entire story. As Allyn downed the last sip, actually more of a gulp, the realization was sobering.

That couple had stumbled upon their answers not in New York, not in L.A., not in Colorado, not even in Florida. Allyn was confident that they had found what they needed in conservative, central Mississippi, of all places. Posted in digital display for anyone with Internet access were pictures of the threesome: the couple's baby, juxtaposed with pictures of Henry Van Deman, MD, and his physician associate, Knox Chamblee, MD. Surrounding the trio was a collection of selected members of the Center's smiling staff whose merits were lauded repeatedly in the personal messages to *wantababynow@ohyeah.com* as well as in the general postings.

The infertility center's ecstasy at being involved in the baby's creation for the *Facebook* couple was plastered all across the faces of the firm's members. Their happiness was genuine; Allyn was sure of it. She could always see through an acting job, even a good one.

Finding her own tears had never been an obstacle for an actress of her caliber. In fact, during the last four years, she had twice cried her way to a Golden Globe and a third time to another Oscar. Yet the tears now were genuine and personal, actually expressing relief more than simply joy. Staring at her computer screen, Allyn was drawn to the digital photographs of the baby, the couple, and the doctors as though they were sensual. Never before had she truly felt fulfilled in life, but now the answer was obvious. This couple had shared their story as they employed a surrogate to make their family. Allyn decided that she would not need a surrogate.

She would go to Mississippi. She would do it all herself, well, almost.

———————————————————————————

Before Tinker had set up shop in Canton, Allyn Saxton had made her first trip to the South. No one knew about her traveling there except for a slip made to a hairdresser when Allyn was forced to reschedule an appointment due to the trip – the *faux pas* that eventually fell into Minor Leblanc's email. She reasoned there would be no paparazzi at the Jackson-Evers International Airport, and she was absolutely right. She had to admit her surprise that no one at all recognized her either in first class or in the terminal, and she had not even worn one of her best disguises. The connection in Dallas had gone smoothly as well, as she melted into the crowd both at the gate and in the Crown Room, where she avoided alcohol per Dr. Van Deman's instructions.

It was the departure from LAX that had been tricky, and that came as no surprise. She was on her own turf there. Exiting the limo, she recognized an obnoxious freelance Los Angeles photographer who was a regular contributor to *Celebrity World* magazine. Considered by most of Allyn's peers as greatly over-compensated for his spoils, the young guy made a successful practice of being everywhere. He peppered her with questions such as "Hey, Allie, you slummin' it this time and takin' commercial?" followed by "Wasn't 20 percent off the top enough for *Mountain Over the River*? So, then, aren't you at least gonna spring for first class?"

Her curt reply was, "I'm going to visit my grandmother," wanting to yell, "You jerk," but refraining. The paparazzi were bad enough on an average day without truly hating the celebrity target.

The truth was that the querying photographer would have seen through a similar, but still false, answer had she retorted, "I'm going to see my mother." Allyn Saxton had not spoken to her mother in 14 years, a fact that had been the subject of repeated exposés on *Entertainment Tonight* and other such broadcasts. To her astonishment during a recent syndicated television interview, the subject was broached by a female talk show host. Allyn had long since abandoned any emotion about the estrangement from her mother, and the host's surprise question was met with an even, "I don't discuss that. You know that, Mava." A written follow-up statement from Saxton's agent to the producer of *The Mava Show* made clear that his client would not be a return guest.

Her visits to the Deep South were not for pleasure or to visit, although she hoped to realize a pregnancy from them, and her travel there was to be incognito, the old-fashioned kind. Had the paparazzi stayed on her tail from L.A., Allyn planned to fabricate a quick story about doing a character study, research for a yet-to-be-announced project possibly to be filmed in the South.

After all, there were lots of southern writers and southern novels available for screenplay development, lots of fodder for prolific actors and actresses who had a yearning to produce their own projects, so the lie could easily escape detection. She herself had considered such ventures, believing that *Executive Producer Allyn Saxton* had a nice ring to it and would play well in a film's credits. Saxton felt the distinction placed an actor a notch further above the rest of the cast even though she or he might already have top billing.

That narcissistic reflection was absent from her trips to see Dr. Van Deman, however, and so was the need to manufacture the story. After her initial phone call to the Center, use of a fictitious name was no longer necessary. Once she spoke personally with Dr. Van Deman, he scheduled her initial and follow-up appointments himself, touting sensitivity regarding her privacy. He even provided his private cell number and encouraged Allyn to call anytime she had problems or questions or needed to change an appointment time.

On the subject of her efforts at total privacy, her initial contact with Van Deman's office had not gone as smoothly. When calling the Center from her own private cell number, *Mary Smith* was the only name she could conjure when asked to identify herself. When the scheduling secretary refused to place her on hold and immediately summon the doctor to take a new patient query, Allyn realized that *Mary Smith* did not muster the same response that *Allyn Saxton* would have.

Although she had rehearsed her lines repeatedly before making that first call to the Henry Van Deman Center of Reproductive Technology, she was forced to leave a quiet and polite message with the secretary, someone named Mia. However, she remained hopeful that her *Facebook* friend's doctor would personally and promptly return her call.

Hanging up with an embarrassed, almost self-deprecating grin, Allyn was sure the doctor would have fallen all over himself to accept her initial call had she provided her true name, that is, if he had been able to get a blubbering, star-struck secretary off the phone first.

The Van Deman Center was growing, its patient base expanding, even beyond the United States. The original marketing efforts put in place by Henry Van Deman were paying off and beginning to do so in a big way, but Van Deman vowed that his ingenuity and vision intended to attract and maintain patient loyalty would never be discarded. And he expected his new associate, Knox Chamblee, to keep the same credo.

When, during Van Deman's return call to Mary Smith, he discovered that he was conversing with Allyn Saxton, the doctor was certain that scoring someone of her caliber had been a direct result of his marketing design. "What a coup!" he said under his breath. After all, he had pulled her away from every other reproductive medicine and surgery center in the world. Of course, unknown to Van Deman, Saxton's decision to use his services had come from her own homemade research protocol developed over a glass of wine or two, working her laptop in the privacy of her own bedroom suite.

Once her initial telephone consultation with Dr. Van Deman was completed, Allyn planned to proceed with his recommendation of ovulation induction, artificial fertilization by a preferred donor, and then impregnation through one or more implanted embryos. She had made the decision to achieve motherhood without the aid of a husband, significant other, or even insignificant other to serve as a sperm donor. Allyn had chosen this physician from the Internet, planning to turn herself over to him in the most personal of ways. He was a substitution for what she had not been able to get any male member of the species to do for her naturally.

She was at peace with her choice but still felt the need to reinforce her decision. Before undergoing treatment by someone she would meet only briefly before therapy began, she returned to the Web. Allyn again read through Internet blogs and several *My Space* entries, all elaborating happy Van Deman endings from an assortment of sterile, afraid they-were-sterile, mateless, same-sex, or mixed-sex couples – one particular touching story involved a threesome – that sought to produce offspring.

Her follow-up "research" unearthed stories of implanting donated human embryos in women who were carriers of such diseases as cystic fibrosis and certain types of leukemia so that their offspring could be healthy. Another story of hope involved two women, one from Tennessee, the other North Carolina, each of whom sought to preserve their ability to have a baby after undergoing treatment for non-Hodgkin's lymphoma. The treatment was expected to be curative, but at the same time would destroy the ovaries. Each woman felt triumphant after successful superovulation induction cycles under the direction of Dr. Van Deman. They now had multiple numbers of healthy eggs safely frozen through the Van Deman cryopreservation program which were available for them to use later in having babies.

Saxton came across another moving discourse about a nice-looking, traditionally sexed couple who had been involved in a horrific car accident just after their third wedding anniversary. The man and woman, both in their mid-twenties, had for several months been trying to conceive when they were sideswiped by an 18-wheeler while traveling on a major interstate. Although the husband and wife miraculously escaped neurological devastation and death, there were significant physical consequences; the wife fell victim to internal pelvic injuries and the husband was left nearly sterile. A day or two prior to the wreck, the couple had suspected – based on an ovulation predictor test kit – that they

had at long last conceived, but even with the most modern of
pregnancy tests, there would have been no way ever to know.

Allyn sent an anonymous gift to the physically and emotionally
scarred couple, who hinted in their lengthy *My Space* discourse
that their union could be in jeopardy as a result of their trauma
and disillusionment. Two separate checks for just under ten
thousand dollars each, drafted in such a way to prevent
detection of the source and a red flag from the IRS, appeared on
their doorstep. The couple found their way to the Van Deman
Center, where they became patients of Dr. Knox Chamblee.
Strangely, this act of charity brought Allyn relief as it eased
any quilt she harbored over using wealth to overcome the
consequences of her chosen lifestyle, while twists of fate instead
had left others childless.

Another story electronically linked to the previous one
chronicled the tribulation of a policeman's wife who believed
she was losing her mind as well as her tubes and ovaries from
endometriosis. The woman's rambling discourse detailed how a
bird had been trying to get to her just like the endometriosis that
was eating her alive; she believed that she was the object of God's
hatred and the devil's love. Allyn Saxton found sadness in that tale
as well, but decided that one expensive act of kindness at a time
was enough for her confused conscience.

Although Allyn was committed to carrying a baby successfully
for nine months and then giving birth, she had long ago faced
childlessness not as a physical dilemma but as a social one. She
was certain that she would have found motherhood naturally and
perhaps been a better wife – and certainly had better husbands –
had she not lived under the spell of Hollywood.

Nonetheless, as she powered down her laptop and closed the
cover, she decided that the only story that truly interested her was
that of Allyn Saxton. She realized that life as a celebrity had also

been an important dream for her – one that she had been able to realize without the aid of the Van Deman Center.

Besides, somebody had to be Allyn Saxton. She had not crawled her way there from the age of ten for nothing. And soon Allyn Saxton would be complete.

Chapter

10

◆◆◆

THE AUDITION

Santa Monica, California 1982

"Hurry up, Allyn, we need to be there by ten o'clock, or they'll cut you." The voice swept up the stairs, sharp edges of aggravation ricocheting from the banister to the opposite wall. Parke Saxton swallowed hard, trying to suppress the growing anger as she hammered out again, this time with a touch of motherly understanding ... just a light, insincere touch. "Please, Allyn, for heaven's sake, hurry up!"

There was purpose to Parke Saxton's anger, an intense style modeled precisely to match the moment or the carelessness of its recipient. An easy illustration was the anger unleashed on her ex-husband when necessary, which was often the case and always disparaging. Quite unlike any irritation directed at their only child, the fury she had unleashed on that philanderer was indeed murderous or at least could have been. Her scorn was relentless and physical and would have continued to be so had he not finally deserted the family.

To the contrary, she had never struck her daughter Allyn, but had certainly come close. While the child could expect an attention-getting shake of her shoulder along with the, "Now, you listen to me, young lady," 8-year-old Allyn Saxton would never have fathomed a strong slap across her flawless face.

"Allyn! I know you want to look your best, but, Doll, we'll be late if you don't come on down." Allyn's mother decided to lower the decibels of her screaming a bit; no need to strain the voice and alert the neighbors. Somehow Parke Saxton held back from stomping her right foot a second time; it was throbbing from the first and her knee ached from the jolt.

Earlier in the week during her routine study of the entertainment rags, she had spotted this open casting call in *Variety*, a mere snippet that signaled a last minute replacement opportunity for an acting job in Hollywood. "Somebody probably got sick and had to cancel out, poor thing," she sneered to herself. "And I'm sure she was just perfect for the part." Shaking her head in mock grief, she added, "No doubt a gifted young girl."

Parke Saxton never questioned her own daughter's natural and consistent ability to dance, sing, and perform comedy or drama. For a ten year-old she was off the talent charts, particularly when it came to improvisational performances – another reason her auditions always went so well. "Oh, I really am so sorry for that other girl," a grinning Parke Saxton said aloud to herself when first noticing the *Variety* ad and circling it with a black Flair pen. Her daughter was not going to miss this audition, and shame on that other girl's mother for letting her own daughter get sick.

"Like everything else for my Allyn, this part was just meant to be. Just meant to be," she declared with authority as she folded the paper and slid it into a zippered section of her oversized purse, firmly closed the zipper, and slapped the side of her purse softly. The notice of the much anticipated casting call had remained safely there until today, and Parke was ready for her daughter to conquer the opportunity.

"Come on, Allyn. Please!" Parke again screamed at the foot of the stairs. She wanted to yell 'dammit' but had sworn off the foul language, a trait that had garnered frequent criticism from her ex-husband – one of his few correct opinions about her, or so she thought. Still there was no response, and there were no footsteps hurrying down the hall toward the stairs; in a house the size of the Saxtons' there was no way to miss them.

"Allyn, for gosh sakes!" Again Parke wanted to say worse, much worse, but held back. Besides, strong language just was not working anymore with her headstrong daughter. "This could be your big chance," she pleaded, stamping her right foot on the foyer rug, a reflex this time. "That big break we've ... you've ... been waiting for."

"But, Momma, my hair ... I don't think it's been up in rollers long enough." Finally an answer emanated from Allyn's bathroom and a surprisingly calm one at that.

"Allyn, please! Look, Doll, we have wasted so much money with that agent. I'm not paying him another cent. We ... you ... can get this part without him!" she yelled again up the stairs, trying to tone it down as much as possible, any deliberate calm forgotten as the urgency of the message began to sink in with her daughter. "That S.O.B," Parke mumbled, knowing that the only money paid to the agent had been his standard commission for the several roles he had booked for her daughter. "Your agent has just about sucked me dry with this thing."

"OK, I'll take it down!" Allyn returned at a level slightly below a shriek. Then in a much more muted but determined tone the girl turned her head side-to-side, eyes remaining fixed on the mirror. "Maybe the wings will hold anyway."

She grabbed the supersized, pink-colored aerosol spray can from the vanity and in the same motion released most of its contents on her thick blonde hair, gluing the surface strands together. As Allyn was forced to hold her breath, the hairspray fog erased her reflection in the makeup mirror that covered the entire wall above her vanity. Even with the aid of the glaring, bare light bulbs that lined the edges of the glass, the mist was impenetrable.

"Doll, you're going to grow up to be the spitting image of Farrah Fawcett," her mother had said so many times to her, although Allyn disagreed. She believed herself now to be more beautiful than Farrah Fawcett. Allyn Saxton was more than simply the ten-year-old version of the television star; she was better.

"Allyn, please hurry, or like I said, we'll be late." Changing her method to that of a plea, Parke tried moving closer by taking a few steps up the stairs. Stretching her neck in the direction of Allyn's room, she stressed, "Last month we, I mean you, missed that part on *Dallas* by five minutes. I know that you would have been fantastic in the screen test with Larry Hagman." The television producer had been searching for a blonde female child to play yet another illegitimate child of J.R. Ewing but later dropped the plotline.

"Your TV mother was going to be Val Ewing, and you would have been Lucy's younger half sister, for heaven's sake!" Parke then lowered her voice to salvage some strength as she reasoned, "Of course, after a couple of seasons Allyn would have been ridiculously taller than that short, dumpy girl who plays the part of Lucy Ewing.

Listening to her mother needle her again about the missed Dallas audition, Allyn realized that Parke was never going to let that one go. She had immediately accepted the responsibility for the screw-up, at least to herself, but would never admit the error to her mother. Flirting in the hall after school had been her downfall, and the cute new boy who had changed schools was irresistible. Without even much thought, Allyn blamed the whole fiasco on the history teacher who had kept the class overtime, causing her to miss the audition.

"Oh, what's her name? I can't believe I've forgotten that actress's name again, the one who plays Lucy." Parke's frustration mounted with fresh regret over the lost role on the top-rated Friday night soap opera. To confuse actors or actresses was way out of character for her. "Anyway, Larry Hagman would have insisted that they hire you for the part. I'm sure of it." Allyn had endured this discourse to the near point of memorization. "Our, I mean, your sorry agent was right to arrange that audition, said he had the inside scoop and a connection with the casting director who owed him some sort of favor. That is one thing that worthless S.O.B has done right!"

"Charlene Tilton, Mom. Her name is Charlene Tilton. She plays Lucy on *Dallas*. I can't believe you didn't know that. Everybody knows that," Allyn announced with pleasure as she materialized at the top of the stairs, her Farah Fawcett blonde wings motionless as she trotted down the steps, the trim of her skirt bouncing in unison at the top of her thighs.

The dress was brand new; her mother had picked it up last week at a boutique on the Strip. Allyn's mom had made it a rule that she was always to have a new outfit for every audition, something moderately expensive and contemporary unless the casting call warranted a different direction. The ritual had become an accidental good-luck charm, ingrained when Allyn won her first role on television, a guest shot on the long-running situation comedy series *One Day at a Time*.

The new-outfit ritual was birthed from the "charm" of a clumsy redheaded girl who stood a head taller than Allyn in the audition line for a part on the series. Waiting with her own mother outside the studio office and standing just ahead of the Saxtons, the redhead dropped a hairbrush while wrestling with a mane that would have made Little Orphan Annie jealous. Jerking down impulsively to retrieve it from the sidewalk, she lost her grip on the orange Shasta she had been drinking, emptying the soda down the front of Allyn's outfit.

Allyn's ensemble for the *One Day at a Time* audition had actually consisted of something from the back of her closet, a leftover from a year ago that was too large for Allyn then but was now flattering, at least without orange soda stains. As the other mother let out a blood-curdling scream, everyone around assumed correctly that the spill was only a careless mishap, not a ruthless effort at sabotage.

Allyn's reaction was reflexive and then motionless: opened jaws stretched wide enough to accept a small man's fist, arms stiffly positioned down at her side, palms turned up in questioning shock as the orange liquid soaked her chest and stomach, reaching her underwear in short order.

Parke Saxton's own reaction surprised even her. Instead of a primordial, motherly scream or the urge to strangle the brainless girl and level the equally dense mother, all she said was, "Allyn, don't panic and don't move. It was just an accident, and it's going to be OK. I'll be right back."

In 1982 the Saxtons drove a station wagon, a Chrysler model that would eventually become obsolete with the arrival of the minivan. Hanging in the rear of the new Town & Country wagon was a clean, fresh ensemble adorned with price tags and out on approval from Bloomingdale's the day before. Deciding that it was really too expensive, Parke had planned to return the outfit the next day.

All of a sudden, the expensive ensemble from Bloomingdale's had become a bargain.

Parke Saxton ran back to her car, reinspected the clothes, judged them spectacular for the television show, and then returned to the audition line. She realized that she had not taken a breath since leaving her beautiful daughter drenched in orange soda. "The least you can do is hold our place in line," she glared at the other mother, who was now weeping. "We'll be right back," she added although Mrs. Clumsy understood perfectly.

Parke was nearly forced to carry Allyn back to the station wagon, her daughter's arms still stiff as though frozen but her knees bending adequately to allow her torso to be pushed along. Once inside the car, Allyn limbered up enough to change clothes with her mother's help. Both soon realized what Allyn already knew, that her panties were orange and sticky in the crotch.

"Mother, why didn't you bring me some extra panties?" an immodest Allyn cried, pulling the underwear down to her ankles.

"Why in God's name would I have brought you some extra panties?" was her mother's angry response. "Well, hell, just don't wear any then," Mrs. Saxton ruled, pulling the wet orange-stained underwear down from her daughter's ankles and over her shoes, before throwing the garment across to the back seat.

When Allyn returned to her rightful place after redressing, of sorts, in the car, progress had been made toward the front of the line. "Annie" had stopped sobbing as the mother fitfully attempted to repair the redhead's cosmetics, a hopeless effort to hide the freckles. Turning from her mother's powder puff to acknowledge Allyn, "Annie" burst into fresh tears, more copious than before.

"It's OK now. Stop crying, Tabitha. That girl's changed her clothes, so it's no big deal now. You didn't mean to spill your Shasta. I'm sure, that girl and her mother understand that," Annie-Tabitha's mother consoled without taking her eyes off her hysterical daughter.

"I'm not upset over spilling my drink on her, Momma! I'm upset over how great that girl looks now in that new outfit. She wouldn't be looking so great if it wasn't for stupid me!" Annie-Tabitha belted, certain that the improved Allyn would sink her. The ensemble from Bloomingdale's, originally considered by Parke Saxton as too pricey, had suddenly become perfect, turning Allyn's chief competition into mush.

The clumsy girl's assumption of the worst for herself was right on target. Her tear-stained mascara and grief-stricken, bloodshot eyes, perhaps more than Allyn's fresh appearance or even talent, helped to seal the director's choice. The guest role in the sitcom episode went to talented, spontaneous, pretty, and perfectly dressed Allyn Saxton, no underwear notwithstanding. The tall, freckled redhead and her can of Shasta had made wearing a virgin ensemble the rabbit's foot for this rising child star in commercial entertainment. Also, she would never again wear underwear to an audition.

In the ensuing months, Allyn Saxton garnered multiple television credits and once she landed her first movie role became a consistent top choice of producers. She was a child star who was just as comfortable being chased by a psychotic killer as playing a comedic younger or older sister. Professional child actor status was cemented to her name as there seemed to be no end in sight to her career. That celebrity status easily survived adolescence and young adulthood, as Mother Saxton refined her managerial ropes as Allyn matured and withdrew from her mother as many a teenage girl does, celebrity or not.

Compensating herself with funds left after Allyn's blocked trust was satisfied under California law, Parke Saxton became a protective wall enclosing her daughter. Without a father to interfere with her system of management or any other relative who could come close, she kept a hand-written, daily journal cataloging her single-handed success in transforming her daughter into a megastar.

The journal entries were usually made late in the evening, after the third or fourth glass of cheap chardonnay poured from a 1.5 liter bottle. Much of the longhand was simply a scrawling summation of notes made on little scraps of paper torn from an old envelope and stuffed into her purse or into the back of the journal itself. The treatise grew thick in time as Parke became even more verbose with her record keeping.

As her daughter exploded into an international celebrity, the journal's outline became obsolete since by that time Parke Saxton had become only an observer, an outcast from her daughter's life. Her daughter's star became no one's creation but Allyn's, although her mother would never agree.

Regarding the terminated relationship with her mother, the reasons were actually a mixture of outgrowing a need and a violation of property – Allyn's acquired sexual property. When Parke was discovered a second time with Allyn's own love interest, the daughter chose to erase that and the previous liaison from memory – a goal made much easier by having no further contact with her mother.

Even without further involvement in her daughter's life, Parke Saxton held to her belief that from the moment Allyn was conceived, she and she alone had molded her daughter's talent and success. And she would do so again. Any idea that could even remotely advance Allyn's career – a truly unnecessary task since by that point Allyn Saxton was a household name – was dutifully recorded in a hurried scrawl and added to the journal. For that reason, Parke kept self-adhesive note tablets strategically placed around the house, including by every telephone.

Sometimes the blurbs were only recollections from years past, but they were still important to Parke in crediting herself for the accomplishments of her only child. The never-ending journal, which to any other reader would have resembled a poorly constructed, self-absorbed memoir, was treasured by Allyn Saxton's mother as a painstakingly authoritative collection of prose, worthy of the Pulitzer Prize. She believed that she possessed a one-of-a-kind manual on how to make a movie star from nothing.

However, the star that was Allyn Saxton had not been created but had grown from the inside like that explained in the Big Bang theory. Her star was no one's creation.

————————————————————————————

"Dr. Van Deman will see you now, Ms. Smith." An incognito Allyn Saxton placed the magazine on the side table next to where she had been sitting. It was last year's well-thumbed *Sexiest Man Alive* issue, and she still disagreed with the editor's 2007 pick. Despite the sunglasses, the lobby's fluorescent light had allowed her not only to admire the photographs but also to read the articles.

At previous visits, Van Deman had come to the waiting room himself to retrieve her, but had called her this morning with the news that he would be running a little late. She assumed that even doctors had car trouble from time to time.

If Allyn thought her disguise for this visit to be particularly clever, the front desk clerk proved it by unceremoniously registering her as a routine patient. With newly dyed hair, courtesy of a 24-hour rinse purchased unrecognized at a local Walgreen's, Allyn pulled the short strands down into her face as much as possible. The shortest of the uneven ones were left to rest comfortably on the top of her sunglasses.

After Allyn signed in as Mary Smith, the busy secretary waved her into the lobby, where she sank into a single seat quietly guarded by an overpowering, thick-leaved houseplant. She had never before waited for Van Deman in the public areas, but fortunately for her, the space was almost empty. The only others present were a guy sitting around the corner dressed in a policeman's uniform and a pale, nervous-appearing woman clinging to him.

Saxton found some strange sense of satisfaction in having to wait a while this morning to see Dr. Van Deman. Maybe her celebrity status really made no difference. Maybe she was being treated just like anyone else; that was good, although she had begun to wonder how much longer today's wait was going to be. She had grown weary of the home decorating and movie star magazines.

Somewhere between the age of 16 or 17, Allyn Parke Saxton II felt she had taken charge of her life, even as her mother remained her legal guardian and financial executor at the time. However, by then, Allyn had become a movie star, not in the sense of every American teenage girl's dream, but a real, academy award-winning, headed-for-a-star-in-the-Groman's-Chinese-Theater-sidewalk movie star. There was then no star embedded in the sidewalk, no signature, no footprints, no, not yet, but Allyn and her mother were already enjoying the choicest of Hollywood's embellishments, courtesy of the fortunate film producers and directors who had cornered the young Miss Saxton for their projects.

While many, if not most, adult actors and actresses of that time were competing for the action fantasy or lovesick dramas of the early- to mid-nineties, motion picture houses were clamoring for scripts suitable for Allyn, a maturing, though striking, teenager transitioning beautifully into womanhood. In many instances, Parke insisted on script revisions before she would allow her gifted daughter to commit to a project, whether the medium was television, Broadway, or film.

By the time she was 25, Allyn Saxton was a multi-millionaire, with no end in sight to the value of her image. In contrast to her mushrooming career, the prospects of many of Allyn's peers were dwindling to parallel her mother's fading influence. Having become an adult, she still generally agreed with her mother's past career guidance but at the same time welcomed the true business and personal control that adulthood had granted.

In marked contrast, when she was first ushered into the medical exam room by Dr. Van Deman as a nearly middle-aged adult, Allyn Saxton no longer felt in control of her life. She had discarded every sexual or platonic relationship as it became no longer meaningful to or productive for her, those finales typically erupting when the person either exerted too great an influence or was no longer of value.

Allyn thought back to that first actual phone contact with Van Deman when she correctly identified herself as Allyn Saxton instead of Mary Smith. "Miss Saxton, I'm so sorry that I was not able to talk with you when you first called about our services here at the Center," Henry Van Deman had said on the return call. "Actually, I believe that your ... your assistant might have been the one who initially called requesting me."

"No, Doctor, I called myself," she was swift to answer. At that time Allyn had decided to take charge of her life situation and did not want anyone else to receive credit.

"Oh, of course. How efficient." Allyn had found Van Deman's voice rich and authoritative, with a clipped enunciation she found strange for Mississippi, until she remembered from his website bio that he hailed from New York. "I was with patients when you first called, and as I'm sure you will come to realize, I ... we ... are very busy here, yet remain personal. My associate, Dr. Knox Chamblee, and I, as well as all of our staff, devote a wealth of time to each case, concentrating on the specific objective of each client. You see, each client, each patient, is different. And, of course, I will be handling your case personally. It is uniqueness that makes this business of healthcare so fascinating."

And a business it was. That fact became clear to Allyn Saxton on her initial visit to the Center. Despite the universally-known reality of her 10 to 12 million-dollar salary per motion picture, she did not see herself as the rich one in the consultation room when she sat across from Van Deman. *I wonder how much*

money this guy makes? she remembered thinking. He wore
what she considered to be a conventional doctor's outfit – a
monogrammed, white-starched lab coat, a male version of one she
had worn during a recent guest shot on *Grey's Anatomy*. Instead
of his tailored Italian slacks and shoes and light blue, tightly
woven Pima cotton shirt with French cuffs, her white TV lab coat
had covered a wrinkled blue scrub suit above tennis shoes.

Even Van Deman's cuff links appeared pricey as intricately
carved, antique onyx should. The cuff links and sleeves framed
strong hands, which somehow still appeared agile, almost
delicate. Allyn watched the doctor take a pen from the surface
of his desk, a rich mahogany piece that would have been at home
at any Beverly Hills antique shop. The writing instrument was
Montblanc, and the pride of mastering it was evident in the
deliberate series of notes he recorded in outline form concerning
her medical, sexual, and reproductive history. Dr. Van Deman
spent little time delving into her social history, either married or
familial, because the facts were already well-known to anyone who
watched television or had an Internet connection.

Her medical history was that of a healthy 34-year-old female,
who was one year shy of what obstetricians termed *advanced
maternal age*. Saxton admitted to smoking an occasional cigarette
but had given up the regular habit five years prior. She was drug-
free in the sense that she only drank a glass of wine a few days a
week, and only expensive *pinot noir* at that.

Allyn Saxton's surgical history included a mini-face lift and
saline breast implants but was topped by a devastating childhood
procedure: a tonsillectomy which cost her a recurring role on
the eighties television series *Growing Pains*. The history of
the tonsillectomy was duly noted, but Van Deman missed the
significance of the lost television role, which Allyn mentioned for
levity's sake. Her career had more than survived it.

On the contrary, her devastated mother barely got over that one. As far as regular exercise, workouts were mandated by a personal trainer and the wardrobe of her acting roles, not to mention the need to escape tabloid criticism warranted by any significant swing in weight, regardless of direction.

Again, Van Deman employed his Montblanc to circle areas of interest on her completed history form. "How long did you have unprotected, monogamous sex with any one partner and not get pregnant?" was next, meant simply to serve as a frank assessment of her degree of fertility or infertility. That question garnered a blush from Allyn, the only personal query to cause one up to that point.

As far as partners were concerned, her sexual history had been long, varied, and protected – interlaced with streaks of monogamy particularly during her two marriages, at least on her part, and always strictly heterosexual, again at least on her part. The secular importance of those details rested merely in objectively analyzing the potential causes of her failure to conceive, Van Deman had explained. This was not a divorce settlement or social work evaluation.

The law of averages would suggest that if Allyn had participated in unprotected sex with several male partners, then at least one or more of those men would have been fertile, thus giving her the opportunity to conceive if she were physically up to par. Of course, while her own reproductive system might have been functioning normally, the miracle remained that she had somehow avoided contracting sexually transmitted diseases or developed an abnormal Pap smear.

"I am glad to see that you have no history of STDs, Miss Saxton," Van Deman observed at that first face-to-face encounter, again referencing the medical history questionnaire he had downloaded and printed from Allyn's material submitted via his website. "We'll go ahead and check for those, just to be sure. That is, if you don't mind, Miss Saxton," he clarified as she nodded unconcerned. The physician again scrutinized the medical history questionnaire, diligently highlighting sections by circling them with the tip of his Mont Blanc, relieved to find her so healthy. As the pen neared the paper, he handled it as precisely as a fine surgical instrument approaching human tissue.

"Of particular concern is that any contracture of Chlamydia or gonorrhea could have damaged your fallopian tubes, or even ovaries or uterus," he commented. As though he could read the growing question in her mind, Van Deman added, "Of course, we're going to work around that, aren't we?"

Van Deman followed with several other questions that had not been on the pre-appointment online questionnaire. At least, Allyn did not remember seeing them on the list and believed she could not have missed these: *Did you try multiple positions or different times of day when you were trying to get pregnant?* was met with a flushed face that surprised even Allyn. *Do you actually enjoy sexual relations?* followed.

"Well, Doctor, let me explain." Allyn fought the urge of feeling embarrassed and foolish over meeting with this doctor, certainly a qualified professional but still someone she had just met. Never would she have imagined such personal, almost provocative, questions. All she wanted was a baby, one that came from her own body.

"You see, uh, Dr. Van Deman," she worked to answer, "I only seldom tried to get pregnant with either of my husbands or my boyfriends. Neither husband wanted a baby with me, so they were sure to wear a raincoat if they caught on that I was coming onto them at certain times of my cycle. You know what I mean – don't you, Doctor?"

"Yes, I think I do," Van Deman responded while redirecting his attention from the printed patient questionnaire to a computer screen, highlighting a few areas of the monitor with a pen stylet.

"And then for a time with my latest boyfriend – I mean fiancé," Allyn continued. "He didn't want to have a baby either, even though we were planning to get married. Of course, I don't think being married really entered into that A-hole's reasoning anyway," she added, glancing away and brushing clear a thick blonde strand that had fallen into the field of her right eye. "He had the nerve to tell me he didn't want a pregnant figure to get in the way of my career. I think he thought he might miss a party or a premiere or two!" Allyn opened up in frustration, then rambled. "That whole line of thinking is just B.S., pure B.S. Don't you agree, Doctor? Just look at what Julia Roberts, Angelina Jolie, and Gwyneth Paltrow have done. They've been pregnant and had babies, even twins, and they're still around. Pregnancy didn't slow them down a bit. Not one bit."

This time, Van Deman paused and looked up from the thin laptop where he had just typed a short encrypted note, clarifying and adding information drawn from the candid, personal discourse of this international personality. He saved the short abstract to a separate file in his hard drive, believing he might need to share it later with someone. That someone was sure to agree that his new patient exuded a raw beauty, a look that screamed attraction even without the benefit of a professional makeup artist or hairstylist, although the hat worn earlier did trash her look.

"So, Ms. Saxton," Van Deman interjected, "in summary, you believe that you have truly never had the opportunity to conceive, that is, in a natural way. By *natural*, I mean between a consenting man and a woman having frequent, unprotected sexual relations." This last statement directed across the desk to Allyn Saxton was more than a summation. It was presented as an open question, no answer necessary.

Henry Van Deman had always considered himself a smart man and an industrious one at that. Now, he just felt lucky. Sitting across from him was one of the most stunning women he had ever seen, inarguably an opinion shared by millions of people around the world, although very few of those outside her industry would actually catch a flesh-and-blood glimpse of her or learn the true, intimate secrets that tabloids could only drool over. How any normal man could have resisted her sexually, particularly if she was in the mood to conceive, was beyond him.

Not only was Allyn Parke Saxton a dazzling beauty who wanted to have a baby with or without a husband, she was also the very thing Van Deman had sought as the foundation of his medical empire: a member of a clientele with indisputable resources and an appetite for the extremes of technology. As he again glanced across at her, he noticed how the neck, although thin, was muscular all the same, making a perfect balance with the rest of her feminine, athletic physique.

Nonetheless, scoring a patient like her had been beyond Van Deman's imagination. During his recruitment spiel to Knox Chamblee, he predicted an infertility facility so advanced that, despite its relatively obscure location, it would attract patients whose resources could put them anywhere. The accounting projections regarding the Center's financial success were not a true fabrication, but during that discussion Van Deman amazed even himself with such a stretch of the imagination. When someone of Allyn Saxton's stature scheduled and fortunately kept her first appointment, his vision of a celebrity-filled practice destined to monopolize the field seemed more than grandiose self-confidence.

Notwithstanding his ego, from the first moment of Saxton's face-to-face consultation as a new patient, Van Deman wondered how she had landed in his lap. From reviewing her submitted profile, he knew that she had answered the online question *How did you hear about Dr. Van Deman and his associates?* with *From a friend.* Henry left it at that.

Van Deman's motions were deliberate as he lifted his face and eyes, then closed the laptop, finished with the initial interview. He then returned the expensive pen to rest in his left front pocket. As the physician stood, he let his eyes drop to her chest just as she looked away as though to check her purse. The patient's upper arms were taut with carved, still feminine biceps that erupted from the short sleeves of an expensive silk blouse. Her ample breasts worked in perfect proportion with her torso: either the kind work of God or the precise efforts of a well-trained plastic surgeon, and a pricey one at that. Either way, Van Deman would have the answer in moments, although he thought he recalled breast augmentation from her surgical history.

Walking toward the door, he explained, "We will need to do a basic physical, although I have reviewed the recent examination records you sent us from your gynecologist in California. It seems that you have not had a complete work-up including a Pap smear and screens for cervical infection in more than a year," Dr. Van Deman said as Allyn groaned with a hint of sarcastic humor, as if the doctor expected it. "Patients always say they never get used to that sort of thing," he shrugged as he moved toward the door.

"Everything to prepare for a routine GYN exam is laid out for you in the treatment room next door. Not to insult you, Ms. Saxton, but it is certainly wise to have thorough STD testing before initiating our procedures. So today we'll get caught up with that as well."

Awaiting her in the next room was a lightly starched, white cloth examination gown, neatly pressed and draped across the head of an electrically adjustable examination table. Resting nearby, Allyn would find matching disposable slippers, similar to those available in high-end hotel suites, except that those provided by the Van Deman Center of Reproductive Technology were finished across the top with a pink *VDC* monogram.

With authority, Dr. Van Deman walked to the exam room door and opened it quickly and purposefully, motioning for Allyn to enter. Masking her dread of the examination was simple, one of the attributes of being a professional actress. It was unnecessary for her to recognize his regal air; she simply obeyed. Besides, he was a doctor.

Allyn now found herself staring at the entrance to the examination room, almost crushing her new Marc Jacobs handbag in the crook of her left arm as she reached to close the door with her right. It had taken several steps to cross the space although she was unaware of having taken them. Feeling the doctor's pause at the exit door of his office to the hall, she almost jerked to attention as the announcement broke the silence. "I'll be with you in just a short minute, Ms., uh, Smith," he said in an attempt at humor about her fictitious name, "and then we'll begin the exam." He could not keep a movie star waiting. Van Deman believed that.

However, there would be a wait, more than just a short one. Van Deman still carried a standard pager, a small black model set to a soft vibratory signal that fit snugly on his right hip. Even with the availability of his iPhone, which seldom if ever left his person, the pager was useful as back-up and for quick messages from within the Center or from the hospital, though most of his patient procedures were done in house. This page was from his own receptionist: *Dr. Pecunia is here.*

Letha Pecunia – the appointment had been forgotten, overshadowed by Saxton's arrival. House calls made by in-demand psychologists like Dr. Pecunia or by any other medical professional, other than those in nursing, remained rare in most areas of the country. However, *house call* was not the most accurate nomenclature for the meeting; it was in essence an office call.

Van Deman transferred his pager to his left hand to punch in the number for the Center's operator. He stood outside his private office/patient examination room suite for a moment, holding the receiver of the slim wall mount phone. Letha Pecunia had saved him on more than one occasion. Her specialty was in counseling professionals like herself, many just as well-educated as she, if not more so.

No one in his office knew that Pecunia was a psychologist; she billed herself as a consultant or advisor. In the situation of the Van Deman Center, she was a medical practice advisor. Her $500 per hour fee plus travel expenses was paid by the administrator and business manager of the practice as part of the overhead, and no one was the wiser.

Henry Van Deman, MD, needed her.

It was Pecunia's practice to come to the patient on his or her own turf, since the types she counseled were not fond of flaunting weakness or indecision. Of course, she started out with a back door entrance and exit to her small office to serve the important types, but soon found her niche in traveling to deliver on-the-spot psychological therapy.

Her confidential list of clients continued to grow and included large corporation CEOs, a university president or two, several United States congressmen, and even a recent President.
Of course, there were other physicians as well; most were departmental chairmen in medical schools and principal members of medical firms like Van Deman. Those were the individuals who made the tough decisions.

The majority of her counseling sessions were designed to probe insecurities and self-perceived weaknesses in leadership with an occasional marital infidelity concern thrown in. Basically, Dr. Pecunia was an ear. That ear had heard countless examples of emotional ignorance and a dearth of true, objective decision-making skills. Many a CEO and CFO had asked her, "What about me and my needs?"

As would be expected of a psychologist, most of Pecunia's sessions focused on emotionally-charged issues. Many times these concerns dealt with unexpected executive worry over balancing corporate profits with the welfare and needs of the little guy. Ruining lives by swallowing businesses whole or in completely dismantling other companies occasionally resulted in sleepless nights.

The quandaries her clients seemed to face often were judged by Pecunia as having common sense solutions. Those were the easy hand-holding situations, the minor situations in which $500 an hour plus travel-expenses sometimes even made Pecunia feel guilty. Smart, rich professionals were so emotionally immature, she had thought time and time again.

In contrast, the situation with Henry Van Deman was different from most. There was no avoidance ritual, no internal smokescreen where feelings and emotions had been rejected. Beginning with their first session, Pecunia was surprised at Van Deman's preplanned auto-psychoanalysis. She was confronted with that which many counselors dread – healthcare, financial, or whatever – an initial encounter where the client seems prepared to make a verbal dissertation.

Fortunately, Pecunia's experience had fortified her for a lengthy history lesson as the first hour was quickly spent. She was not surprised to learn of Van Deman's noteworthy medical training, nor was it unexpected that it was a lengthy one, especially for a board-certified physician with a medical specialty. She forced her own concentration through a course of events attributed to Hurricane Katrina, which spirited him away from a larger metropolitan area to Canton, Mississippi.

As the discourse approached the end of the first hour, she wished for a less comfortable chair and wondered why her new client had scheduled the consult in the first place. Had he had concerns about his present life or even after-life concerns, he had not vented them. The first $500 was tallied by then, and Pecunia was certain that when Van Deman finally did get around to the real reason for the consultation, he would have already resolved his problems or at least assumed he had. He was that kind of individual who did not go to the bathroom without an in-depth analysis of the need.

As the secretary escorted her to Dr. Van Deman's office for this second scheduled consultation as Saxton waited in the adjacent exam room, the psychologist hoped for more than Part II of the Biography of Superdoctor: Henry Van Deman, MD. Perhaps in store for Pecunia was a nasty eruption blaming his parents for emotional insecurities or lost opportunity or, more calmly, a request for advice regarding how to handle a difficult physician partner.

She hoped he might even vent some repressed hostility toward a past or present spouse or sexual partner, female or even male. The doctor's sexual preference had not been broached during their first session; however, nothing but heterosexuality was implied through voice inflection and facial and hand gestures. For whatever was troubling him, there seemed to be no target for blame.

"Look, I need you to talk to me, to talk this thing through with me. There isn't anyone else I can discuss this with." Van Deman's greeting was hurried – no salutation, no hello, not even a smile accompanied the dismissal of his secretary with a flick of his right hand, as though waving off a mosquito. His demeanor was a welcome one for Pecunia, one of getting down to business.

"Yes, OK, I'll, uh, just sit down here, across from your desk, like I did during our last session, Dr. Van Deman." Psychologist Pecunia took the same much-too-comfortable upholstered chair positioned approximately six feet from Van Deman. He remained standing as he lifted the pen from his desk, rolling the Montblanc between his right thumb and middle finger.

He turned to stare through the floor-length window behind his desk, a curiosity for Pecunia in that closed plantation shutters completely obscured the outdoors. The previously unobstructed view of the building's exterior rear garden had been a pleasant distraction for Pecunia during their initial consultation, and to her disappointment Van Deman showed no sign of opening the blinds. As her client continued to stare at the window as though studying nature through the opaque slants of blonde-colored wood, Dr. Pecunia decided to compile a few notes on the discourse.

"Don't you want to open the blinds a bit, Dr. Van Deman?" she asked, before really considering the question.

"Well, I really hadn't planned to. I've actually gotten used to their being closed." The pen was spinning faster between the thumb and forefingers of his right and left hands, and to Pecunia's surprise he never dropped it. "I guess the cleaning people closed the blinds a couple of weeks ago to dust them, after I complained to my office administrator that the service had been slipping recently. And slipping isn't a good thing, considering how much I pay those jokers," he remarked.

"Dr. Van Deman, you're not paying me to discuss cleaning supplies," she interrupted.

"Anyway, I found them closed one morning," he continued, ignoring her comment, "and I haven't raised them since. I've gotten used to it. Sort of like the privacy."

"Dr. Van Deman, you do not seem the type person to shield

yourself from the outside world. I remember the view through your office window to be so lovely – several white crape myrtles were in bloom, I believe. And today the drive up from the airport was so pleasant, the weather so lovely, not nearly as hot as when I was here before. I think you ..."

"You're right, Dr. Pecunia," Van Deman's turn to interrupt. "I'm not paying you $500 an hour to discuss cleaning supplies or the weather. Why don't you just go ahead and call me Henry?"

"I see. Very well. *Henry* it is." She cleared her throat softly and pressed, "Okay, Henry, what *are* you paying me to do for you?"

"Sex. I want to ..."

Pecunia cleared her throat more deeply in interruption. "Henry ... Dr. Van Deman ... Henry, I'm afraid I don't understand." Letha Pecunia was a short woman. *Petite* was not an accurate descriptive term for the prominent psychologist in that the term implies a diminutive physique. To the contrary, *dumpy* was simply too unkind. Truthfully, she was too intelligent and well-educated to be labeled as dumpy; height was Pecunia's only petite feature as her figure was overpowered by grossly oversized breasts, fused to her hips in such a way to void the belt line. Van Deman wondered if her neck had been omitted during embryological development.

Whatever her client's forthcoming remarks, Letha Pecunia, Ph.D., dreaded them. Despite her office wall covered with diplomas and educational certificates, sex was her least favorite dimension of psychological counseling. Besides, Van Deman was handsome – tall, clearly more than six feet, with confident, sharp features and a head full of neatly cropped, blonde hair. He was physically fit, as well, and looked significantly younger than 52 years old – not the type to be missing out on sex, whatever the orientation.

"Dr. Pecunia, I am the one who does not understand," Van

Deman countered in response to her interruption. "My entire professional career revolves around sex, artificial sex. Manmade sex, if you will." Suddenly he looked away from the closed blinds, jerking his face toward Pecunia, momentarily interrupting his discourse. "I could just as easily have said 'female-made sex,' so, no professional sexism implied and no pun intended," he chuckled, showing the first inkling of amusement since Pecunia had come face-to-face with him.

"All right, I see," she lied, tilting her head to her right in a soft nod, trying not to squirm in her chair while mustering the aura of a compassionate, problem-solving counselor who wanted to push things along. Unlike she first assumed, this discussion did not seem to be heading toward a paranoid discourse on infidelity or corporate concern over inappropriate sexual attractions between employees or patients. *But where is this going?* she wondered as she not-so-subtly shifted her hips in the chair.

"These patients, they come to me as a last resort," Van Deman continued. "They've been everywhere else to solve their problems, starting first with a local medical practitioner of some sort, sometimes a gynecologist, but not always. By the time they make their way to me, most have had an operation or two or three to correct infertility issues, with many of those procedures actually performed by people who knew what they were doing. These women, along with some of their male partners or sperm donors, have already taken several types of fertility-enhancing medications."

"Yes, yes, I see." Another counseling nod went unnoticed, with this one appearing even more perplexed. Van Deman also missed the slight pull to the right corner of her mouth along with the crooked inch rise of the eyebrow above.

"You know what's so strange about this, Letha?" he queried. Pecunia looked up from the pad where she intended to take notes, having only recorded the date and time up to that point and now somewhat taken aback that he had called her by her given name. "The odd thing for me is … and that's why I have you here with me; all of this is just what I wanted," he expressed in frustration, tossing the pen to his desk and raising his right arm in an abrupt wave, gesturing around his office and ending at the closed set of window blinds, as though directing her to the obscured view. "I wanted to be the last resort for these people – the answer, the resolution to infertility, their victorious result."

She took advantage of the few moments of silence that followed as her client turned again to stare at the closed view of the outside garden. "Well, Henry, is that not what you have here? I took the liberty of perusing your website before our initial appointment and was definitely impressed. Your published success rates for the types of reproductive problems you treat must be the envy of most other hospitals or clinics. And the glowing testimonials from people from all over the country – you cannot put a price tag on that kind of free advertising. Why, there were even several from overseas!"

"You just don't get it. For your exorbitant fee, you just don't get it, do you?"

Taken aback at his abruptness, she jerked her head to the rear, "Well, I guess, I'm afraid that I don't. What do you really mean?" she asked, dropping the scribe pretense.

"These people think that I am God."

"Of course, they do. Certainly they have placed a great deal of faith and money in …"

"No, they really believe I am God, the Almighty … that I can create life, that I am the essence of life."

"Henry, these patients are infertile. They come to you knowing that this is a medical clinic; that you're just …"

"Do you suppose God decides when life will happen?" Van

Deman interjected in autonomous tone, no answer expected.

"Well, yes, I mean, religious doctrine teaches that God created the earth and its inhabitants and that He controls mankind. The answer to your question rests in what a person truly believes. You seem to believe in God; you are the one who has brought up the concept. What do you think?"

"I think that my patients are correct. They have good judgment. No, they possess excellent judgment. That good judgment is shown by the fact they have come to me to be treated."

Nervously, Dr. Letha Pecunia scribbled *God* on her pad, wondering if this was all beginning to come together: a God-complex of some sort. At least she now had some symptoms and a few concrete characteristics that could work into a problem-oriented diagnosis. Over the last several years, she had dealt with several obsessive-compulsion cases with grandiose delusions like the one unfolding in front of the dark window. As a chill ran through her, she fought shivering. She could not remember a compulsion that seemed so literal, so encompassing – a God-complex that was obviously a reality for its holder.

"Henry, I believe our time for today is up," she said, trying to disguise her relief. Anyway, I believe that your secretary told me that you needed to cut it a little short today – that you had an important patient from California."

"She can wait. After all, she wants me to be God. She expects me to be God. The reality of all this, my dear Dr. Pecunia, is that I fear that I want to be God."

Again, the psychologist scrawled the word *God* on her pad.

"Dr. Pecunia, I am God," was the icy response, terrifying in its finality.

Reminder, you have a patient waiting appeared in green print on the black background of Van Deman's pager. *Patient probably anxious, very.*

"You're right, I have to go, Dr. Pecunia ... Letha. My time for this session was indeed limited. I'm sorry that I did not plan better. This particular patient who is waiting has traveled quite a distance to see me. She's rather important, at least she thinks she is – and I guess that she is. Most people seem to think so."

"I'm sure that she is. Aren't all of your patients important?" she asked rhetorically, expecting no answer and receiving none.

"My secretary will be with you in a moment. She'll show you out and schedule our next visit. Of course, I'll look forward to getting your bill."

"And I'll look forward to sending it to you," she quipped.

————————————————————————

As instructed, Allyn Saxton had undressed, donned the breezy examination wardrobe, and sat on the end of the examination table to wait for the doctor to complete her first visit. She found repetitious the supplementary questionnaires left in the room for her to answer, particularly those related to family history, but she had come a long way for a result and had no intention of doubting the method. However, the wait for the doctor's additional attention did seem more protracted than that typical for L.A., affording her ample time to thumb through four current magazines discovered in a corner periodicals basket. Her picture was on the cover of two of them, the two that looked the worse for wear.

Holding the gown to her chest, Allyn slid off the end of the table in hopes of finding something else in the room to pass the time now that the magazines were memorized and discarded. She considered getting out her Blackberry and playing some computer games, although she had never used it much and was not sure she knew how.

Instead, her eyes drifted around the room as she began to study the area more closely. The corner basket had already been worked over. The cabinets lining the walls of the room probably contained only medical supplies, and since all but one were fitted with a recessed cylindrical lock, Allyn correctly assumed they were off-limits. She did try the one door left unbarred and found nothing but paper drapes, boxes of Kleenex, and tubes of lubricating jelly.

All that was left to explore was what resembled an oversized laptop computer mounted flush on a type of console, standing near a couple of padded stools not far from the foot of the exam table. Allyn assumed that the electronic wizardry was an extremely up-to-date ultrasound or sonogram machine. When she had not become pregnant, she had undergone several such tests in doctors' offices in California where her pelvic organs were probed and measured and photographed.

Understanding that she had visited a Los Angeles gynecologist, her lawyer once joked that Allyn could skip the next movie deal and garner early retirement if, instead of her smiling, flawless face, an ultrasound image of one of her internal sexual organs should grace the cover of an entertainment magazine.

As Allyn remembered the attorney's endless laughter over his off-color humor, she caught her own smiling reflection in the monitor mounted at eye level on the nearest wall. "A financial fantasy ... making lots of money at my expense, my own personal expense. Where have I heard that before?" she asked rhetorically, straightening her hair a bit as she took advantage of her outlined image. "Gosh, what an A-hole he is – funny, but a real A-hole."

"I'm sorry. Did you say something?" Dr. Van Deman's voice startled her as hurriedly entered the room without knocking.

"Oh, no, Dr. Van Deman. I was just looking at this flat screen monitor," she answered on cue, as though improvising a line on stage. "Just wondering if I could get *Showtime* or something like that on it. You know, I would've even settled for the *Food Network*: Rachel Ray, even Paula Dean." As he started to respond, she added, "I read all your magazines while I was waiting, and you could definitely use some fresher ones."

Van Deman smiled politely, mixing in an air of slight embarrassment at having kept Miss Saxton waiting. He knew that Allyn Saxton's gorgeous, unveiled face was all over the front cover of most of the magazines scattered throughout the Center; he had seen patients poring over them. "Miss Saxton, I am indeed sorry for having kept you waiting so long."

"No problem. I'm used to directors and producers and even photographers taking their time. I guess, Doctor, that you're sort of a producer," she quipped, resuming her assigned spot by walking from the wall monitor over to the examination table, her gown in tow. She hopped back on the end of the table as gracefully as she could as Van Deman stared transfixed.

"That monitor is wirelessly connected to our UM-KAO1 ultrasound or sonogram here, the latest available. Very high-definition." Van Deman ran his hands across the smooth top of the precious machine's console. His hands appeared just as smooth, his long fingers professionally manicured, but still masculine. "We use this gem for egg retrieval and sometimes embryo implantation. Most patients like to watch what we're seeing in the console, so we give them the opportunity on the monitor."

Van Deman looked back to Allyn Saxton, a beautiful woman, who, like so many, had put off nature's normal directive to procreate. Now it was up to him. "Yes, Miss Saxton," he proposed, "we show the inside of the female human body to our patients, the inside of their bodies in high-def."

As she hid behind a false name, Van Deman guided Allyn from that first appointment through ovulation induction, egg harvesting and artificial insemination, and then embryo freezing since she decided against immediate implantation into her uterus. He explained to an appreciative Allyn Saxton that his sole management of her case was centered around maintaining strict confidentiality, even though employee understanding of HIPPA regulations and plain, simple, professional standards were firmly in place at the Center.

Apart from her movie-star status and much to his relief, Allyn Saxton had accepted those policies and procedures over which he had full control. Once more, from the moment he discovered the identity of Mary Smith to be Allyn Saxton, every aspect of her evaluation and care was handled with kid gloves, and only by Henry Van Deman himself. Much to his regret and without justification, he had shared the advent of his prized catch with Knox Chamblee. *Maybe I just wanted to brag a little*, he thought. For up to that point, Van Deman had not considered the possibilities.

In spite of guaranteeing her absolute secrecy, Van Deman knew that others might still learn of the star's involvement with his Center. However, any buzz to that effect would have been much more likely had she been treated in a media-rich, major metropolitan area. He doubted if Saxton would ever divulge the origins of her pregnancy since the famous generally value their privacy, and she seemed no different.

While the marketing potential of treating a client the caliber of Saxton could have been endless for the Van Deman Center if the story were leaked to the media, this was a dramatically different situation. His personal interest in her case mandated absolute secrecy about her identity and her medical records as well. His main fear was not that his treasured young associate would violate Saxton's privacy, but that Knox Chamblee would begin to ask too many questions and probe a little too far.

Chapter
11
◆◆◆
THE DEMONSTRATION

When Wesley Sarbeck first signed them in at the reception kiosk just beyond the front foyer, he was reminded of checking in for a flight at the airport. Having never before seen that type of electronic patient registration system in a doctor's office, Wesley wrapped it nicely in his modernistic opinion of Dr. Van Deman and his methods. That night in the hospital waiting room, Dr. Henry Van Deman had convinced him that the future was here for Wesley and Carrie Sarbeck and nothing was too bizarre or impossible.

Fortunately, Wesley had passed his test and proven his own fertility. Had he not, then he and Carrie would not have progressed to this point. The stipulation to their finally becoming parents lay in the fact that their baby must have at least 50 percent of the couple's genetic material. That assurance would complete their objective, at least Wesley's objective. Carrie Sarbeck had stopped voicing an opinion. She considered her body only as an incubator.

"You'll need to submit some additional samples, Mr. Sarbeck," the cheery lab technician had announced on their previous visit as she handed him another sterile container. "We need to have lots of healthy sperm to pick from," she added. The donor's ova, the other half of the genetic material that would grow into the Sarbeck child, had already been frozen fresh and stored and would be thawed, as Van Deman explained, to be fertilized by Wesley's own contribution.

Had Wesley not paid the final installment of the fees due the Van Deman Center two weeks previously, he and Carrie would not have progressed this far through the process. Miss Wax had been satisfied as well, and Wesley assumed that the egg donor's estate had received its share.

He had never mentioned the murder of Cheryl Choice to Carrie because the death was nothing but a sideline factor in their becoming a family. Choice had been merely a donor-for-hire, selected for her attributes and her price, her eggs long ago collected and fresh frozen for potential use by a couple like Wesley and Carrie Sarbeck. All they had needed was a suitable egg donor – one whom they could afford, one who passed for resembling Carrie, and one who was fortunately fertilized by Wesley.

During the trial-run embryo implantation, Dr. Van Deman told them, "We will implant two viable embryos into the uterus and then freeze the others. Therefore, we could get twins although it is quite possible that only one embryo will survive to become a fetus. Implanting two, of course, increases our odds of getting at least one healthy baby. That's what you want, isn't it, one healthy baby, Mr. and Mrs. Sarbeck?"

Wesley nodded in the affirmative. "But we would be thrilled with twins. Who wouldn't be?" he looked over to Carrie for affirmation, receiving none. "Sure, Doctor, going from no baby to two babies would be quite an adjustment, but we would definitely be thrilled, Doctor. Yeah, thrilled!" he rebounded from her silence, working to suppress the anxiety in his smile.

Carrie's expression remained solemn as a fresh tear seeped unabated from the corner of her right eye. She continued to stare at her tiny, feminine hands as they rested in her lap, a faint tremor obvious.

"Earlier in the development of this technology," Van Deman ignored Carrie while playing to the receptive member of the two-person audience, "we would have implanted three or more embryos to increase our chances of one surviving as a full-term, bouncing, healthy baby. But now with improved techniques and equipment, the embryo survival rate has soared to the point that most embryos survive processing and uterine implantation, leading to a successful pregnancy."

Wesley nodded eagerly. He was following the doctor's line of reasoning and hoped that his wife was absorbing some of it. They would discuss it later. She would come around.

"So you still put in two embryos, Dr. Van Deman, just to be sure we get at least one; but a lot of times people like us wind up with two. Is that right?"

"Yes, you're correct, Mr. Sarbeck. Gosh, I must call you *Wesley*. I feel that we have come such a long way since our first meeting that night in the hospital when your wife was in such danger," Van Deman replied, as he glanced over at the wife, finding not a hint of appreciation for his saving her from bleeding to death.

"We will introduce two healthy embryos in Carrie," he maintained with authority, "fully expecting both to implant successfully. As you know, her uterus has been converted into a receptive human incubator for your baby, or perhaps even babies."

Van Deman noticed Wesley's growing enthusiasm, surpassing apprehension as he continued to define the process for Carrie's artificial conception. "Yes, we will introduce these growing human cells that we observed to glisten under our microscope. Dr.

Chamblee, the laboratory assistants, and I fully expect them to continue to divide exponentially into babies, or at least one baby. Sounds simple at that point, doesn't it, Wesley?" Dr.Van Deman added somewhat lightheartedly to the lone member of his captive audience.

"Of course, you will have some legal and ethical options regarding any excess embryos, that is, over the two we plan to implant. From the union of your sperm and the donor eggs, my team and I certainly expect three, and possibly four, healthy, viable embryos to be leftover once we have successfully implanted the best two of the group."

"Options?" Wesley inquired, the reaction that Van Deman had learned to expect.

"Sure, options. We, that is, you, should strongly consider having any unused embryos frozen fresh in their present state of active cellular division. Then, you can use them later, if you like, or you can even donate the remaining embryos to some other less fortunate childless couple."

Wesley realized that he should have read more about this whole process, or at least done an Internet search of the terms *frozen embryo* or *frozen human eggs*, or even of *Henry Van Deman, MD.* "So, Doctor Van Deman," Wesley attempted to summarize, "what you mean is that if something doesn't work out this time, then we'll have the other embryos to fall back on. We'll still have some more options, like you just said."

"Well, yes, that's true. But we fully expect everything to 'work out this time' as you say. You and your wife should fully realize your dream." Van Deman paused briefly as he gave another quick look at the wife, trying to ignore her increasing hand tremor, but at the same time hoping she would become more responsive. He made a mental note to double check with the Center's psychologist about the patient screening protocol.

"Yes," Henry Van Deman, MD, stated in near oration, "you should fully realize your dream of becoming parents as you benefit from our experience and matchless reproductive techniques.

"Incidentally, I thought you, the two of you, would find it fascinating to see a digital photograph taken through our microscope of what will soon become your baby." As though on Van Deman's cue, the door from the hall opened into the examination room.

"Mr. and Mrs. Sarbeck," Van Deman placed an increased emphasis on *and Mrs. Sarbeck* in a renewed effort to bring her into the discussion. The effort was not lost on Carrie, although she couldn't have cared less. "As you may know, this is my associate, Dr. Knox Chamblee," Van Deman introduced. "While I attend to another patient, I've asked Dr. Chamblee to show you photographs of your embryos in the blastocyst stage. This will be your baby's or babies' first photo or photos, you might say." Van Deman let out a soft laugh, sounding almost corny in Knox's opinion, as the attempted icebreaker went unanswered.

Van Deman had planned to turn the Sarbecks over to Chamblee, and after the day's encounter with the female half, he was even more delighted with his decision. The couple would quickly warm up to Knox, he hoped, since younger physicians can sometimes muster patience from absolutely nowhere.

By Van Deman's design, there had been little opportunity for the Sarbecks to develop a cozy, personal doctor-patient relationship with him. Although name-brand recognition was essential to the success of the Center's marketing efforts and continued profitability, there were simply too many steps, too many people involved for a strong emotional bond to develop between the Center's founder and each patient or couple.

The ultimate purpose of the Van Deman Center for

Reproductive Technology was to produce healthy offspring for its clients. Whether or not he personally met every client was ultimately irrelevant, because he considered every conception to be a Van Deman baby.

Pursuant to that philosophy, the majority of the Sarbeck medical history and the infertility treatment preliminaries had been gathered by the chief technician of the embryo culture laboratory. This arrangement had allowed Van Deman to maintain little hands-on contact with the Sarbecks after the initial treatment of Carrie's last ectopic pregnancy and his resulting conversation with Wesley.

This divestiture of the patient workload was another reason Van Deman had taken Dr. Knox Chamblee into the practice. To Henry's delight, Chamblee seemed to mind his own business while actively building his own practice. As the younger doctor moved further into the Sarbecks' treatment room and approached the computer keyboard, it was obvious from the chill that the first-photo baby humor had been lost on this couple, particularly on the female half.

On the other hand, Van Deman's introduction of Chamblee began to stir even Carrie Sarbeck, who raised her head briefly for the appealing new doctor before returning to stare blankly at her trembling hands. She remembered having noticed Dr. Chamblee walk through the outskirts of the waiting room once, finding him attractive.

"Sure, I'll be glad to show them their blastocysts," the younger doctor answered, though Van Deman had already left the room. As Dr. Chamblee typed a few rote commands on the keyboard, he said, "Look at the screen on the wall and the first image should appear in just a few...Well, there it is – in microscopic high definition."

Wesley looked in the direction of the wall monitor, and Carrie surprisingly followed, her response noted only by her husband. She raised her head sufficiently to see images on the sleek screen mounted high and flush with the surface of the nearby wall.

"This is one of the two blastocysts we plan to implant. In our laboratory we have emphasized very healthy *in vitro* conditions so that the union of the egg and sperm – we call that union a zygote – can grow and divide rapidly into more cells. You may already know that *in vitro* is Latin for *within the glass*, meaning that in our case we are recreating a natural function of the human body in a controlled environment outside the body. The familiar concept of a test tube baby is really way too simple. Medical reproductive technology has come a long way since that term was first used."

Wesley Sarbeck liked this guy, Chamblee. He spoke in plain English, and Wesley followed Chamblee's explanation with a weak grin of understanding and authentic anticipation of finally becoming a father. Even though the Sarbeck baby, seen for the first time as only as a clump of blue-colored material, would contain none of his wife's genes, he had hoped that this demonstration would afford her a physical, if not yet emotional, attachment to this whole *in vitro* process, whatever the derivation.

As a result of the work of these doctors, Carrie would be carrying a healthy baby in her womb for nine months, just as if Wesley had put it there in the intimacy of their bedroom. However, to his continued disappointment, his wife remained uninterested and totally rigid, save for her ever-trembling hands. He hoped Carrie would eventually warm up to the new doctor.

"This technology is so much more than a reaction in a test tube," Dr. Chamblee clarified. "The blastocyst shown in this digital photography is composed of nearly 100 growing cells and is the form in which the living embryo will be implanted in the uterus," Chamblee defined as he highlighted a dark object in the center of the screen with a laser pointer pulled from his jacket pocket. To Wesley, the perfectly round thing appeared almost three-dimensional, nearly popping off the screen.

"This particular collection of cells will become the placenta and the inner collection will develop into a baby, your baby," enthused Dr. Chamblee. After retracing the object's thick, round luminescent blue border that encircled an area mimicking the moon's surface, he explained, "We have scheduled the actual embryo transfer for day five of your reproductive cycle, Mrs. Sarbeck." Expecting some verbal reaction or perhaps a hint of curiosity, he paused for a moment to look over at Carrie.

The pause went unanswered, and Chamblee returned his attention to the screen and his pointer. As he redirected his voice toward the much more receptive husband, he added, "Of course, your hormonal treatment has geared the lining of the uterus to be friendly to the blastocyst, which after all of the cellular division is completed, we will refer to as an embryo. This is really the step where ..."

"Doctor, this all seems so unnatural – so against God," Carrie blurted, startling even Wesley, as she could not help thinking again about the bird, pounding its beak against her bathroom windowpane on the day that Wax visited their living room. While its relentless pounding should have exhausted the animal, the bird followed by hurling its entire body against the glass. The more the bird worked to reach her, the more the window was smeared to prevent Carrie from viewing the happy home next door.

"Carrie, honey, we've already worked through that." More concerned than embarrassed, Wesley buried his face in his hands as he shook his head side-to-side. He could think of nothing positive to say, nothing to discount what he considered an absurd reaction from his irrational wife.

Uncertain as to how to react, Dr. Chamblee decided to ignore the woman's comment and continued. "Mrs. Sarbeck, we anticipate that the embryo will then invade the lining of your uterus to accomplish pregnancy. *Invade* is probably not a good word. *Attachment* or *implantation* is perhaps a better way to think about it."

He waited a moment, anticipating some off-color remark from the wife. But she was quiet, again downcast. "It is after this implantation in the healthy, receptive uterus that the blastocyst should ... no, we're going to remain upbeat here ... that the blastocyst *will* grow into a baby, your baby. We like to think of all of this well-timed, coordinated process as creating a natural pregnancy situation."

With that, Chamblee advanced to the next image which showed two of the round objects. He highlighted them with the laser pointer.

"By transferring two healthy embryos in this blastocyst stage, we improve the odds of a successful implantation. Our hope and plan is that at least one blastocyst will attach itself to a uterine lining made healthy by all the hormones we have given you. The result will be that the Sarbecks will receive at least one healthy baby, though there is a very good chance that we will get twins as I think you may have already been told."

The reinforcement of that possibility, planned to be the last of Chamblee's presentation, was definitely met with surprise. As Chamblee closed that particular computer program file, Carrie Sarbeck slid to the floor as her husband immediately bent to hover over her.

"However, this *in vitro* fertilization technique using blastocyst transfer on day five has a very low risk of triplets, and that is a plus – I can assure you!" he ad-libbed hurriedly while rushing to attend to Mrs. Sarbeck's limp body.

Somehow Carrie Sarbeck recovered to the degree necessary

to undergo the trial embryo transfer, the actual purpose of the day's trip to the Center. "Are we hurting you, Mrs. Sarbeck?" Chamblee asked as he inserted a thin specially designed latex catheter through the opening into the uterus. The diameter of the catheter was made to fit the cervical canal so that pain from instrumentation would be minimal.

Carrie merely shook her head, "No."

"Remember, you can watch the catheter placement procedure, if you like, Mr. and Mrs. Sarbeck, by studying the wall monitor," Dr. Chamblee added, as he maintained focus on his work, going through the trail run of placing a human embryo in her uterus. During the entire procedure, Carrie Sarbeck's demeanor remained unchanged, almost resigned to the procedure, practically martyred. She was repeatedly offered the opportunity to look at the video monitor, but refused to watch the manipulation of her body.

While Wesley was fascinated by Dr. Chamblee's work and wanted nothing more than to stare transfixed at the monitor on the wall, he could not ignore his wife's face, drained of emotion. He thought it better that she start to cry again or even cry out, preferring that she emit an endless supply of tears than simply play dead. Wesley forced himself to accept her behavior as a perpetual assumption of disappointment – anguish that arose from a feeling of eventual failure. He wished instead that her behavior represented simple anxiety or dread over having the procedure itself.

For Carrie, Wesley knew that there was to be no real physical pain from the procedure. With the administration of the accompanying sedative, Dr. Chamblee had assured them of that. He had hoped that by now his wife's optimism over the expected outcome would have matched his, that in about thirty-eight weeks they would finally become parents and be a real family. The possibility now seemed so real, so promising. After all, their day had come. Following all the hormone injections, pills, schedules and sonograms, their day had finally come.

But Wesley was wrong. Carrie was not afraid.

"All right, Mrs. Sarbeck, your body is ready. Everything should go just fine," Dr. Chamblee announced with a smile, beginning to question his senior partner's patient selection but comfortable in the fact that he himself had seen the women's signed consent for treatment.

"I know that you're nervous, Mrs. Sarbeck. Let me go ahead and call you *Carrie*," Chamblee said gently with true empathy. "But when you and" – he looked over at the information shown on the laptop to be sure of the husband's name – "Wesley, come back in a few days, we'll have everything all lined up for you. Everything will go just fine," Knox Chamblee comforted, searching for the best in bedside manner as he removed his latex surgical gloves and walked over to the waste receptacle.

"Pretty soon it will be Carrie and Wesley Sarbeck's big day!" Chamblee added as he retrieved the laptop, motioned for the assistant to help the couple from the room, and left for his private office to chart the procedure.

———————————————————

"Carrie, can't you be excited? This is it, for God's sake. This is the day they're really going to do it for us," Wesley said when they returned later to the Center.

Tinker Murtagh noticed the young couple in the lobby as they walked away from the kiosk to sit on the small upholstered couch waiting for them in a corner across the room. The actual day of embryo implantation had come. Through Tinker's electronic eyes, the two appeared far from suitable for the loveseat ahead.

"This won't be my baby, Wesley. I've told you that over and over and over again," Carrie responded, her arms folded across her chest, her face pale and stony. "It'll be yours and that woman's, but it won't be mine." Carrie thought about the picture in the photo album of the smiling blonde egg donor: a rich, beautiful person who was nothing but a delighted arrogant woman celebrating Carrie Sarbeck's loss.

As Wesley tried to pull his wife close, Tinker watched the guy place his left arm around the woman as the couple sank deeply into the richly upholstered chair. "Well, maybe the two are lovebirds, after all," the ever-optimistic Tinker said to himself, but then returned to his Sudoku puzzle.

As she seemed to relax a bit in the comfort of the cushions, Wesley resurrected a sliver of hope that Carrie was going to snap out of this. *Dammit, this is her big day, too!* he thought, but wanted to scream – the big day for her, for their, embryo implantation. Nothing had been left to nature, nothing left to chance.

From the start, Dr. Van Deman had assured them that quality control systems would assure that everything would proceed smoothly during the actual embryo implantation. They had paid him and Dr. Chamblee good money for that quality and reassurance – a lot of money, in fact, for someone on a policeman's salary; a lot of money, in fact, for anyone on any salary.

Now that the day had actually arrived, Wesley fought the sight of the grotesque murder of his future baby's genetic mother. He thought of her beautiful photograph as a blonde in Lucille Wax's album, and the nod of approval he coaxed from his depressed wife as she peeked out through the cracked open bathroom door. Miss Wax never saw the nod, but he did, and only for a moment, when Carrie seemed to avert her eyes after a cursory glance at the photograph he had selected.

The Sarbecks were now ready – at least, Wesley was ready. Over the last several weeks he had prayed for patience with his wife, but with his prayers unanswered, he was losing the battle. Carrie Sarbeck's enthusiasm over their having a baby was no longer dwindling; it was now nonexistent.

"I'm tired, Wesley," she had said without emotion when learning that her husband had written the first check payable to the Van Deman Center. "It's not about the money. It's just become all too mechanical. There's no love in it," she said in monotone. "I'm not even a part of it." The cool in her voice was not lost on Wesley, but he rallied, rationalizing her distance and lack of affection as only temporary.

"Things will be different," he had told himself throughout the fertility treatment process, and he repeated the reminder, hoping for an inkling of encouragement. "All I have to do is get Carrie pregnant just one more time, even like this, even though it seems fake. Once she's holding our baby in her arms, a baby carried to term in her own body, things will be different."

Instead of seeing the now-deceased egg donor in Lucille Wax's expensive photo album, he saw Mrs. Wesley Sarbeck. After finally becoming the mother of a healthy baby, Carrie Sarbeck again would be the girl he married, the one filled with optimism, life, and enthusiasm.

"She'll come around. I know she will."

Chapter

12

•••

THE INVESTIGATION

After an exhaustive investigation by the Jackson Police Department, the only potential witness identified at the Cheryl Choice shooting was Minor Leblanc, except that at this point the investigators had eliminated him as a suspect. After repeatedly questioning Leblanc in what he would exaggerate to others as brutal interrogation, the JPD determined that the personal shopper was simply doing his job that evening and that his job did not include murder.

The police rightfully believed his innocence, particularly when the first officer on the scene described Leblanc's shocked demeanor. Not only did Officer Wesley Sarbeck's initial discoveries help to clear Leblanc, but the DNA, fingerprint, and ballistic studies, as well as the absence of motive, cleared him as well – not to mention that the detectives simply did not consider Minor the murderous type.

Once Minor Leblanc was eliminated as a suspect, the police focused their attention on husband Gregg Choice. While his philandering would soon be uncovered, police detectives found Mr. Choice a businessman focused on achievement but still reasonably distraught over his wife's death. Choice's profitable chain of athletic clubs and retail fitness equipment outlets had begun with the locally thriving Jackson Sports Emporium, before marching across the Southeast to Atlanta and swinging up to the Highlands in North Carolina. More recent acquisitions and expansions included a facility in Santa Monica, California, and two, soon to be three, in New York City.

The necessity of being away from home to build his growing physical fitness empire had come easy for Gregg Choice, the police decided. There had been no children with his present and only wife, no children to distract him from his own interests – personal, business, or otherwise. He was home enough to attend the gala charity functions at the Jackson Country Club, to play in a sufficient number of croquet matches to keep the couple's membership current in the local Canton Wicket Society, and to sign checks for the administrative secretary who manned his small corporate office in a renovated early 1900s building on Capitol Street in downtown Jackson.

Sporting a six-foot four, muscular frame that was more striking than imposing, the blond-haired, blue-eyed Gregg Choice was a natural choice to excel in sales related to the athletic equipment and program industry. His classic, chiseled facial features were etched in the magnetism required to reel in as many male business contacts as female. Regardless of his personal business success and physical good looks, envy seldom found Gregg Choice.

A few months prior to her death, Cheryl and Gregg had celebrated their ten-year wedding anniversary. For her, the festivities consisted of joining her tennis team for lunch in honor of their first-place league record and, for him, a plane trip to Hilton Head for another ribbon-cutting ceremony. He was to unveil another exclusive health club facility there, his most upscale yet. The "cutting" was the Choice trademark mini-gala, consisting of a small herd of local exercise enthusiasts gathered via engraved invitation.

The draw was an opportunity to try out the latest in computerized cross trainer treadmills, ellipticals, vibration machines, strength training equipment, and abs devices with personal trainers on hand for instruction and health tips. Sample yoga and Pilates classes led by celebrity-guest fitness experts were in high gear in Choice's carpeted or polished wood floor classrooms that jutted off the main exercise theatre.

Freshly processed or squeezed juices – carrot, cucumber, spinach, pumpkin, watermelon, papaya, orange, and beet extracts – were available at refreshment stations scattered throughout the spacious facility with chilled bottled spring water as an alternative. Oversized apples and bananas filled custom Niermann Weeks containers for the hungry. As usual, the advertising consultants under contract to Gregg Choice arranged for extensive regional media coverage of the event, and Choice basked in the attention.

Unlike, previous years, it was no longer Cheryl's custom to accompany her husband to the posh ribbon-cutting ceremonies. However, she was not missed; there was always a girl available for the rich, charismatic Mr. Choice. When doctors upset Gregg and Cheryl with his diagnosis of male sterility after Cheryl's inability to conceive a baby with him, he had begun to flaunt that charisma with many women, undaunted.

With no apparent concern over getting a mistress or pickup girlfriend pregnant, he enjoyed the secondary benefits of his sterility but gambled dangerously with the risks of contracting and spreading sexually transmitted diseases. Through a false sense of security, his seemingly careful selection of girlfriends overrode the necessity of safe sex. As Cheryl seriously contemplated divorcing Gregg, her secret practice of donating her eggs became an even more twisted outlet of revenge against her cheating husband. By the time of Cheryl's death, she was certain of his extramarital affairs and had stopped having sex with him many months previously.

As a result of Gregg Choice's infidelity, the Jackson Police Department had come across a smorgasbord of out-of-state girlfriends in their weeks of investigating the death of his wife, and with the help of local authorities had questioned each one. All were unaware of the others, each with a verifiable alibi and each without any commitment from Cheryl's widower. Nonetheless, Mr. Gregg Choice had a solid alibi himself, courtesy of his appearance at the International Fitness Expo in Los Angeles. Serving as a featured speaker on exercise and fitness goals, his live television interview from the convention center happened to coincide with the proposed timeline of his wife's death. Consequently, the JPD had no choice than to push the charismatic Gregg Choice to the bottom of the suspect list.

At no point did Lucille Wax appear in the investigation of the murder of Cheryl Choice. Purposefully, Choice had left no records that could trace her to Miss Wax, and for fear of discrediting her own lucrative ovarian donor trade, Wax was not about to volunteer any information. Anyway, she could not fathom any connection between her client's participation in her program and the murder. Again, the tiny matter regarding Lucille's recent discovery of the jimmied door lock at the rear entrance of her office was something that she chose not to think about.

Therefore, after long weeks of homicide investigation, the murder of Cheryl Choice remained unsolved, with no major or minor suspects or any prospects. The Jackson Police Department's murder investigation would eventually settle to the dregs of the cold case files. The culprit had done a masterful job, the unnecessarily gruesome aspect of the crime adding confusion to all the possible motives and suspects.

Chapter
13
◆◆◆
THE BLUE JAY

"That girl looks like Hell," Tinker Murtagh said aloud to himself in reference to the sight of Carrie Sarbeck with Wesley and Knox Chamblee in an examination and treatment room. As he checked his laptop for the other panel screens available to him, he added, "Not much goin' on anywhere else either."

More and more, he had begun to equate his electronic surveillance of this medical facility to watching the blend of a television soap opera and a movie from the silent film era, though he had never seen the latter genre. Even without the benefit of formal introduction, Tinker Murtagh had nevertheless, by doing simple website research, grown familiar with a few of the players observed during his monitoring of the Van Deman Center. When he first took this job, broke through the encryption of the Center's surveillance system, and logged into its video files, he did what most potential patients or clients of the Van Deman Center of Reproductive Technology would do: he went to the company website. There, the link designated as *STAFF* allowed him to place names with the faces as the professional color photographs of Doctors Van Deman and Chamblee topped the two columns of secondary staff members.

Murtagh had watched as the taller, older doctor, whom he knew as Dr. Van Deman, left the room where the woman and man remained. Although he assumed the couple to be man and wife, he muttered, "Well, you never know these days."

Murtagh's mutter turned to a chuckle as he followed Van Deman down the hall, playfully alternating the camera source between front and rear views. "Gee, Fella, you really don't look as pretty now as you do on your website. No way, José!" He zoomed in, enlarging the doctor's determined face, not a stern visage, but not a happy one either. "Anyway, how old is that picture you have plastered all over the Internet, Doc?"

Van Deman rounded the next corner as his observer continued the monologue. "Oh, so you say the difference in how you look to me is just in the quality of video feed. Not enough pixels? Well, Hot Shot. You're the one who paid for this crappy system."

Tinker's laughter was so deafening that for an absurd moment he feared that Van Deman would hear him. The thought then garnered another laugh, even louder than before.

"OK, OK, Oh Brilliant One," he persisted as Van Deman slowed in the corridor to stop at the next closed door. "Maybe you're right, Doc. The reason you don't look as good is that I'm forced to view you only in black and white. Never will see you in color, you know. At least, not in the flesh," he said as his laughter dropped to a chuckle as Henry Van Deman seemed to rap once on the door before entering the room.

Waiting inside was Allyn Saxton. She had been lying supine on the examination table, waiting for Van Deman, clutching the sheet that covered her lower half. When hearing the door open, she sat up on the edge of the table just as Tinker clicked to bring the interior of the large room into full view. Assuming it to be rarely used, Tinker was surprised that he had never before been inside this space. However, by referencing the building's layout grid, it had been effortless to pinpoint Van Deman's new location and bring up the room panel to full panoramic view.

While the doctor appeared to greet the woman waiting in the room, Tinker scanned the space, realizing that the large area was equipped similarly to the previous room he had been surveying, the one containing the younger doctor and the male and female couple. He kept that last examination room pulled up, but reduced it to the lower right-hand corner of the computer screen. She was the same woman Murtagh had seen earlier that morning, entering the front entrance wearing a wide-brimmed hat that he thought looked less than discount-store quality.

Having found the woman's dress more intriguing than the day's number puzzle, he had followed her from the parking lot, observing every angle as the oversized chapeau was no match for the facility's multi-directional 2.4GHz surveillance cameras. He saw her face and body from every perspective and confirmed her identity.

When Tinker first had the revelation that the hit involved was Allyn Saxton, the name at the outset meant little to someone who paid little attention to celebrity. Then the name rang a bell from a popular TV comedy airing a few years back, leading Murtagh to discover that the website of one of the major television networks offered free reruns of the show. Between crossword and Sudoku puzzles, Murtagh enjoyed a couple of episodes of the 1980s sitcom that preceded the star's major break into cinema.

His client had supplied some background information detailing that Allyn Saxton had received several treatments at the Center prior to his taking this job. Even though Tinker was not a scientist, at least not a medical scientist, lots of doctor visits sounded reasonable to him, considering the ultimate plan of the old sitcom star.

Van Deman had designed Saxton's room and the identical

treatment room where Chamblee and the Sarbecks remained to be adjacent to the microscopy lab and the embryo storage facility. An airtight passage, no more spacious than a shoebox and similarly shaped, had been installed at counter height in the shared wall between the two treatment rooms and the laboratory.

Doctors Van Deman and Chamblee utilized this chamber as a transfer mechanism when harvesting human eggs. After retrieving the eggs from the donor's ovarian follicles in the treatment room under the guidance of an ultrasound or sonogram, the physician would then use sterile technique to place them into a Petri dish.

The dish and its cargo were then gently placed inside the chamber, and with the door closed, the chamber itself was left airtight. This maneuver ensured that the positive pressure system inside the embryo culture lab on the opposite side of the wall was maintained, permitting its state-of-the-art filtration system to remove even the finest of solid particles from the air.

Such quality controls were designed and proven to eliminate contamination from all sources – thus the facility's designation as a laboratory of distinction by the International College of Laboratory Sciences, a certification proudly displayed on a wall plaque in the lobby. With the aid of this design, along with the implementation of rigid antisepsis, airborne contaminants were prevented from entering the embryo culture room. As a result of these airtight controls, Drs. Van Deman and Chamblee produced human blastocysts of the highest quality.

While Tinker maintained his watch of Van Deman and the Saxton woman, Chamblee was attending the Sarbecks upon their return to a nearby room. Wesley had somehow coaxed his wife from the lobby into proceeding with the day's scheduled implantation of the actual embryos.

"But, Doctor, I don't want to get AIDS." Knox was taken aback by the wife's panicky interruption as she held open a celebrity magazine, particularly when she had been so strangely silent during their previous encounter and again today, up to that point. "Mrs. Sarbeck, there's no cause for concern. Your donor's oocytes, or eggs, were cryopreserved, you see. That's something that not all fertility centers can do," he reassured.

Carrie Sarbeck remained stricken.

"You see," Dr. Chamblee continued, focusing his attention on Carrie but including Wesley, "all egg and sperm donors, no matter who they are or where they have come from, are thoroughly screened for STDs – Chlamydia, gonorrhea, syphilis, hepatitis, in addition to HIV – those words may be offensive, but are factors that must be considered in this day and time. Also, by successfully freezing the freshly harvested eggs, we can wait out the longer incubation period associated with the AIDS virus should the donor have been exposed and her test not yet showing positive."

"See, Carrie, that's not a problem. Getting AIDS from this whole thing is not a concern," Wesley reinforced. He had studied all of the printed information supplied by the Center and was well aware of the rigid egg donor screening and follow-up. Per signed agreement with their donor, the doctors were to run an HIV blood test on her six months after the actual donation to allow for the typical viral incubation period to pass, making sure that the donor's AIDS test remained negative. "Has a scare of getting that been your problem with this from the get-go?" Wesley Sarbeck released his wife's hand and walked around the room in a tight circle, totally perplexed.

Carrie Sarbeck failed to answer as she pictured the blue jay smashing its beak against her bathroom window. Had she responded, the answer would have been, "No."

Assuming the infection issue settled, Knox Chamblee pushed on. He had another embryo transfer to perform within the next hour. "As I said earlier, once the donor's eggs have been fertilized and the cells start to divide, we check them daily. In fact, the same technician is assigned to each particular case so that there is little variance during the observation process. So, when the technician detected at least eight divided cells in your embryos, then the blastocyst soon followed, and here we all are, ready for transfer."

"That's what we're going to do today. Isn't that right, Doctor?"

To his surprise, Carrie had again spoken, though her voice was weak. "Yes, that's right, Mrs. Sarbeck. We went through an implantation trial during your last cycle, on Day 19. Therefore, you and your husband are here today for the real thing. Our high-powered microscope has detected eight divided cells or more in each embryo, just like I showed you before in the digital photographs. Happily, we have several healthy blastocysts for transfer and implantation into your uterus."

Carrie said nothing in response. Instead, she returned to her magazine, which Knox noticed to have remained on the same page as earlier – an article on Allyn Saxton.

"So, we do have that now, Doctor? Don't we?" Wesley asked, still perplexed as he looked over at his wife, now idly thumbing through the magazine.

"Yes, we do." Knox felt as though he was hopelessly repeating himself, but, nevertheless, forced patience. "In your case, we will be transferring two blastocyst embryos. They are extremely healthy-looking. Here, take a look at your actual embryonic blastocysts." Knox popped a couple of keys on the computer and the evidence materialized on the wall monitor.

"Are two enough to put into Carrie, Dr. Chamblee?" Wesley asked without as much as a glance at the blue, round-shaped structures on the flat screen that appeared exactly to him as the ones he was shown the other day. Carrie looked up from the magazine at him, her stare now penetrating.

"Yes, as healthy as your embryos are, two should be sufficient. In the case of older female recipients, we sometimes transfer three or more."

"Damn you, Wesley!" Carrie Sarbeck flung the magazine at her shocked partner. "What do you think I am, a damned rabbit, or maybe a hamster?" Her husband silently fielded the opened copy of *Inside Beauty* before it knocked over a container of hand washing liquid on a nearby counter.

"Uh, well, I see," Chamblee remained smooth. "I guess then that two will be OK – with you both?"

Carrie reserved comment, her complexion somewhere between pink and boiling lobster red. Her husband calmly refolded the magazine and returned it to the nearby magazine rack. "Yeah, we're ready, Doctor. Just go ahead and get it over with," Wesley nodded as he spoke, his reply a mixture of disgust and frustration with a just hint of defeat.

Chamblee pushed ahead with the procedure as the lab tech joined them in the room with the needed supplies, including the embryos. "Don't worry. Just like in the trial run, this won't be any more uncomfortable than getting a Pap smear," the doctor said as Carrie groaned.

Meanwhile, Tinker Murtagh was more interested in what was transpiring in the adjacent room between Dr. Van Deman and Allyn Saxton. Earlier in the job, Murtagh had considered slipping into the building in advance and installing some additional surveillance equipment. Although he was not surprised that Van Deman's private office was not fitted with cameras like the other areas, he still resented being barred from that space.

He had flipped from screen to screen, following Saxton from the moment she had entered the parking lot that day and walked to the building's front entrance. After she left the patient waiting area, she had spent only a relatively short time in Van Deman's office before moving to the examination room.

"Stay focused, man," Murtagh said aloud to himself – the same admonishment issued whenever he watched the other patients' examinations, particularly when the doctor or one of the nurses opened a condom package to cover the sonogram probe just as Van Deman was doing now. He had learned to think of the probe as a *vaginal ultrasound transducer* after an Internet search led him to the appropriate term. The ultrasound or sonogram probe looked like something else to Tinker, something that he would never expect to see covered with a condom.

Tinker was relieved that she had come back from California and this was to be one of her last visits to the Center, maybe the very last. His job was nearly finished. He smiled, thinking about the money he was going to make, not his usual stipend, but enough. The order had been simple, and he would carry it out with ease because he was Tinker Murtagh. *Just get all of it. I don't care how you do it – just get all of it.*

Tinker then refocused on the preliminaries to that money as he watched Van Deman leave Saxton on the examination table and enter the embryo culture room through the short hall. After first donning a disposable surgical cap and shoe covers, the doctor next dressed in face mask and surgical gloves. While Murtagh had noticed others doing the same when entering, this was the first time he had seen Van Deman at all inside the embryo culture room. Typically, the same two women employees performed all the work in that area, sitting for hours staring into microscopes and typing information into computers.

In contrast, the embryo culture room was at the moment free of employees. Rushing to the work space counter, Van Deman pushed aside the waiting chairs and hurriedly entered several commands on the keyboard of the nearest computer. Since the lab's computers were not networked with the Internet, Murtagh was unable to log in directly to Van Deman's screen and, therefore, had no remote control view of Van Deman's computer work. As had been the case with the two regular lab employees, Tinker was forced to manipulate the room's security camera to peer at any information displayed on the computer monitor.

Today was an even greater challenge. In the case of Van Deman, his standing to bend over the computer screen and keyboard rather than sitting at the counter forced Murtagh to strain the camera around the back of the doctor's head and back to visualize what he was doing. In cat-and-mouse fashion, Murtagh traced the doctor's every action with the high powered, hidden camera. *Van Deman knows the camera is here; he has to. He built this building*, thought Tinker.

As he expected, Murtagh prevailed. While Van Deman continued to pound the keyboard, Tinker followed the electronic images popping in rapid succession in front of the physician and recognized the display as the same electronic forms used by the laboratory personnel. Titled with apparent patient names and medical record numbers, the information was flanked by a small digital photograph inserted as further client identification.

Henry Van Deman halted abruptly when the name *Mary Smith* appeared in the upper left-hand corner of one of the electronic pages, followed, as expected, by a medical record number that was actually a short combination of numerals and letters. Recognizing the photo of Mary Smith as that of Allyn Saxton, Murtagh jotted her patient ID number in a blank space found on the front cover of his new Sudoku book.

In addition, he scribbled the column headings: *PRE-CYCLE PROTOCOL, OVULATION PROTOCOL, LUTEAL SUPPORT PROTCOL* in a tight space on the back. Tinker read the headings aloud, stumbling through most of the pronunciations as Van Deman scrolled through the electronic form, replete with more terms and lined spaces to the point that it resembled an Internet merchandise ordering form.

Tinker remained focused on Van Deman's computer screen as he zoomed in and around the doctor's torso, spotting other prominently displayed numbers and letters, his efforts aided when his subject began to alternate attention between the computer and the laboratory's large microscope resting nearby on the counter. Labeled as *Day 1* though *Day 18* were other columns and tables filled with abbreviated information that meant little if anything to Tinker Murtagh as he studied the magnified monitor. Van Deman scrolled down until he reached a space entitled *Cryopreservation*. As the doctor's hand moved the cursor to the right, Tinker slowly pronounced C*ryopreservation* and felt proud at what he assumed was a bona fide effort.

To the right side of the screen was a string of capitalized words followed by symbols: *Egg Harvest #, Frozen #, Successful Thaw #, Non-Viable Egg #, Embryo Cell #*, and *Blastocyst #*. Then followed the headings: *Date Thawed, Date Fertilized*, and *Date of Transfer*. Murtagh assumed correctly that these areas stored the information related to the number of eggs obtained, the number frozen and thawed for later use, and then the number that were actually fertilized and grew. From what he could see, he clearly understood that the stored information pertained to patient Allyn Saxton.

"Yeah, this is it," Murtagh triumphantly announced to himself.

Van Deman then shifted his body, inadvertently blocking Murtagh's view. It only took seconds for Van Deman to stop the cursor and enter some information on the computer's key pad. "Shit, I can't tell what he's doing. Anyway, doesn't matter. All I need to see is the entry code to that freezer," Tinker exploded.

As Murtagh strained unsuccessfully to follow Van Deman's every move, the physician used the fourth finger of his right hand to hit *Delete* in the *Successful Egg Thaw* column. As fast as the numeral *7* vanished from that data space, Van Deman replaced it with a *2*. He next entered the numeric differences in the *Non-Viable Egg* column, which suddenly registered *5* instead of *0*.

Despite all the computer wizardry strewn throughout the Center, Tinker was dumbfounded to catch Van Deman next pull a sheet of self-adhesive paper labels from a drawer in the cabinet below the work surface, grab an ordinary pen from the holder by the computer, and hurriedly write something on the label at the top of the page. After peeling away the label, Van Deman sprinted to the oddly shaped unit that Tinker knew as the embryo freezer, the same area that earlier disappointed him when the action there failed to become pornographic. He thought about the liquid nitrogen delivery man and the cute female employee who had followed the guy a few days ago as he serviced the embryo freezer.

Tinker redirected with high-power focused zoom as he caught the doctor entering a numbered security code on the lighted LCD panel embedded on the front of the freezer. Tinker made a note of the code. As the freezer responded and the top of the unit rose deliberately to meet him, Van Deman adhered the small paper label to the thin clear cylinder held in his left hand and returned it to the embryo storage unit.

Murtagh had never been interested in the frozen semen stored in the lower levels that contained potentially viable sperm. It was the female counterpart tucked away in the upper section of the counter-high machine that was his monetary target – the single tiny compartment assigned to 1216DS – the compartment assigned to Allyn Saxton, not Mary Smith.

Despite swift direction of the camera to what Van Deman had manually printed on the paper label, Murtagh was successful only in capturing the freezer's security code. However, he was certain of one fact: the embryos that the important doctor had returned to that freezer belonged to Allyn Saxton.

"There, I hope that was not too uncomfortable, Mrs. Sarbeck,"
Knox Chamblee said, as the assistant followed his insertion
of the embryo transfer catheter with an abdominal sonogram
transducer. Consisting of an inner and other sheath, the flexible,
cylindrical device passed easily as expected to within one
centimeter of the top of Carrie's medically primed uterus. In
contrast to the egg harvesting procedure, this technique generally
produced minimal patient discomfort, obviating the need for
analgesic premedication. Such was the situation for Mrs. Wesley
Sarbeck; she did not flinch.

As Chamblee proceeded with the planned transfer of the two
healthy Sarbeck blastocysts through the uterine catheter, Carrie
Sarbeck remained stone-faced. Her steady, shallow breathing
reassured Knox that she was physically stable and without pain.
Gee, what a flat affect! he thought again in amazement, and
then checked the husband, whose facial expression repetitively
projected complete fascination with the proceedings. Wesley
Sarbeck firmly held Carrie's limp hand as the sonogram
technician traced the release of the catheter's fluid into the
extremes of his wife's womb.

"Look, Carrie, that's our baby. It might even be our babies,"
Wesley's excited emphasis on the plural accentuated the emotion
in his voice. Focusing on the broad video monitor, mesmerized
at the miracle on display, Wesley ignored his wife's indifference
as she merely stared blankly ahead. Carrie saw and felt nothing
in particular as a clear shield abruptly covered her face. Moments
later, the hysterical blue jay reappeared, pounding mercilessly
against the clear covering as it had done against her bathroom
window.

Maybe she had been wrong all along, she thought, watching

the panic-stricken bird smear the shield like it had previously done on her window. Maybe the bird had not been trying to tell her something or to change her but really desired to harm her, to stop her. Now he bird's actions seemed much more direct, even vengeful. Maybe the bird wanted to protect these embryos that had just been forced into her, protect them from a fate similar to that of their real mother.

"When is this gonna be over?" an aggravated Carrie Sarbeck broke her silence as she mentally shooed away the frantic blue jay.

In the lower right hand corner of his laptop screen, the Sarbeck saga continued to play silently for a disinterested Murtagh. He had missed the motions of Chamblee's instructions to Carrie to lie motionless on the treatment table for twenty minutes, preferably thirty, now that the embryo transfer procedure had been successfully accomplished. He also missed the patient's response.

"Not a problem," Carrie remarked softly, in defeat. "I'll just lie here motionless for you, Doctor. Sure, I'll lie very still – right here until I die."

"Next we'll need for you to take estrogen and progesterone hormones," Chamblee moved on, ignoring the remark and inwardly wanting to punch Van Deman for recruiting this weird situation.

"For how long, Dr. Chamblee?" the anticipation was obvious in Wesley's voice.

"For 12, maybe 14 days. Then we hope to ...," Chamblee hesitated, "... No, let's certainly be optimistic. We will have a positive pregnancy test at that time. Then, as soon as we document a viable pregnancy by sonogram, we will get the two of you to an obstetrician."

Wesley Sarbeck smiled at the doctor's words as he let his wife's hand go. His was a confident, victorious smile.

By now, Van Deman had returned to Allyn Saxton's room, where the procedures and patient instructions would be the same as those for Carrie Sarbeck. Purposefully he scheduled no assistant, his design to remain alone with Saxton throughout her treatment. Having performed the procedure countless times with a successful pregnancy rate approaching 100 percent, he was undoubtedly capable of controlling the sonogram transducer and simultaneously completing the embryo transfer without an assistant. He alone had prepared the two blastocysts for the embryo transfer.

Saxton had done her part to ready her body. After the initial evaluation and instruction at the Van Deman Center, she had returned to California to administer the self-injectable vials of hormones and swallow the oral medication as directed and shipped to her by Dr. Van Deman. While it had been Saxton's intention that her efforts remain cloaked in secrecy, she believed she and her doctor had done well in that regard also.

The news that followed was disturbing, at least at first, her disappointment apparent as Dr. Van Deman entered the room. "The intracytoplasmic sperm injection process, or what we refer to as *ICSI*, technically went well indeed," he announced. "Two eggs were successfully penetrated by your donor's sperm. I observed the process myself. Unfortunately, we had only two eggs to work with; the other five failed to survive the freezing and thaw process."

The actress in Allyn Saxton relied on her talents to stave off her disillusionment. "But, Dr. Van Deman, you took seven eggs from me. I saw those eggs on the sonogram you did. What happened?" The news was not all bad, she realized. It definitely could have been worse. Besides, she had never been able to conceive with a human being; why should she expect a machine and some magic potions to work to the contrary?

"Well, you're right, Miss Saxton," Van Deman was dogmatic. "We successfully harvested seven fresh ova from your ovaries last year after you underwent ovulation induction protocol. And we were prepared to proceed at that time with fertilization and embryo implantation into your uterus as you had originally planned with us."

"I know. I know," she interrupted. "But I changed my mind. I ... I got cold feet. It's just that simple. I got cold feet."

"We here at the Center understand how that can happen. Becoming a parent is a serious thing even when it happens of your own volition – spontaneously – with or without planning. And it can be ..."

"A scary thing," Allyn interrupted. "At least that's what it became for me at that time. I can get so emotional. Sometimes it has to do with the role I'm playing; I think I was reading a script about an autistic child or something like that when I decided to call off the embryo implantation. I just couldn't go through with it then – wasn't sure if I really wanted to be pregnant after all."

"For that reason we then offered to freeze your eggs, a process that not all reproductive facilities can afford their patients. And I, we, have perfected the process. Your seven eggs were freshly frozen until you were ready to get them back; however, as I said, only two survived the thaw process."

Van Deman had viewed a recent television documentary studying the facial expressions and eyebrow movements of a politician suspected of not telling the truth. He hoped that unlike the politician, his own countenance matched that of legitimacy. "So we had only two eggs available at this time to fertilize with the sperm of the donor you selected. I'm sorry. Less than perfect is not the norm around here."

Allyn Saxton smiled at Dr. Van Deman. She had grown more comfortable with him, even though she had never really felt uncomfortable. Her selection of an infertility specialist from the Internet had turned out to be a good one. There was no doubt that Henry Van Deman, MD, was a smart man, one with an outstanding record of success in his specialty. Once she had decided to renew her efforts to get pregnant, Allyn was grateful that he had preserved her eggs in case her plans changed. Not only had he saved her from having to restart the entire process, she was a year younger when she had created the eggs – a year that could be subtracted from her advancing maternal age.

On the other hand, Allyn felt the shadow of lost optimism over Van Deman's unexpected news today. "Dr. Van Deman," Allyn began, fighting the quiver in her voice, "you explained to me once that you prefer to transfer four embryos in cases like mine, cases in which the woman is older. So, if I just receive two, what should I realistically expect? It seems like that literally cuts my chances in half of this happening at all – that I'll get pregnant this time."

"Generally, we do transfer four blastocysts or embryos in cases of higher maternal age and hope that at least one implants and survives," Van Deman replied. "But in many of those situations, the person has chosen to proceed with the treatment against higher odds, such as in cases of chronic health problems or even more advanced maternal age. For example, many patients are actually in their mid-forties or older and are smokers. Some suffer from high blood pressure, are overweight, or have other issues. Of course, in your case, Allyn, none of that applies to you."

Van Deman paused for a few moments, hoping that some of his speech had sunk in. He had chosen his words carefully. Seeing Saxton's worried face relax a bit, he felt somewhat relieved as well. "Even though we were successful in obtaining only two healthy embryos in your case, Allyn, your prospect of having at least one healthy baby is nearly certain. You realize, of course, that you may be blessed with a twin pregnancy – don't you?"

Allyn nodded. She was feeling better as confidence in her body and Dr. Van Deman was returning.

"Today we are fortunate to transfer two healthy blastocysts from the pair of eggs that did survive and for the reasons just discussed, it remains highly likely that both transferred embryos will find favor in your uterus and grow. We could see the birth of two healthy babies – barring any unusual obstetrical complications, of course," Van Deman cautioned. Then with a subtle grin he continued to elaborate in a feeble attempt at humor. "It does seem strange that the OB guys consider someone like you as at an advanced maternal age. You, Miss Saxton, look to be in your twenties."

"Oh, thank you, Dr. Van Deman," Allyn blushed. She suddenly felt 80.

"Allyn, perhaps there is one thing that we have not discussed fully."

"What is that, Dr. Van Deman?" Allyn's thoughts had drifted backward for a few moments, back to the question of whether or not she was actually doing the right thing. She wondered if she really understood the ramifications of this artificial fertilization and of finally becoming a mother.

"I just mentioned that twins are a very real possibility. But should the fertilized eggs split, then we, I mean you, could wind up with triplets, or rarer, quadruplets."

"Dr. Van Deman, oh, please! Please, stop there." Allyn raised both hands, palms facing forward similar to a cop halting traffic. "You better go ahead and get this over with before I change my mind again."

Allyn then reclined per instructions and Van Deman began the embryo transfer procedure. She accepted the doctor's offer to observe the process on the video monitor, the same implantation procedure that Carrie Sarbeck had received in the other embryo transfer room. Yet Allyn Saxton did not absorb the sonographic image of the catheter sliding into her uterus, nor did she feel it. Instead she concentrated on her decision to have this procedure and the resulting change in her life that would result. In so doing she tried to envision the face of the anonymous Caucasian donor she had chosen from the bank of frozen sperm available through the Van Deman Center.

Unhindered by any obligation to match the physical characteristics of a spouse or even a significant other, she had fought the banality of choosing an Adonis, Greek-god physical type; but nevertheless still came close with her selection of a six foot-two, graduate student in the arts who played intramural soccer and basketball. He was also identified as an accomplished pianist and guitarist with thick, dark hair complete with a slight natural curl. Once more, there was no known family history of genetic defects or hereditary illness, nor even a tendency toward male-patterned baldness.

Before proceeding with injection and fertilization of her ova by this particular man, Allyn was reassured that the donor's banked sperm had been successfully thawed and used for impregnation on three previous occasions, each time successful. All three clients, none of whom lived on or near the West Coast, were well-satisfied with the results.

Van Deman noticed that Saxton had remained perfectly at ease, no labored breathing, no signs of anxiety. She seemed resigned to receiving only two of her embryos on this day instead of the expected four, though she had listened thoroughly to his instructions and had followed his treatment advice to the letter. Allyn Saxton would be pregnant with at least one baby, maybe two, or maybe more if the two transferred embryos should divide spontaneously. In today's discussion with his movie star patient, Van Deman had been sincere in his prediction.

That was where his sincerity ended. Dr. Van Deman never intended to implant more than two embryos. It was true that when Saxton chose to discontinue the fertilization process months ago, all of Allyn's harvested eggs were frozen just as Van Deman had promised. However, his promises stopped there.

Van Deman held steadfast in the belief that Saxton would finally resume her plans for *in vitro* fertilization. While it had been difficult to delay his own plans, he did not want to jeopardize some semblance of success for this prominent client. When he found her ova so receptive to the thawing and fertilization procedure which followed, he decided that healthy Allyn Saxton would have a satisfactory pregnancy with the implantation of only two embryos.

Consequently, the remaining five eggs thought lost by Allyn Saxton were fertilized to wait safely in a dehydrated state, stored inside tiny straws within the embryo freezer unit. Organized and labeled per code, the eggs lay suspended at the six-cell stage of growth courtesy of a special solution kept frigid by liquid nitrogen. Van Deman felt confident that the additional five embryos harbored the same potential to grow into full-term babies, just as did the two actually returned to Saxton. Before being implanted, all that the remaining, precious embryos would need was a 12-hour thaw and a recipient other that Allyn Saxton.

Through the watchful eye of Van Deman's own cameras, Murtagh had observed the day's entire physician-patient interaction. Except for the consultations with Allyn Saxton in his private office and the couple of times the doctor had been to the men's room, Tinker had missed none of Van Deman's movements and had found nothing out of the ordinary – just business as usual.

However, Tinker's ignorance led him to miss the true significance of the doctor's seclusion in the embryo culture room.

During the 12 critical hours before Saxton's procedure when Van Deman labored there alone at times, Tinker observed what seemed to him to represent no more than routine medical or research procedures. In his eyes, Van Deman was merely flipping between the room's computer keyboard, large microscope, and freezer in the embryo culture lab. Tinker's downfall would be that during that 12-hour period there was no technician or other physician to interfere with Van Deman's actions.

Chapter
14

•••

THE SPILL

Mia did not argue with her afternoon assignment to handle the patient checkout window. Since her clandestine morning invasion of the embryo storage area with the deliveryman, she had walked softly around the Center, failing to refuse any clerical task or errand. Once more, she expected no mileage reimbursement when she drove her own car on those errands. She wanted no trouble. Despite her constant paranoia, no one ever mentioned her infraction of the off-limits-area rules.

As the weeks passed, Mia became more comfortable in believing that no one other than Rizzo, the liquid nitrogen delivery man, knew anything about it. Since another guy had replaced him, she assumed that he had quit over the extra route and his resulting marital difficulties. Having had no further contact with Rizzo, she felt her secret safe – but she would take nothing for granted.

The fact that the Center's administrator was passing along increased daily responsibilities to Mia advanced her perception of trust. Of course, neither the other employees, the administrator, nor Mia –not even Knox Chamblee – knew of the tireless security cameras with or without the attached Tinker Murtagh, nor did they know of the digital video records of her infraction.

The recording of her rules violation remained sealed in storage, of interest to no one, particularly not Tinker, who lost interest when she did not have sex with the delivery guy. While Van Deman's dreams of a state-of-the-art fertility center had included this Big Brother concept, he had never found the need to access the archived security footage, the longevity of which was determined by the storage capacity of the digital system.

Mia had remained the first employee on site every morning, punctual in her promise to have the building open for the other employees. After her ritualistic wipe down of the employee break room and kitchen with disinfectant, she used the remaining extra time to peruse the *Help Wanted* section in the newspaper – just in case she needed an opening.

In spite of the addition of job hunting to her morning ritual, Mia failed to spot any opportunity that matched her present compensation and benefits, while she promised herself that if the opportunity arose, she was out of there.

"I'm using another one of those throwaway cell phones to call you," Van Deman said after leaving the treatment section of the building complex and exiting a rear entrance onto the enclosed patio area. There he could talk privately, since no employee breaks were scheduled during that time. Once more, patients never drifted through the door to the patio with its threatening designation *Center Personnel Only - Emergency No Exit Only*. The doctor's call could be as long as thirty minutes while Saxton remained completely motionless during the required post-embryo transfer period, keeping her legs elevated on the treatment table, waiting for her doctor to return.

The interaction between Van Deman and Saxton stalled for the moment, Murtagh needed a bathroom break himself and decided this was as good a time as any.

"My private office line is designed to be secure, but there would be phone records in case she gets suspicious later. But that's not going to happen. I've got her convinced. You remember, of course, that I've got a great Doctor's bedside manner." Van Deman issued a weak laugh that was not reciprocated as he stood on the patio and continued on the cell phone.

"Yes, the remaining five embryos that I fertilized were perfect when they underwent the freezing process," he continued. "You need to lighten up a bit over this," he spoke into the piece of numbered plastic that had cost him $28 at Target. The question from the other end was predictable.

"Of course, the five embryos are absolutely genuine Allyn Saxton, 50 percent, that is. As soon as they are thawed, they should resume the cellular division process at exactly the stage at which I halted it. Just as the two thawed embryos that Saxton actually received will flourish, the growth of the others will be jumpstarted as well, as though they had been freshly harvested ready for implantation."

Van Deman anticipated the question which followed and answered before asked, "Our records will clearly reflect that the other five eggs she left in storage failed to thaw properly and were destroyed as mandated." There was a pause as Van Deman wrinkled his face in aggravation, "Oh, yes. The Van Deman Center will survive any audit."

The conversation progressed. "This thing worked well when we were living together in New York, and it'll work well down here. As long as you don't divulge the true origin of the embryos, no one will ever suspect a thing. It's OK for the buyer to think that they originated from a movie star and were fertilized by a tall, blonde-and-handsome doctor like me, but it has to stop there. We can grow this embryo reassignment deal into a nice little sideline cash business, even better than before." Van Deman laughed in satisfaction while his former business partner and lover on the other end skipped the joke. "Don't worry," he continued. "Lighten up. You wanted to resume this trade, and now it's happening."

For a moment Van Deman assumed that the call had been dropped, but then he heard an *OK* in response. "Look, I'll keep you in the loop and let you know when her pregnancy test is positive. Now that we have completed the transfer, Saxton will have to take some more hormone meds, estrogen and progesterone, along with low-dose aspirin – nothing that she hasn't had to do already to get this far. Once she's happily pregnant with a singleton or twins, she'll quit thinking about her long-lost, other five embryos. "

Silence resounded from the other end, though Van Deman thought he might have heard a sigh.

"The next few weeks will tell. I'm confident that everything will move along smoothly from this point." Van Deman was sure he detected an even more pronounced sigh at that point, although the coverage with the throwaway cell was not as reliable as that of his usual vendor. "I'll call you when we have evidence of fetal heart activity by ultrasound. Remember, you're working with Henry Van Deman."

The Center's administrator had assigned Mia magazine duty, a tedious task, but one she considered well-suited for Miss Evans. Aware of Mia's obsession with order and cleanliness, the administrator assumed the young woman qualified to gather magazines strewn about the building over the past several days and return them to the central patient waiting area. Most of the day's patients who had already checked in for procedures or evaluation had finished and departed the building, leaving many of the treatment rooms empty and free for retrieval of discarded periodicals.

The assignment was one of the menial ones; Mia knew that, but nevertheless welcomed the opportunity to get moving, circulate, and free herself from the phone or assisting patients with using the Center's computerized check-in kiosk. As she left the front area of the building and began walking the corridors, she wished for her iPod and recently downloaded collection of Danye West songs. "Boy, getting caught around here jiving with earplugs – that would land me out on the street for sure!" Mia laughed wryly to herself.

The cellular service provider remained unclear at intervals, but despite the broken syllables Henry Van Deman understood and responded, "Yes, I'm sure Saxton is not suspicious, not suspicious in any way."

Still concerned, the voice hesitated, clearly not as confident as Van Deman and beginning to regret his pushing to resume their *little sideline, cash business* as Van Deman now called it. When Allyn Saxton was on location in Manhattan a couple of years ago, he had done her hair, wardrobe, and makeup and had gotten to know her well. She did not strike him then as the naïve, gullible type – except in her choice of men.

"Well, I will admit that initially the patient did appear disappointed at my news that only two blastocysts had survived. *Au contraire*, when I explained to her that the two available for implantation were as robust as any I have ever produced, Miss Saxton seemed more than satisfied, particularly when I informed her that her embryo transfer had proceeded nicely and that having twins was likely. Be optimistic. Saxton will never suspect a thing, and neither will anyone else."

Mia stopped to retrieve an empty Diet Coke can resting atop an open issue of *Architectural Digest*, the messiness left on an end table squeezed between two loveseats. As she lifted the can, wishing that she had brought along a small garbage sack, she noticed Dr. Van Deman through the window. He was standing alone on the back patio, talking on a cell phone, seemingly immersed in the conversation, as he used hand gestures and cutting arm movements for emphasis. Mia had never seen either of the doctors in that area commonly used by employees.

"He's got such a nice office over there," she flipped her free hand in the direction up the hall. There was no one around to hear her comments, as her thoughts raced. "Why would he want to go out there and use the cell phone? I guess the cell reception isn't as good inside as out. I'd never know 'cause Big Sista won't let us use our cell phones inside on the job.

"You can't tell me big-bad Van Deman would stand for crummy cell signals anywhere around this place, 'specially not in his own swanky office!" Mia defied in soliloquy. As she placed her hands on her hips, bent at the wrists, the not-quite-empty Diet Coke can she was holding in her right hand tilted forward. The last slurp of thin brown fluid splattered to the floor at the foot of the patio door, but not before spotting her skirt and shoes.

"Damn! I just washed and dried this thing," Mia nearly shrieked, catching herself. Relieved to see the contents of a nearly empty Kleenex box on the table, she reached for the last of the fresh sheets and looked down to wipe her dress and shoes. Next would come the floor. "I hope the lazy, sloppy so-and-so who left this can is satisfied," she muttered as she wiped furiously, wishing for a paper towel since the Kleenex did not withstand her obsessive blotting.

"Like I said, I'll call you when my patient's pregnancy test is positive. You'll know that Allyn Saxton is pregnant even before the media," Van Deman said as he reentered the building. The door to the patio opened as Mia picked tiny wads of tan-colored Kleenex from the floor. So intense was her effort that she did not see Dr. Van Deman coming toward her.

"Let's don't talk any more until then. You let me handle Allyn Saxton." As Van Deman clicked off and said, "Bye," he was glancing back at the patio, as though checking to see if he was being followed. Until now having had no doubts about pushing ahead with plans to withhold Saxton's embryos and broker them through his old boyfriend, the battle with the developing indecisiveness had left him a bit shaken.

"What the hell!" spewed Van Deman to the resistance felt against his right leg when entering the hall from the patio, headed in the direction of Saxton's treatment room. So determined had been his step that the tall, lanky physician in his upper fifties was unable to avoid the light-skinned black girl, hurdling over her in a maneuver so smooth that it appeared to have been rehearsed.

Mia's scream was more from shock than from the pain of Van Deman's affront to her shoulder. As they collided, the doctor's cell phone flew from his hand, breaking into several pieces as it bounced along the floor. Not realizing the device was a throwaway, Mia was more concerned over the potential loss of the boss's expensive cell phone than of the damage to her throbbing shoulder.

His anger and surprise were obvious. "I was having a private conversation out there. What are you doing here anyway, young lady, Miss ...?"

"Mia. My name is Mia Evans."

"I don't care what you damn name is. Were you trying to eavesdrop on my private conversation?"

"Oh, no, sir, I wasn't," Mia answered, forgetting about the remaining mess on her clothes and the floor, her voice so weak with shock and fear that she was not quite sure that she had even replied. "I promise I wasn't listening," Mia emphasized, hearing words come out of her mouth this time. She thought for a moment, trying to see if she could even remember anything the doctor had been saying as the door opened. His words were so rapid, so bossy. He had said the word *saxton*, no, the name *Allyn Saxton*.

"Sir, I didn't even know you were out there," she lied. "I was told to go around the building and pick up magazines. I always do as I am told." Van Deman maintained his stern, suspicious stare as she grasped for a better explanation. "I ... I stopped here to get that Diet Coke can," she paused, pointing to the now dented aluminum that had bounced down the hall during the collision. "I didn't realize that it wasn't completely empty, so a little spilled."

In retort, Van Deman glanced around, finding the floor in the immediate vicinity spotless, except for the area near the soft drink can.

Mia struggled, "I am a very neat person. I wiped up all of it with a couple of tissues. I promise, sir."

"You know, young lady, I do need to know your name. Here, stand closer so I can read your employee ID badge to be sure I've got it." Mia obeyed, accidentally dropping a few bits of wadded Kleenex from her trembling, delicate hands. "*Mia Evans*," Van Deman read from the plastic badge clipped to the right collar of her blouse. "That's a nice name. I don't think I've ever known any Evanses."

"My folks are from Milwaukee, originally."

"Oh, I see. Well, Miss, I guess it is *Miss* Evans?" Van Deman summarized rhetorically, with a satisfactory sense of resolution that even Mia could detect. He looked down at her coldly. "Why don't you just go on back to Milwaukee, because ... you're fired!"

Van Deman picked up the cracked cell phone and let it drop into the side pocket of his white lab jacket as he pushed his way around the girl, leaving a few small pieces of black plastic in his wake. Although he did not physically touch her as he walked past, the air seemed to part with such force that Evans' body shook, knocking open her clenched hand and tossing the remaining bits of paper back to the floor.

"Oh, my Lord! What did I do?" Mia asked in disbelief, but not loud enough for the fast-paced Dr. Van Deman to hear, had he cared.

By then, the chief doctor had cleared the next corner and redirected his path to his private office. Once inside, he locked the door and logged into the administrative file of the Center's hard drive, accessing the employee staff. He scrolled down to *Evans, Mia*, seeing the same smiling photograph as that on the employee badge he had just seen in the hall.

"Evans ... let's see. You've been here for sixteen months, changed your hairstyle a little since you've been working for us," he remarked softly, his voice studied as he further examined her computerized employee record for any outlier. "Oh, and never have called in sick or clocked in late for work? Ummm, that's a first," he noted in sarcastic surprise.

Van Deman scrolled back to the profile at the top of her page and saw that she had a West Jackson address. Van Deman had never set foot in West Jackson and, as far as he knew, had yet to meet anyone who had. Within the given employee information he found no mention of a spouse or children. "I wonder if she lives alone?" he pondered aloud. Then he decided, "She'd probably have an aunt or grandmother around the house if she had spawned a herd of rug rats."

For a record of Mia Evans' address, Van Deman first highlighted *Print* on the computer screen, and then thought better of it. Instead, he retrieved the Montblanc from his front jacket pocket and jotted the address on a syringe-shaped notepad lying on his desk. The pad was colorfully emblazoned with the logo of an infertility drug which encompassed most of the available writing space.

Nevertheless, he squeezed Mia's residential information along one side of the syringe, tore the sheet from the pad, and folded the page in half. Almost in a singular motion, Van Deman stuffed the note in his front jacket pocket, reclipped the pen there, and logged off the computer screen. The memory would note that he had visited the employee records section but that could be explained away as nothing out of the ordinary for any doctor to check now and then, especially the senior member of the Center, the one who signed the payroll checks. The computer access was pure business, plain and simple.

Van Deman suddenly felt pushed for time. He had forgotten Saxton. Her thirty minutes of motionless, post-embryo transplantation was well over, and he hoped she had not gotten dressed and prepared to leave or, worse, actually left. As Van Deman stepped hurriedly across his office floor toward the hall door that led to Allyn Saxton's treatment room, he paused. Staring from his desk was the remainder of the syringe-shaped notepad, the deep imprint of the home address of Mia Evans glaring as if written in neon.

Lunging for the notepad with his right hand, he nearly crushed it before smoothing the paper and forcing it into the shredder near his desk. "There, no one will know I ever tried to find you, Miss Evans," he muttered under the machine's smooth, satisfying hum as it quickly sucked the thin tablet paper through its teeth.

As the shredder stilled, Van Deman darted from his office and continued toward his celebrity patient.

Highlighting that screen panel, Tinker had caught the doctor quickly pushing past the young woman, who did not follow Van Deman, but only stood there in the hall for a moment, motionless. What Murtagh did not understand was that Mia Evans' breathless, frozen stance was the result of a bombshell.

Murtagh minimized her panel and traced Van Deman's movements to the doctor's private office, where he lost him behind the door to the inner sanctum. He re-checked. There was no movement in Saxton's treatment room as she continued to lie on the table, her legs up in the air. Tinker exhausted his fantasy about seeing movie star Allyn Saxton that way and moved on. Since he could not observe Van Deman's actions at the moment, he went back to his circle-the-word puzzle.

"That bastard!" Murtagh would have been able to read Mia's lips had he resumed the watch, her wits collected and her mind starting to spin. "I wasn't doing anything wrong, just cleaning up. Doing what I was told to do. Doing what She told me to do."

Even in her frustration, the overheard fragments of Van Deman's cell conversation began to reverberate in her head. Judging from his tone, the name *Saxton* seemed to have been the focus of the conversation.

"He was pissed that I heard that. He fired me for hearing that name, not for nearly knocking him and his expensive pants to the floor." Mia remained motionless, her thoughts scrabbling. "Why would the S.O.B. fire me for hearing that?" Mia wondered, beginning to question whether the doctor was talking about a patient or a friend or whomever.

"We don't ask questions about stuff around here. This is a medical clinic. We don't talk about patients' stuff around here. Stuff around here is private. We – they've – got rules," Mia spoke softly, though defensively, just as she felt hollow inside about those very rules she formerly ignored in a big way.

Lost as to what should be her next step, Mia could think of nothing but her invasion of the embryo culture lab. The memory of that blunder began to swirl, just as bitter acid rose from deep within her stomach. Somehow that early morning she had escaped detection in the off-limits area and preserved her own job. On the other hand, this time she had really screwed up.

"What have I got to lose?" Mia asked herself. In any case, the two weeks' severance pay promised if she was hired would tide her over until the next job, whether she was tossed today or pressed for another two weeks of work.

"I s'pect I'll be around for at least the rest of the day," Mia predicted correctly. She was also on target with, "I don't think Van Deman will go straight to the administrator to get her to do his dirty work. He'll probably wait until after-hours. That's when she'll escort the lowlife likes of me off his property." Mia wiggled her shoulders sharply and repetitively, as though mimicking being pushed along to an exit, probably the rear one.

"He won't want to dirty his high-priced hands or waste any time with formal good-byes." Mia's shoulder no longer hurting, she began to wiggle both in place as though she were being marched or strutted away. "That Van Deman … he's a real important doctor with lots of important and high-paying patients. Those VIPs need every spare moment he's got to give them." The shoulder movements had become non-stop, highly rhythmic by now.

"Yeah, he'll just brush by that administrator in the hall or maybe remember during a really important discussion with her and say something like, 'Oh, and that black girl. Get rid of her. Get that low-life chick off my property,' " Mia Evans imagined before fantasizing with a satisfied smile, "Yeah, Van Deman'll probably think again about the way I look and say instead, 'Get that cute lowlife chick off my property.' "

With that, Mia stopped the gyrating shoulder routine and pulled her arms in tightly, crossing them across her chest in a self-hug. She thought again about the few words she had heard of the doctor's cell phone conversation. "Why did he get so mad? Was it because I heard the name *Saxton* as he opened the door into the hall? What was the first name, *Allyn*? Is she a patient here?" she puzzled aloud. "That just can't be."

Curiosity about any personal issues regarding the patients had never been of any real concern of Mia Evans. After all, she, like all the other employees, had submitted to a confidentiality agreement when hired, an absolute requirement of the job. When showing up for work, Mia's chief concern was to earn that paycheck to cover her apartment rent, car payment, food, gasoline, and utilities. Somehow she was able to add to her wardrobe from time to time. And Mia had maintained her focus except for the regrettable morning in the embryo culture lab.

But now the situation had changed. For some unknown reason, she was soon to be an ex-employee of the Van Deman Center of Reproductive Technology, and she had to know why. Curiosity now had the best of her.

On a mission, Mia marched toward the front of the building where the main computer terminals were housed, but then thought better of it. "If I go this way, I might run into that S.O.B. and his squeeze." Evans had never imagined Van Deman and his administrator to be lovers, but that thought gelled smoothly in her frame of mind. She was about to commit a major rules violation, if not the most severe breach possible by an employee. And while her formal dismissal papers were pending, she still felt clammy about what she wanted to do – what she was going to do.

Mia made an abrupt U-turn in the wide hall and headed back toward the employee break room and kitchen that she sterilized every morning. From the corner of his eye, Murtagh noticed the sudden movement but was now too close to beating a Sudoku to pay much attention. Mia moved quickly toward the rear of the building and then doubled back through a smaller corridor to a seldom-used section off the main administrative area. In this sparsely appointed office space sat a single computer terminal waiting in suspend mode for Mia Evans.

She had been assigned to this tightly-confined workspace on

multiple occasions, no more than a claustrophobic alcove that most of the other clerical employees sought to avoid. The area had not been in the original architectural renderings but was born out of a last minute construction change to the adjacent room during renovation of the old Masonic lodge.

The original design called for this now shrunken space to serve as a medical transcriptionist's office, a need made obsolete before the Center evaluated and treated its first patient. Dr. Van Deman's acquisition of electronic medical records and voice recognition dictation systems negated the need for a proficient typist and traditional transcription equipment.

This last-minute shifting of resources and sheetrock unintentionally omitted installation of electronic surveillance for the diminutive quarters termed *the cell* by the office staff. The reality was that this shifting of office space had created a spot where Evans could work undetected, even by Tinker Murtagh and Dr. Van Deman.

Murtagh continued to ignore Mia as she made her way through the halls to the little-used workstation that his camera had missed. Had the Sudoku not been so challenging and had he tried to follow her, the effort would have been futile.

Despite the surging adrenaline that called for breaking into a full-out sprint, Mia forced calm and kept her pace to a determined walk. Her immediate fear was that she would encounter someone, anyone, particularly the Center's administrator, working unexpectedly in the drab, forgotten work area. Even the nighttime janitorial service ignored it since the area always appeared to be undisturbed.

Mia was certain she would have a few moments there alone.

"Damn," Mia muttered in irritation, although she wanted to shout in disgust when she made it to the isolated computer. The screen was dark. Shaking her head in frustration and fear that the unit was no longer functional, Evans hit the power button firmly. The computer responded with a soft hum, resurrecting the hard drive from hibernation as the screen displayed the expected series of sign-on images.

Mia then falsely felt the presence of someone else in the room and jerked her head to the entrance of the space in response as she blindly entered her employee identification number and other sign-in information on the key pad. She remained alone; the administrator was not stalking her, nor was Dr. Van Deman.

Relieved, Mia refocused on the fact that no one ever came into this room, at least not very often, and she could work alone. As expected, the system still accepted her personal password and she was in. She typed commands and highlighted icons that brought her to the alphabetized patient roster, to which the clerical staff had unrestricted access. Only the patient medical history and course of treatment were unavailable to the clerical staff except when necessary to schedule specific treatments or procedures.

Linked to the complete names of each patient on the electronic roster was a page of routine information expected in any client profile: dates of birth, mail and email addresses, last four digits of social security numbers, and a combination of available phone numbers. Pasted in the upper left-hand corner was a two by two-inch facial photograph that ranked just above mug shot quality. When quietly checking in new patients, Mia had easily taken some of those digital pictures herself, using the Center's camera, then downloading each image to the correct patient. The photograph served dual functions; it was a method of patient identification as well as an electronic link, or widget, to past, current, and future patient appointment dates and times.

Rather than scan the entire list of names, she directed the cursor to the search function and typed in the name she had overheard from Van Deman's cell phone conversation. "That must

have been what made that guy so pissed at me," she muttered
again as she typed the letters *s-a-x-t-o-n*. *NO INFORMATION
FOUND* screamed at her from a large box that erupted on the
center of the screen. "That's screwy," she responded, then tried a
different route.

Immediately she switched screens to the facility scheduling
option and scrolled down the list of treatment and procedural
rooms. The day had been relatively slow in the Center even with
both doctors working. She first brought up the schedules for the
INITIAL EXAMINATION ROOMS, finding nothing there, and
then pushed the cursor to the *EMBRYO TRANSFER ROOMS*.
There had been two procedures scheduled for the day, the rooms
highlighted in green, indicating that the patients had arrived for
the appointment and the procedures had been completed.

Mia double-clicked on *ROOM 1* and *Sarbeck, Carrie* popped up.
"Well, that's obviously not Allyn Saxton," she noted nervously,
finding her voice unexpectedly weak at the possibility of imminent
discovery. The amateur sleuth felt that her detective work had
spanned hours when in fact she had been in the forgotten room
only minutes.

Remaining in the *EMBRYO TRANSFER ROOMS* section, Evans
then popped down to *ROOM 2*. "There's no name here," her
voice still low though somewhat stronger as her curiosity was
piqued. In the space designated for a patient name, there were
only a series of closely placed asterisks, similar to that associated
with website online passwords or credit card receipts. She paused
momentarily to reflexively count the number of asterisks. There
were five sequential marks, a single space, and then six more.
At no time had Mia Evans ever seen any similar listing on the
Center's software.

She then moved across the page to the assigned space for the
patient medical record number, again not finding the expected

series of non-sequential digits, only a series of asterisks and this time only six. "Our patient numbers are six numerals long, just like this number," she remarked in her normal voice, then briefly retreated from the keyboard and screen, concerned that she may have spoken loudly enough to attract attention.

She looked back around and then jumped up to glance out the office door. There was no one anywhere nearby. Reassured that she remained physically alone, Mia suddenly feared that perhaps someone or something routinely monitored an individual's live presence on the Center's integrated computer system. She assumed that access of each electronic file or schedule left a trail, unless the user only reviewed the information without alteration. Mia quickly squelched that concern, deciding that the administrator was too involved in efforts to keep the physicians, the patients, and the vendors happy to delve into such moment-to-moment pursuits.

Besides, Dr. Van Deman, the ogre, would have assumed that a lowlife such as Mia Evans would run from his building after the *"You're Fired!"* denouncement. No way would she have hung around to straighten pens and pencils and empty the garbage, or whatever else he had been paying her to do – much less play on the computer. Nobody would review the computer file access history unless a specific concern was raised, and, anyway, Mia Evans would not be around if and when that concern arose.

Typically the computer program allowed one to highlight the patient number, double click, and then bring up the patient information screen. Mia hesitated briefly to think things through, to sort out all of the information that had been thrown at her in the last few minutes. If someone had gone to such great lengths to keep secret the identity of that patient in that room, then the access link from the obscured patient ID number to the profile information most certainly would have been disabled. If she went through motions to test this short asterisk series against the patient profile page, would an alarm go off? Would the computer blow up? Would Van Deman materialize behind her chair, grab her straightened hair, yank her head back toward him and then slit her throat ear-to-ear?

She pushed aside those thoughts, closed her eyes, and cringed even as she double-clicked on the asterisks that stood in place of numerals. The computer surprised her.

"Damn!" Mia exclaimed again, then threw her right hand against her mouth as she whirled the small rotating desk chair toward the entrance to the room, certain that someone had heard the expletive. Before her appeared a patient profile page, an apparent direct electronic link from the patient ID number disguised by asterisks, a flaw in the software that the Center's administrator may have detected had she not been so consumed with keeping the physicians, the patients, and the vendors happy.

"Allyn Saxton?" she read the name in the upper left-hand corner, "*The* Allyn Saxton?" she questioned herself in complete skepticism. *The beautiful actress with eternal youth and worldwide celebrity was a patient at The Van Deman Center in Canton, Mississippi?* she thought, again with skepticism.

Despite the patient confidentiality that was assumed and required in any medical clinic or hospital, Mia continued incredulously, "I can't believe that nobody said anything. This just can't be true. Everybody would have wanted her autograph." She looked away from the computer screen as she shook her head side-to-side in wonder. "Must just be the same name – a coincidence, a pure coincidence."

Returning her attention to the patient ID profile page, there in the upper right-hand corner was a two-by-two inch photograph of a woman in a strange hat, no makeup, no visible hair style, and no smile. Mia maximized the color image to full-screen. Mia thought back to a smiling Allyn Saxton on the recent cover of *With It* magazine that lay askew under a lamp on the table where Van Deman had fallen over her a few moments ago. Thinking about the photograph credited to a celebrity fashion show held to benefit hurricane victims, Mia mentally compared the flawless face to the one before her on the screen. "That's her. That's Allyn Saxton. Shit!" she gasped, again clapping her right hand to her mouth as she could practically feel the sting of a disgusted grandmother's slap across her face.

Further down the page were a Los Angeles address, a cell number, and a business listed as an alternate contact person. "I bet that's her agent," Mia decided aloud, imagining what kind of posh home stood at Allyn Saxton's given residential address and the impeccably gorgeous, rich-and-famous types who must grace the interior and grounds. "Brad Pitt, Hallie Berry, Tom Cruise, Will Smith, Jennifer Anniston, Matthew Fox, Usher, Beyonce, Alicia Keys, Nicole Richie, Barack Obama ... they've all been over there. I know they have." Mia stared mesmerized at the Hollywood address, beckoning her in glowing reverse type from the screen's black background.

She shook her head again, wondering if this entire afternoon had been a dream, but knowing that it had not. Somehow one of the most popular, recognizable television and movie stars in the world had wound up way down in Mississippi as a patient in the medical clinic where a nobody like Mia Evans worked. "How did this girl get past me when she checked in for the first time?" she wondered aloud. "I did have a bad cold a couple of weeks back and lost my voice, or it may have been the day I was out with the bad period." Mia seldom missed work, but unknowingly had fallen victim to an Allyn Saxton disguise.

"But I know what happened today. Miss Goody-Two-Shoes had me doing scut work around this place – made me miss Allyn

Saxton's comin' into the place where I work, at least the place I used to work." Mia assumed in frustration and regret. "I wonder who all knew she was here besides the bosses."

As Mia went through the mental exercise of *whys* and *what-ifs* that accompany any surprise information, she moved down the page of personal, non-medical treatment data. The information also detailed that Saxton had been paying for her services in cash and was even ahead on payments.

Waiting for Mia at the bottom of the page was a three character-sized space where the clerk who initially entered the patient information could either type in her initials or choose from a pre-entered list. "Let's see who first checked in this famous chick," Mia mumbled, already suspecting the answer. Assuming that the administrator herself had done the tedious clerical work in an effort to maintain the star's secrecy, Mia hightlighted that box at the bottom of the screen.

The initials *HVD* glared at her. "What the hell?" she declared, feeling another grandmotherly slap. "That A-hole Van Deman checked her in himself, and I guess he took her picture dressed in that corny disguise," she realized as she returned to the rendering of a distorted Allyn Saxton. "I guess no one in the building knows she's been here but him," she concluded, then corrected herself.

"That is, no one but him – and me."

———————————————————————————

Henry Van Deman never mentioned the Mia Evans incident to the administrator of his practice nor the fact that he had fired her because of it. There was no need, since she never returned to work, surprising everyone at the Center except Van Deman. Evans' mother reported her missing once she failed to find Mia in her own apartment, a mother's concern prompted by her daughter's uncharacteristic failure to answer her cell phone or a knock at her door, or even to return voice mail or email for two days.

Mrs. Evans' unease was compounded by Mia's absence from work, a job her daughter had seemed to enjoy, the absence first discovered only when she called the Van Deman Center asking for Mia. The unsympathetic office administrator took the call herself, partly out of curiosity over Mia's absences and her whereabouts.

"I assumed that she had quit and taken another job in some other doctor's office – or that maybe she was out somewhere selling cosmetics, used cars or pink lemonade, for all I know," the administrator rambled, forcing humor that was lost on the concerned mother.

"Of course, Mia did clock out an hour early on her last day here, which was, let's see, yes, about three days ago. You know, Mrs. Evans, your daughter did not even have the courtesy to submit a resignation, much less give two weeks' notice."

With a streak of insensitivity that often surfaced, Van Deman's administrator stressed, "If the truth be known, this really isn't like the Mia that I hired. I could always depend on her." At that, Mia's mother dabbed a tear in the corner of her right eye. "Oh, and when you do talk to her, Mrs. Evans, I would appreciate your telling Mia that even a few days' notice of her plans to quit would have been mere common courtesy."

Before hanging up, the administrator speared in cool sarcasm, "Of course, by not giving me the required two weeks' notice, she loses all the money the Center had contributed to her retirement account." Her pause was tormenting as she uttered, "I'm so, so, sorry."

Mrs. Evans' rising level of anxiety about her only daughter's whereabouts paralleled the administrator's growing disdain, so much so that she blocked out the woman's last comment. Her motherly imagination was consumed with fear that Mia may have run off with a new boyfriend, the latest in a string of undesirables that had become a hot issue between her and her daughter.

"Has anyone besides me called up here looking for Mia?" Mrs. Evans asked the administrator face-to-face when she arrived unannounced at the Center the following morning. Annoyed, the administrator nearly refused to see her without an appointment.

"Well, yes, I told some young man the same thing I told you when he called yesterday before lunch asking to speak to your daughter. 'Sorry, she's AWOL,' I told him. In fact, when the same male called later in the day looking for Mia, this time identifying himself as her fiancé, I told him the same thing. I guess he thought I was trying to hide her from him."

Collapsing into the nearest chair at the response, Mrs. Evans fanned herself with a thin magazine pulled from a side table. *Fiancé* was not a word she wanted to hear. "I told your daughter's boyfriend, fiancé, or whatever you want to call him – I said, 'Young man, I've already explained this to you. Mia LaShay Evans does not work here any longer and never will again, I assure you.' Now, Mrs. Evans, would you rehire someone who walked off the job, leaving you high and dry with so much work to do around this office? I doubt it." The administrator gesticulated, throwing her right hand palm-up, extending her arm to the extreme right in demonstration of the large space she managed.

"Well, Miss, ahh ... ," Mrs. Evans pulled herself from the upholstered chair in the administrator's office and returned the magazine. The administrator's real lack of interest in Mia's disappearance was taken as coldly by her mother as it was intended. "I'm very concerned about my daughter. It's not like her to leave town or change jobs without sharing with me. We've always been close," Mrs. Evans said as she surveyed the room for a Kleenex. Finding none, she dabbed her eyes with the sleeve of her blouse.

There was no sympathy forthcoming from the administrator. In her eyes, rudeness deserved rudeness. "You see," Van Deman's chief employee explained, "with Mia gone, and so unexpectedly, I was left with no one to unlock the office for me and receive early morning supply shipments. Our vendors arrive well before our general opening time and need someone to let them in and sign the receipt. Mia and I had a workable system in which she managed that for me without my having to depend on the night watchman. Your daughter has always been so dependable."

Mrs. Evans detected a hint of softness that quickly returned to reality.

"So, I really don't understand how she could have done this – have turned out to have been so inconsiderate," the administrator rebounded, looking off for a moment and then staring at Evans. "You simply never know how poorly some people have been raised when you hire them. Do you, Mrs. Evans?"

The mother burst into full-blown tears, the sobbing left far behind.

Satisfied, the administrator offered, "May I show you to our front lobby and the door, Mrs. Evans?"

Once the police finally accepted the missing persons report on Mia LaShay Evans, there was an investigation that probed the archived security videos from the Center's digital vaults. The lower level policewoman assigned to the case would be only the second person to study the images, although her perspective differed greatly from that of Tinker Murtagh. Based on employee time records provided by the Center's administrator, the policewoman located the images of Evans clocking out on her last day of work, and at the usual clock out time.

As captured by the basic security system known to all at the Center, nothing appeared out of order. No one was spotted following her to her vehicle, nor did she glance over her shoulder to suggest a lookout. Mia merely seemed to walk calmly from the employee exit through the parking lot to her car. The less vivid images of the basic security camera failed to catch the true detail of her face: a combination of soft tears over her firing, mixed with a look of excitement over her discovery of the Center's top-secret, celebrity patient – Allyn Saxton.

Upon clocking out from the Van Deman Center after her altercation with Henry Van Deman and after her unauthorized computer research, Mia had planned to return to work the next day in hope that the administrator had come to her rescue and rightfully reasoned with Dr. Van Deman. As far as she was concerned, Mia considered her knowledge of the celebrity treatment as nothing more than curiosity on her behalf and her overhearing of Dr. Van Deman's cell phone conversation nothing more than an innocent *faux pas*.

Henry Van Deman's choice of the metropolitan Jackson area for his state-of-the-art human reproductive center and the area's rapid economic and structural growth came into play with Mia's disappearance. Housing and commercial establishments were appearing at nearly every corner, mostly in the suburbs and on the periphery of the city limits, but also in Jackson itself with downtown revitalization booming.

Mia LaShay Evans epitomized the target market for such commercialism; she was an attractive, youthful, employed female, anticipating her own future family and home, who enjoyed shopping, regardless of income constraints. She missed few, if any, of the sprouting clothing boutiques and trendy home furnishing stores that occupied the spreading shopping sectors and strip malls. The areas were designed to look like parks and walking trails – expansive, elaborately designed buildings interlaced with fountains and transplanted, mature greenery – seemingly never-ending construction, regardless of the cost of gasoline or staggering unemployment figures.

A potential nemesis to that physical growth, but of no consideration to its enthralled customers, was an engineering burden known as Yazoo clay. Not indigenous only to the Jackson, Mississippi, area, the thick, gooey layer of mud rock lurks below the topsoil of many parts of the southeastern United States with Jackson and central Mississippi having been granted far more than their fair share.

Extending to average depths of 30 to 40 feet in some places, the distinctively yellow-brown, weathered clay is an engineering nightmare for those choosing to build atop it. Its unweathered cousin, the blue-gray variety, is not much friendlier. The unyielding expanding and contracting forces of Yazoo clay
are such that the construction industry jokes that it has a life and mind of its own, as it cracks foundations and ceilings of buildings and homes while making roller coasters out of streets and highways.

Considering the unstable soil no more than a professional challenge, the architects, engineers, and construction

contractors building in central Mississippi at the time required extensive foundation work to support their structures, particularly when
the design called for multi-storied buildings. Thanks to the explosive commercial interest in the South and the one-upmanship of human nature that does not escape business developers, fresh dirt and a fresh hole could be found anywhere around Jackson at the moment Mia Evans disappeared.

Within the metropolis of Jackson, including the adjacent cities of Ridgeland, Madison, Byram, Florence, Pearl and Flowood, large pieces of equipment mastered by both male and female operators remained on the job around the clock, nights and weekends. Excavating tons of dirt, digging deep beyond the worst of the Yazoo clay, contractors moved it from place to place after hours and under artificial lights, if necessary, to meet strict deadlines – a work ethic that would have made the Egyptian pharaohs proud.

Nevertheless, there were developments on tight completion schedules that still allowed workers to clock out at reasonable hours. One of these sites was destined for the ultimate in upscale shopping hysteria, a money-making Mecca located off Interstate 55, north of Jackson and south of the Center's actual location in Canton. Uncharacteristically, security cameras at the construction site were rare and generally kept in place only in nearly completed sections, where expensive laminates and other finishing materials were ripe for confiscation or just plain vandalism.

Undisturbed by rain, a seemingly endless caravan of dump trucks had hauled load after load of treacherous Yazoo clay for days from this particular site to a location where cracks in walls and shifting pilings were not of concern. As a result, a large hole in the earth remained nice and dry, waiting for a stable layer of fill dirt and gravel, interlaced with systematic drains that would be camouflaged by a hotel's swimming pool section. An enticing oasis of hot tubs, waterfalls, lap lanes, and even a spacious area to float on a raft or simply play water volleyball, the water feature and pool area was to anchor the fitness center of the retail development's five-star boutique hotel.

At gunpoint and well after nightfall of her final day at the Center, Mia Evans was carjacked from her dark driveway and made to drive her Nissan across that same construction site. Terrified, she descended into the excavation area destined for the pool by following the gradual slope of the nearest side. After she reached the depths of the dig and applied the brake, an arm reached from behind to shift the vehicle into park. With the engine still running, Mia Evans was strangled unceremoniously from behind with a piece of garden hose. She was left slumped over the steering wheel, sans murder weapon with the engine stilled.

After a dozer covered the tracks left by Mia's car as she drove across the site to her death, layers of fresh, non-Yazoo fill dirt were compacted around her and the small vehicle. Beginning at the depths of the projected pool area, the fill was, not coincidentally, sufficient to obscure the body of Mia Evans and her Nissan. The tightly sealed soil now begged for the support of gravel, rebar, and concrete, as well as drains and other plumbing, required before the pool itself could be installed.

The next morning's construction crew was a relief team, no member of which had worked the job in the last several days and, needless to say, did not question the progress at the site. Not wanting to be reprimanded for slowing the unexpected level of progress, the job foreman immediately proceeded with finishing to specification the foundation for the pool and water feature.

The guests of the five-star hotel, soon to rise from the earth to adjoin the pool area, would, like the authorities, remain oblivious to what rested below the swimming facility. This elaborate watery tombstone would assure for Mia Evans an undisturbed grave.

Chapter
15
◆◆◆
THE LEFTOVERS

Having already agreed to two future jobs, Tinker was ready to complete his commission in Canton and leave Mississippi. He had decided that shipping the embryos to his client would be too risky, so he would transport them himself. Besides, he wanted to be sure that he received final payment. The surveillance tapes of the actual heist could be a problem if anyone ever cared to view them, but he understood that the digital recorder recycled itself every six weeks. To be sure of his obscurity, he had discovered a method of scrambling or even halting the recording software.

Consequently, if anyone did bring up the recording, there would be evidence of only a few lost minutes. However, if his scheme went as smoothly as planned, those minutes would become only seconds.

While the initial contact with this current client had been by nameless courier, he had brief, follow-up communications by cell phone. The client had asked for a contact phone number, which Tinker provided – a simple thing to arrange, particularly since the job by design was not expected to be lengthy. Since even gas stations had kiosks with hungry executive hopefuls selling cellular

service, he nonchalantly bought a disposable, a no-thrills model
with a prearranged number of minutes – unknowingly similar to
the one Van Deman had acquired earlier.

The particular gas station at which Tinker chose to purchase his
business-related cell phone was located at an exit off I-55 North. The
thriving, 24-hour establishment offered a plethora of hot, mostly
fried, food items, showers for truckers, and novelties and trinkets
designated as Mississippi souvenirs, plus gasoline and diesel fuel.
Mounted security cameras were impossible to miss, meant to ward off
shoplifters and thugs contemplating heists. Tinker doubted if many
of the cameras were even live, except for the ones hanging from the
ceiling near the cash register checkout which served the dual purpose
of thwarting robberies and keeping the sales clerks honest.

When approaching and passing through the front entrance
of the store, Murtagh had been careful to lower his head, keep
his sunglasses on, and turn his face away from the registers. He
purposely managed these maneuvers before penetrating the range
of the camera scanning the front entrance. In added effort to
avoid being identified later, Tinker covered his mouth and face
with both hands as though coughing. He stayed away from the
main checkout area and purchased the cell phone at the kiosk
which was devoid of security cameras. Tinker had surveyed the
situation closely on an earlier visit.

Upon taking the Van Deman job, Tinker had no clue as to the
identity of his client, and still did not, except that he knew the
client had the money, at least the required upfront money. His
minor expenses, including the cell phone package, had been
deducted from that amount as overhead. Tinker understood that
all successful businessmen had overhead; the truly successful
ones, like Tinker Murtagh, kept it low.

As instructed in that initial note which threw him into
cyberspace with Henry Van Deman, Murtagh obtained the short-

term phone and then called the number listed in the note. A voice answered, "*Yes?*" At first Tinker was taken aback, for it was a female voice. It was not that a woman would not or could not deal in such enterprises as this, yet he was momentarily stunned.

The note had detailed that his potential employer would likewise obtain an untraceable cell phone and that only he, Tinker Murtagh, would have the number. Nonetheless, Tinker wondered if the *Yes?* was the curt, hesitant greeting of a female secretary or other underling rather than a savvy, determined, client – the type with which he liked to work. The latter became, for him, the truth and the advance down payment money was immediate once he accepted the terms. The woman's request was succinct; as the initial phone conversation ended, she repeated from the first written contact, "Get it, get all of it."

The woman outlined when Allyn Saxton was to arrive in Jackson and drive to the Van Deman Center of Reproductive Technology in nearby Canton. She was unsure of the exact day but knew a finite range of dates. Saxton had already traveled to the Van Deman place and had left and returned to California, but that was of no consequence to the client's purposes. It was this last trip that was important.

But then she clarified one final item. Desiring Allyn Saxton's human embryos, she wanted only the leftover ones, the extra ones that routinely would not be implanted in Saxton's uterus, but instead left fresh frozen in Van Deman's vault for later use. She was sure there would be leftovers; Murtagh would not have to worry about that.

"Look, lady, if there's nothing there for me to *steal*, that won't be my fault. You'll still owe me the money," he had explained in his matter-of-fact business dialect, a voice free of any Southern inflection.

"Like I said, sir, there will certainly be frozen embryos for you to

... let's see, I'd rather use the term *obtain* rather than *steal* ... for you to obtain for me."

"OK, if you say so, lady. It's your money. But you really don't want me to get all of them from the get-go?" he asked, the Southern inflection creeping back.

"No, like I just explained. Simply the remaining ones. They're supposed to be just as good. I think they use the term *viable*. Once she has her implanted embryos, her fair share, then I want the rest of them. Do I make myself clear, sir?"

"Yeah, whatever you say. Like I said, it's your money," he added as they ended the call.

What the woman did not detail was her reason for not completely depriving Allyn Saxton of a pregnancy that she rightfully deserved and that had escaped her despite being married at least twice with countless lovers in the mix. After all, she, the woman that this Tinker Murtagh assumed was gifted with limitless funds, had been pregnant herself: once. Motherhood had not brought her any long-term pleasure, so why should she spare Allyn Saxton the torture?

Tinker took in the view as Allyn Saxton redressed once Dr. Van Deman dismissed her after the implantation procedure. He generally avoided such study, considering it the borderline behavior of an electronic Peeping Tom. But, after all, a guy could only work so many word and number puzzles, he decided. This girl was good-looking and, in his estimation, seemed all natural in the physical sense.

"It doesn't look like any of those Hollywood plastic surgeons have put this one under the knife. No, it don't," Tinker determined as Saxton seemed to look around the room for anything she may

might have forgotten. She already had the hat that she had worn
earlier and the nondescript handbag.

Uncharacteristically, he felt a twitch of guilt about what he was
about to do, then squelched it. "Let's remain professional here,
Murtagh. Besides, even the hire said she wasn't stripping this
chick completely of her stuff."

Tinker Murtagh was not the type to watch *E!* or *Entertainment
Tonight* on television, much less *Dancing with the Stars* or
American Idol, or to even glance at a *People* magazine.
However, even without a bone of celebrity consciousness, he
still knew who Allyn Saxton was. America and the world loved
her. If she endorsed a product, it became an overnight financial
success. Tinker had even switched his brand of shaving cream
to that smeared across the cheeks of a male actor in a television
commercial just before Allyn Saxton appeared out-of-the-blue
to tackle him.

Tinker decided that she was probably a decent girl, no more
promiscuous than any other of those Hollywood types. He
believed he knew that she had been married before and was not
sure if she was married now, although he doubted it. There had
been no male accompanying her to Van Deman's place.

"What dumbass would let that go?" he questioned while closely
watching her leave the room from that angle.

––––––––––––––––––––––––––––––

The exit of Carrie Sarbeck and her husband Wesley from
the Center about a half hour before that of Allyn Saxton went
uncelebrated in a lower panel on Tinker's screen. Dr. Chamblee
had assured them that the procedure went well, and they were
given a couple of prescriptions for hormone supplements that
Carrie was to take in anticipation of a positive pregnancy test in

a couple of weeks. After that would be more prescriptions, more sonograms, and then routine obstetrical care at the physician's office of their choice.

"It sounds so simple now, Wes," Carrie broke the silence as they approached the new pharmacy near their home.

"That's the first optimistic thing you've said during this whole thing, Carrie. The way you behaved today around Dr. Van Deman and then Dr. Chamblee, particularly Dr. Chamblee, I was afraid they were going to call the whole thing off – like they were raping you, or something, by implanting those embryos in you, our embryos."

"Our ... embryos ...... our ...... embryos .... our .... embryos." Carrie repeated her husband's last two words barely audibly as she struggled to convince herself. In his concentrated effort to pull the car to a stop near the front door without choosing a handicapped spot, Wesley had not heard her response. He was truly excited. They were finally going to be parents – happy parents.

As he put the car in park and switched off the ignition, Wesley leaned slightly forward to retrieve the wallet from his back pocket. For safekeeping, he had placed Carrie's prescription for the necessary hormone replacements inside it, and he wanted to double-check. "Yep, got it right here, Honey," he reported as he pulled the tightly folded piece of paper with the imprinted Van Deman logo from his wallet. "Be back in a minute, unless you want to come in."

Carrie shook her head. "No, I don't want to come in. No."

"After the embryo transfer, the doctor said that all you had to do was lie on that table for thirty minutes, and then you could walk around. So, Carrie, if you want to go in and look around, say maybe at their makeup or magazines or something, then you can."

"I don't care anything about any makeup. I couldn't care less about seeing anyone; and if I did see someone, I couldn't care less how I looked!" she yelled, to Wesley's surprise and for anyone in the parking lot to have heard - had the automobile windows been lowered or one of the doors even cracked.

"Geeze, Carrie," Wesley hushed her, reaching for her after he transferred the prescription from his right hand to the left. "What in the hell is wrong with you anyway, Baby? Just wait here. I'll leave the keys. Why don't you listen to the radio or a CD or something?"

Wesley was relieved to find a short line at the prescription counter inside the pharmacy. Nevertheless, the wait to have the order filled was lengthy. When Wesley questioned the clerk, the complaint was written off to a backlog of unfilled prescriptions called in by other physicians.

"The pharmacist is working as fast as he can, so are the pharmacy techs. You'll just have to wait your turn, sir. I'm sorry, but I don't think it'll be much longer," the sympathetic teenage girl working the cash register behind the counter explained, as was her routine, though she added a smile.

The teenager's gesture was wasted on Wesley, as it was on the others forced to wait. He wished for his police uniform. Dressed as a policeman, particularly if accompanied by a screaming siren or revolving blue light, he always received respect. As the wait in line to have the prescription filled seemed endless, Wesley worried more about his wife and regretted having left her alone in their car. Each time he offered to leave the prescription and return later to pick up the medications, he was told by the smiling girl that the wait would be just a few moments more.

Finally the name Sarbeck was called, and Wesley lurched to attention. He had nearly memorized a newspaper tabloid borrowed from a rack near the register and carelessly returned it. Allyn Saxton's smiling face captured by a telephoto lens as she played on a beach somewhere graced the front of the magazine that now rested sideways for the next customer.

Carrie sat alone in their car while her husband fidgeted in exasperation inside the drugstore. Unlike Wesley, she was ignorant of the time that elapsed. "Our embryos," she repeated, this time in pure monotone with no one around but her to hear, although even she failed to hear her own words. She said again, "Our embryos," but then placed her right hand against her mid-lower abdomen and said this time, "No, your embryos."

She thought back to the day that the Wax woman came over to their house with her wares, the catalogue of women, who under the guise of a donation, were willing to sell their eggs – a natural part of her body that she had lost long ago, something that had been taken from her. Her enthusiastic, though bewildered, husband had finally coaxed her out of the bathroom to choose the egg donor from the woman's high-priced collection, or better yet, merely to approve his selection.

Wesley had selected a donor with blonde hair. She was striking, but not gorgeous. She was well-dressed and radiant. Wesley had told her that in many ways the donor reminded him of her, although Carrie did not believe him. She was surprised that the woman appeared slightly older than she would have imagined, and so said. Her husband offset her remark with, "But this one has a successful enough track record." As Carrie watched Wesley rub his forefinger erratically over the thin Lucite preserving the donor's photograph, he added, "And what's even better is that we can afford her, at least we should have enough money to pay her fee."

"A prostitute. That's what that woman in that picture is, or was!" Carrie broke the silence in the car, easily hearing herself this time. "My husband should have just f'ed a prostitute and then tossed her some filthy, extra money to carry the baby, their baby, not my baby. He could have had lots of prostitutes for what we paid that smiling bitch!"

While shaking her head uncontrollably, Carrie elaborated, "She's not smiling now, is she?"

"Did you say something? Is who not smiling?" Wesley opened their car door and popped into the driver's seat. His excitement had resurfaced now that he had their medication.

"No, ah, I didn't say anything. No, Wesley. I didn't say anything."

"This little stuff is going to keep your uterus in good shape for our baby, your baby. Everything is going to work out fine. I can just feel it." Wesley Sarbeck was defiant as he backed the car out of the parking space and drove toward their quaint home, a place that Wesley knew would come alive in about nine months. "You know, Honey, we might just have to add on."

Just as during the ride home, Carrie Sarbeck was silent the rest of the day. Her husband had taken the entire day off and continued the holiday through the upcoming weekend. He was constantly pestering her with *How are you feeling?* or *Can I get you anything?* or *Have you been taking your vitamins and hormones?* Because she had caught him in the act, she knew that he was checking the supply of her hormone medication to be sure that she never missed a dose. His excuse had been that he was looking for some dental floss in that particular drawer that never held dental floss, toothpaste, or anything of that nature.

Oh, and don't forget to take a baby aspirin. Remember, Carrie, Dr. Chamblee said to take one 87 milligram aspirin every day because they think that may help prevent rejection of the embryo ... or ... help with implantation ... or something like that. This repeated reminder made Carrie cringe, a look she hid as she sat before her cosmetics mirror the next morning, forcing herself to apply some blush and mascara, even a smear of lipstick.

Her husband seemed so optimistic, so happy. Never once did he mention that the money that her childless, spinster aunt had given them was nearly gone. Seven hundred dollars was all that was left in that account. She had gone online with the bank a couple of days ago and checked. Drs. Chamblee and Van Deman had been paid in full for the embryo transfer and the follow-up exams and treatments for this most recent cycle. If she was indeed now pregnant and the pregnancy stuck, Wesley's family health insurance plan through the JPD had maternity benefits and the $700 should come close to covering their out-of-pocket expenses.

As of now, however, the presumed pregnancy had cost an additional $10,000 about which her husband would never know. He could never know. There was no way.

Carrie Sarbeck had been left her family's sole heir when her maternal aunt died the previous year, long before Carrie and Wesley had ever heard of Lucille Wax or embryo transplants. Her aunt lived in a Jackson-area retirement home where there was no equity, and her remaining modest, well-worn furnishings ranked slightly above rejection status from the Salvation Army donation center. The will had been simple; everything went to her wonderful niece, Carrie Sarbeck. However, with no car, no home, and no desirable worldly possessions to speak of, there was really nothing to bequeath. She simply had been a very sweet old lady who already had given her last dime to the cause: one last chance to propagate her family through her niece.

Carrie had gone through her aunt's things alone. She unearthed a few old family photographs packed in an antique cedar chest, some of which included her mother and most of which she had already seen in duplicate form. There were old bank statements and income tax records that long ago should have been shredded and discarded. A few pieces of American Brilliant cut and pressed glass were found wrapped in boxes, and Carrie welcomed them to her own home as treasured collectibles.

The real surprise was that her aunt had maintained a safety deposit box at a local bank. Carrie found the key in a tiny cloth pouch in the bottom of her aunt's cluttered jewelry box – cluttered with scraps of note paper, old credit card receipts with matching expired cards, a few quarters and a nickel or two, and a few unused but clearly obsolete first class postage stamps. The key was stamped with the name of a downtown bank that had undergone several corporate buyouts but still maintained the branch location indicated on the metal key.

Carrie slid the cloth pouch in a purse compartment and forgot about it over the ensuing days of handling funeral arrangements and clearing up paperwork at the retirement home. Fortunately, her aunt's Social Security and other retirement benefits had kept her bills at the facility current so that there were no financial obligations in that regard, nor was anything due the funeral home since her aunt had maintained a comprehensive, paid-up funeral expenses plan that covered her simple but tasteful funeral and burial.

Months later Carrie absentmindedly reached into the seldom-used compartment of her purse where the safety deposit box key waited. Reminded by the texture of the cloth pouch, she groaned, "Oh, well, the last thing to take care of." Carrie could not deny that the minimal, but all encompassing, details surrounding her aunt's death had kept her diverted from her infertility woes and obligations.

Having nothing constructive planned for the day as usual, Carrie decided to drive downtown to her late aunt's bank. She would not be missed; Wesley was to be on police duty the rest of the day and would, in fact, soon be assigned more night duty, a work change she felt unfair due to her husband's advancing seniority with the Jackson Police Department.

"That must be why the overdue notice was returned in the mail marked *UNDELIVERABLE*. Your aunt must have already died when we sent the notice out," the bank clerk explained with a nervous laugh. The clerk in the safety deposit department was polite but clearly embarrassed at having to inform Carrie that the rent on the safety deposit box was overdue by just over six months. "But I'm sorry," she continued, "the fee of $85 will still have to be taken care of before I can let you into the box. How would you like to pay ... cash, personal check, debit card, or credit card?"

Carrie reached for the wallet in her purse. Since Wesley sometimes overreacted to unexpected expenses appearing on their credit card or bank statements, she felt it best to pay in cash, and was surprised that she had enough in her wallet to cover her late aunt's overdue balance. Satisfied, the clerk thumbed through a file of elongated, heavy paper forms and extracted one. Handing it to Carrie, she asked her to sign under her aunt's most recent signature, dated over four years ago, about the time she entered the nursing home.

Once the delinquent payment had been made, the only other requirement for Carrie to gain admission to her deceased aunt's safety deposit box was presentation of a valid driver's license, a photocopy of which the clerk stapled to the signature card before placing both in a separate, much thinner file. Not required was a death certificate, lawyer's directive, or will designating Carrie Sarbeck as beneficiary or executrix of her aunt's estate.

After the clerk inserted both the bank's key and the key that Carrie possessed into the lock and turned them, the door of number 2418 popped open and the clerk swung it forward. As a customer courtesy, she reached inside the shallow space for the handle, pulling the thin metal box to a place within Carrie's easy reach.

"There ya go!" the bank clerk pronounced, grinning as she turned to exit the walk-in vault. Then she stopped and pointed toward of a set of cubicles located just outside the door to the large vault. "Oh, and you can take the box into one of the private stalls over here and then return your key to me as you leave. Unless, of course, you want to continue to rent the box. Just let me know."

Carrie was tiring of the bank clerk. As her remarks faded, Carrie forced a nod of recognition without watching the clerk exit the area. Instead, she listened for the woman's footsteps against the tile floor until she knew that she was alone. There was going to be nothing in her late aunt's lock box but some four-year-old air. Nevertheless, she wanted privacy in dealing with it.

Carrie took a long, deep breath. She was beginning to regret her venture downtown to the main Jackson branch of the conglomerate that had been her dear aunt' s longtime and trusted financial institution. It was not even the bank to which she and Wesley subscribed. Consequently, she had wasted an afternoon fighting traffic to clean out this lock box, not to mention the expensive gasoline burned on a mission that was certainly not urgent, nothing but a rather unnecessary formality.

If she hurried, she might have time to run by the grocery store and cleaners before Wesley got home. That way, the whole afternoon would not be a waste. He was her husband and he meant well, and for some reason he wanted to have children with her. Their difficulty in so doing had monopolized her thoughts. "Wesley loves me, and I don't know why. I know I should do what he wants about having a baby." Carrie remained alone in the room surrounded by individually numbered thick, steel doors, protecting the secretly stashed valuables of hundreds of the bank's customers – the value of those contents no doubt considered subjective in many cases.

The futility of the moment was Carrie's chief concern as she stared up at the steel door that had sealed her aunt's safety deposit box. Again she assumed the metal compartment housed within to be empty or at least filled with outdated paperwork representing nothing substantial. Her aunt's current will had been on file with the administrators at the nursing home and had already been executed.

Meanwhile, Carrie was certain there was no undisclosed life insurance policy since her aunt had been frank about the status of her financial arrangements. Upon her aunt's admission to the nursing home, the only life insurance policy still in force had been assigned to the corporate owners of the retirement facility and had been used to fulfill her aunt's financial obligations there.

Carrie was forced to stand partially on tiptoe to reach the pale, grey-colored metal box, just visible inside the dark, narrow space of box number 2418. She gently pulled against the thin handle and it failed to budge. Thinking it stuck against the compartment walls from lack of use, she jerked the box gently forward and back. "This thing's not stuck. It's heavy," she muttered to an empty room.

Of course, Carrie Sarbeck had never felt the weight of $10,000 in cash, arranged in rubber-banded bundles of tens and twenties with a few fifties and hundreds mixed in.

Carrie cracked the lid of the metal box for a peek inside even as she worked to balance herself and lower the box to waist level. The sight of a sea of green money forced the lid shut as she guiltily looked around the vault. "There must be some mistake. The clerk must have unlocked the wrong box. This can't be Aunt Syble's safety deposit box." Then she reconsidered. "No ... no, I watched that girl put Aunt Syble's key that I brought with me in the slot to this compartment and then match it up with the bank's key. She was running her mouth the whole time but, still, there can be no mistake," Carrie continued to mutter, trying to convince herself. "The door to the compartment would not have opened if the keys didn't match, so if she had pulled the wrong key ..." Carrie shut up once she completely lifted the lid and gawked at the interior of the metal box, brimming with money.

Again she looked around, more frantically this time. She remained alone in the room, but certainly there were security cameras. Someone was watching her or could watch her or might watch her later. A wave of guilt, which washed through Carrie as though she were a thief, passed as quickly as it came, only to be replaced by several jumbled thoughts. *Well, if this was Aunt Syble's money – and it must have been, I still don't know where she got it, and no one knows it's there, I guess, because it's been there for at least four years ... and it wasn't mentioned in her will, but Aunt Syble must have had a reason not to mention it – she must have assumed that I would eventually find it because I would be the one to find the key. There was no one else who cared anything about her but me, but it really doesn't matter why this money is in this box because it's mine now – it's definitely mine now. It's not Wesley's; it's mine.*

Carrie held one end of the closed box tightly, pushing the weight against her stomach, cradling it as she bent over. She looked nervously through the opened vault door toward the private cubicles surrounding the periphery of the walk-in vault. Human nature wanted her to dump the money out of the box in the first cubicle she could reach, spread out the bundles in piles, and count every last bill.

Then Carrie looked down at her purse, resting on the floor under the column of safety deposit boxes. She realized that it was not roomy enough to hold the cash. *How am I gonna get all this money out of here without being seen?* she wondered. *Thieves are everywhere, and no one in this bank needs to know about this money.*

Carrie considered sliding the metal box back into its slot, closing the door and coming back later. She immediately negated that option, having already closed out the box and not wanting to deal again with the talkative clerk. Nor did she want to reopen the issue with anyone else regarding her rights to a dead relative's safety deposit box.

The most realistic option was to move to the nearest cubicle, coolly place the closed box full of money on the counter of the work area, gently close the door to the space, and in a nondescript, though businesslike manner, quickly walk to one of the tellers and request a sack or some other container. Besides, she was there to clean out her aunt's lockbox. No one would dream that it contained a bundle of cash. And, again, she simply did not want to draw more attention to herself. Feeling even more the thief, she fought to squelch the thought. This was her money now.

She chose the realistic option. There were no other safety deposit box customers nearby and the distance to the nearest teller was not far. He appeared to be a pleasant man, probably mid-twenties, in the process of dismissing one bank customer with no others in line. Carrie Sarbeck headed in his direction, wanting to remain clear of the grinning female clerk.

The walk toward him seemed much longer than expected as Carrie moved with her body turned at an awkward angle, allowing her to keep an eye on her precious work cubicle located immediately outside the vault. Just as she reached the man's counter he flashed a *NEXT WINDOW PLEASE* sign in her face, or at least it seemed that way to Carrie. "I'm sorry, Ma'am. It's time for my break. One of the other tellers will be happy to help you." He showed no remorse as he gestured with his right hand up and down line of bank teller windows, none of which was void of a customer.

"Oh, please. All I need is a bag or sack or some sort. I'm closing my aunt's, I mean, my safety deposit box and I forgot to bring a larger purse with me." When he appeared to balk, she added a lie, "Please, please help me. You see, I'm in a terrible rush. I left my baby at home with my neighbor to babysit, and she is due to go to work in just a little while."

Carrie caught him glancing at his watch and spotted the pack of Marlboro Lights in his front shirt pocket. "My neighbor works as a nurse at University Medical Center in the neonatal intensive care unit, you know, takes care of all those tiny, sick, premature babies. I can't make her late for work. She works three to eleven." Carrie's spontaneity surprised even her as it seemed to spark a hint of pity in the young man. "Like I said, she takes care of those poor little babies."

"OK, just a minute." The male teller glanced at his watch – this time nervously. Nicotine withdrawal was a powerful thing, and because the round trip to the outdoor patio where smoking was allowed would take 10 of his 15 minute cigarette break, he was anxious to get rid of the persistent woman. He would have to push for a raise next quarter since he was breaking his back to please customers.

Carrie watched as the guy trotted over to a walk-in closet located in a corner at the end of the row of teller windows and then breathed easier when he instantly emerged with a cloth bag imprinted with the institution's well-known logo.

"That's plenty big," Carrie said under her breath, relieved.

"There you go, Ma'am." The teller plopped the empty bag on the counter of his window, almost knocking askew the *NEXT WINDOW PLEASE* signage. There was no *Is there anything else I can do to help you?* as he practically jogged away from her, headed to the exit.

Empty money bag in hand and in turn skipping the thank you, Carrie quickly returned to the cubicle that had not left her sight, certain that no one had gone near it as she had dealt with the obstinate bank teller. Fighting her uneasiness, Carrie first took a seat in the plastic chair provided in the cubicle. She felt that each sound she made, whether softly scooting the chair across the linoleum floor to be nearer the working surface or even lifting the lid to the metal cash box, would echo throughout the bank building, drawing attention to Carrie Sarbeck and her loot. Carrie reconsidered bank security cameras and looked above her noting nothing that resembled them. "Surely, they give customers a little privacy around here," she muttered.

Carrie knew that the most expedient and prudent action was to empty the money into the bag, walk normally from the bank, find her car in the parking garage, get in it, and drive home as carefully and inconspicuously as possible. Yet, human nature prevailed. While stuffing each bundle into her treasured bank bag, she roughly counted the cash by thumbing through each stack, most of which were grouped by denomination. "There's close to eight or nine thousand dollars in here, probably more," she marveled softly, although she wanted to squeal in delight, an emotion that for quite some time had been missing from Carrie Sarbeck.

Just as she was reaching for one of the last bundles of twenties in the last layer of money, Carrie unearthed a sealed envelope, engraved with the initials *SWA* on the closed flap and taped facedown to the bottom interior of the box – Aunt Syble's personal stationery. Her heart skipped several beats as she pushed aside the wad of money to expose completely the note, and then stared at it, dumbfounded.

For the moment, the money did not seem important. Once Carrie began to pry one corner of the envelope loose from the brittle tape, the entire piece popped up. She held the sealed envelope in both hands, turning the front side toward her, and stared at the name, her given name, written there in her Aunt Syble's unmistakable script. Unnecessarily concerned about discovery as she heard a pair of voices pass near her closed booth, then fade, Carrie thought that maybe she should drop the note into her purse to open later. However, she decided against it. Barring a bank robbery, no one was going to disturb her anytime soon; the bank was far from closing for the afternoon.

She tore open the top the envelope, careful to preserve the engraved *SWA* on the back and the handwritten *Carrie* front side and read:

> *My dearest Carrie,*
>
> *No doubt you are surprised to find this money. In case you have not completed the count, it amounts to $10,000. I have placed it in my safety deposit as sort of an emergency fund for myself, and, since you have found it, it seems that I never needed it. However, it was for the possibility that I might need the money before I died that I decided not to mention these savings in my will. Besides, your being my only remaining relative meant that you would locate my safety deposit box key and remove the contents.*
>
> *It has been my pleasure and privilege to help you and your husband have a baby with the money I have*

already given you, and I do hope that things will work out or have worked out well for you by now in that regard. Even if you have not been able to give birth by now, I do hope that you still have options. I know that becoming a parent has been difficult both physically and emotionally for you. As you know, I have grieved over your difficulties in having a baby, believing that you inherited those problems from my side of the family. For that reason, please use this money as you see fit. Since I have left you cash, it will remain our little secret. Telling Wesley about this is your choice.

Won't it be wonderful for you to have your own baby? A human being that belongs to you and to God, that came from your body—I am confident that the doctors will find a way to make this possible for you and Wesley. To me, Wesley has always seemed like such a nice boy, being a policeman and all ... a good provider, for sure, a solid man. He deserves a baby that I know you want to give him, and will eventually.

You and Wesley both have such wonderful features, shining from within and without. Those features will combine to create a baby that will grow to be the best of you both. The world will look at that baby and scream, "That beautiful child belongs to Carrie and Wesley Sarbeck. And Syble Ann Waters is that baby's great aunt. No question about it!"

Love,
Aunt Syble

Carrie finished reading the note in tears. The last few written words recorded in her beautiful script *The world will look at that baby and scream, "That beautiful child belongs to Carrie and Wesley Sarbeck. And Syble Ann Waters is that baby's great aunt. No question about it!"* raced through her head, reverberating against her skull, hitting the sides like a richoqueting billiard ball. She refolded the note, stuffed it back into the envelope, and dropped it into the bag of cash.

A few minutes later Carrie found herself sitting behind the steering wheel of her car, keys in the right hand, poised to slip into the ignition. The last thing she remembered was grabbing the money bag and hurriedly heading for the bank's exit door. "The money!" she screamed in panic as she threw her arms toward the right passenger seat, finding it empty. She next groped the floorboard of the car, finding the bank sack pressed tightly between the back of her legs and the edge of the driver's seat. "Oh, thank you, thank you!" she cried, eyes shut as though in prayer, money bag now squeezed into her chest.

However, prayer was not the answer for Carrie Sarbeck.

While driving home that day, Carrie dismissed the grocery store, the clothes at the cleaners and a few other errands that Wesley expected her to complete. She forgot that there would be nothing to prepare for supper without dropping by the grocery. She thought of nothing but the way she could truly be the mother of Wesley's baby.

In the masterfully written note, her wise aunt had been clear from the grave that this additional money was to make Carrie Sarbeck happy. The funds Aunt Syble had given when alive were meant for the Sarbecks as a couple, as a future family. But this money was designed for Carrie, Carrie Sarbeck, alone. She needed to use the money in a way that would make her truly feel like the mother to her husband's baby. She would never feel that way if the radiant woman with the blonde hair were still alive.

She thought again of her afternoon spent as a recluse in her bathroom as the bird pounded the window pane and the human egg broker worked her husband downstairs. She remembered how the bird's beak smeared the window as it pounded the glass so forcibly that she assumed that at any moment the glass would be smeared in blood. The bird was trying to help her, trying to communicate with her, trying to tell her to do it.

Once the egg broker had left her living room that afternoon, Carrie went to her own jewelry box and extracted her aunt's brittle, yellowed note left to her under the money in the safety deposit box. She unfolded and reread it.

Wiping her eyes with her sleeve and at the moment thinking about the best use for the money, she sobbed uncontrollably. Her aunt's words were so idealistic, so innocent, and certainly not meant to be critical of any path on which she would embark with her husband in becoming parents. Despite the money spent, the selection of an egg donor to their liking – or at least to her husband's liking –, and the personalized treatment she had received at the Van Deman Center, Carrie realized at that moment that she would never feel that the baby she was to carry was actually hers.

The child that she would present to the world, the one she would be carting to daycare, play groups, and birthday parties, never truly would be hers. The child that she would dress, clean up after, help with homework, and worry about when a teenager out late at night would never truly be hers. This baby would merely be the biological product of her husband's sperm and the woman he had picked from Lucille Wax's catalogue.

Carrie held the note in front of her face with both hands that day and between sobs whispered, "I know, Aunt Syble, that I approved of that woman as the egg donor. I looked at her picture and her byline, and I consented to using her. Well,

Wesley had already selected her from the donors in our price range, but I approved her. I didn't want to look at any other pictures. I didn't care who he picked. I just didn't want to disappoint him."

Suddenly, a surprised Carrie no longer felt the need to cry as her stifled sobs ceased. She firmly held the note even closer to her face and added defiantly, "The problem, Aunt Syble, is that the egg donor will be the mother of my baby, not me. Even when I carry the baby in my own uterus for nine months – that baby they are making in the medical office – the baby will still be hers. That blonde-haired woman will be the mother of Wesley's baby, not me."

Carrie lowered the yellowed envelope to her lap; she was free of tears, but ripe with resolve. "I have let you down, Aunt Syble. I am so, so sorry. As long as that woman we – he – just picked is alive, no matter where she lives, even if it's in another town or state or even country, she will always be the mother of Wesley's baby. As long as she is alive she will be the mother of my baby, Aunt Syble, not me."

"As long as she is alive," Carrie Sarbeck repeated with a determination that sounded distant, as though someone or something else had spoken this time. Scanning her aunt's letter, she found Syble's script smooth and determined, matching the way she felt.

After having reread the letter that day and cowering under the bird in her bathroom, she finally knew what she had to do. There was only one way in which she could ever feel that the baby was as much hers as Wesley's.

The problem was how to do it.

Chapter

16

•••

THE PAYBACK

Earlier in Wesley's career in law enforcement, he shared more of the events of his day or night as a policeman with Carrie, a practice not unusual for any young professional. No secrets were divulged. Every arrest made, every citation issued was a matter of public record. In fact, for a few of the truly early years, she made a hobby of watching for newspaper articles as well as television or radio news announcements about various police raids or criminals apprehended.

Something caused Carrie to remember one particular case, washing her with a chill that left her toes and fingers numb and her head light. She realized that she had stopped breathing for a few seconds and believed that her heart had stopped beating. It was an anxiety attack, she realized.

But the anxiety was not from fear that her husband was in danger from the moment he finished his training and was placed on the streets in active police duty. The anxiety was from her excitement over what the bird had been trying to tell her with the window smears that might as well have been blood.

For some reason, Carrie retrieved the memory of one of her

husband's earlier arrests of a Jackson man accused of murder. The legal proceedings that resulted from a gunfight in a declining motel on Highway 80 landed one Eduardo Luna in Parchman Prison in the Mississippi Delta until his sentence was reduced on appeal followed by an early parole for good behavior.

It was her husband's courtroom testimony that actually reduced Luna's sentence, and Eduardo was present in the courtroom that day to appreciate and register the effort. Since Carrie had begun to share her husband's interest in the case, she welcomed Wesley's suggestion that she attend the day's proceedings. Carrie admired Wesley's professionalism on the witness stand – looking fit, trim, and very important in his police officer's uniform.

The jury of twelve righteous citizens, anxious to squelch a rising wave of criminal activity, sought to punish Luna, but not to the degree that one might have assumed. The man that Luna had shot and killed had been his accomplice in a liquor store robbery that had been successful until an employee of the Crockett Motel housekeeping staff overheard the two men arguing over the spoils. A pair of fifths of Jack Daniels consumed between nine and eleven o'clock in the morning had sparked the disagreement. The woman bypassed her manager, who was happy to have any clientele no matter how seedy, and called 9-1-1 to alert the police.

Not only a liquor store bandit, but also a derelict father to three illegitimate children by three different women and head pimp of the Crockett Motel brothel, Eduardo Luna's accomplice in the liquor store heist was viewed by the jury as even lower on the food chain. This juried opinion of the man whom Luna had shot that morning and Officer Wesley Sarbeck's eyewitness account of the gun battle led to leniency for one Eduardo Luna.

The clincher for the jury's decision was found in Sarbeck's testimony detailing how Eduardo prevented his accomplice from dropping one of the other officers by shooting his own derelict buddy first. The jury seemed to forget the fact that Luna and the bad-dad pimp were engaged in a drunken battle over the split of cash stolen from a mom-and-pop liquor store on Gallatin Street. And the jury ignored the obvious – that a furious Luna wanted his accomplice dead regardless of where the gun was aimed.

Carrie vividly remembered the trial held in the courthouse in downtown Jackson. Despite being conducted several years ago, it was something that she could never forget, and she was certain that Eduardo Luna had not forgotten it either. During a recent supper conversation, Wesley mentioned that Luna, out on parole, had made an unannounced visit to police precinct headquarters to thank his savior personally for the accurate account of the shooting. Luna was now gainfully employed as a stock boy at a mega-discount store in south Jackson and had turned over a new leaf – all credit given to Officer Wesley Sarbeck.

Times remained hard though for Eduardo Luna, it seemed, with a sick mother, lots of medical bills, and no decent place to live. Anyway, life was better due to a shorter prison sentence – all because of the pertinent courtroom testimony of Officer Wesley Sarbeck. Eduardo was still not sure how he and his family were going to make it, but they would, somehow.

Carrie Sarbeck believed she had that *somehow* for Eduardo Luna.

On her second try, she found him stocking merchandise at the twenty-four-hour mega discount store around 1:30 a.m. Wesley was still working the precinct graveyard shift, giving her the opportunity to seek out Eduardo. Of course, he did not recognize her when she called his name, interrupting his replenishment of toilet paper rolls to a row of sparse shelves.

"Yes, Ma'am. Can I help you find something?" Eduardo Luna asked, alarmed at hearing his name from a stranger. He did not feel threatened. The woman standing above him did not look like a cop or an old girlfriend. He feared that this woman had recognized him from the publicity about his trial for murder, something that he hoped by now had been forgotten.

"Yes, Mr. Luna, you can help me. I'd like to call you *Eduardo*, if that's OK."

"OK, sure. *Eduardo* is fine."

"My husband is Wesley Sarbeck, the police officer who testified for you at your murder trial. You came by the precinct the other day and thanked him. You told him that if he ever needed a favor from you to let him know."

" Did Officer Sarbeck send you down here, Miz Sarbeck? This is sort of an unusual hour to be out shopping, don'tchathink?"

"No, no. My husband doesn't know anything about my being here. And you're not to tell him, understand?"

Luna stood from his crouched position over the boxes of multiple varieties of Charmin to get a better look at this woman. She was about his height, certainly not as stocky as he, on the youngish side, not beautiful or even pretty, but not ugly either – fairly nice breasts from what he could tell, probably not a screamer. All in all, if she somehow had the hots for him, he decided that he would gladly oblige.

"What do you want me to do for you?" he grinned as she missed the growing implication. "I don't get off until six but I might be able to take a break out back for a few minutes."

"No, this is something that will take some research, a little investigation on your part, I would expect. But someone like you should have plenty of the right connections."

"I don't think I understand," Luna asked, wondering if this freak were into multiples or some other kinky stuff.

"Do you understand how much $10,000 is?"

"Ten grand?" Eduardo Luna dropped the package of large roll, super soft absorbent on the floor. "Lady, what kind of shit are you into?"

Carrie's radar never did detect his sexual references as she pushed on. "I need you to kill someone for me, a woman." Luna was speechless as his eyebrows rose in astonishment. "I don't have her name or where she lives. But I believe she lives in Mississippi, Louisiana, or maybe Tennessee – not too far away. She might even live right here in Jackson. I can tell you the name of the person who would have that information. Her name is Lucille Wax. I don't want you to hurt Miss Wax, mind you. In fact, the source of this hit might be revealed if she was hurt or if anyone knew that you were poking around in her business.

"Look, lady, are you for real?"

"My husband confided in me about your sick mother and the rat-infested apartment where you live with her. The money I'm offering you would go a long way toward helping out, wouldn't it, Eduardo?"

Luna glanced around furtively. He knew there were security cameras everywhere in the building, but anyone interested would assume he was helping a customer. He retrieved the package of toilet paper from the floor and placed it on the shelf. He needed the money, badly.

"Is this for real? Is this some kinda setup or something?"

Carrie removed an envelope from her purse. "This is a down payment of one thousand dollars. Maybe that will cover some of your upfront expenses. You'll get the other nine thousand when I know she's dead."

"Look lady, I'm not so sure," he argued, although not convincingly. "Your husband having some big affair with this bitch or something?"

"No, he's not having an affair with her, not in the way you think. We've gotten what we need from her, and I need for her to be gone, away from this world. That's the only way I can ever be happy. Something's – someone's telling me to do this."

As his mind raced with temptation, Luna watched the color of Mrs. Sarbeck's eyes nearly change. There was no way to miss it. Maybe she was crazy, but he needed the money nevertheless. Boy, did he ever need the money.

He had murdered before, although he really did not count the shooting at the Crockett Motel in his repertoire, the only murder for which he had been apprehended. After being granted parole from that screw-up, he had promised himself that he would go straight. But there was just no way. This here was a gift – one that he needed and could not refuse.

"OK, one more time," he relented, pushing the packages of toilet paper flush to shelf edge.

"What'd you say?" Carrie leaned in closer.

"I'll take the job, but I've got to have a third up front. And you'll have to round it up to $3500."

"I thought you might say that." Carrie slyly pulled from her purse another envelope containing $2500. "In exchange for this little extra advance, I want this job done quickly, like within the week."

"OK, you got it. No problem."

"You'll get the rest of the money the night after it's done. I'll meet you in the parking lot next to the piles of garden soil. We better not be seen together again in the store."

"Good idea, lady. It's almost like you done this before."

"Well, I've seen enough TV."

Luna grinned as he bent to continue his transfer of packages from the cardboard crate to the shelves in the personal products section. "Well, then from TV you already know that my kind don't like to be double-crossed." He straightened again to look at Carrie Sarbeck in the eye. "After all, if I'm able to track down this bitch that you want me to snuff out, then I can do the same to you."

As Eduardo chuckled, Carrie Sarbeck went expressionless.

Eduardo Luna earned the rest of the money, completing the hit within the time constraints set by his new client. Just as punctual with payment was a satisfied Carrie Sarbeck. Even with the difference in hair color, she delightfully matched the smiling newspaper photo of the murdered Eastover woman to the one she remembered from Wax's catalogue. As promised, the balance due Luna was transferred unceremoniously in the parking lot near the stack of 20-pound bags of organic topsoil.

There was no discussion in the Sarbeck household regarding the murder of the Jackson socialite, each member of the tiny household harboring a different reason for avoiding the subject. Like any tenured professional, Officer Wesley Sarbeck had long ceased venting at home the specifics of a day's – or night's – work and was not about to resume the confidences with the Choice murder case. Keeping mum his involvement with the death of Cheryl Choice was facilitated by the local media's failure to identify him by name as the initial officer on the scene.

Even by successfully avoiding the subject, Wesley cringed in fear that his sensitive wife would eventually recognize the victim as the donor of half of their baby. And while Carrie was afforded multiple opportunities to make the connection and much to her husband's relief, she never commented on the subject.

Also ignored by Carrie was the file photo of Cheryl Choice. Reminiscent of the color rendering in the Wax catalogue, it ran on the front page of the *Clarion-Ledger* and *Northside Sun* newspapers. Likewise, her picture frequently appeared on local television newscasts along with updates on the police investigation and interviews from Choice's devastated social contacts.

Wesley believed that had Carrie discovered the connection between their baby and the murdered Jackson socialite, she would have been completely torn apart. His fear was not that Carrie would have disapproved of Choice's true identity, but that her learning of the violent end for the natural mother of her baby would further taint her view of the future.

As each day progressed toward the birth of that baby, Wesley Sarbeck was confident that his secret was safe.

Chapter
17
◆◆◆
THE EXECUTION

The planned break-in at the Van Deman Center was finally ripe for execution. Between word and number puzzles, Tinker Murtagh had concluded that the job was to be much simpler than many of his others. Allyn Saxton's embryos were lying in wait for him, frozen in the Embryo Culture Lab in the funny-looking contraption to which he had the digital lock combination. The nitrous oxide-supplied freezer just happened to be located below a structurally weak area of the roof, weak enough to afford easy, unauthorized entrance through a vented area while remaining strong enough to prevent collapse under his weight.

Disabling the electronic security system for the Van Deman Center would not be a problem for someone like Murtagh. To do so meant no more than breaking through a computer firewall. Van Deman had skipped the locally owned burglar and fire alarm companies, opting instead for a nationally based security system that operated through the Internet. As long as the Internet connection remained live, so did the monitoring system. Since the Center maintained high-speed, cable Internet access backed up by direct phone line access along with a natural gas-fueled electric generator in case of power outage, the ability of the security monitoring service to receive notification of a breach seemed certain. That is, of course, if the breach was reported in the first place.

And that was where Tinker Murtagh's magic came into play.

Murtagh had already determined the weekend, Sunday morning in particular, to be the Center's most vulnerable. Through his observations and research, it seemed that any of the weekend work required of the laboratory technicians in checking or tending to embryos or lab specimens was always shifted toward Saturday, leaving them at least one day at home and out of Van Deman's clutches. This arrangement appeared to play smoothly, even though the duo of two laboratory technicians apparently worked in rotation and from an on-call system. Seldom would the same person have Saturday duty on two consecutive weekends, or at least that was what Murtagh had deduced from his time involved on this job.

Consequently, he decided that this Sunday, two days away, would be the day. He would enter the building that morning, in broad daylight, parking his vehicle a few blocks away in the weed-infested parking lot of an abandoned convenience store building. IIis dented, dirty black pickup would blend nicely there with the other abandoned vehicles, the empty and mostly broken beer and wine bottles, and the other trash including used condoms and a needle and syringe or two. The street traffic in the Mississippi Bible Belt would be minimal this Sunday morning, like any other Sunday morning, he thought, particularly if he aimed for church time, say, eleven o'clock to noonish. No one would be around. No one would see him.

However, he knew there would be the problem of the worthless day security guard. This particular Sunday, the older of the two would be on duty, at least if the schedule ran true to form. No alarm would sound on Tinker's intrusion; he would take care of that. Even if the alarm system were still in place, the alarm was installed as silent on-site, with notification immediately sent to the local police with a page to the guard.

But there would be no alarm. Immediately before leaving for the site, Tinker was to disable it via his laptop and the free web access provided in the motel room that had served him well during the planning stages of this heist. In less than twenty minutes, he would be in and out of Van Deman's facility and back to his motel room to reactivate the alarm by way of his ability to breach Internet passwords. The offline time for the monitoring service could be even shorter if he chose to access the Web via his laptop, using the encrypted wireless Internet network that encircled the walls of the Center.

"That won't work, Shithead. That'll put your truck too near the scene," he said, breaking a pencil imprinted with *Circle 8 Suites* on the shaft by stabbing it lead-point first into a nearby notepad. He had almost speared his Sudoku book, but selected the motel notepad instead. He could carry his laptop with him on foot, he reasoned, but wanted to skip the extra baggage.

"I need to get me one of those expensive hand-helds for the next job. It'd be just easier to break through the wireless encryption, get on line, and get what I need done with one of those toys," Tinker resolved as he tore through the pad with the splintered end of the wooden pencil. "I can definitely afford a Blackberry or an iPhone after this job. Shit, Tinker Murtagh is expected to be top-of-the-line and look that way, too."

Tinker leaned back on the desk chair as it rocked backwards, nearly reaching the end of the bed. Another story was the 185,000-plus miles on his truck's odometer that caused him to covet a new vehicle.

Up to that point, Tinker had received half of his agreed-upon fee. In earlier days he demanded only a third up front, but as his reputation grew successful in conquering the unusual and often complicated heists, so did his requirements. As long as the money promised was good and received on time, he cared little to nothing about the source. However, this client, who wanted the frozen Saxton embryos, had become careless about anonymity. So, during a slow day of preparation, Murtagh surrendered to commonplace curiosity and easily traced the electronic payment through a myriad of dummy accounts to a bank in California.

The name associated with the checking account was Parke Saxton.

Murtagh's quick background check of Parke Saxton revealed that his no-longer secret client was actually the mother of Allyn Saxton. He wasted no time or energy in uncovering his client's rationale for stealing her own daughter's embryos. Other than some tabloid gossip that Allyn Saxton and her mother had been estranged for years, and despite the mother's desire to the contrary, there was nothing for him to discover during a brief Internet search of the subject.

Even Tinker Murtagh could not pull-up a record of the afternoon when college-aged Allyn was surprised to find her mother nude in a hot tub with a boyfriend, Allyn's boyfriend. The first incident was not the severing point. In fact, the two later laughed over the absurdity that either had found the guy in the hot tub attractive. It was the second incident, five years later and involving another Allyn Saxton boyfriend that destroyed the mother-daughter relationship. The fact that the tryst occurred in Allyn's own apartment bedroom was a moot point; Allyn had earmarked that lover as her next fiancé. She never again communicated with her mother, much less the new ex-boyfriend.

Allyn's break from Parke Saxton had been an easy one, since her post-college, adult career as a television and up-and-coming film celebrity was igniting and no longer needed a mother's push. Allyn Saxton was going to be an even greater star in Parke's absence. She was going to build a career as well as a family without her mother.

To the contrary, the break had been difficult for the mother, who surprisingly felt guiltless for her sexual gratification at her daughter's expense. *Allyn owes me for my sacrifices. She has her whole life before her, including the pick of the litter – any man she wants. Allyn Saxton would be nothing without her mother* was her maternal reasoning. While Parke Saxton remained financially afloat without her daughter's involvement, she was unable to squelch her obsession over her daughter's seemingly unstoppable career in the entertainment industry.

True, as an enormously attractive woman in her own right and at a mere 46 years old, that obsession had deeply violated her daughter's personal life. Now in her mid-fifties, the still eye-catching woman had passed beyond her physical needs, turning only to the emotional ones. Parke Saxton truly regretted having had sex with her daughter's boyfriends, her repentance reaching beyond the discovery of those two careless times, since there had been many others about which Allyn knew nothing. As Parke Saxton repressed her own envy of her daughter's international celebrity, her compulsion had become to recreate the close emotional relationship she once had with Allyn. To that end, she would use her daughter's own flesh and blood.

Parke's compulsion had led to the hiring of a string of professional investigators who, disguised as paparazzi, followed Allyn Saxton to the extent that her mother could afford. That trail wound through her daughter's disastrous, childless marriages and her unsuccessful, defeating treatments for infertility. It was a last-resort effort that led her daughter to a state-of-the-art infertility clinic in Mississippi, of all places. Wiretaps of her daughter's conversations with a Dr. Van Deman revealed plans which would result in seven fresh human embryos, each composed of half Allyn Saxton's blood – Parke's blood – with the other half donated by some male of Allyn's choosing. If Parke knew her daughter as well as she had before, and she believed she did, then that male's DNA would be highly desirable.

Regardless of when Allyn chose to have the appropriate number of embryos implanted, the investigators reported that there would be some number of unused embryos left for freezing and later use. Her daughter could then have others implanted for a future pregnancy or pregnancies, donate them to another infertile woman or couple, or even destroy or dispose of the healthy tissue in some other way. Parke did not want her blood to be given to someone else or find its way into a science experiment. Why shouldn't she be the recipient? The doctors in California could give her the hormones necessary to let the embryos grow inside of her uterus, just as the doctor was doing for Allyn. All Parke had to do was get those embryos out of Mississippi.

As another Allyn flourished inside her womb, she would have a second chance at being a mother. Even if the baby turned out to be a boy, or even if she had twins or even triplets, things would be different this time. Her life would return to one of fulfillment and remain that way.

Her most recent PI, the most costly of the string, put her in touch with Tinker Murtagh. Parke's personal private detective himself refused to broker the embryo deal, claiming that to do so reached well beneath even his own level of conscience. Thus, the novice Parke Saxton, with her traceable method of payments led Murtagh to her true identity, a meaningless discovery to a man only interested in money.

On the other hand, the remainder of his fee from Parke Saxton would never make it to Tinker's greedy pockets. After he disabled the security cameras monitoring the Embryo Culture Lab and deactivated the building's general security system, neutralizing the older security guard had been simple – nothing that strong rope and duct tape could not manage. Tinker then dropped into the embryo culture lab via the roof's ventilation system positioned above the embryo freezer as planned. However, a flabbergasted Tinker Murtagh found empty the freezer compartment assigned to patient number 1216DS.

Tinker had planned to be inside the building for no more than seconds, but this discovery blew his timing. After his expletives, he composed himself long enough to double check his records by removing the laptop from his slim backpack. He was grateful that he had decided to bring his computer along. Once rebooted, the laptop files confirmed that he had the precise location for the hit and the correct codes and patient number. Tinker could only stare longingly into the vacant freezer compartment. That was the correct spot, for sure, and it was flat empty. Murtagh considered, though briefly, lifting other stored frozen embryos and substituting them for the required missing ones. However, even Tinker Murtagh had scruples, though he was befuddled over the possibility of a Murtagh failure and the loss of the remaining fee.

Despite the clock, Murtagh next brought up *Video Archives* on his laptop screen and scrolled rapidly through those pertaining to the Embryo Culture Lab. His eye caught the series of frames beginning at 2:03 a.m., the morning following Allyn Saxton's embryo transfer and Van Deman's unseen alteration of the numbers of her viable eggs and embryos remaining in storage.

"What the ....!" Murtagh screamed. "I must've been asleep and didn't go back and review the video. Damn! Of course, I was asleep. No one ever goes into the lab at that early hour, particularly not that asshole Van Deman!"

Tinker slowed the video to several seconds per frame to watch Henry Van Deman, MD, remove the cylinder labeled *1216DS* and belonging to Allyn Saxton from the freezer. Van Deman then placed it in a small case resting on the counter nearby. Van Deman then closed the embryo freezer, punched in the digital security code, picked up the case from the counter, and exited the lab. In Murtagh's shocked rage he imagined the doctor to stare directly at the thumb-sized security camera and wink at his observer before closing the door leading to the next room. His reason for removing the frozen embryos from their assigned location was unexplained.

"That f'ing thief!" Tinker yelled, as he slammed shut the laptop, crammed it into its slot in the backpack, and crawled back out of the building onto the roof through the ventilation system.

Murtagh had not often felt a failure. In fact, he could not remember the last time. His own reaction to this debacle would be to disappear, to vanish without any further contact with the woman in California. Maybe that woman did deserve an explanation for not getting what she had ordered, he considered, but then he reasoned that he was right to keep the investigation fees earned to date. He had worked hard, after all, and had new assignments waiting.

Had Tinker Murtagh chosen to decipher the doctor's scheme and draw upon even a slice of imagination, he might have supposed that Dr. Henry Van Deman was gathering a private, secret stash of human embryos. Had he known of Van Deman's cell phone conversation, the one partially overheard by lowly Mia Evans as it emanated from the employee patio, he might have gathered a clue that the freezer would be empty of Saxton's remaining embryos. Had he been able to listen to the full length of the call, and from both ends of the conversation, Murtagh could have discovered Van Deman's purpose for collecting embryos, particularly those belonging to Allyn Saxton, and his plans for additional profits. Had he been privy to another call made by Van Deman later that day and from the same cell, then he would have known what was planned for the light-skinned black girl who torched his imagination as she seemed to flirt with the chemical deliveryman.

Had Tinker drawn upon the imagination and mental acuity that had made him a whiz at both paper puzzles and the computer, then he might have predicted the unlikely Van Deman scenario. Tinker could have exposed Henry Van Deman's twisted betrayal of the Hippocratic Oath and his patients' trust.

And Tinker Murtagh would have been dead right.

EPILOGUE

About five months later

"Get those firm buns off my sofa and back on that elliptical walker, or they won't be firm much longer. Doc, you're not paying me to watch TV."

"Look, Ihle, I'm just taking a short break. I was up late last night." Dr. Chamblee was propped on the communal leather couch available in the lounge between the men's and women's dressing areas. After several successful completions, he had not registered for another full course of Boot Camp, but instead signed up for the Saturday morning *a la carte* option.

"Oh, up late on call at the hospital, Doc?" Coco Ihle looked and acted tough. It was part of the aura of what she well knew her students referred to as *Boot Camp*. However, she always picked one or two favorites from each series of fitness classes, and Dr. Knox Chamblee ranked highly each time her participated.

"No way, Ihle. My partner and I are rarely called in after hours. I left that bugger back at my old practice up in Montclair - taking a lot of emergency hospital and crap like that. Sometimes one of the emergency rooms around here will call Van Deman or me and ask us to come in for a complicated ectopic pregnancy case or if one of our own infertility patients has shown up in the ER with a treatment complication. But that's rare, thank goodness."

Coco had pulled a clipboard from inside a nearby cabinet to study the student roster of her upcoming torture session, totally uninterested in the medical practice detail. However, she loved to have physicians as clients, particularly when she could turn the tables and make them sweat. "Well, then what were you doing out so late, Doc?" she probed.

"Believe it or not – I had a date!"

"Whatcha mean *Believe it or not*? You're a good-lookin' guy, and besides, you're a walking billboard for Body-by-Coco-Ihle!" she laughed, although the humor was meant as complimentary both to Knox Chamblee and herself. She considered Knox a body sculpting success story. He had paid close attention to her directives in class and never missed a paid session. While his physique had filled out nicely as a result of the vigorous exercises and training, he had not overdone it. He had lost the detracting soft spots, keeping his body trim without overly bulking up. "But Doc, a date? I thought you were saving yourself for me," she frowned jokingly, shaking her head side-to-side.

"You're too busy up here cracking the whip to have a steady, Ihle. And I need a steady – I'm getting on up there in age. I'm on the second half of thirty, you know."

"OK, ol' man. Who's the lucky girl?"

"That's just it. I hope she feels lucky. She graduates soon from law school at Ole Miss and already has this great job with a corporate firm downtown, the one across from the capital building. We've been going out for a couple of months and hit it off right off. I've got 10 years on her, but she likes the mature type, I guess."

"Shoot, that girl knows she's found herself a rich doctor – forget marrying one while he's still suffering in medical school. She's gonna snag you now that the diploma's on the wall and the wall's holding up a swanky office building like yours, Doc," she winked as she gestured defiantly with her clipboard and walked toward the entrance to the gym. It was time to shout some orders; Coco Ihle was having withdrawal.

"Oh, by the way," she paused. "Tell the lucky girl that there's a special discount on this fall's session – applies to any girl who's engaged to hunky Knox Chamblee. But let her know that if she messes him up, I've got a few special machines out back that would love to say hello."

Smiling, Knox shook his head as the commander left the lounge, leaving him alone. His throbbing headache from a late night out was beginning to ease, and Knox was beginning to feel up to a little treadmill before heading home for a nap. He reached for the bottled water left resting on the end table and grabbed the remote to turn off the television where a replay of a recent installment of *Endless Entertainment!* was well underway. The figure on the screen caught his eye. It was an obviously pregnant Allyn Saxton walking out of a swanky restaurant with a couple of heavyweights in tow whom Knox assumed to be bodyguards.

"Having declined to be photographed for months and seeming to be in virtual seclusion, a spokesperson for New Universe Studios has confirmed that Allyn Saxton is going to be the next Hollywood mom, " the female reporter beamed in an inset that popped up in the lower right-hand corner of the screen. "The star of the soon-to-be-released sequel to last year's blockbuster *Mountain Over the River* has declined to name the father and has not been romantically linked to any one in months since her last well-publicized breakup. So, I guess it's anyone's guess." The reported shrugged her shoulders as the cameras caught every Saxton movement, particularly the awkward shots of her wedging into the waiting limo. Saxton's belly was much larger than that to be expected for 22 weeks of pregnancy.

"However, *Endless Entertainment!* has confirmed that Saxton is pregnant with twins! That's right, twins!" the female reporter beamed as though she were the unknown father. "Our source in Hollywood says that Saxton's Los Angeles obstetrician assures her that she and her unborn babies are doing just fine." The reporter glowed as though the world could now rest in peace. "Now, back to you, Miles, for the latest in New York."

Chamblee followed through with hitting the power button on the remote. Hearing this news about Allyn Saxton, he realized that Van Deman had not updated him on the outcome of the Center's secretive, celebrity patient from months ago. From the swollen appearance of the movie star and the confirmation that she was carrying twins, the timing seemed just about right. Curious, he broached the subject with his partner the following Monday and was met with another "None of your business."

Having recently earned full practicing and financial partner status in the Henry Van Deman Center, despite no name change for the facility, Knox felt within his bounds to inquire about the celebrity, but dropped the subject at the unexpectedly curt response. Chamblee fought offense, but instead wrote off Henry's abruptness to, perhaps, physician disappointment over a decision by the exclusive client to choose another facility for infertility treatment. Consequently, he never again mentioned the name to Van Deman. He and Henry had consistently worked well together in growing the Center in scope and profitability with seldom if ever the slightest disagreement concerning patient care, operational business, or staffing concerns.

However, as the months progressed, Van Deman drew more into himself, keeping much of the information pertaining to his own patients uncharted and doing more and more of the minor procedures and lab work himself. Touting concern over the lengthy, tedious working hours of the laboratory personnel, he would insist, "Here, I'll do this myself. Why don't you go out to the patio and take a break?" The techs always accepted the offer. "My dear, I'll save you for the hard stuff!" he joked, as the technician would trot off to the rear patio. Van Deman never

failed to produce a plausible excuse for any practice deviation
from the Center's standard policies.

As a result of his increasing suspicion and concern about
Van Deman's actions and even while he grew more and more
financially secure, Knox frequently began to wonder if he had
made the right decision to join Henry Van Deman in medical
practice. He wanted security – a worthwhile, productive, but still
predicable, career in medicine. Likewise, Dr. Knox Chamblee
desired the same on a personal level. He was prepared to get
married, settle down, and raise a family.

Often, he thought that he should never have left his old practice
in Montclair.

THE END

About the Author

Darden North, MD, is a board-certified obstetrician/gynecologist who lives in Jackson, Mississippi, where he practices medicine at Jackson Healthcare for Women, PA. He and his wife Sally have two young adult children, as well as two dogs and a granddog. North's first novel *House Call* (hardcover 2005, paperback 2007) was awarded Finalist in Mystery/Suspense by the 2008 Next Generation Indie Book Awards. His second novel *Points of Origin* (hardcover 2006) was recognized in Southern Fiction by the 2007 Independent Publishers Book Awards. Both *House Call* and *Points of Origin* were nominated in Fiction by the Mississippi Institute for Arts and Letters and by the Southern Independent Book Association. North is a member of Mystery Writers of America, the Mississippi Writers Guild, Sisters in Crime, and the Independent Book Publishers Association. He has participated as an author panelist in such literary presentations as "Murder in the Magic City" (Birmingham, AL), "Author! Author! Shreveport's (LA) Celebration of the Written Word," and "Murder on the Menu" (Wetumpka, AL).

A few years ago, Darden North hung up his golf clubs for a laptop – but on occasion is still spotted with a croquet mallet or garden shovel. He is writing a fourth novel as he continues to deliver babies and maintain a full gynecological practice.

The author can be contacted through his website *www.dardennorth.com* and welcomes reader comments.